P9-DNK-266

WARRIORS

EXILE FROM SHADOWCLAN

WARRIORS

GRAPHIC NOVELS

Graystripe's Adventure
Ravenpaw's Path
SkyClan and the Stranger
A Shadow in RiverClan
Winds of Change

Tigerstar and Sasha #1: Into the Woods
Tigerstar and Sasha #2: Escape from the Forest
Tigerstar and Sasha #3: Return to the Clans
The Rise of Scourge

WARRIORS
EXILE FROM SHADOWCLAN

CREATED BY
ERIN HUNTER

WRITTEN BY
DAN JOLLEY

ART BY
JAMES L. BARRY

An Imprint of HarperCollins*Publishers*

Warriors: Exile from ShadowClan
Created by Erin Hunter
Written by Dan Jolley
Art by James L. Barry

HarperAlley is an imprint of HarperCollins Publishers.

Exile from ShadowClan
Text copyright © 2022 by Working Partners Limited
Art copyright © 2022 by HarperCollins Publishers
All rights reserved. Manufactured in Bosnia and Herzegovina.
No part of this book may be used or reproduced in any manner whatsoever without written permission except in the case of brief quotations embodied in critical articles and reviews. For information address HarperCollins Children's Books, a division of HarperCollins Publishers, 195 Broadway, New York, NY 10007.
www.harpercollinschildrens.com
Library of Congress Control Number: 2021951514
ISBN 978-0-06-304327-5 (hardcover) — ISBN 978-0-06-304326-8 (pbk)
22 23 24 25 26 GPS 10 9 8 7 6 5 4 3 2 1
❖
First Edition

WARRIORS

EXILE FROM SHADOWCLAN

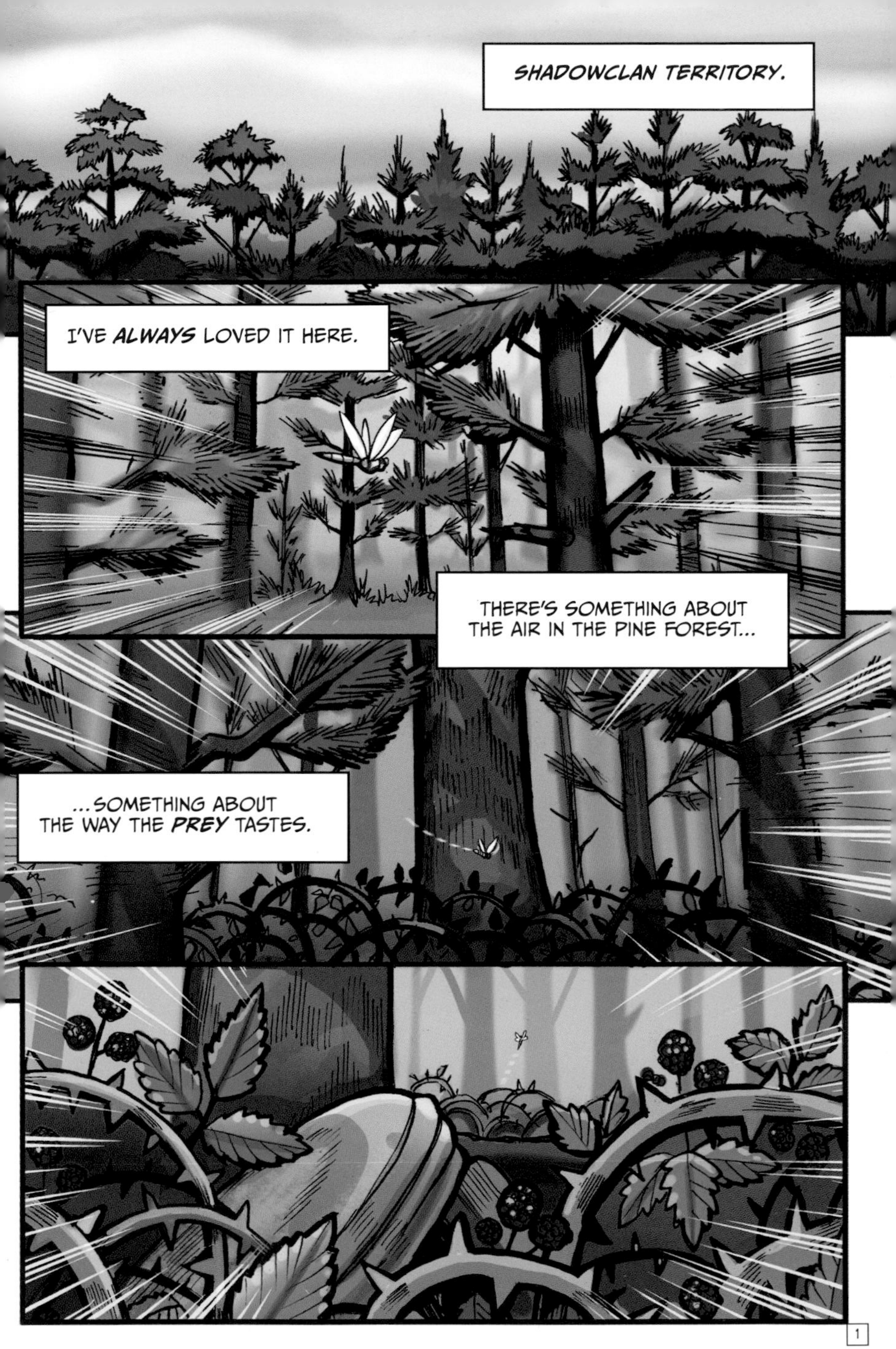
SHADOWCLAN TERRITORY.
I'VE ALWAYS LOVED IT HERE.
THERE'S SOMETHING ABOUT THE AIR IN THE PINE FOREST...
...SOMETHING ABOUT THE WAY THE PREY TASTES.

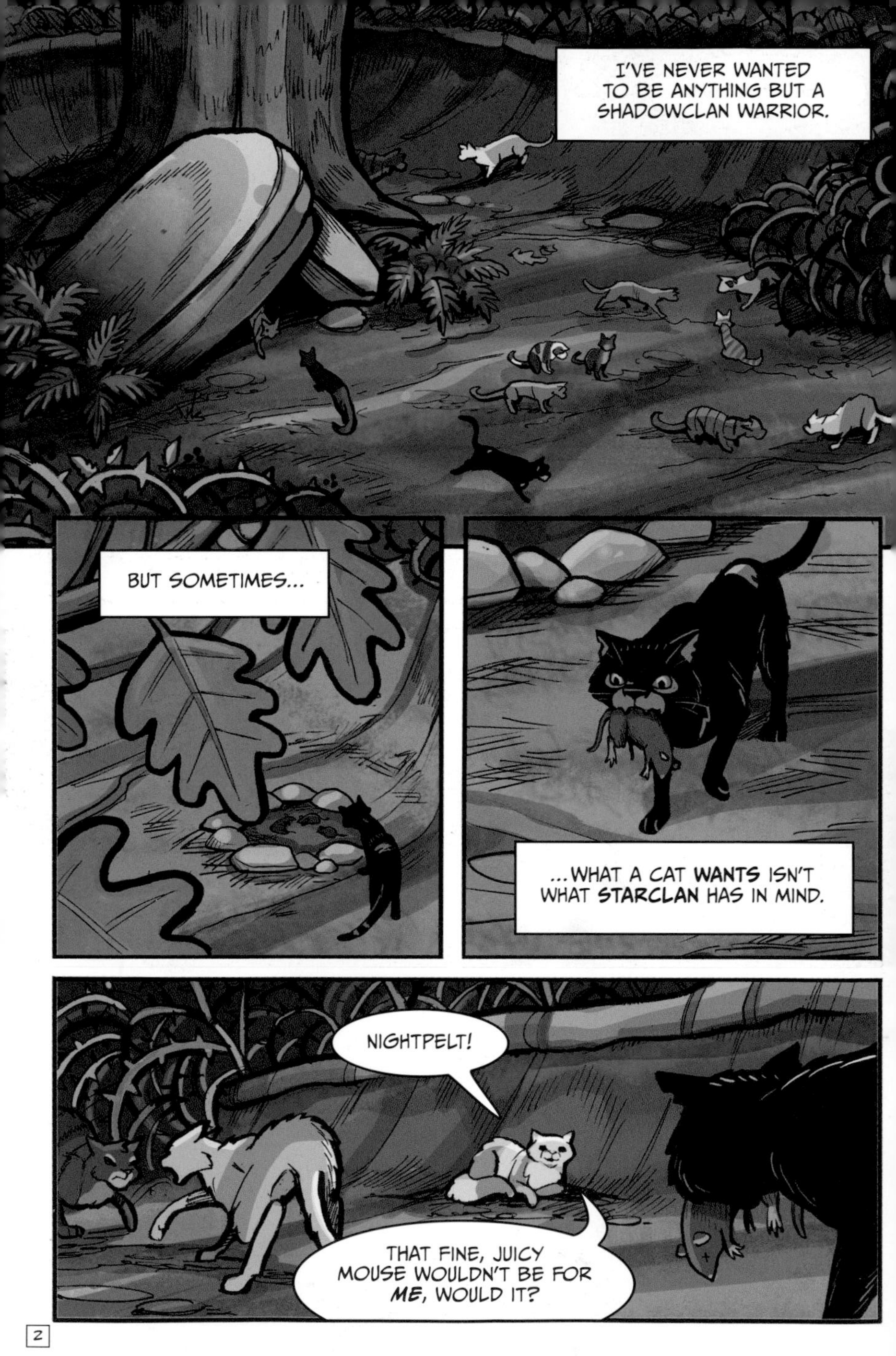
I'VE NEVER WANTED TO BE ANYTHING BUT A SHADOWCLAN WARRIOR.
BUT SOMETIMES...
...WHAT A CAT **WANTS** ISN'T WHAT **STARCLAN** HAS IN MIND.
NIGHTPELT!
THAT FINE, JUICY MOUSE WOULDN'T BE FOR *ME*, WOULD IT?

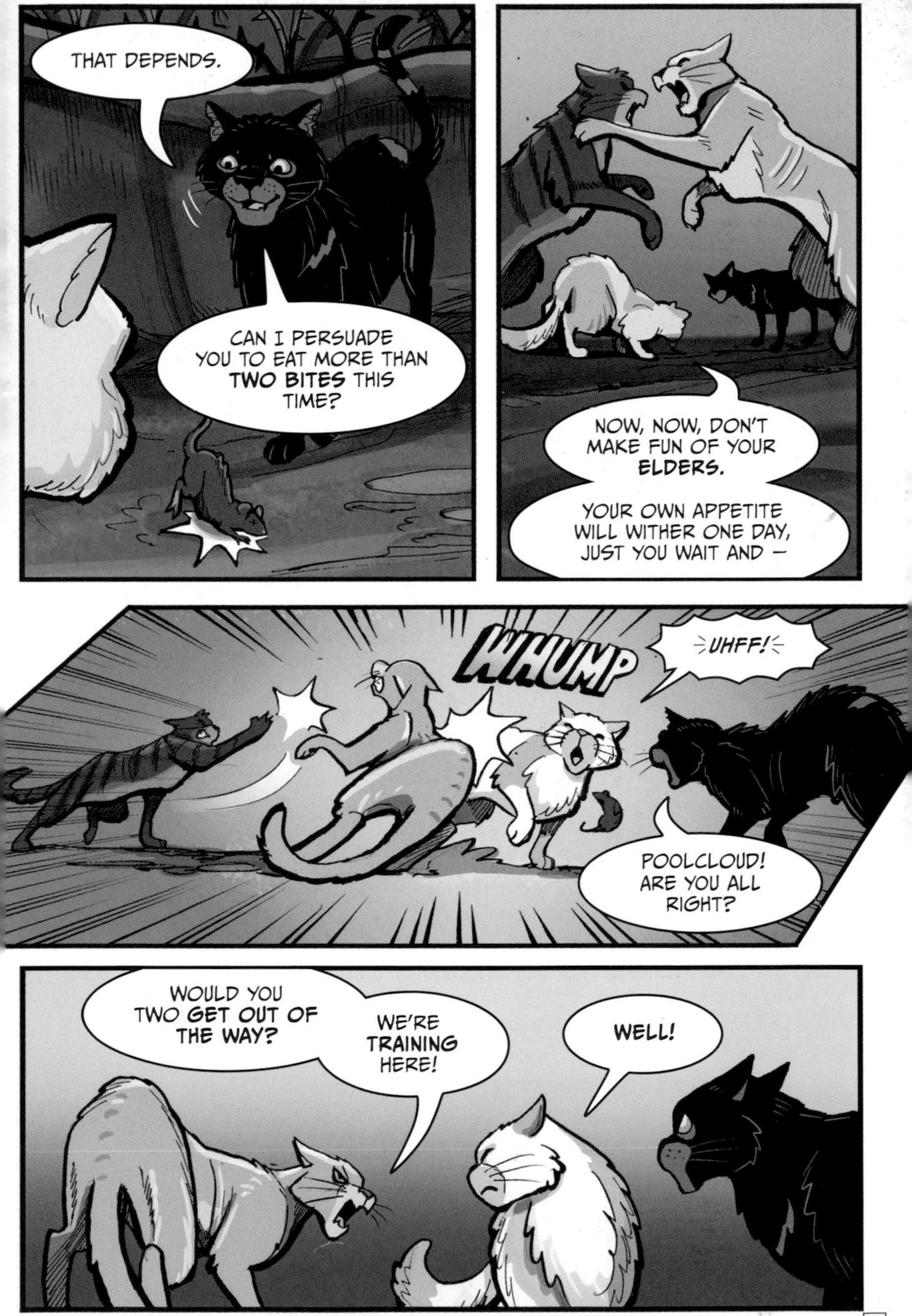
THAT DEPENDS.
CAN I PERSUADE YOU TO EAT MORE THAN **TWO BITES** THIS TIME?
NOW, NOW, DON'T MAKE FUN OF YOUR **ELDERS.**
YOUR OWN APPETITE WILL WITHER ONE DAY, JUST YOU WAIT AND –
WHUMP
UHFF!
POOLCLOUD! ARE YOU ALL RIGHT?
WOULD YOU TWO **GET OUT OF THE WAY?**
WE'RE **TRAINING** HERE!
WELL!

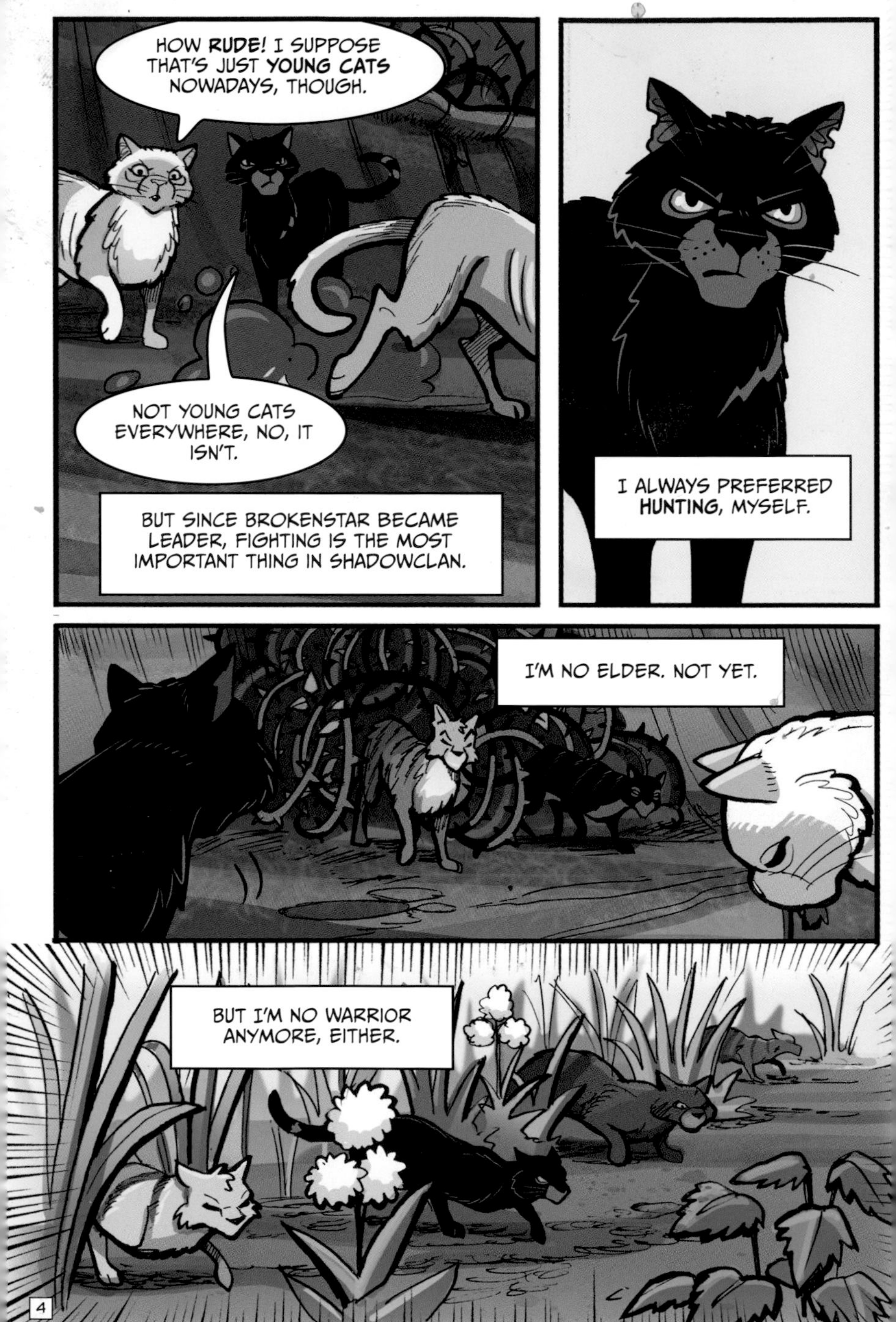
HOW RUDE! I SUPPOSE THAT'S JUST YOUNG CATS NOWADAYS, THOUGH.
NOT YOUNG CATS EVERYWHERE, NO, IT ISN'T.
BUT SINCE BROKENSTAR BECAME LEADER, FIGHTING IS THE MOST IMPORTANT THING IN SHADOWCLAN.
I ALWAYS PREFERRED HUNTING, MYSELF.
I'M NO ELDER. NOT YET.
BUT I'M NO WARRIOR ANYMORE, EITHER.

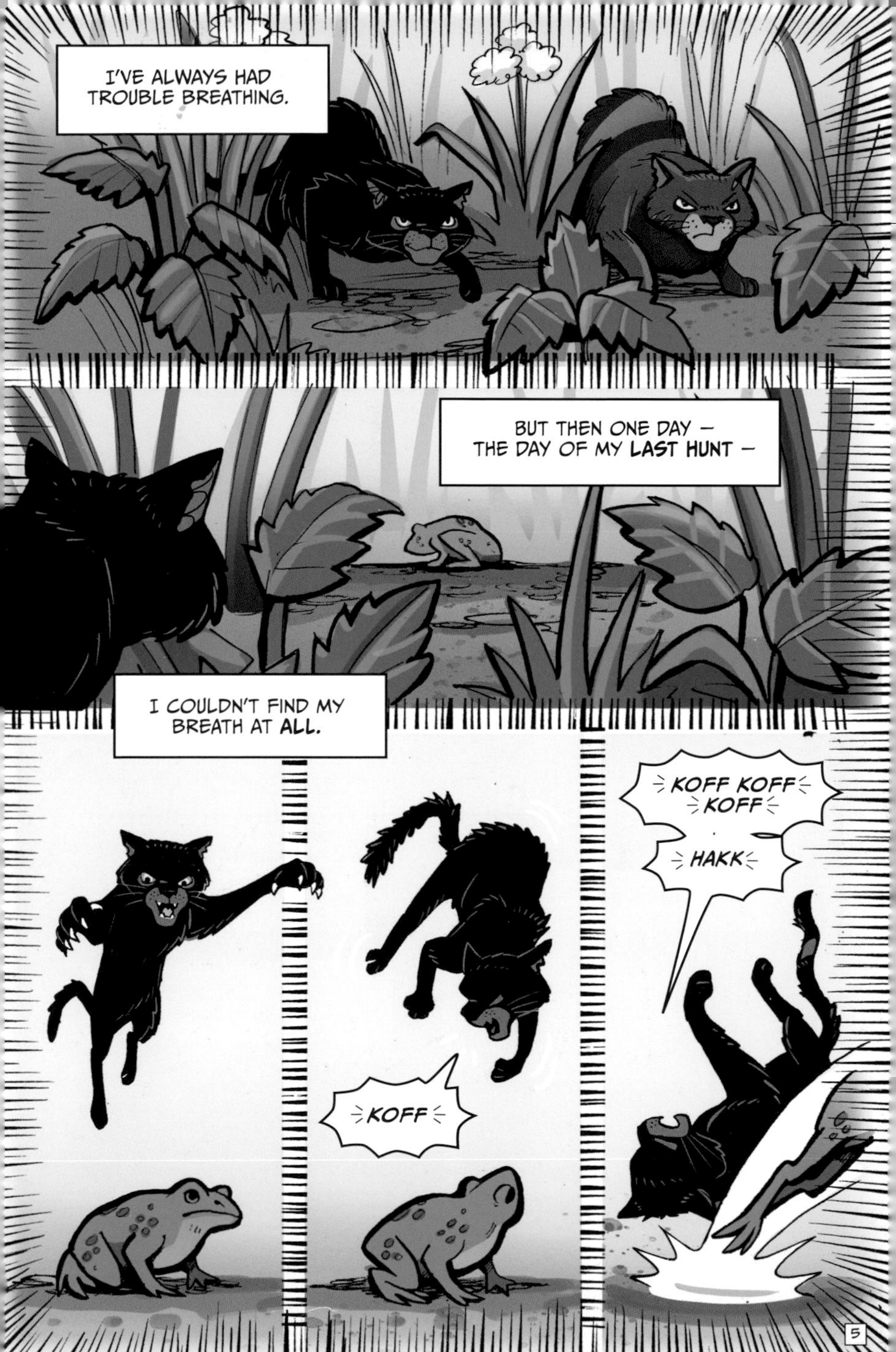
I'VE ALWAYS HAD TROUBLE BREATHING.
BUT THEN ONE DAY — THE DAY OF MY LAST HUNT —
I COULDN'T FIND MY BREATH AT ALL.
KOFF
KOFF KOFF KOFF
HAKK

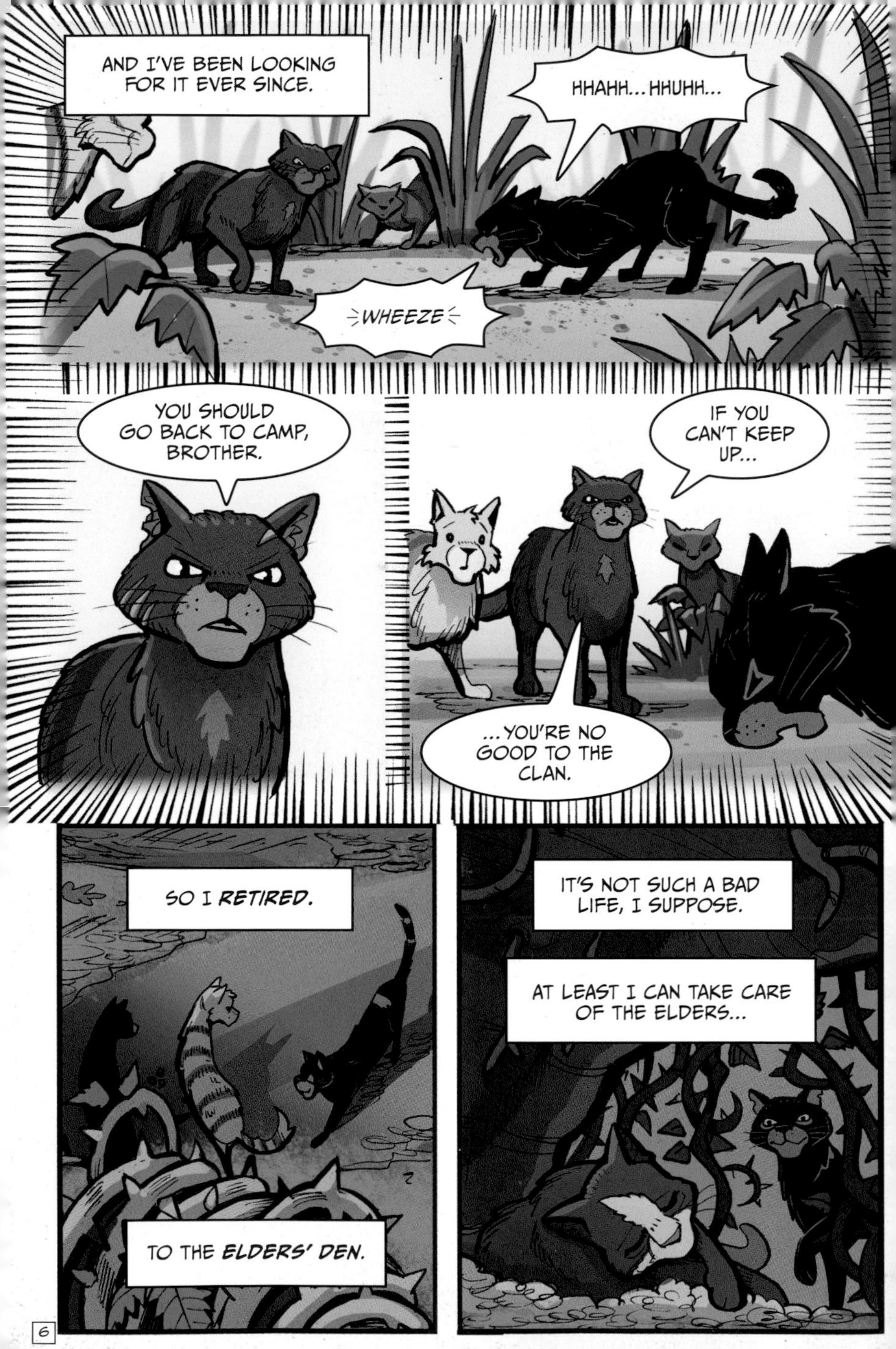
AND I'VE BEEN LOOKING FOR IT EVER SINCE.
HHAHH... HHUHH...
WHEEZE
YOU SHOULD GO BACK TO CAMP, BROTHER.
IF YOU CAN'T KEEP UP...
...YOU'RE NO GOOD TO THE CLAN.
SO I *RETIRED.*
TO THE *ELDERS' DEN.*
IT'S NOT SUCH A BAD LIFE, I SUPPOSE.
AT LEAST I CAN TAKE CARE OF THE ELDERS...

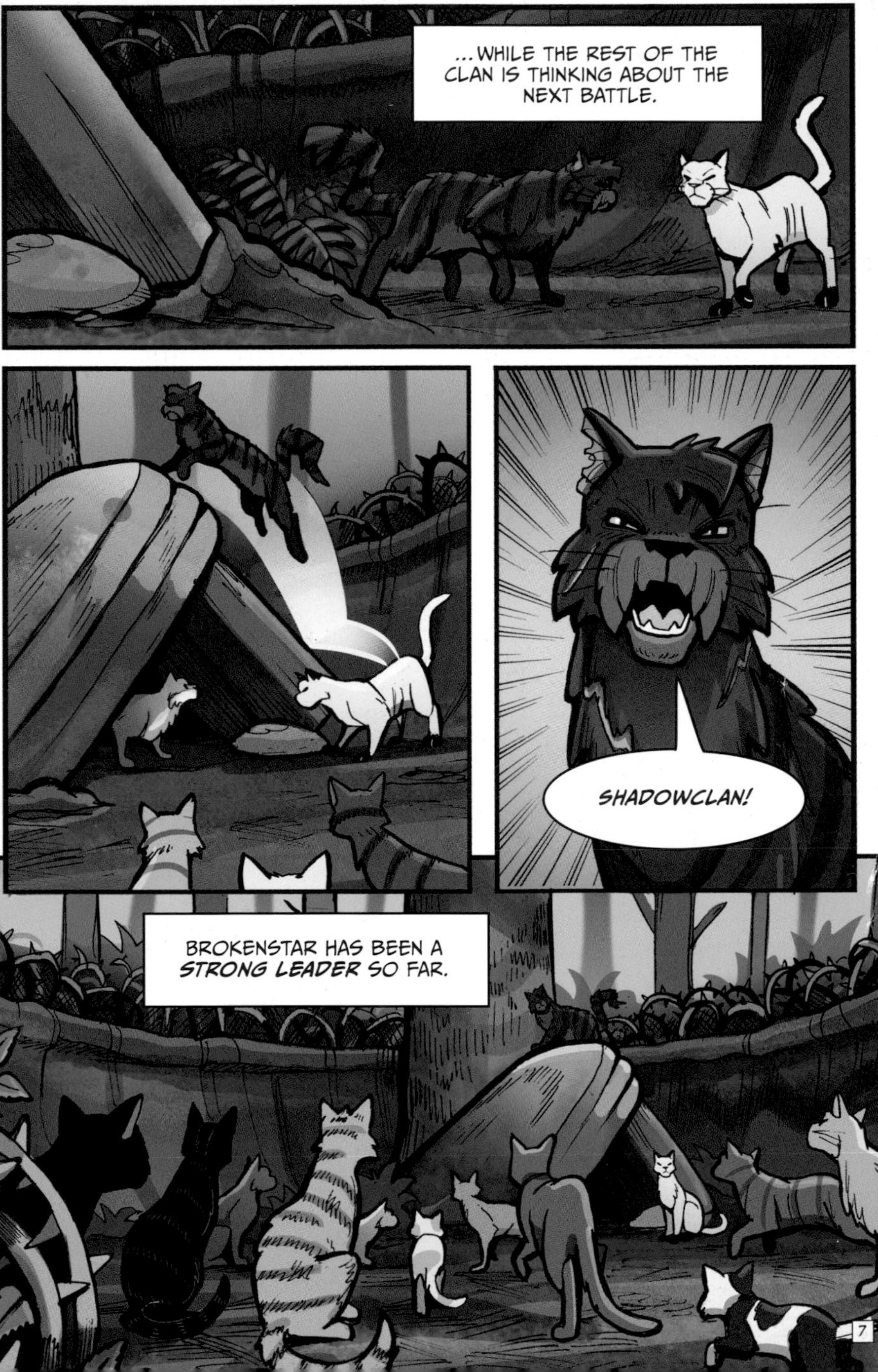
...WHILE THE REST OF THE CLAN IS THINKING ABOUT THE NEXT BATTLE.
SHADOWCLAN!
BROKENSTAR HAS BEEN A STRONG LEADER SO FAR.

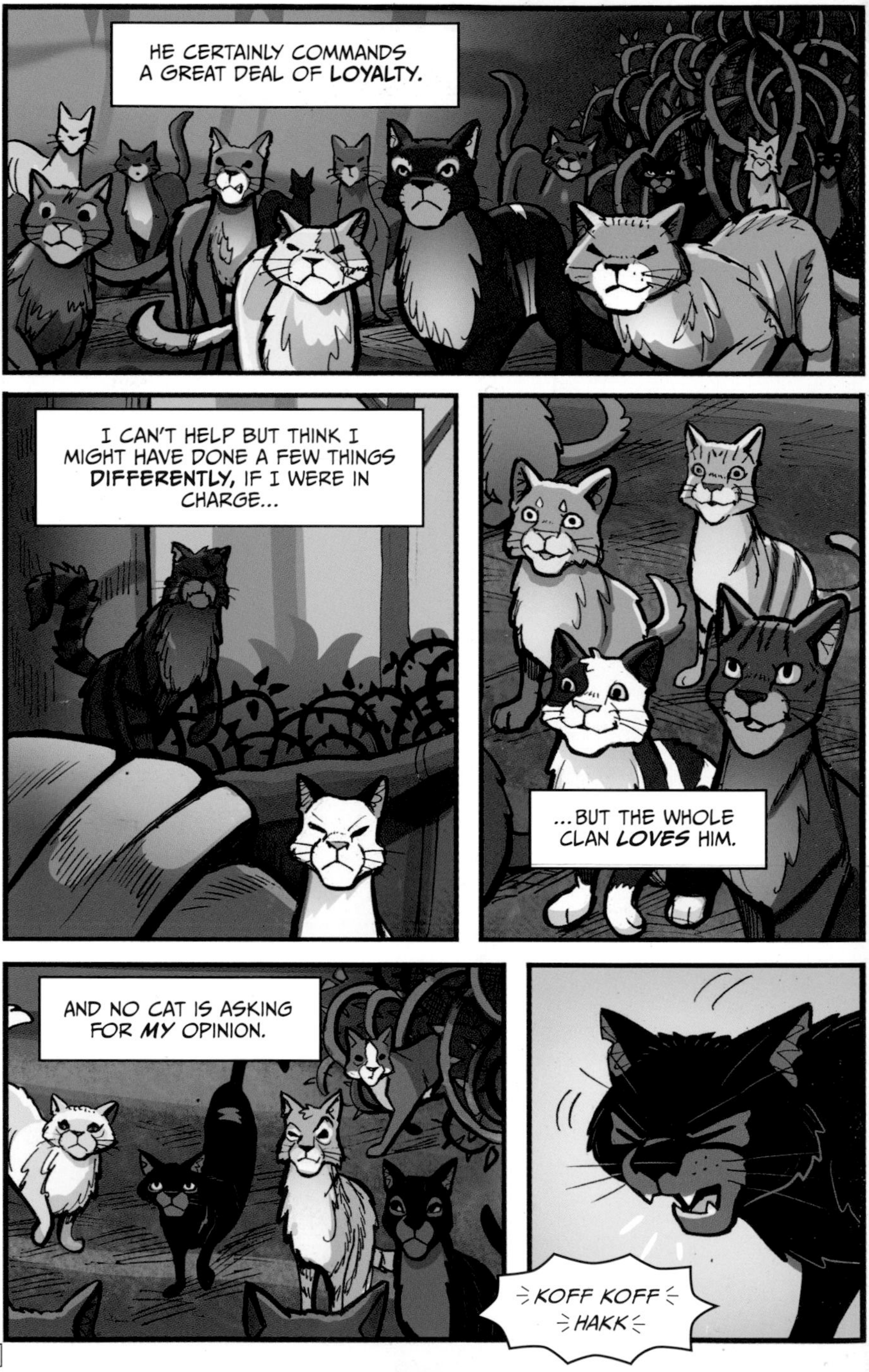
HE CERTAINLY COMMANDS A GREAT DEAL OF **LOYALTY.**
I CAN'T HELP BUT THINK I MIGHT HAVE DONE A FEW THINGS **DIFFERENTLY,** IF I WERE IN CHARGE...
...BUT THE WHOLE CLAN ***LOVES*** HIM.
AND NO CAT IS ASKING FOR ***MY*** OPINION.
KOFF KOFF
HAKK

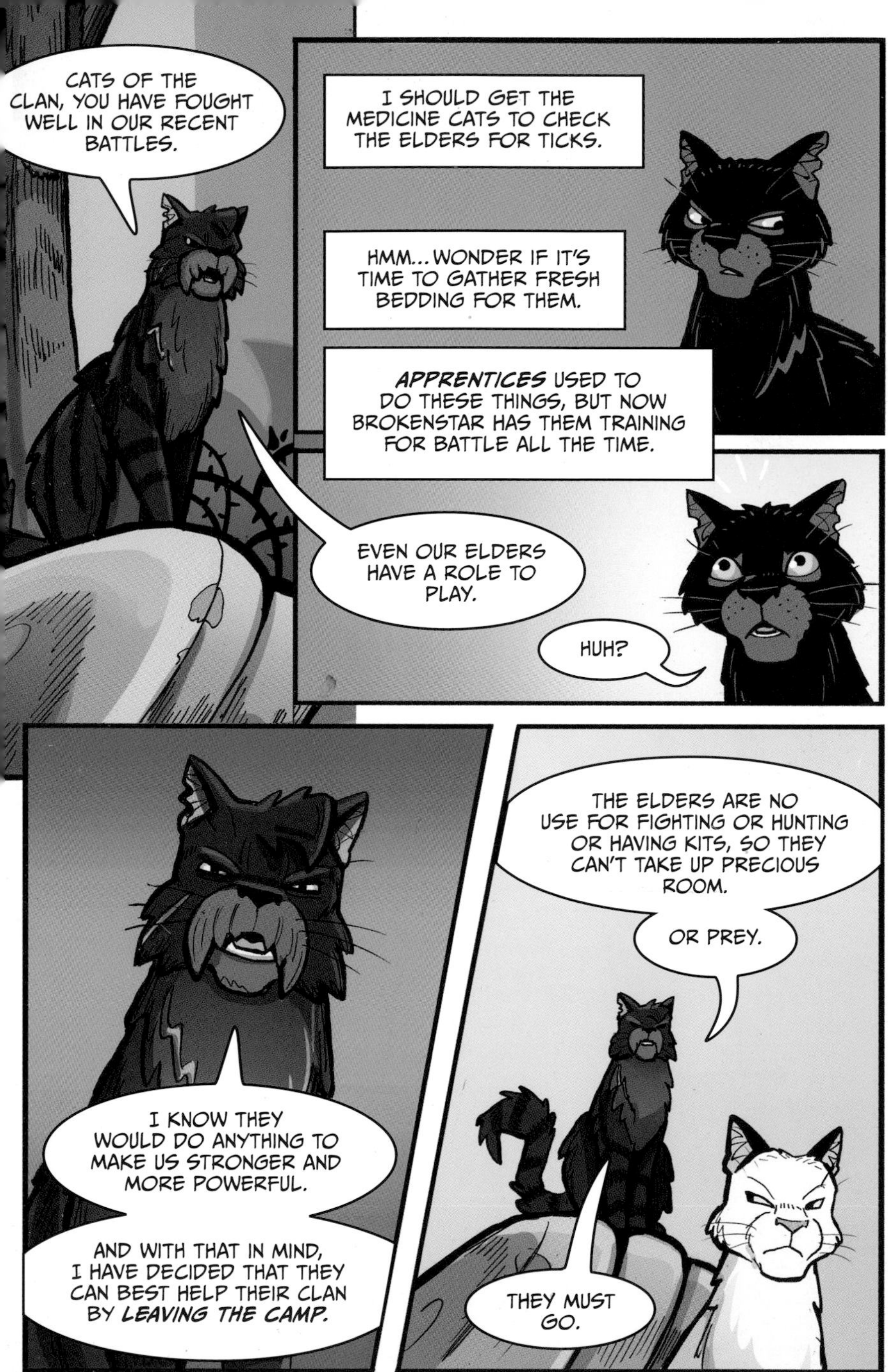
CATS OF THE CLAN, YOU HAVE FOUGHT WELL IN OUR RECENT BATTLES.
I SHOULD GET THE MEDICINE CATS TO CHECK THE ELDERS FOR TICKS.
HMM...WONDER IF IT'S TIME TO GATHER FRESH BEDDING FOR THEM.
APPRENTICES USED TO DO THESE THINGS, BUT NOW BROKENSTAR HAS THEM TRAINING FOR BATTLE ALL THE TIME.
EVEN OUR ELDERS HAVE A ROLE TO PLAY.
HUH?
I KNOW THEY WOULD DO ANYTHING TO MAKE US STRONGER AND MORE POWERFUL.
AND WITH THAT IN MIND, I HAVE DECIDED THAT THEY CAN BEST HELP THEIR CLAN BY LEAVING THE CAMP.
THE ELDERS ARE NO USE FOR FIGHTING OR HUNTING OR HAVING KITS, SO THEY CAN'T TAKE UP PRECIOUS ROOM.
OR PREY.
THEY MUST GO.

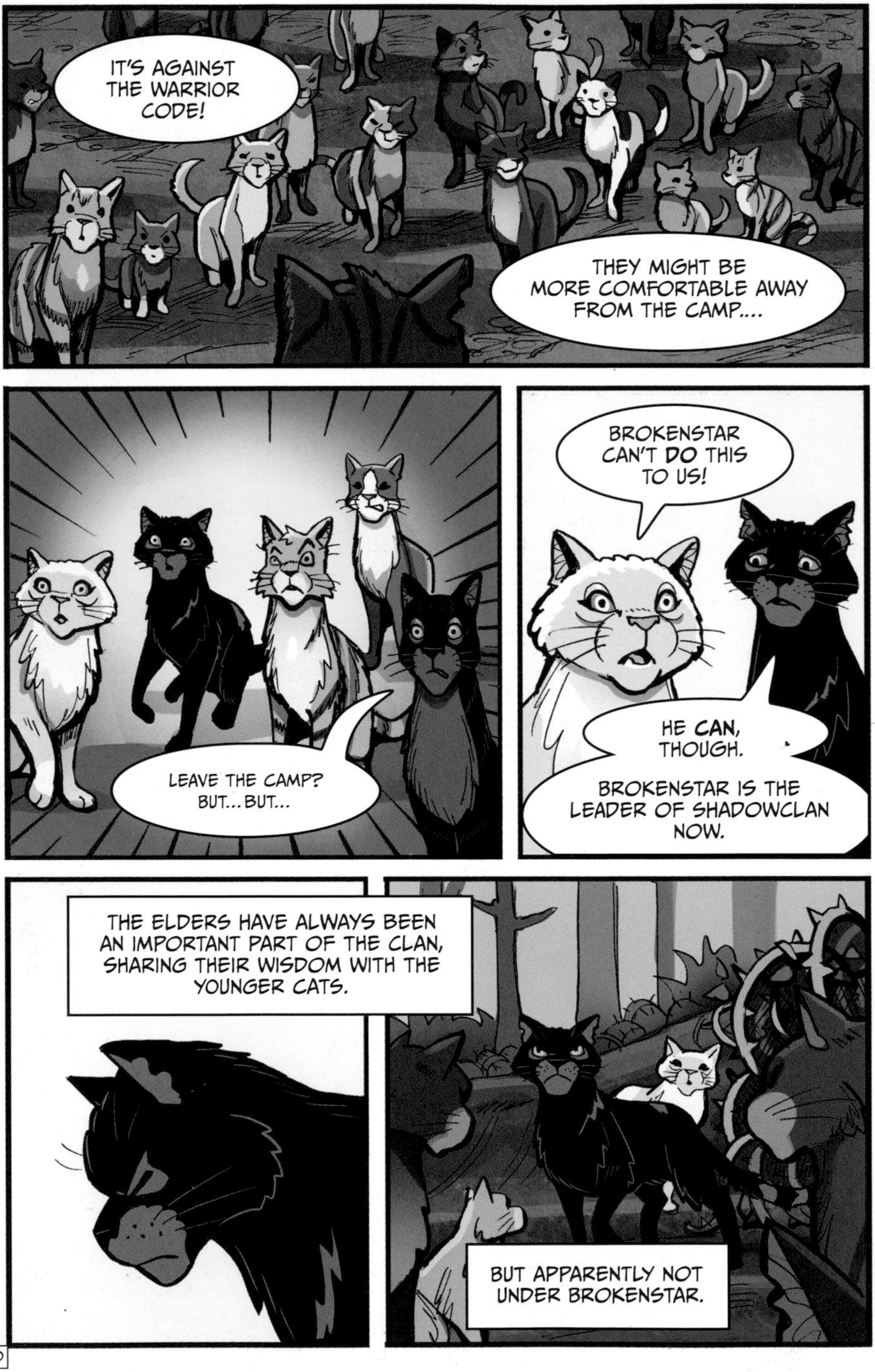
IT'S AGAINST THE WARRIOR CODE!
THEY MIGHT BE MORE COMFORTABLE AWAY FROM THE CAMP....
LEAVE THE CAMP? BUT... BUT...
BROKENSTAR CAN'T DO THIS TO US!
HE CAN, THOUGH.
BROKENSTAR IS THE LEADER OF SHADOWCLAN NOW.
THE ELDERS HAVE ALWAYS BEEN AN IMPORTANT PART OF THE CLAN, SHARING THEIR WISDOM WITH THE YOUNGER CATS.
BUT APPARENTLY NOT UNDER BROKENSTAR.

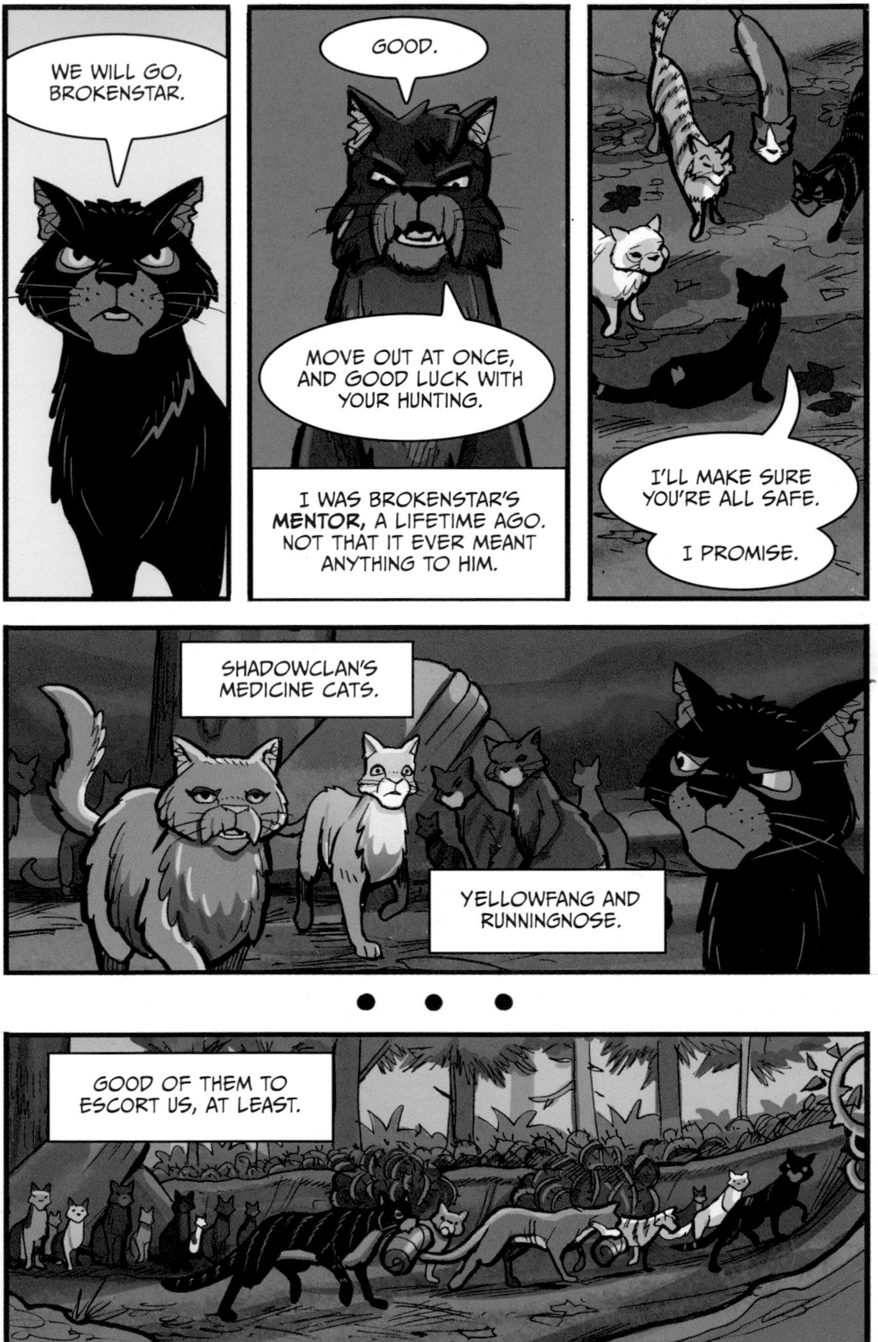
WE WILL GO, BROKENSTAR.
GOOD.
MOVE OUT AT ONCE, AND GOOD LUCK WITH YOUR HUNTING.
I WAS BROKENSTAR'S **MENTOR,** A LIFETIME AGO. NOT THAT IT EVER MEANT ANYTHING TO HIM.
I'LL MAKE SURE YOU'RE ALL SAFE.
I PROMISE.
SHADOWCLAN'S MEDICINE CATS.
YELLOWFANG AND RUNNINGNOSE.
GOOD OF THEM TO ESCORT US, AT LEAST.

THIS IS **WRONG**.

THE ELDERS HAVE WORKED HARD ALL THEIR LIVES FOR THEIR CLAN. THEY DESERVE TO BE PART OF IT.

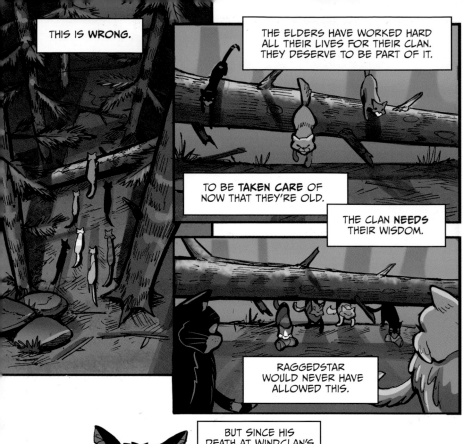

TO BE **TAKEN CARE** OF NOW THAT THEY'RE OLD.

THE CLAN **NEEDS** THEIR WISDOM.

RAGGEDSTAR WOULD NEVER HAVE ALLOWED THIS.

BUT SINCE HIS DEATH AT WINDCLAN'S PAWS...

...ALL BROKENSTAR HAS WANTED TO DO IS AVENGE HIS FATHER.

EVEN WHEN HE WAS MY APPRENTICE, ALL HE EVER WANTED TO DO WAS FIGHT.

BROKENSTAR WANTS TO MAKE SHADOWCLAN MORE POWERFUL THAN ANY OTHER CLAN.

THAT'S A GOOD THING — ISN'T IT?

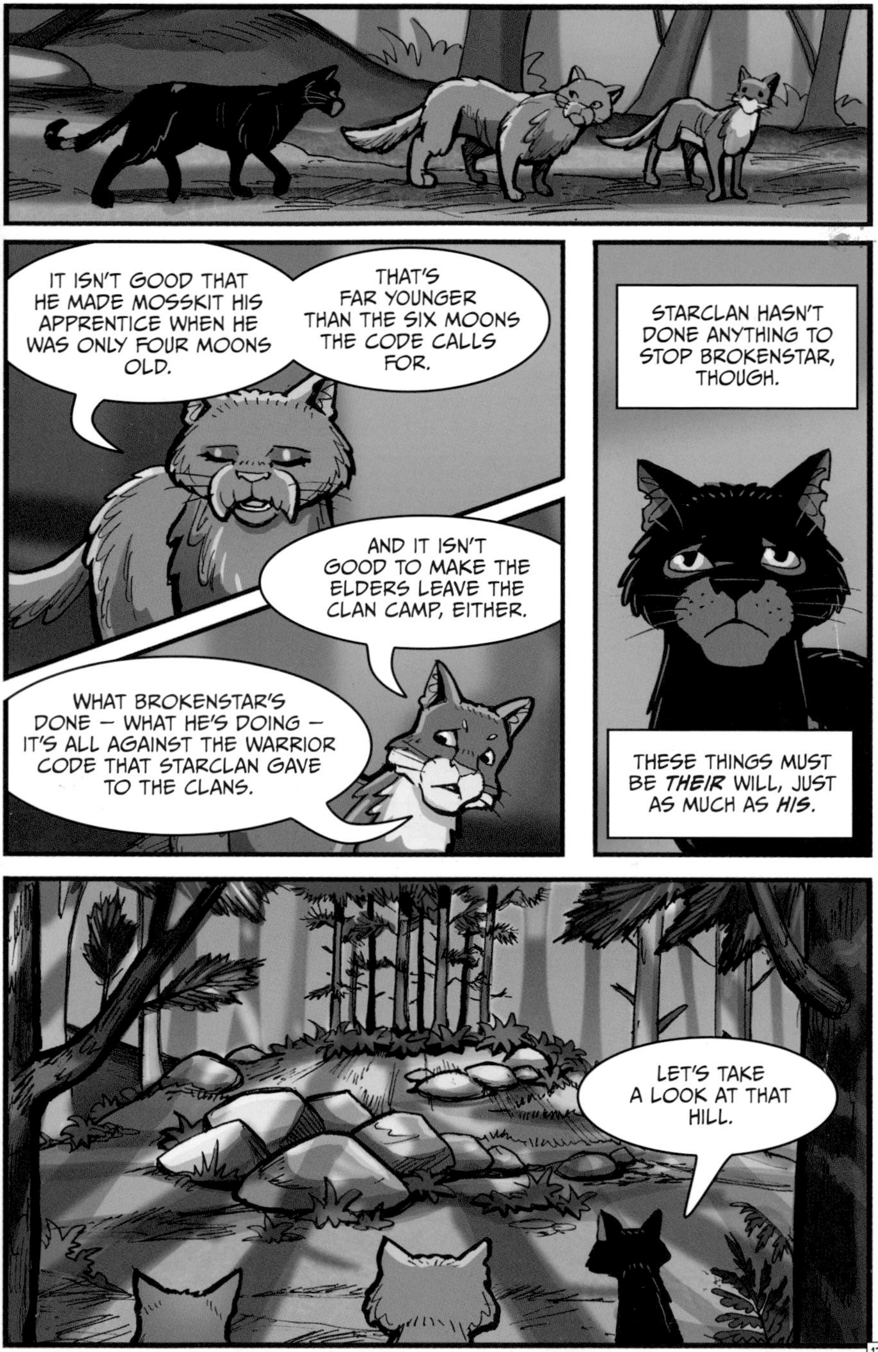
IT ISN'T GOOD THAT HE MADE MOSSKIT HIS APPRENTICE WHEN HE WAS ONLY FOUR MOONS OLD.
THAT'S FAR YOUNGER THAN THE SIX MOONS THE CODE CALLS FOR.
AND IT ISN'T GOOD TO MAKE THE ELDERS LEAVE THE CLAN CAMP, EITHER.
WHAT BROKENSTAR'S DONE — WHAT HE'S DOING — IT'S ALL AGAINST THE WARRIOR CODE THAT STARCLAN GAVE TO THE CLANS.
STARCLAN HASN'T DONE ANYTHING TO STOP BROKENSTAR, THOUGH.
THESE THINGS MUST BE *THEIR* WILL, JUST AS MUCH AS *HIS*.
LET'S TAKE A LOOK AT THAT HILL.

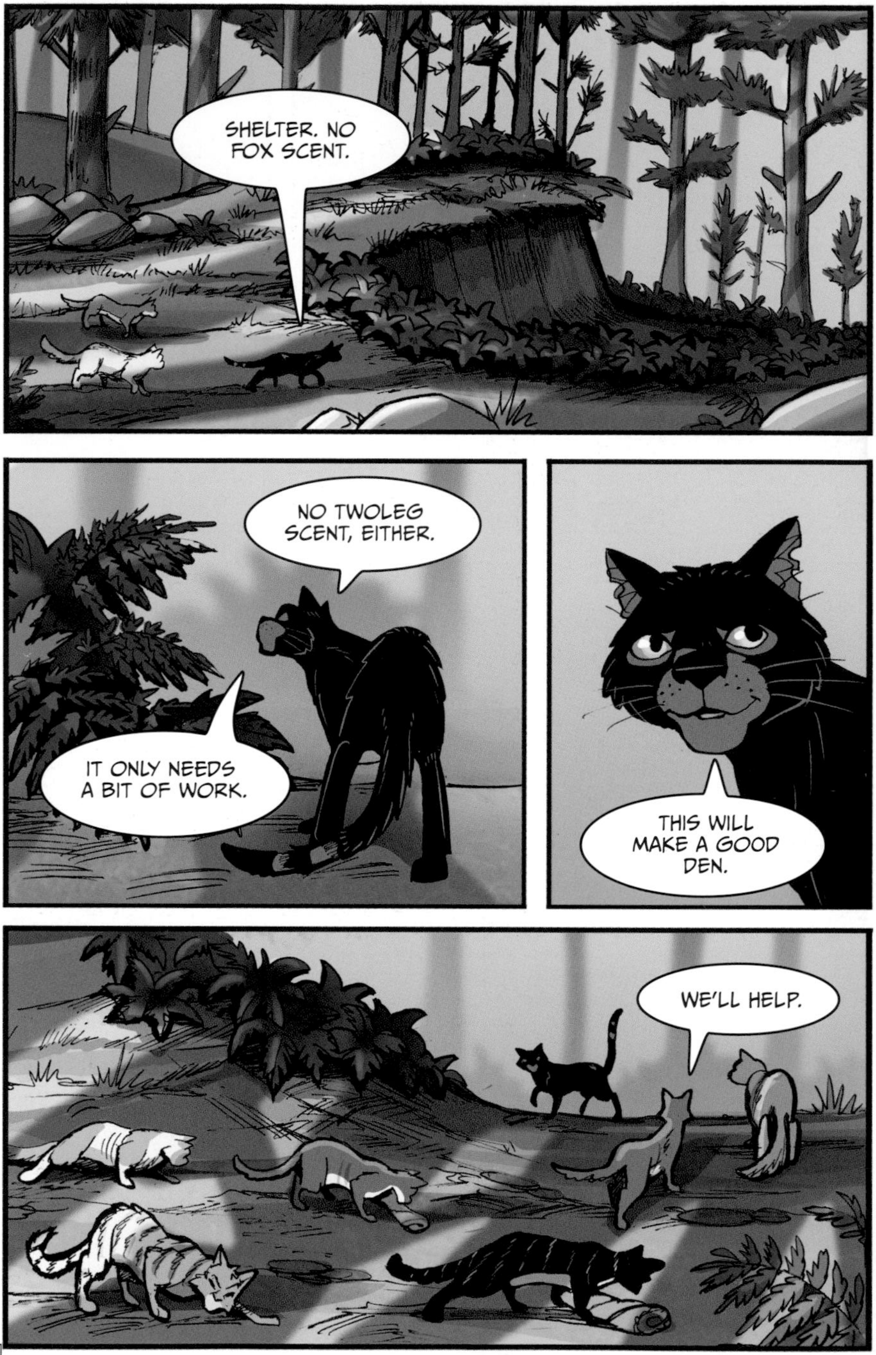
SHELTER. NO FOX SCENT.
NO TWOLEG SCENT, EITHER.
IT ONLY NEEDS A BIT OF WORK.
THIS WILL MAKE A GOOD DEN.
WE'LL HELP.

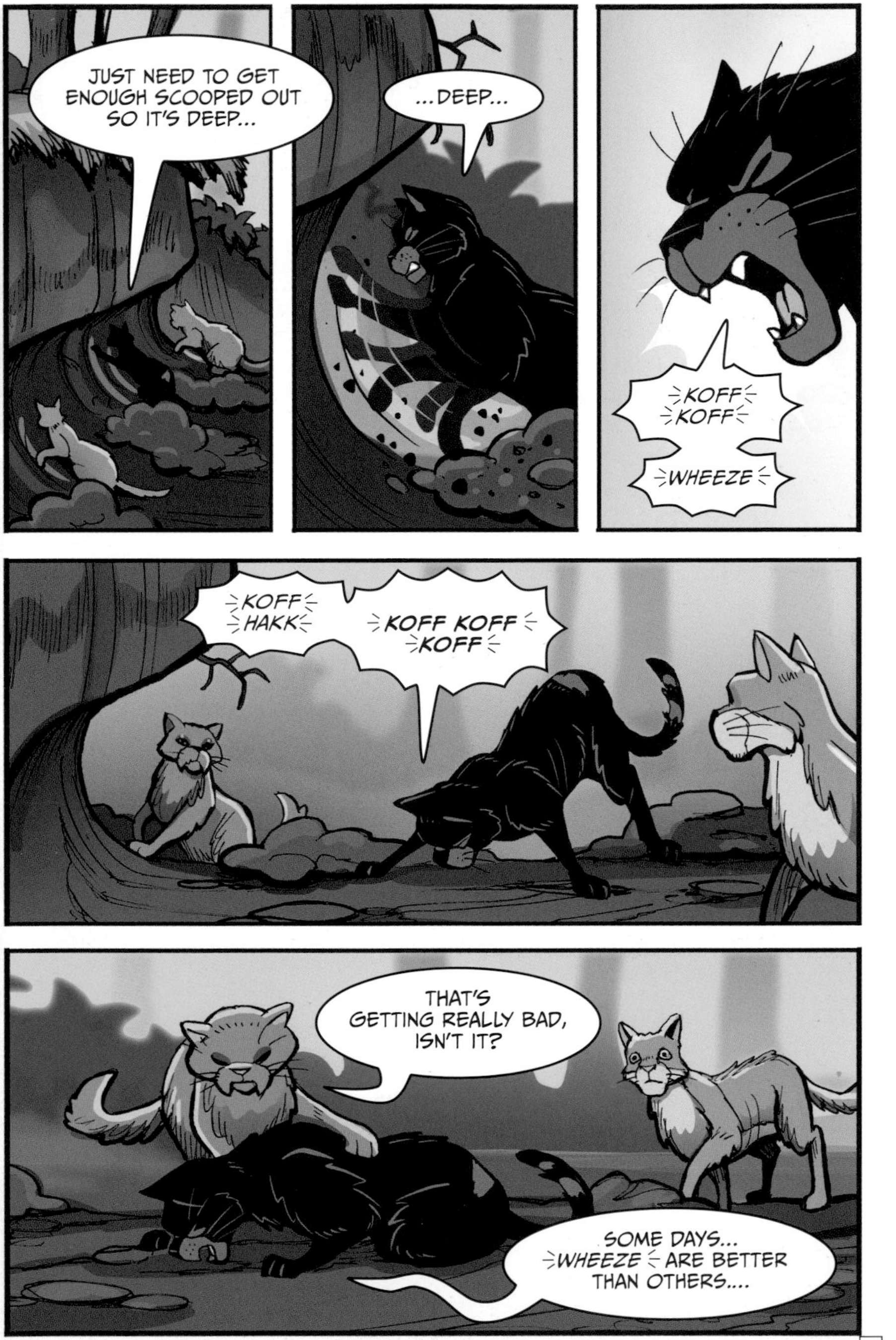
JUST NEED TO GET ENOUGH SCOOPED OUT SO IT'S DEEP...
...DEEP...
KOFF KOFF
WHEEZE
KOFF HAKK
KOFF KOFF KOFF
THAT'S GETTING REALLY BAD, ISN'T IT?
SOME DAYS... WHEEZE ARE BETTER THAN OTHERS....

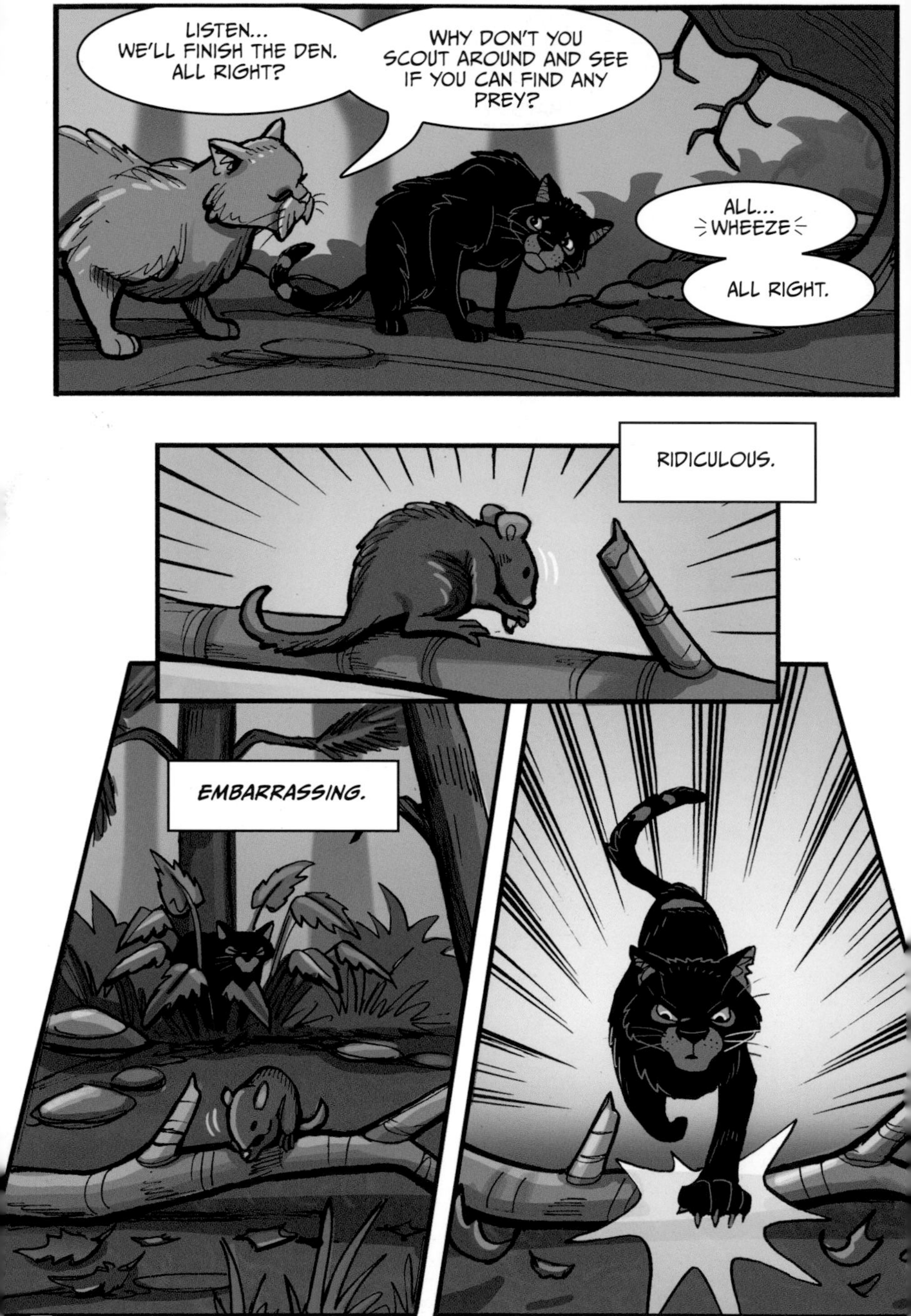
LISTEN... WE'LL FINISH THE DEN. ALL RIGHT?
WHY DON'T YOU SCOUT AROUND AND SEE IF YOU CAN FIND ANY PREY?
ALL... WHEEZE
ALL RIGHT.
RIDICULOUS.
EMBARRASSING.

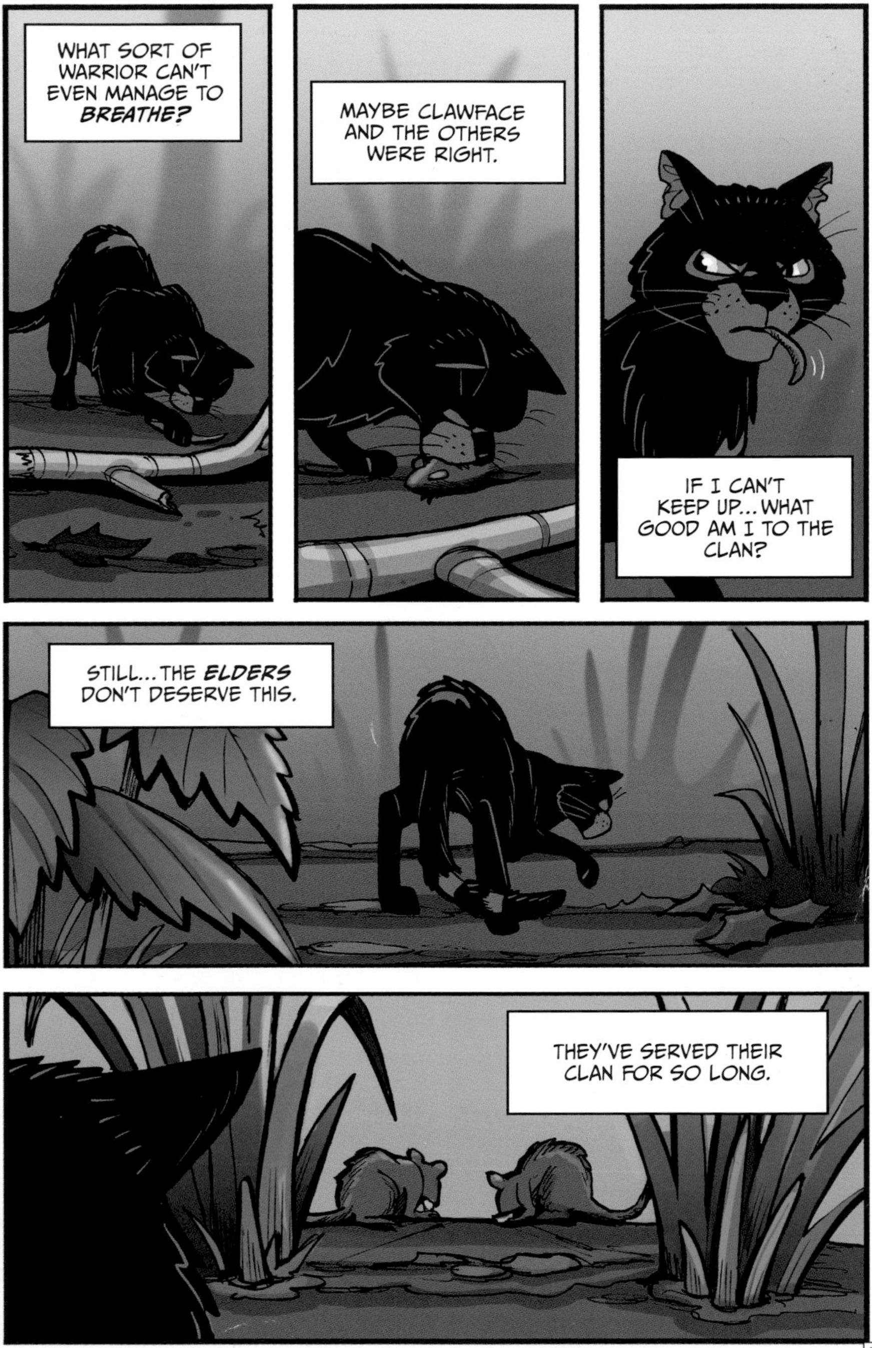
WHAT SORT OF WARRIOR CAN'T EVEN MANAGE TO *BREATHE?*
MAYBE CLAWFACE AND THE OTHERS WERE RIGHT.
IF I CAN'T KEEP UP... WHAT GOOD AM I TO THE CLAN?
STILL... THE *ELDERS* DON'T DESERVE THIS.
THEY'VE SERVED THEIR CLAN FOR SO LONG.

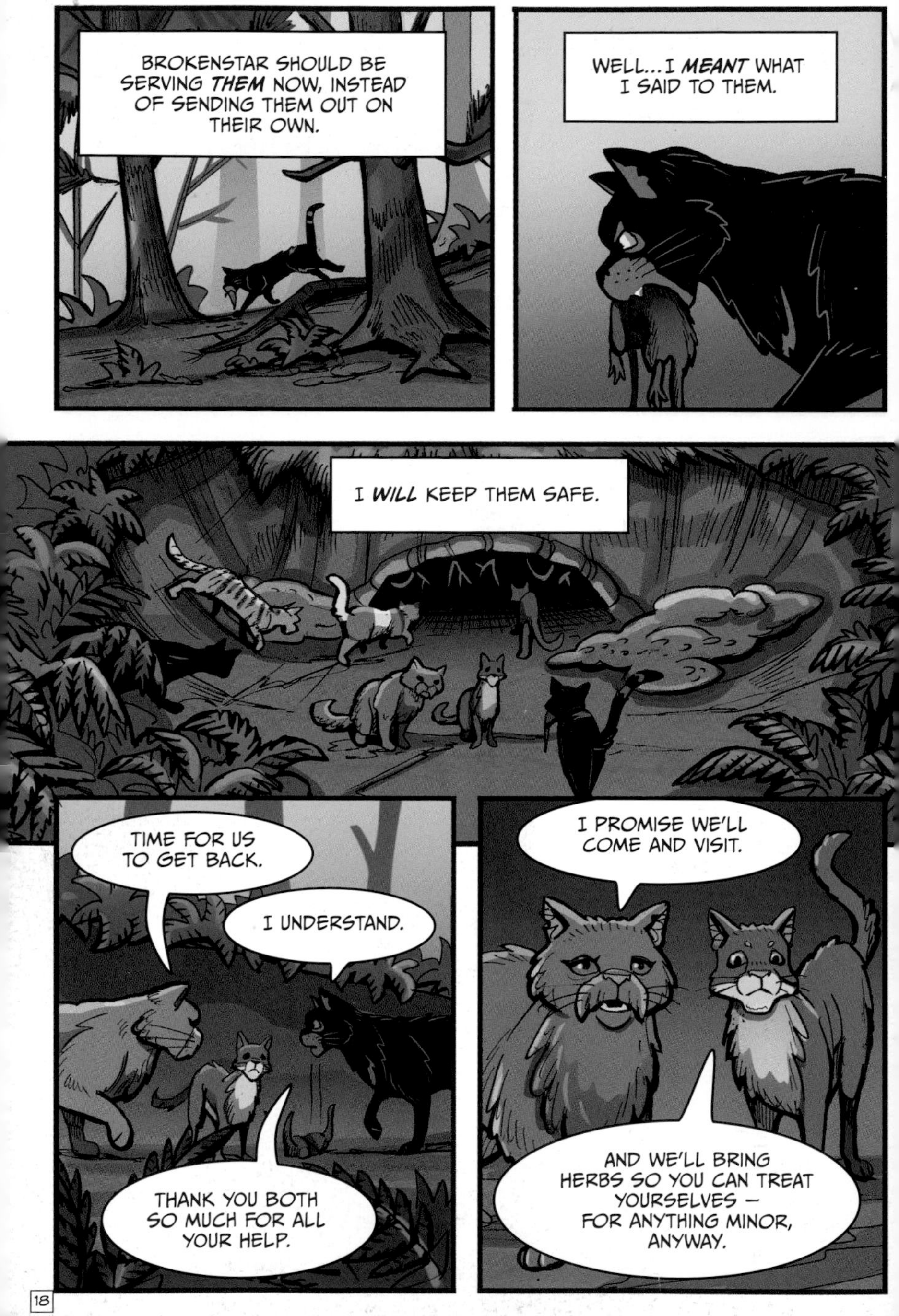
BROKENSTAR SHOULD BE SERVING *THEM* NOW, INSTEAD OF SENDING THEM OUT ON THEIR OWN.
WELL... I *MEANT* WHAT I SAID TO THEM.
I *WILL* KEEP THEM SAFE.
TIME FOR US TO GET BACK.
I UNDERSTAND.
THANK YOU BOTH SO MUCH FOR ALL YOUR HELP.
I PROMISE WE'LL COME AND VISIT.
AND WE'LL BRING HERBS SO YOU CAN TREAT YOURSELVES — FOR ANYTHING MINOR, ANYWAY.

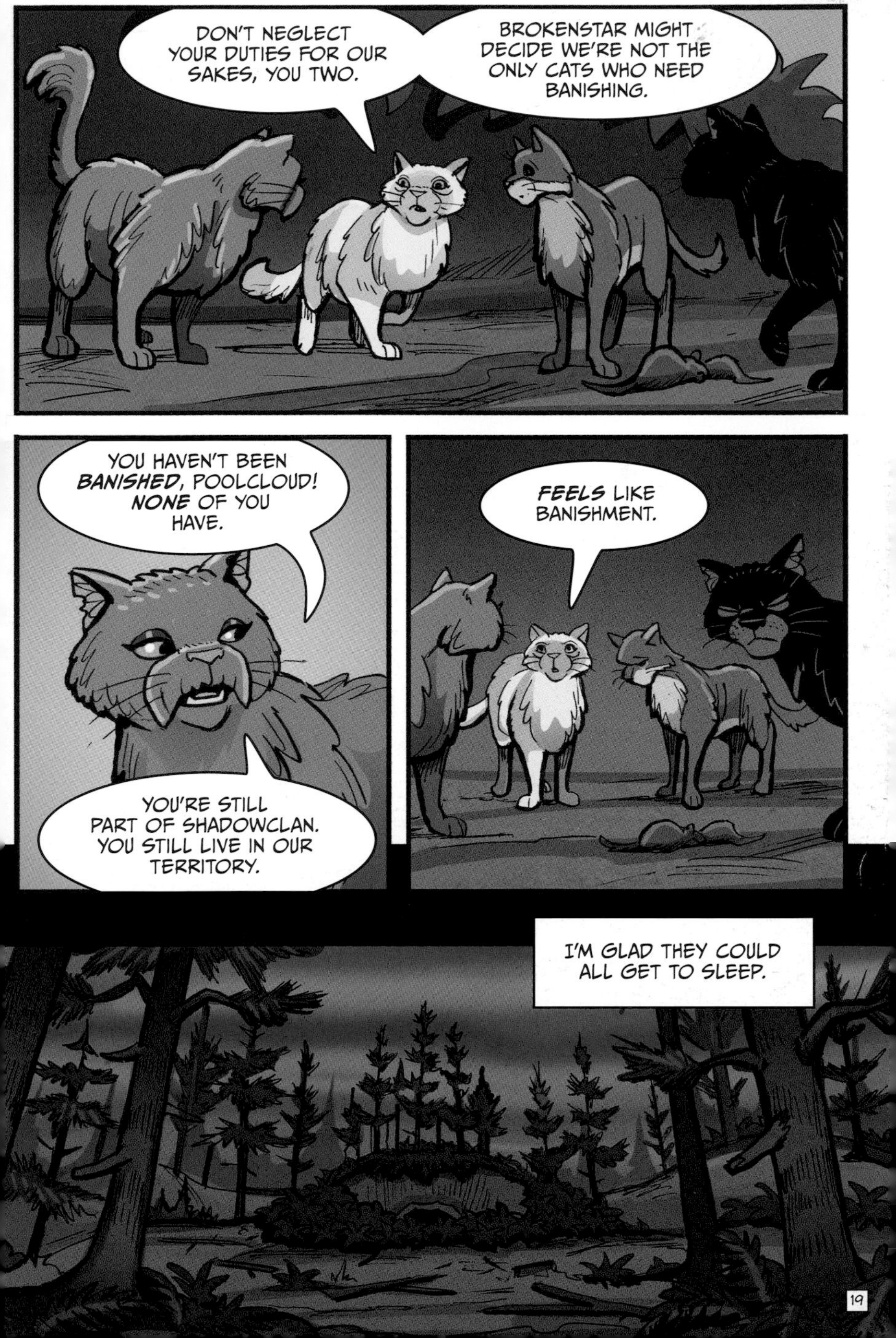
DON'T NEGLECT YOUR DUTIES FOR OUR SAKES, YOU TWO.
BROKENSTAR MIGHT DECIDE WE'RE NOT THE ONLY CATS WHO NEED BANISHING.
YOU HAVEN'T BEEN *BANISHED*, POOLCLOUD! *NONE* OF YOU HAVE.
YOU'RE STILL PART OF SHADOWCLAN. YOU STILL LIVE IN OUR TERRITORY.
FEELS LIKE BANISHMENT.
I'M GLAD THEY COULD ALL GET TO SLEEP.

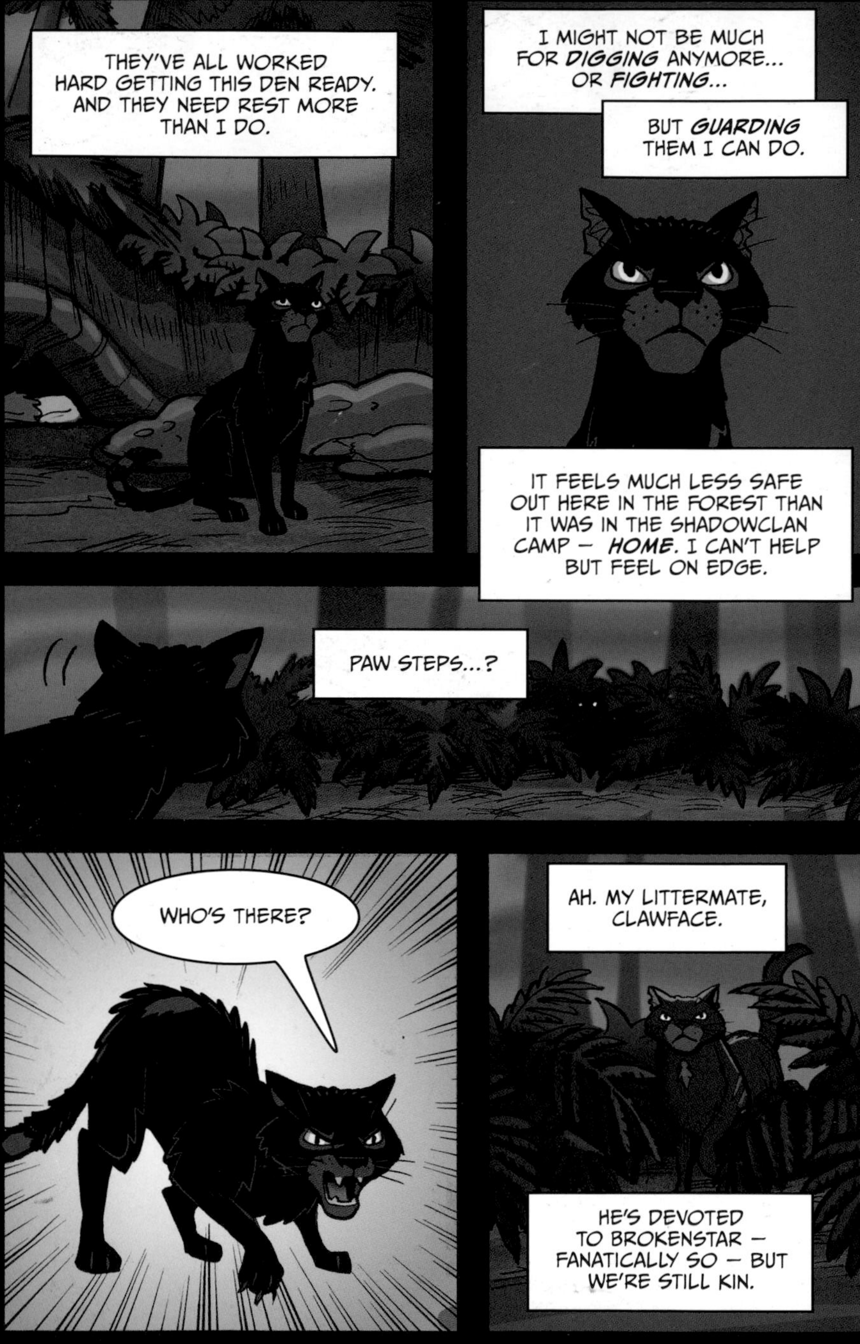
THEY'VE ALL WORKED HARD GETTING THIS DEN READY. AND THEY NEED REST MORE THAN I DO.
I MIGHT NOT BE MUCH FOR DIGGING ANYMORE... OR FIGHTING...
BUT GUARDING THEM I CAN DO.
IT FEELS MUCH LESS SAFE OUT HERE IN THE FOREST THAN IT WAS IN THE SHADOWCLAN CAMP — HOME. I CAN'T HELP BUT FEEL ON EDGE.
PAW STEPS...?
WHO'S THERE?
AH. MY LITTERMATE, CLAWFACE.
HE'S DEVOTED TO BROKENSTAR — FANATICALLY SO — BUT WE'RE STILL KIN.

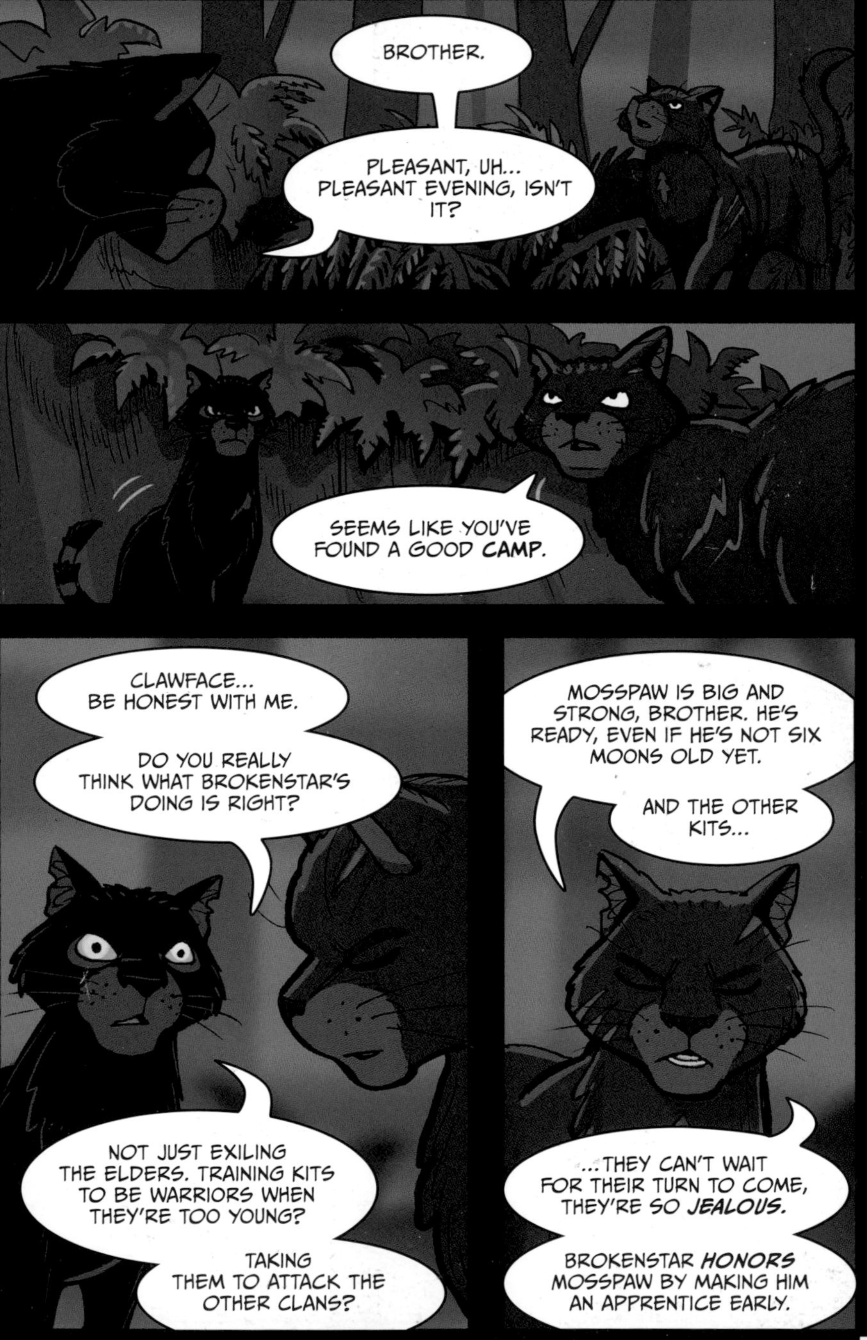
BROTHER.
PLEASANT, UH... PLEASANT EVENING, ISN'T IT?
SEEMS LIKE YOU'VE FOUND A GOOD **CAMP.**
CLAWFACE... BE HONEST WITH ME.
DO YOU REALLY THINK WHAT BROKENSTAR'S DOING IS RIGHT?
NOT JUST EXILING THE ELDERS. TRAINING KITS TO BE WARRIORS WHEN THEY'RE TOO YOUNG?
TAKING THEM TO ATTACK THE OTHER CLANS?
MOSSPAW IS BIG AND STRONG, BROTHER. HE'S READY, EVEN IF HE'S NOT SIX MOONS OLD YET.
AND THE OTHER KITS...
...THEY CAN'T WAIT FOR THEIR TURN TO COME, THEY'RE SO ***JEALOUS.***
BROKENSTAR ***HONORS*** MOSSPAW BY MAKING HIM AN APPRENTICE EARLY.

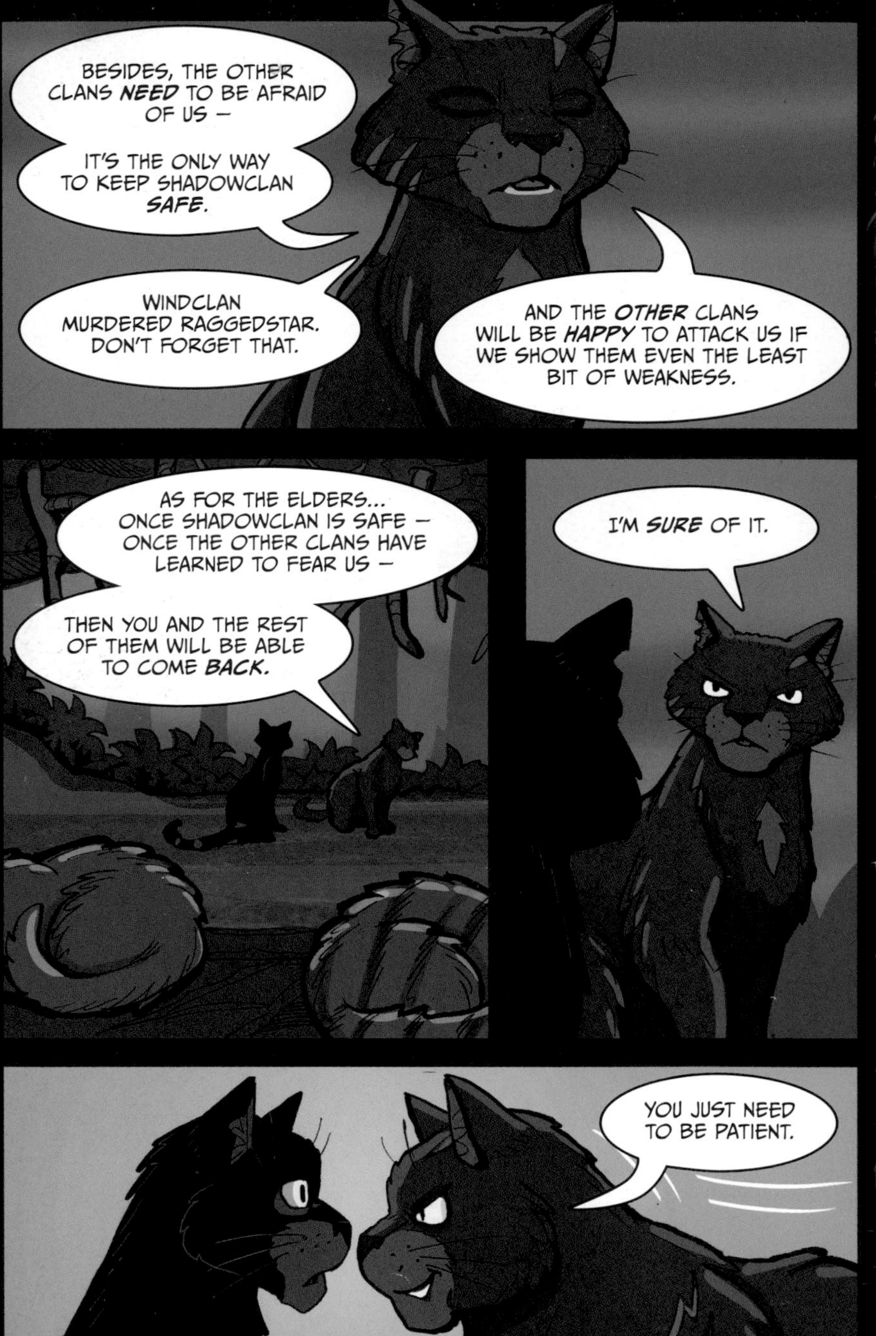
BESIDES, THE OTHER CLANS NEED TO BE AFRAID OF US –
IT'S THE ONLY WAY TO KEEP SHADOWCLAN SAFE.
WINDCLAN MURDERED RAGGEDSTAR. DON'T FORGET THAT.
AND THE OTHER CLANS WILL BE HAPPY TO ATTACK US IF WE SHOW THEM EVEN THE LEAST BIT OF WEAKNESS.
AS FOR THE ELDERS... ONCE SHADOWCLAN IS SAFE – ONCE THE OTHER CLANS HAVE LEARNED TO FEAR US –
THEN YOU AND THE REST OF THEM WILL BE ABLE TO COME BACK.
I'M SURE OF IT.
YOU JUST NEED TO BE PATIENT.

PATIENT?

...WE'RE GOING TO HAVE TO DEPEND ON EACH OTHER.

LEAF-BARE IS COMING. IF THE ELDERS AND I ARE GOING TO SURVIVE...

AND ALL OF THEM WILL HAVE TO DEPEND ON *ME*.

I WON'T LET THEM DOWN...

...BUT *PATIENCE* HAS NOTHING TO DO WITH IT.

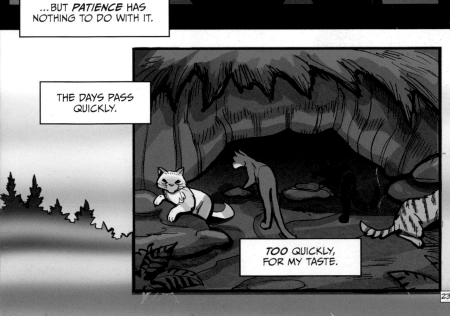

THE DAYS PASS QUICKLY.

TOO QUICKLY, FOR MY TASTE.

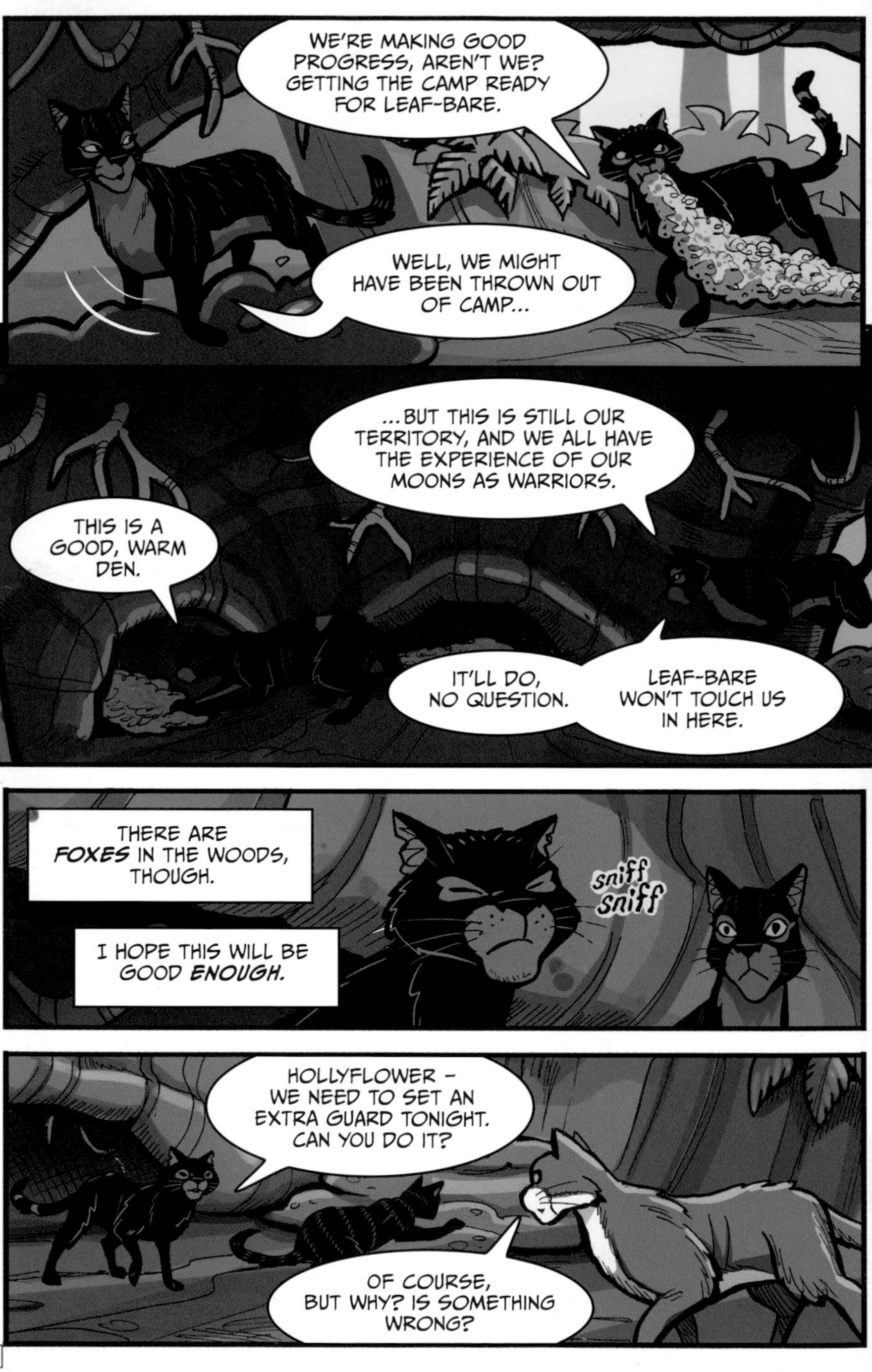
WE'RE MAKING GOOD PROGRESS, AREN'T WE? GETTING THE CAMP READY FOR LEAF-BARE.
WELL, WE MIGHT HAVE BEEN THROWN OUT OF CAMP...
...BUT THIS IS STILL OUR TERRITORY, AND WE ALL HAVE THE EXPERIENCE OF OUR MOONS AS WARRIORS.
THIS IS A GOOD, WARM DEN.
IT'LL DO, NO QUESTION.
LEAF-BARE WON'T TOUCH US IN HERE.
THERE ARE FOXES IN THE WOODS, THOUGH.
I HOPE THIS WILL BE GOOD ENOUGH.
sniff sniff
HOLLYFLOWER – WE NEED TO SET AN EXTRA GUARD TONIGHT. CAN YOU DO IT?
OF COURSE, BUT WHY? IS SOMETHING WRONG?

MAYBE NOT.
WE JUST NEED TO
BE VIGILANT.

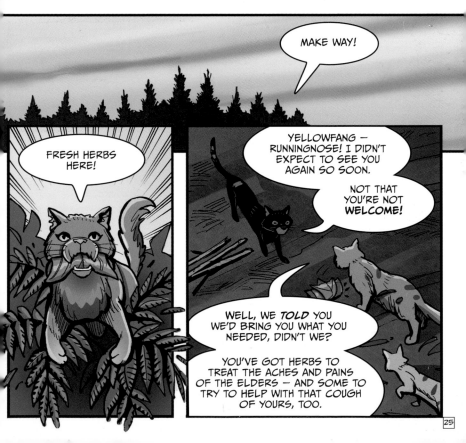

MAKE WAY!

FRESH HERBS
HERE!

YELLOWFANG —
RUNNINGNOSE! I DIDN'T
EXPECT TO SEE YOU
AGAIN SO SOON.

NOT THAT
YOU'RE NOT
WELCOME!

WELL, WE *TOLD* YOU
WE'D BRING YOU WHAT YOU
NEEDED, DIDN'T WE?

YOU'VE GOT HERBS TO
TREAT THE ACHES AND PAINS
OF THE ELDERS — AND SOME TO
TRY TO HELP WITH THAT COUGH
OF YOURS, TOO.

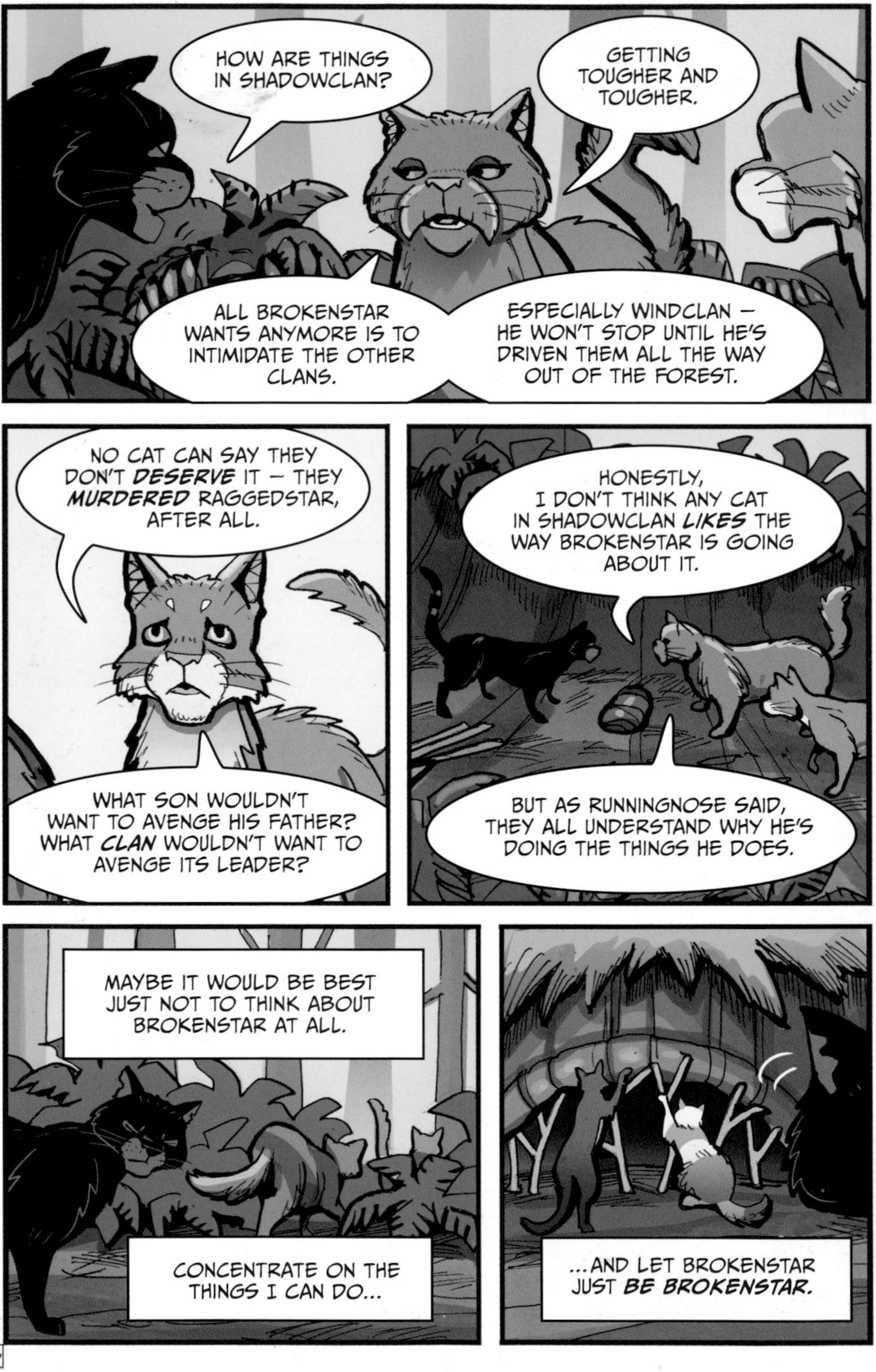
HOW ARE THINGS IN SHADOWCLAN?
GETTING TOUGHER AND TOUGHER.
ALL BROKENSTAR WANTS ANYMORE IS TO INTIMIDATE THE OTHER CLANS.
ESPECIALLY WINDCLAN — HE WON'T STOP UNTIL HE'S DRIVEN THEM ALL THE WAY OUT OF THE FOREST.
NO CAT CAN SAY THEY DON'T *DESERVE* IT — THEY *MURDERED* RAGGEDSTAR, AFTER ALL.
WHAT SON WOULDN'T WANT TO AVENGE HIS FATHER? WHAT *CLAN* WOULDN'T WANT TO AVENGE ITS LEADER?
HONESTLY, I DON'T THINK ANY CAT IN SHADOWCLAN *LIKES* THE WAY BROKENSTAR IS GOING ABOUT IT.
BUT AS RUNNINGNOSE SAID, THEY ALL UNDERSTAND WHY HE'S DOING THE THINGS HE DOES.
MAYBE IT WOULD BE BEST JUST NOT TO THINK ABOUT BROKENSTAR AT ALL.
CONCENTRATE ON THE THINGS I CAN DO...
...AND LET BROKENSTAR JUST ***BE BROKENSTAR.***

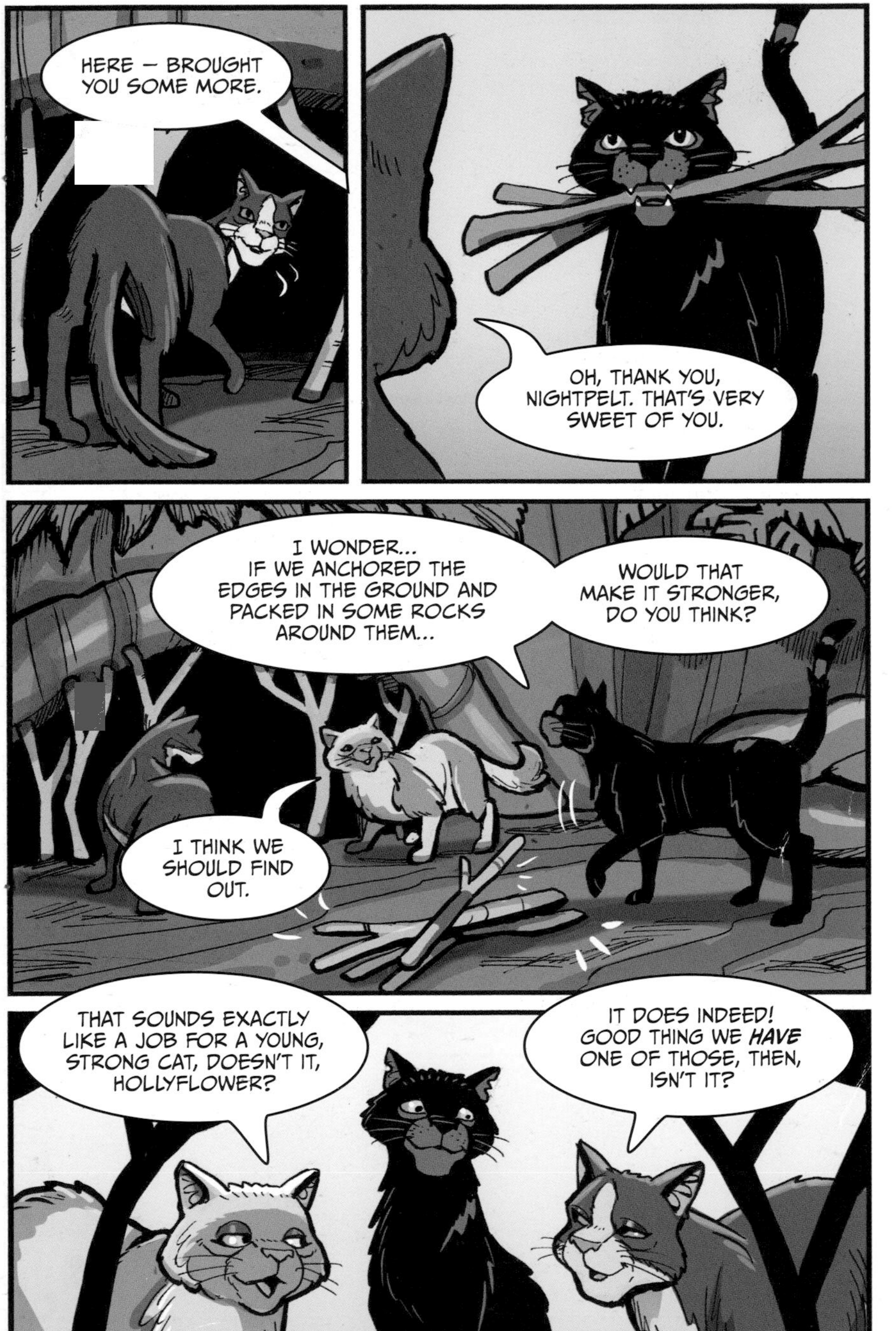
HERE — BROUGHT YOU SOME MORE.
OH, THANK YOU, NIGHTPELT. THAT'S VERY SWEET OF YOU.
I WONDER... IF WE ANCHORED THE EDGES IN THE GROUND AND PACKED IN SOME ROCKS AROUND THEM...
WOULD THAT MAKE IT STRONGER, DO YOU THINK?
I THINK WE SHOULD FIND OUT.
THAT SOUNDS EXACTLY LIKE A JOB FOR A YOUNG, STRONG CAT, DOESN'T IT, HOLLYFLOWER?
IT DOES INDEED! GOOD THING WE *HAVE* ONE OF THOSE, THEN, ISN'T IT?

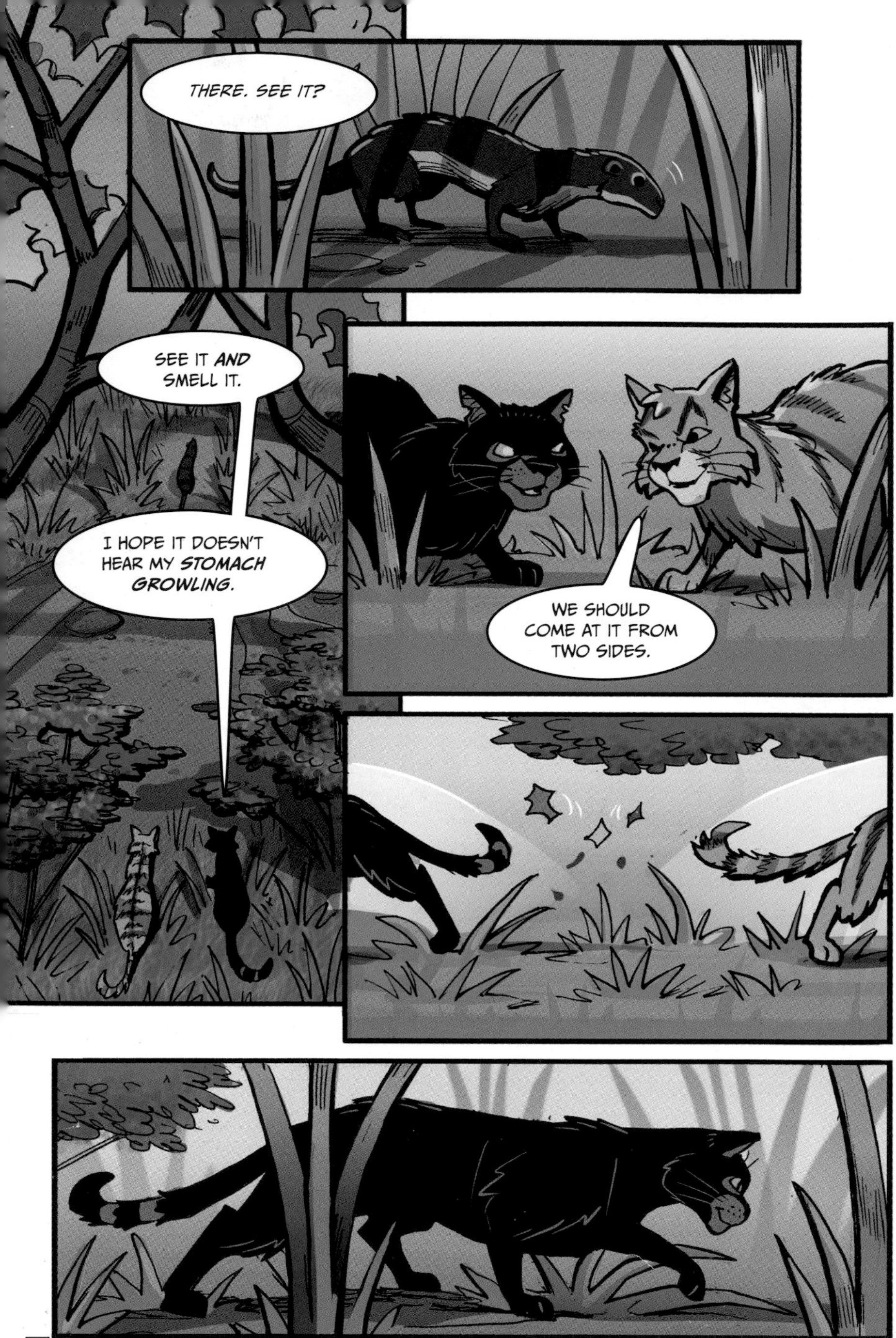
THERE. SEE IT?
SEE IT AND SMELL IT.
I HOPE IT DOESN'T HEAR MY STOMACH GROWLING.
WE SHOULD COME AT IT FROM TWO SIDES.

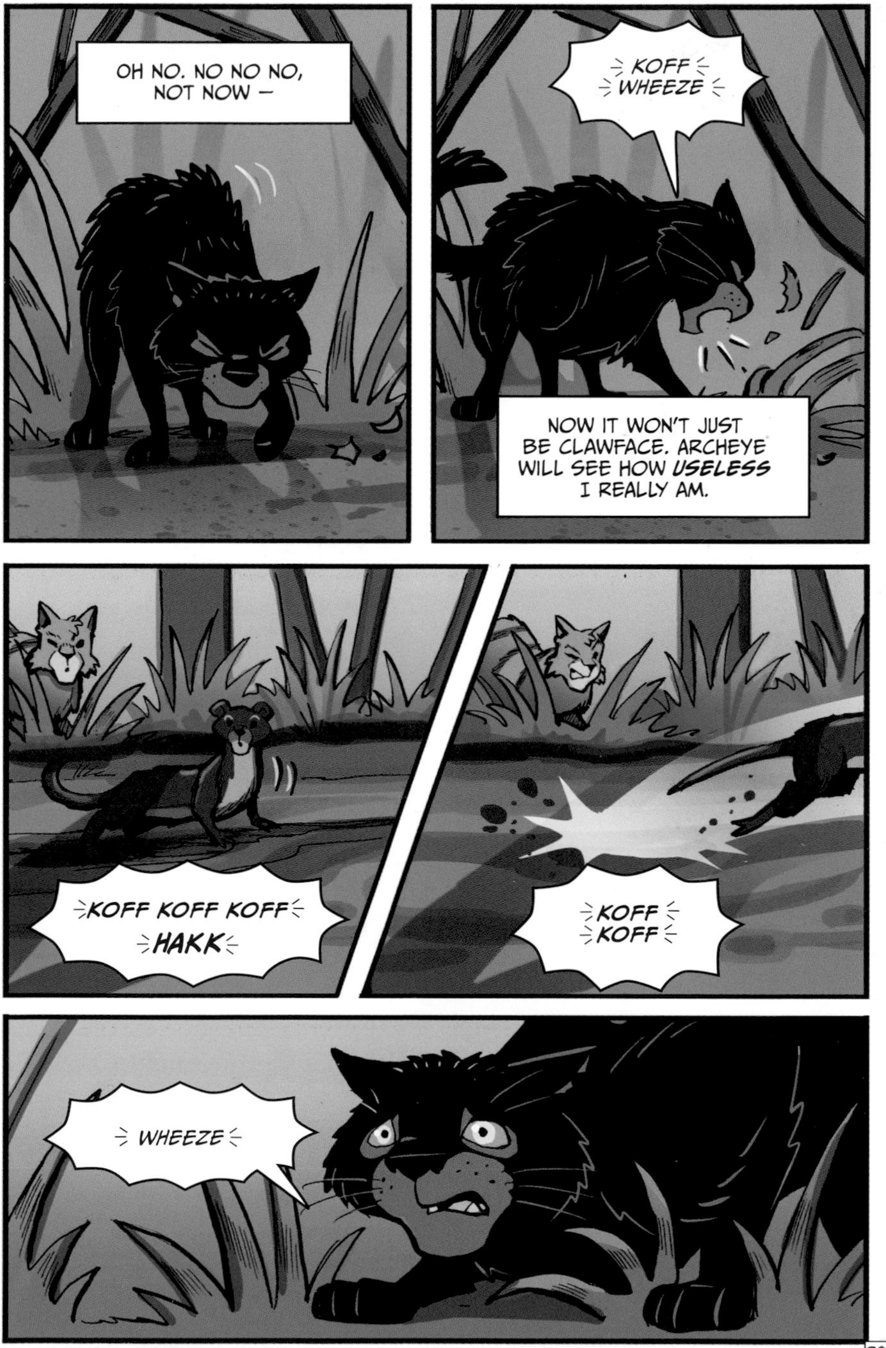

OH NO. NO NO NO, NOT NOW –
KOFF WHEEZE
NOW IT WON'T JUST BE CLAWFACE. ARCHEYE WILL SEE HOW *USELESS* I REALLY AM.
KOFF KOFF KOFF HAKK
KOFF KOFF
WHEEZE

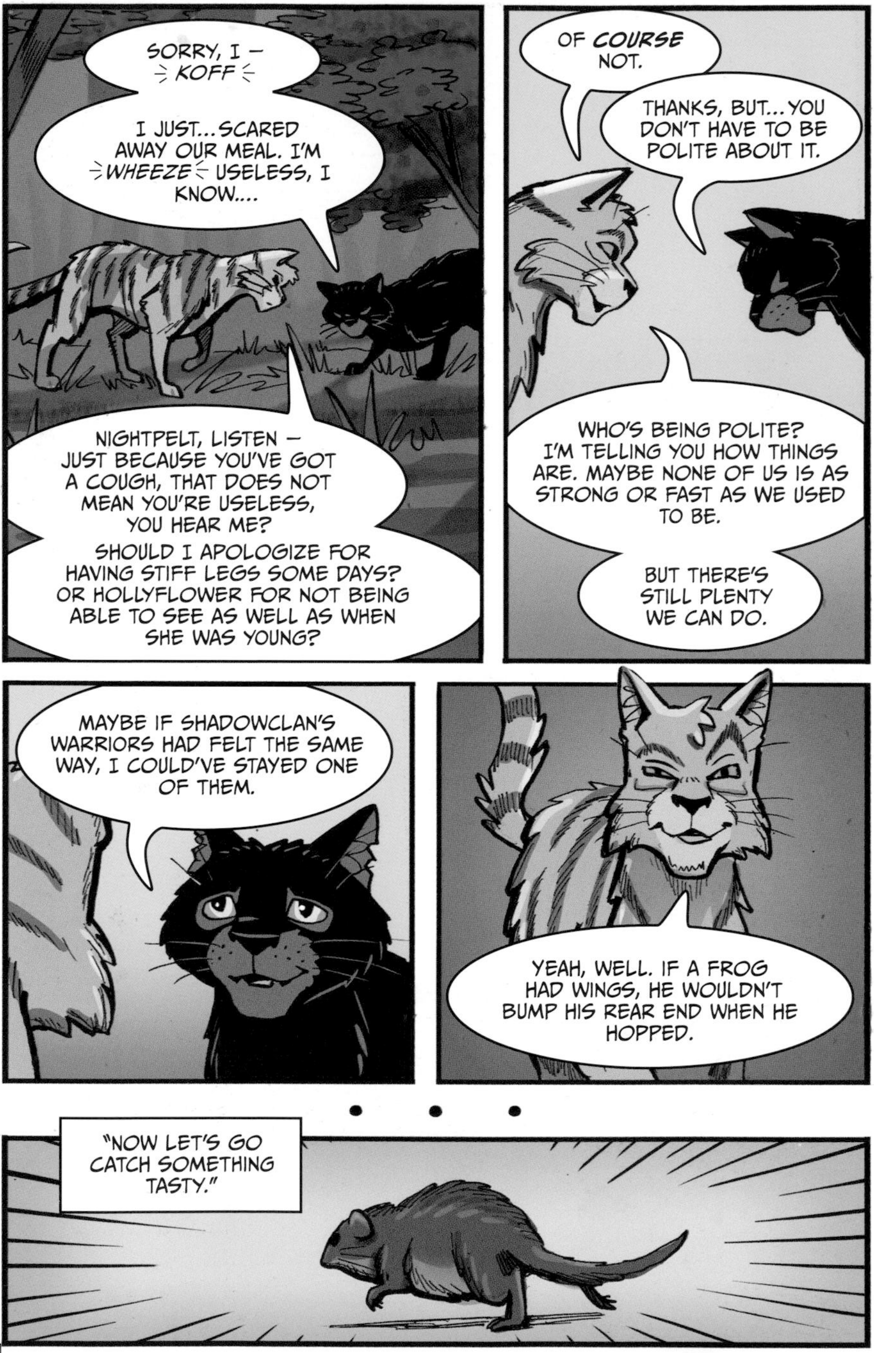
SORRY, I — KOFF
I JUST... SCARED AWAY OUR MEAL. I'M WHEEZE USELESS, I KNOW....
NIGHTPELT, LISTEN — JUST BECAUSE YOU'VE GOT A COUGH, THAT DOES NOT MEAN YOU'RE USELESS, YOU HEAR ME?
SHOULD I APOLOGIZE FOR HAVING STIFF LEGS SOME DAYS? OR HOLLYFLOWER FOR NOT BEING ABLE TO SEE AS WELL AS WHEN SHE WAS YOUNG?
OF COURSE NOT.
THANKS, BUT... YOU DON'T HAVE TO BE POLITE ABOUT IT.
WHO'S BEING POLITE? I'M TELLING YOU HOW THINGS ARE. MAYBE NONE OF US IS AS STRONG OR FAST AS WE USED TO BE.
BUT THERE'S STILL PLENTY WE CAN DO.
MAYBE IF SHADOWCLAN'S WARRIORS HAD FELT THE SAME WAY, I COULD'VE STAYED ONE OF THEM.
YEAH, WELL. IF A FROG HAD WINGS, HE WOULDN'T BUMP HIS REAR END WHEN HE HOPPED.
"NOW LET'S GO CATCH SOMETHING TASTY."

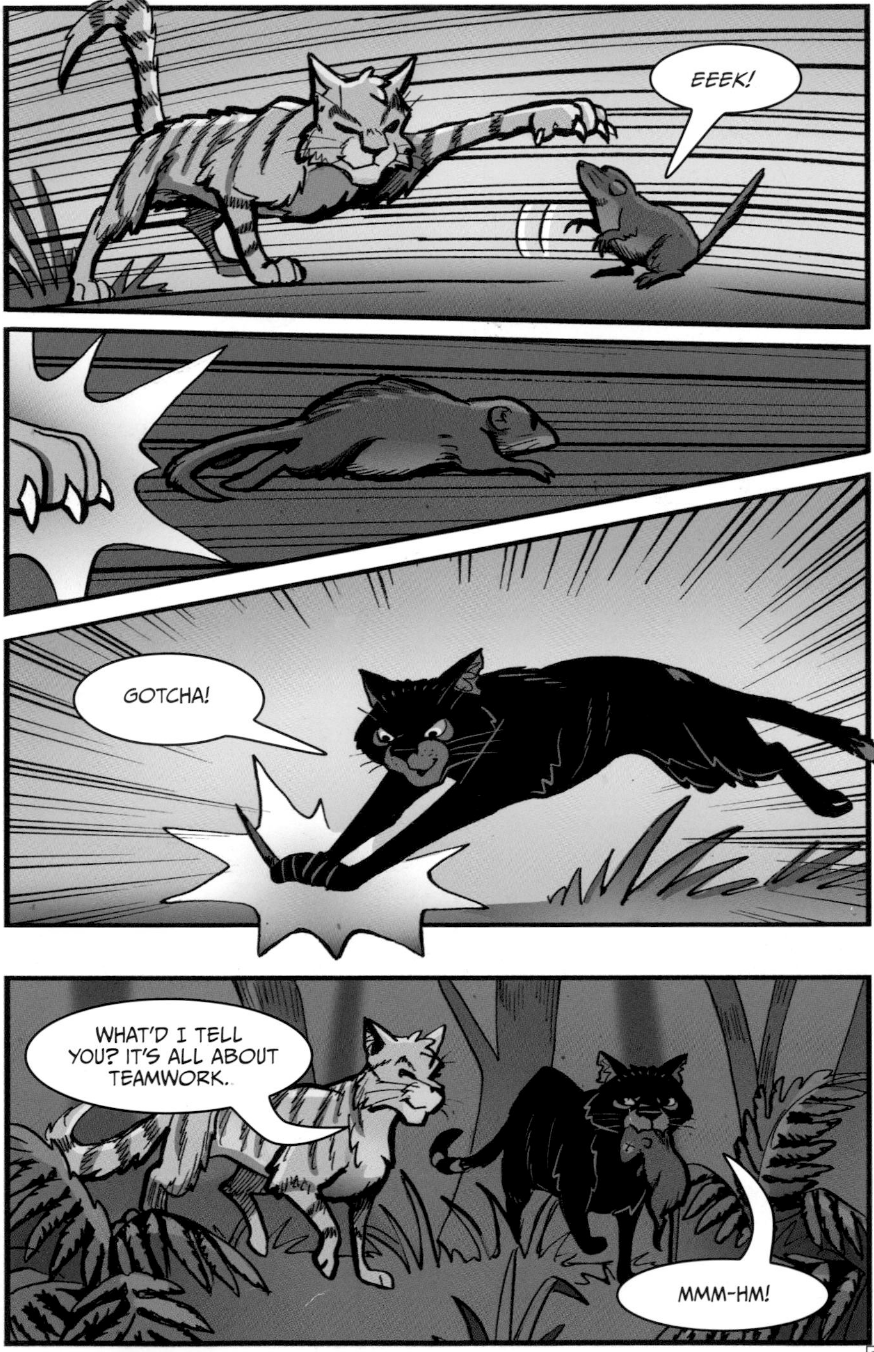
EEEK!
GOTCHA!
WHAT'D I TELL YOU? IT'S ALL ABOUT TEAMWORK.
MMM-HM!

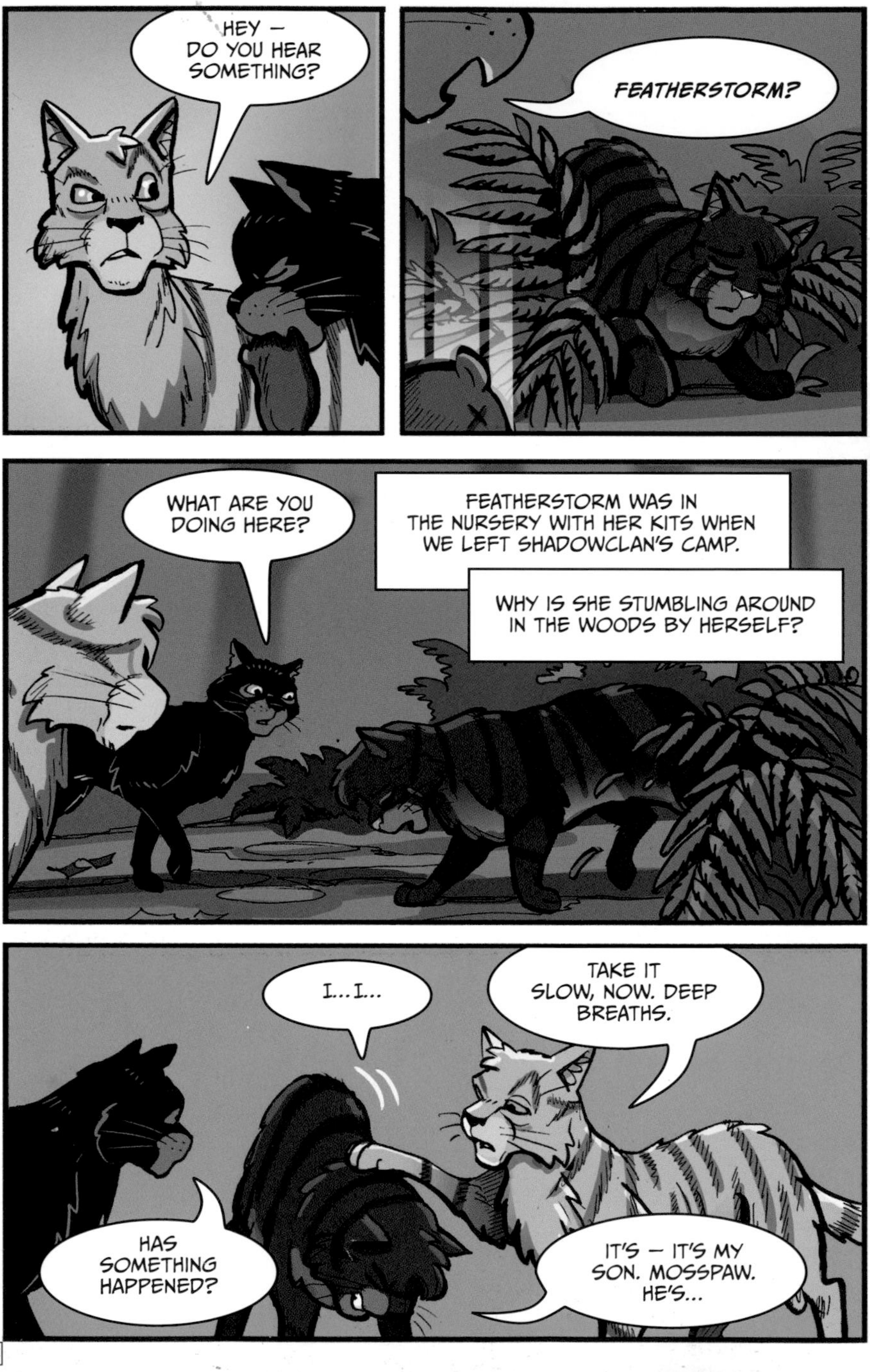
HEY — DO YOU HEAR SOMETHING?
FEATHERSTORM?
WHAT ARE YOU DOING HERE?
FEATHERSTORM WAS IN THE NURSERY WITH HER KITS WHEN WE LEFT SHADOWCLAN'S CAMP.
WHY IS SHE STUMBLING AROUND IN THE WOODS BY HERSELF?
I...I...
TAKE IT SLOW, NOW. DEEP BREATHS.
HAS SOMETHING HAPPENED?
IT'S — IT'S MY SON. MOSSPAW. HE'S...

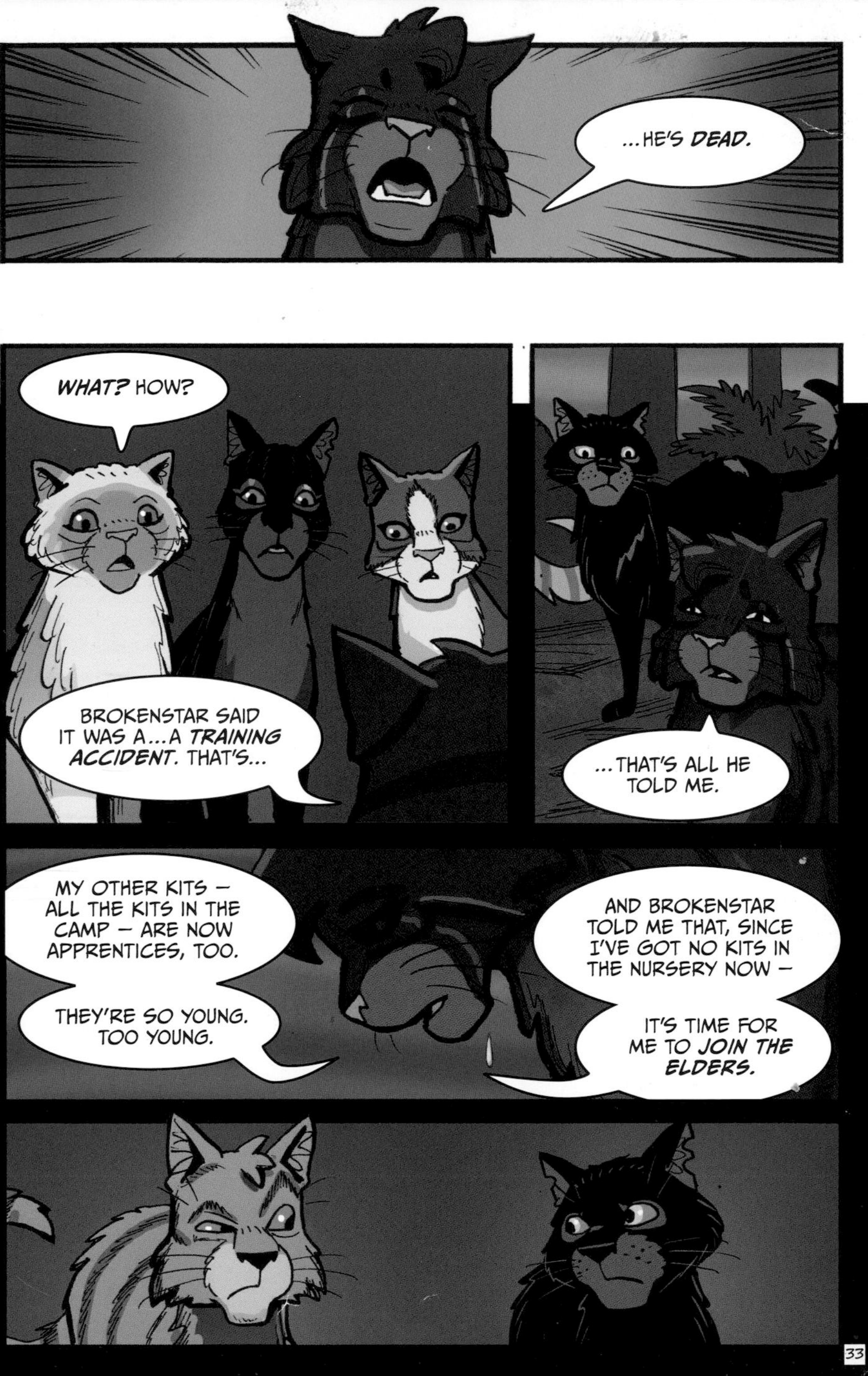
...HE'S DEAD.
WHAT? HOW?
BROKENSTAR SAID IT WAS A...A TRAINING ACCIDENT. THAT'S...
...THAT'S ALL HE TOLD ME.
MY OTHER KITS — ALL THE KITS IN THE CAMP — ARE NOW APPRENTICES, TOO.
THEY'RE SO YOUNG. TOO YOUNG.
AND BROKENSTAR TOLD ME THAT, SINCE I'VE GOT NO KITS IN THE NURSERY NOW —
IT'S TIME FOR ME TO JOIN THE ELDERS.

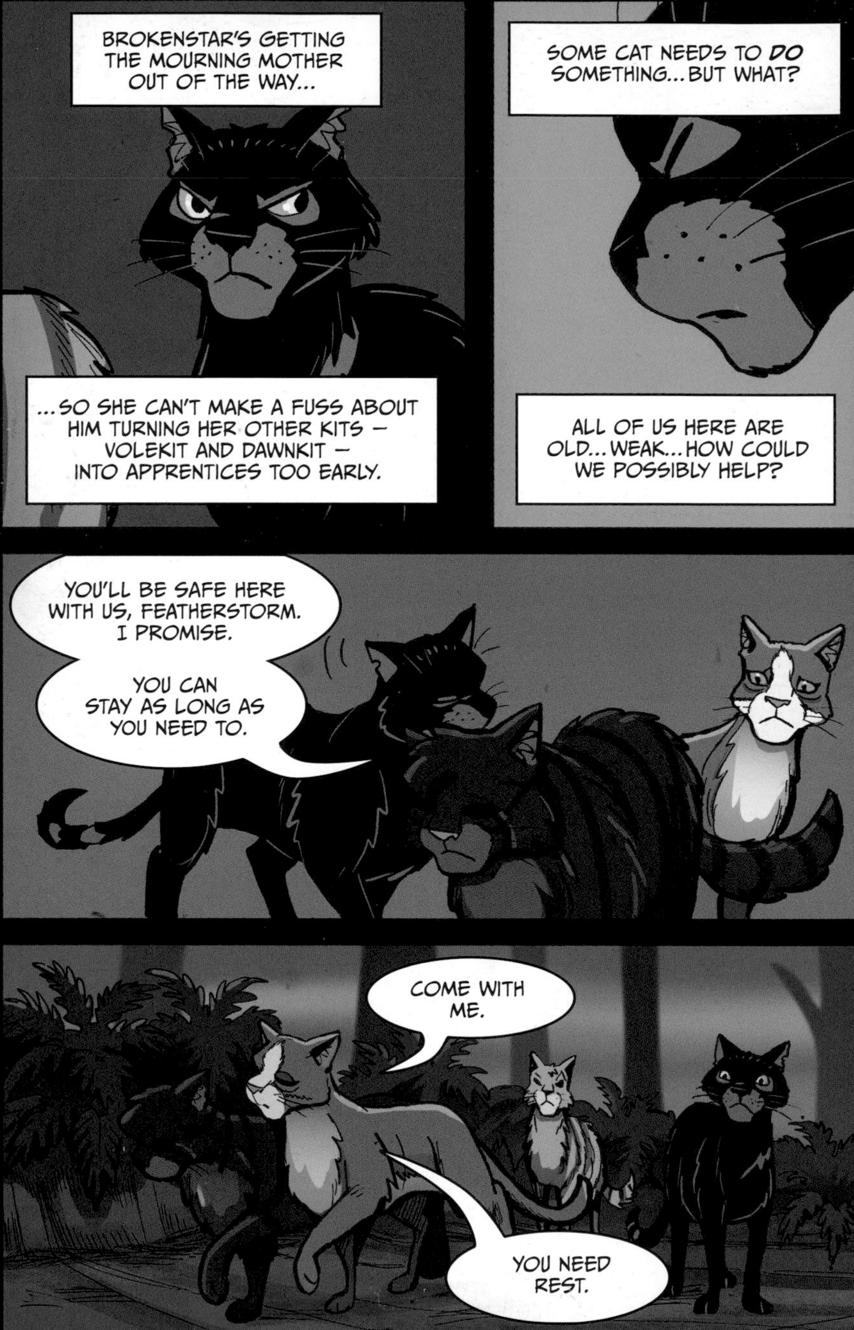
BROKENSTAR'S GETTING THE MOURNING MOTHER OUT OF THE WAY...
...SO SHE CAN'T MAKE A FUSS ABOUT HIM TURNING HER OTHER KITS – VOLEKIT AND DAWNKIT – INTO APPRENTICES TOO EARLY.
SOME CAT NEEDS TO *DO* SOMETHING... BUT WHAT?
ALL OF US HERE ARE OLD... WEAK... HOW COULD WE POSSIBLY HELP?
YOU'LL BE SAFE HERE WITH US, FEATHERSTORM. I PROMISE.
YOU CAN STAY AS LONG AS YOU NEED TO.
COME WITH ME.
YOU NEED REST.

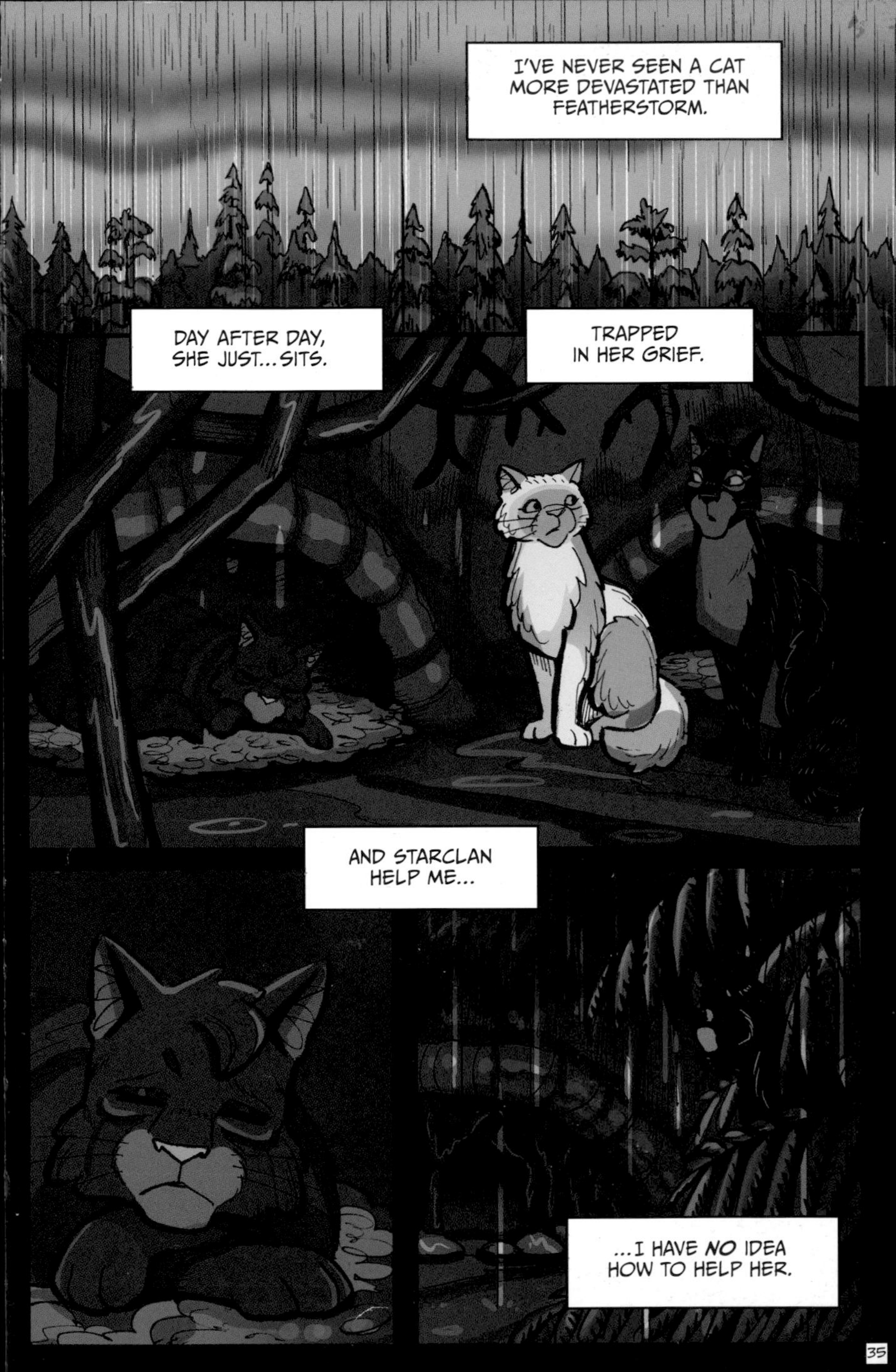
I'VE NEVER SEEN A CAT MORE DEVASTATED THAN FEATHERSTORM.
DAY AFTER DAY, SHE JUST...SITS.
TRAPPED IN HER GRIEF.
AND STARCLAN HELP ME...
...I HAVE NO IDEA HOW TO HELP HER.

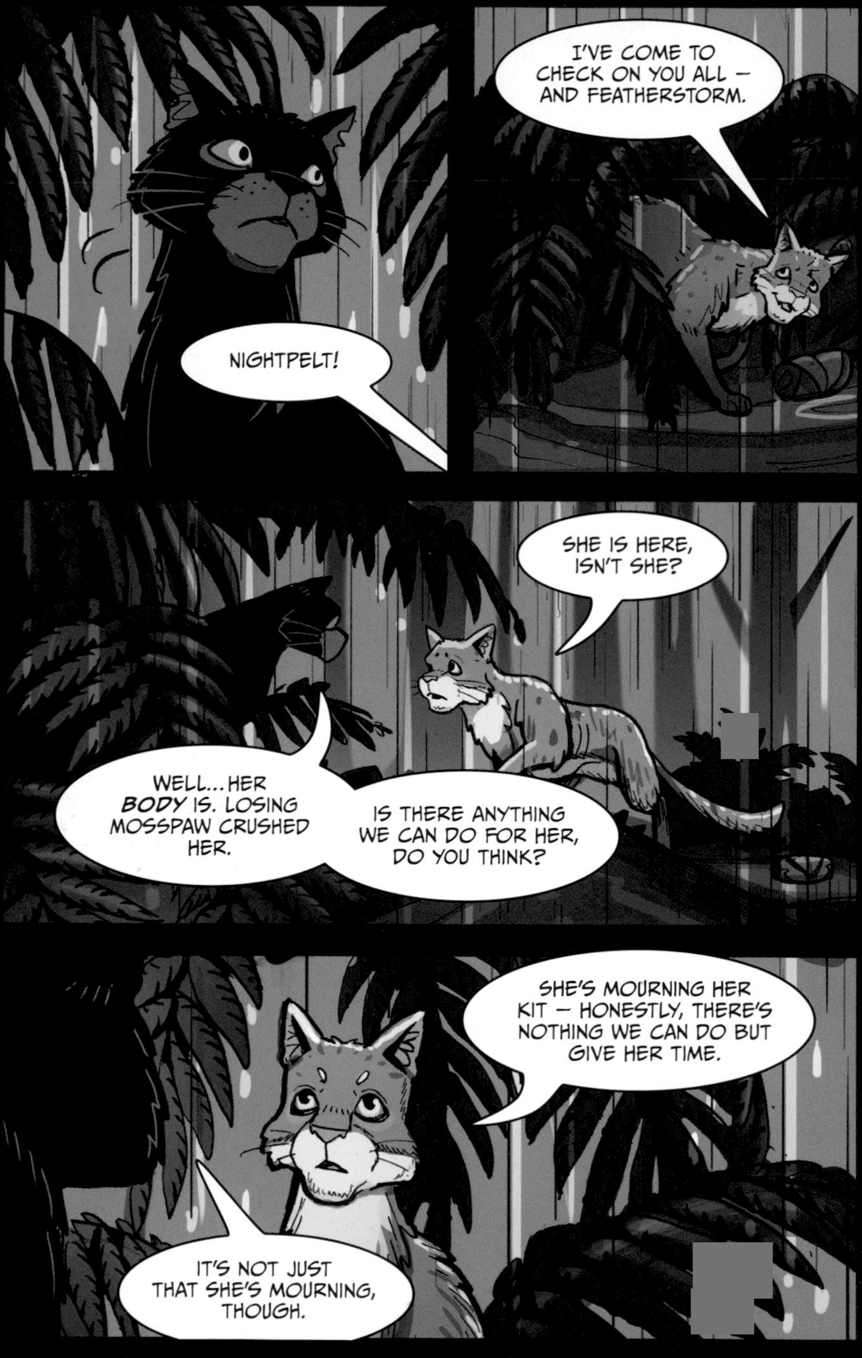
NIGHTPELT!
I'VE COME TO CHECK ON YOU ALL — AND FEATHERSTORM.
SHE IS HERE, ISN'T SHE?
WELL...HER *BODY* IS. LOSING MOSSPAW CRUSHED HER.
IS THERE ANYTHING WE CAN DO FOR HER, DO YOU THINK?
SHE'S MOURNING HER KIT — HONESTLY, THERE'S NOTHING WE CAN DO BUT GIVE HER TIME.
IT'S NOT JUST THAT SHE'S MOURNING, THOUGH.

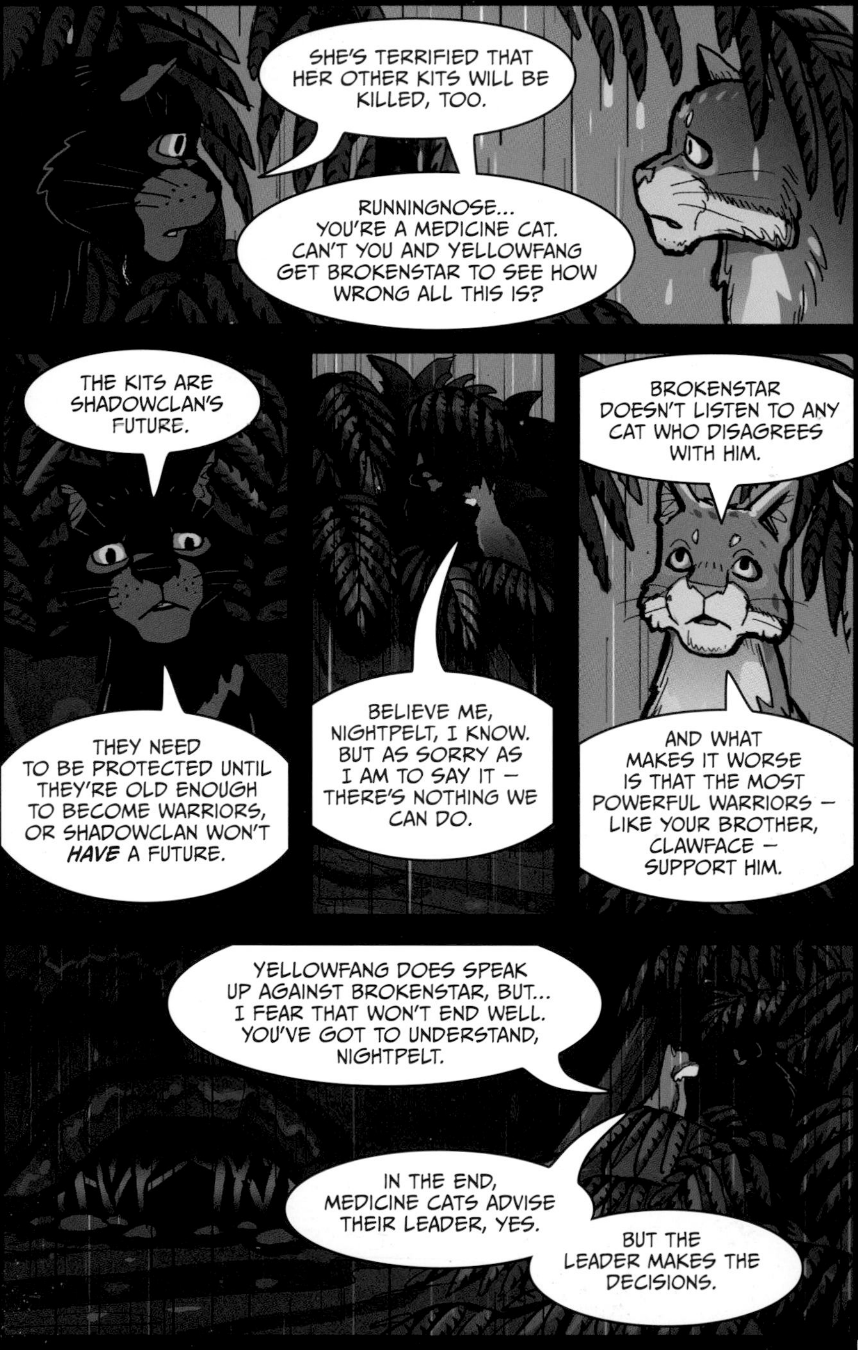
SHE'S TERRIFIED THAT HER OTHER KITS WILL BE KILLED, TOO.
RUNNINGNOSE... YOU'RE A MEDICINE CAT. CAN'T YOU AND YELLOWFANG GET BROKENSTAR TO SEE HOW WRONG ALL THIS IS?
THE KITS ARE SHADOWCLAN'S FUTURE.
THEY NEED TO BE PROTECTED UNTIL THEY'RE OLD ENOUGH TO BECOME WARRIORS, OR SHADOWCLAN WON'T *HAVE* A FUTURE.
BELIEVE ME, NIGHTPELT, I KNOW. BUT AS SORRY AS I AM TO SAY IT — THERE'S NOTHING WE CAN DO.
BROKENSTAR DOESN'T LISTEN TO ANY CAT WHO DISAGREES WITH HIM.
AND WHAT MAKES IT WORSE IS THAT THE MOST POWERFUL WARRIORS — LIKE YOUR BROTHER, CLAWFACE — SUPPORT HIM.
YELLOWFANG DOES SPEAK UP AGAINST BROKENSTAR, BUT... I FEAR THAT WON'T END WELL. YOU'VE GOT TO UNDERSTAND, NIGHTPELT.
IN THE END, MEDICINE CATS ADVISE THEIR LEADER, YES.
BUT THE LEADER MAKES THE DECISIONS.

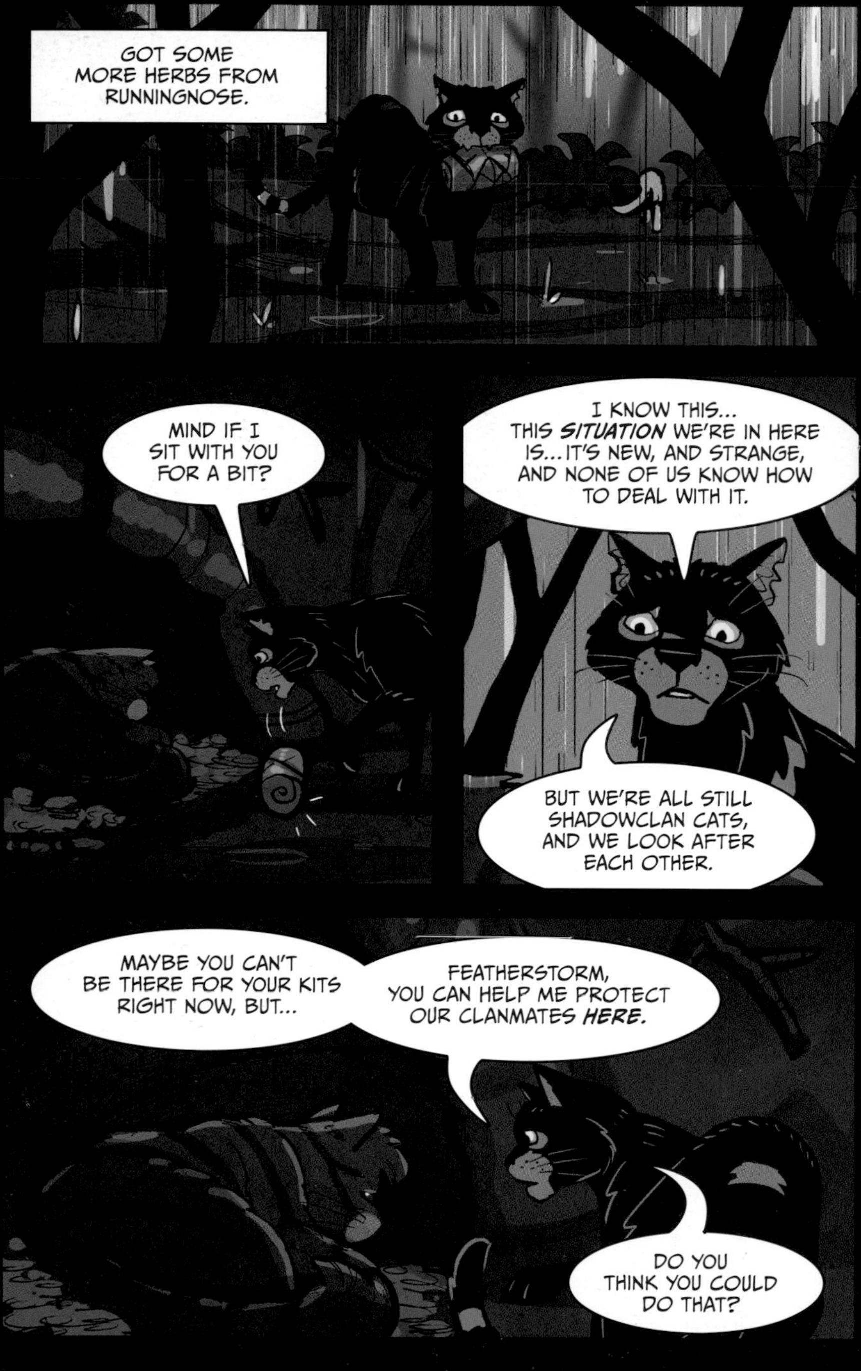
GOT SOME MORE HERBS FROM RUNNINGNOSE.
MIND IF I SIT WITH YOU FOR A BIT?
I KNOW THIS... THIS *SITUATION* WE'RE IN HERE IS...IT'S NEW, AND STRANGE, AND NONE OF US KNOW HOW TO DEAL WITH IT.
BUT WE'RE ALL STILL SHADOWCLAN CATS, AND WE LOOK AFTER EACH OTHER.
MAYBE YOU CAN'T BE THERE FOR YOUR KITS RIGHT NOW, BUT...
FEATHERSTORM, YOU CAN HELP ME PROTECT OUR CLANMATES ***HERE.***
DO YOU THINK YOU COULD DO THAT?

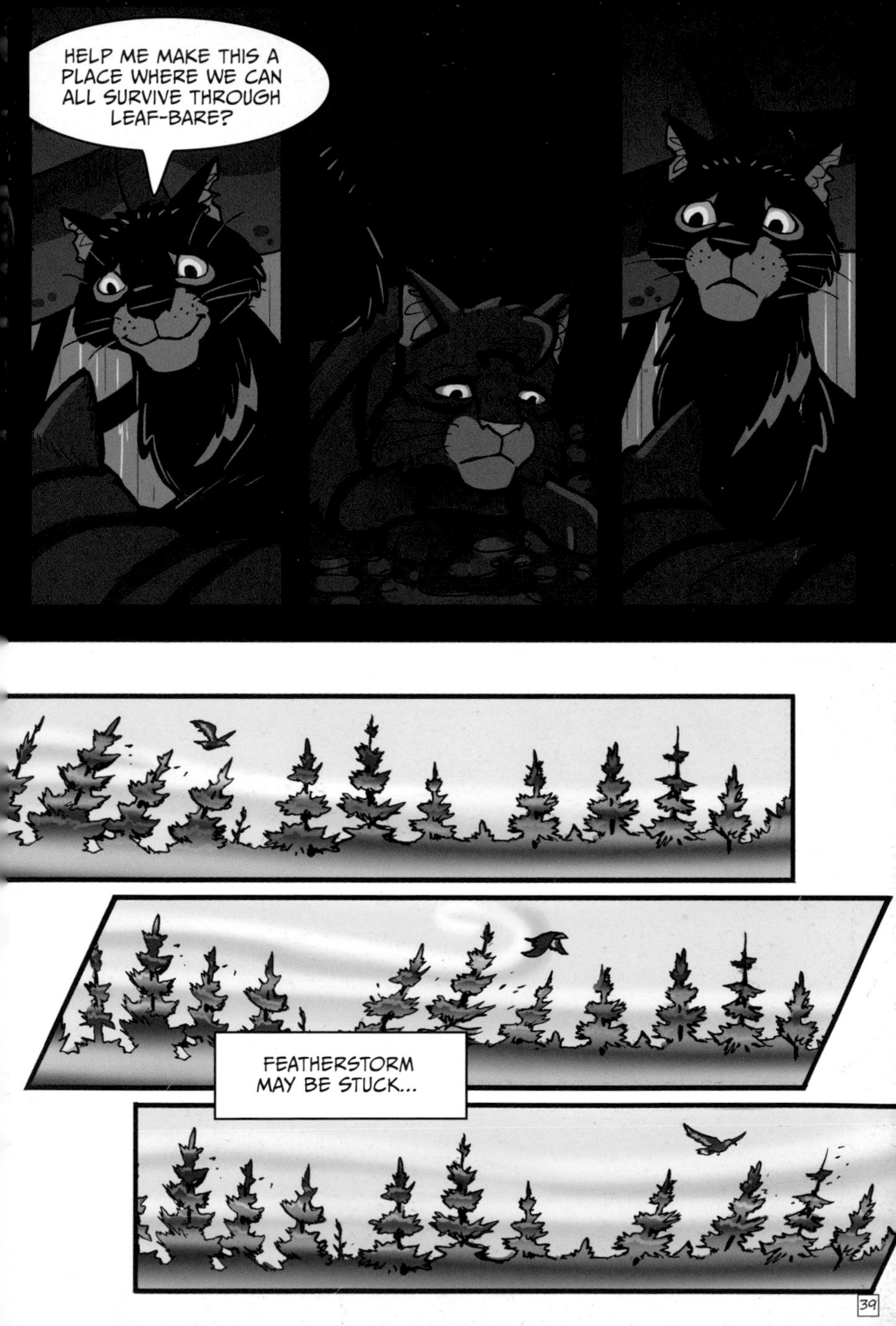
HELP ME MAKE THIS A PLACE WHERE WE CAN ALL SURVIVE THROUGH LEAF-BARE?
FEATHERSTORM MAY BE STUCK...

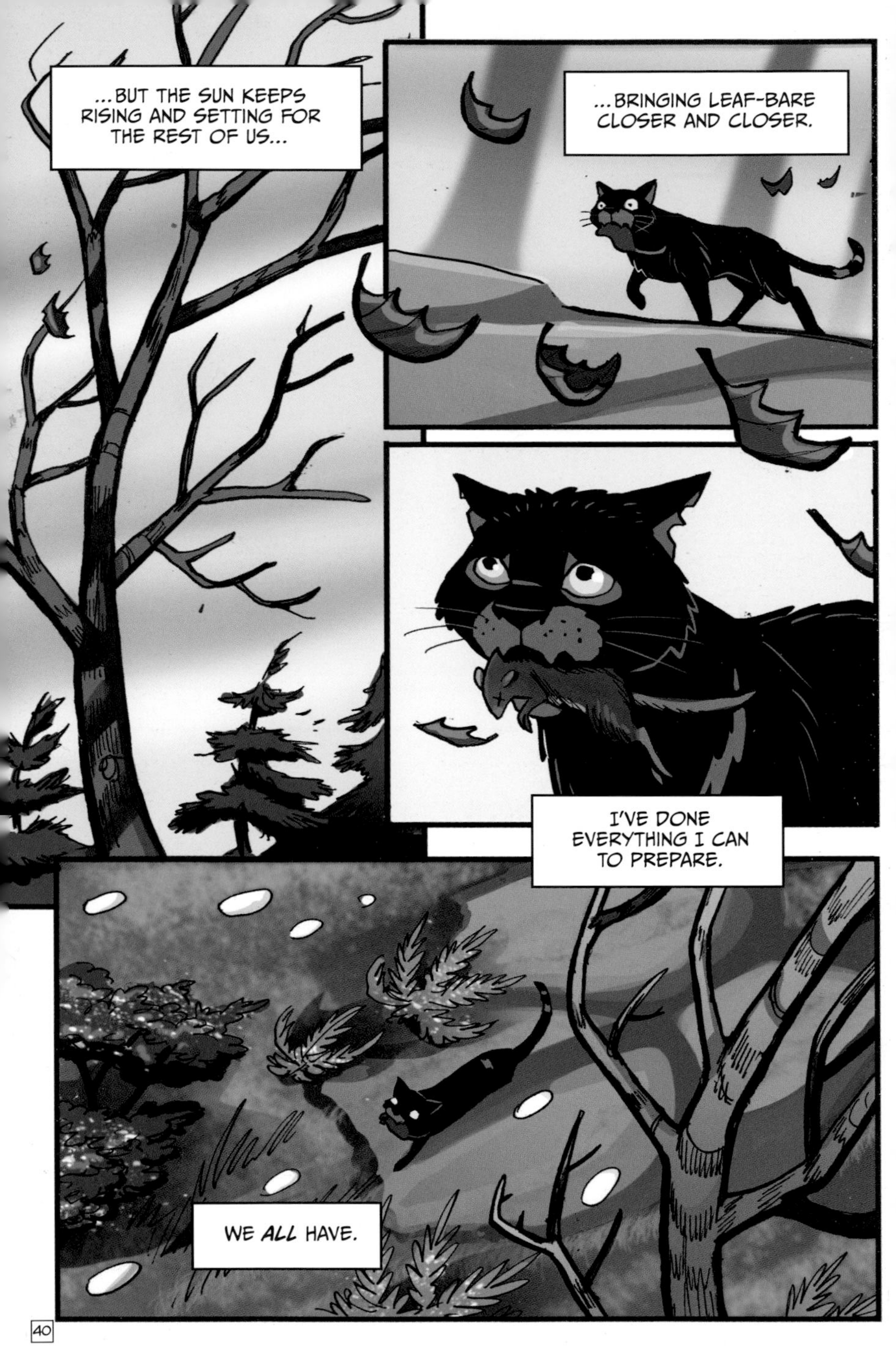
...BUT THE SUN KEEPS RISING AND SETTING FOR THE REST OF US...
...BRINGING LEAF-BARE CLOSER AND CLOSER.
I'VE DONE EVERYTHING I CAN TO PREPARE.
WE *ALL* HAVE.

NOW THERE'S NOTHING ELSE BUT TO WAIT...

...AND, STARCLAN WILLING, SURVIVE.

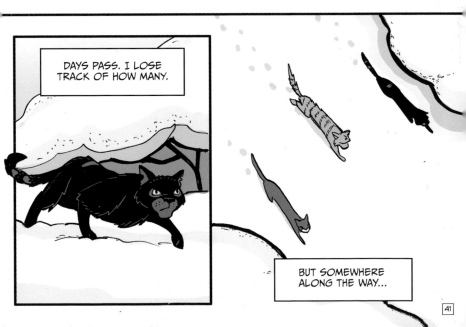

DAYS PASS. I LOSE TRACK OF HOW MANY.

BUT SOMEWHERE ALONG THE WAY...

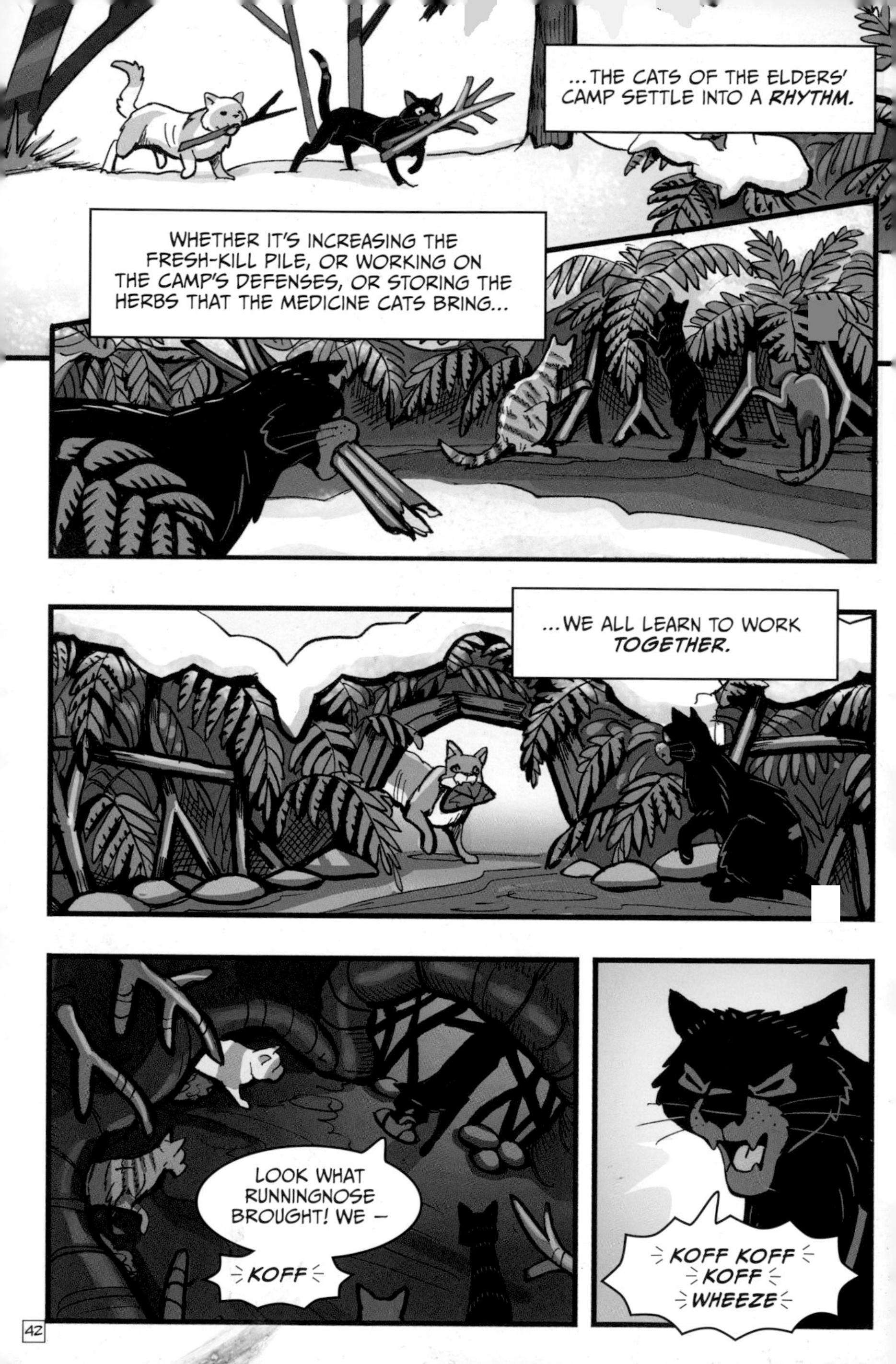
...THE CATS OF THE ELDERS' CAMP SETTLE INTO A *RHYTHM.*
WHETHER IT'S INCREASING THE FRESH-KILL PILE, OR WORKING ON THE CAMP'S DEFENSES, OR STORING THE HERBS THAT THE MEDICINE CATS BRING...
...WE ALL LEARN TO WORK *TOGETHER.*
LOOK WHAT RUNNINGNOSE BROUGHT! WE —
KOFF
KOFF KOFF KOFF WHEEZE

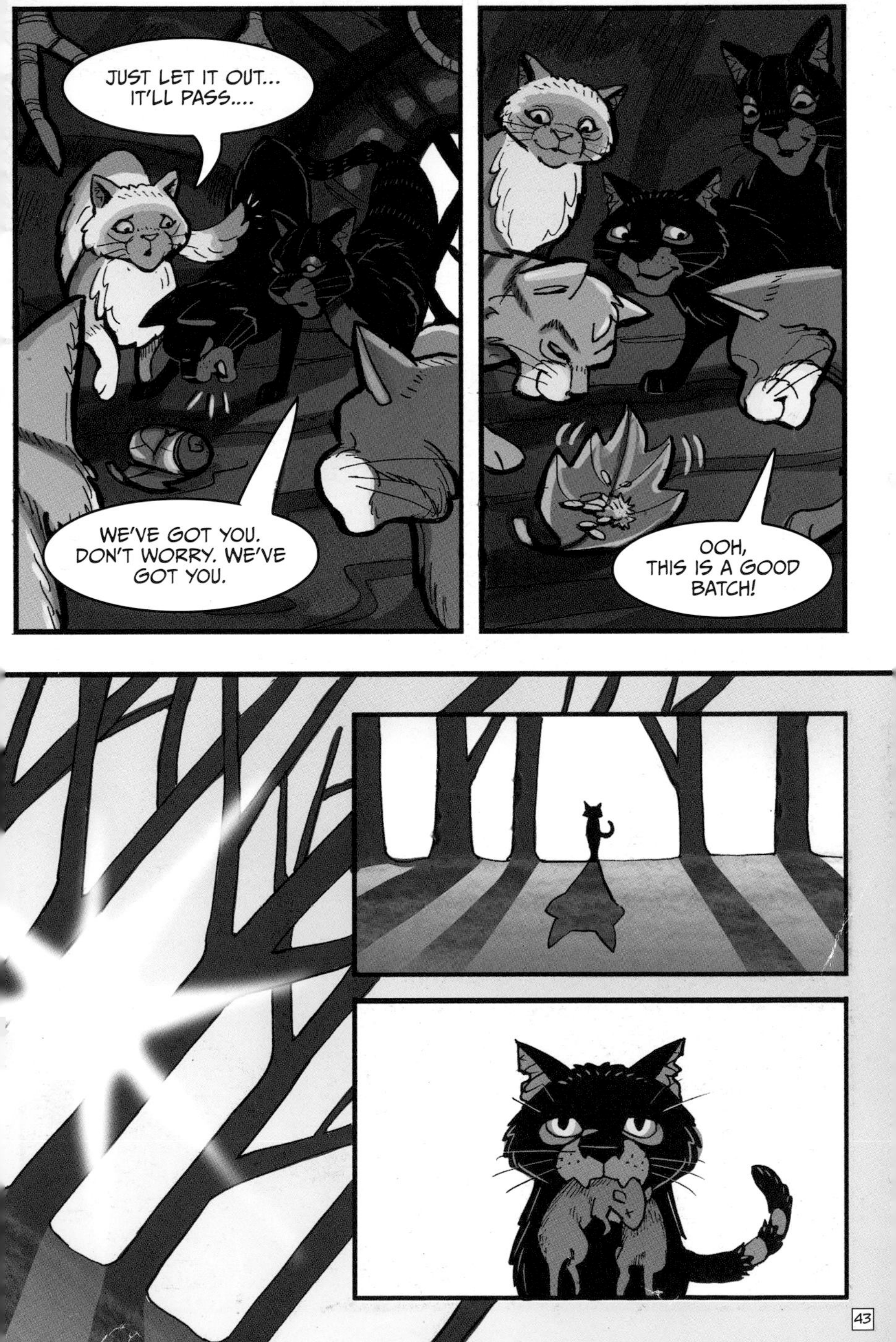

JUST LET IT OUT... IT'LL PASS....
WE'VE GOT YOU. DON'T WORRY. WE'VE GOT YOU.
OOH, THIS IS A GOOD BATCH!

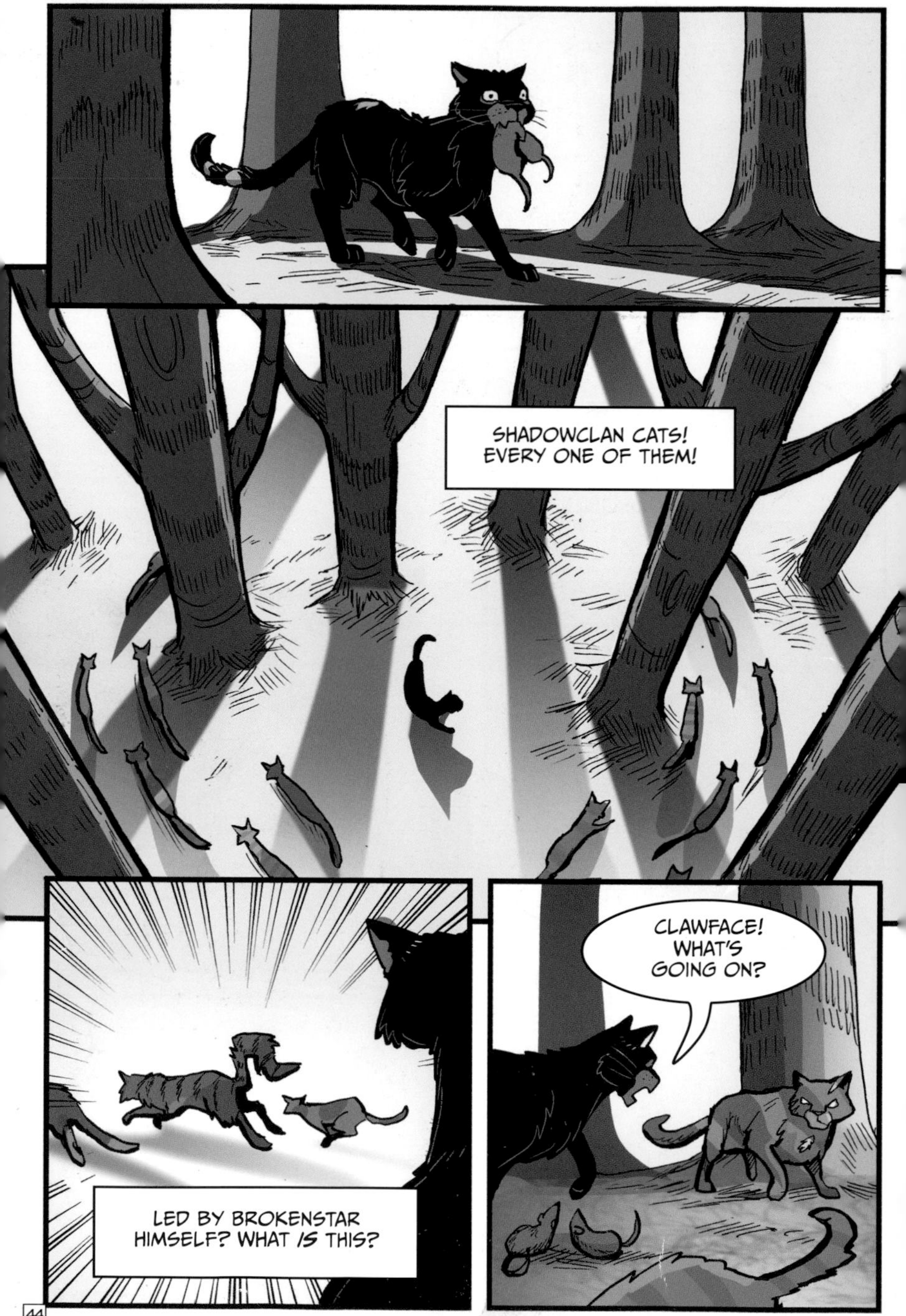
SHADOWCLAN CATS! EVERY ONE OF THEM!
LED BY BROKENSTAR HIMSELF? WHAT *IS* THIS?
CLAWFACE! WHAT'S GOING ON?

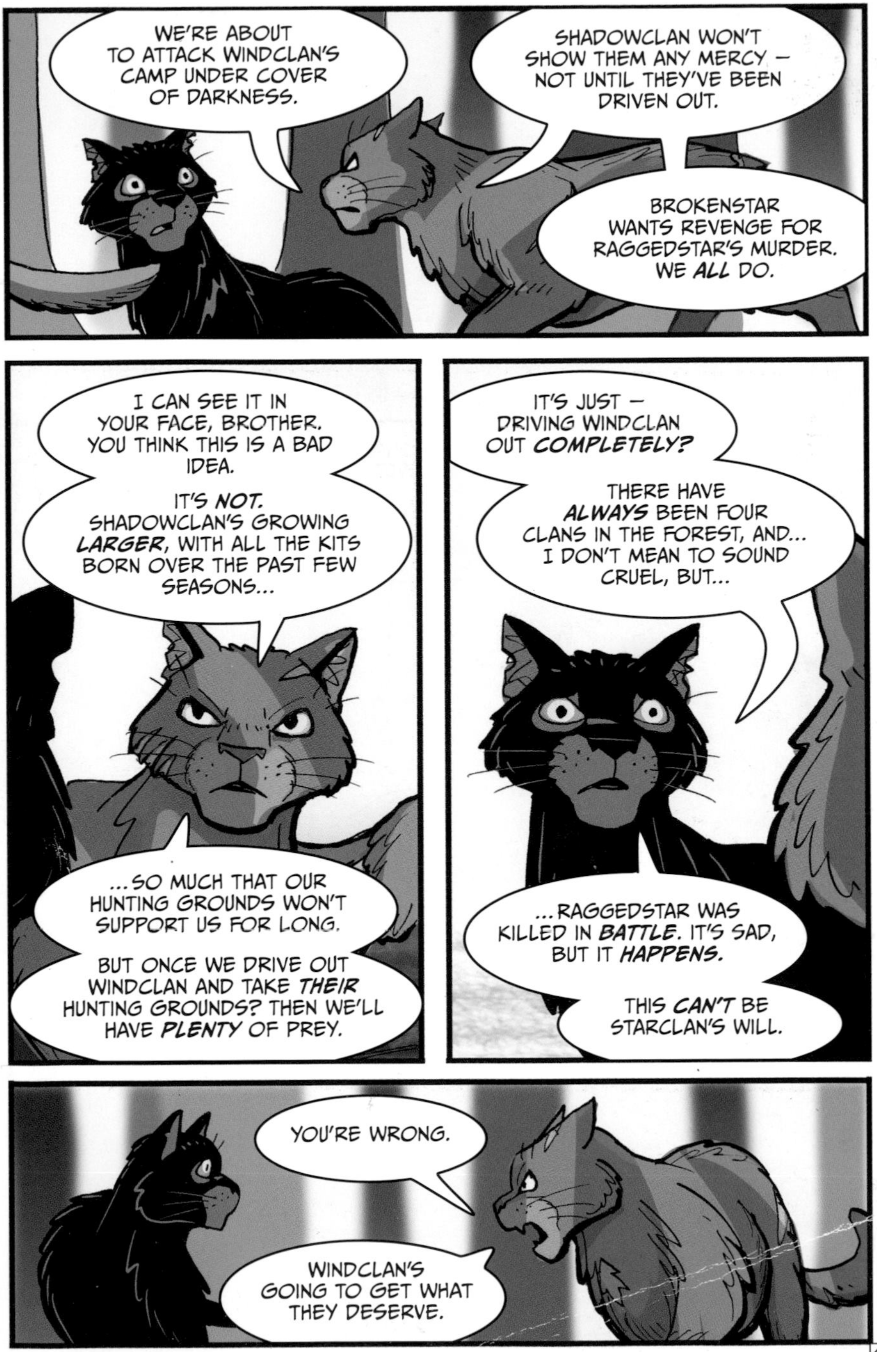
WE'RE ABOUT TO ATTACK WINDCLAN'S CAMP UNDER COVER OF DARKNESS.
SHADOWCLAN WON'T SHOW THEM ANY MERCY – NOT UNTIL THEY'VE BEEN DRIVEN OUT.
BROKENSTAR WANTS REVENGE FOR RAGGEDSTAR'S MURDER. WE *ALL* DO.
I CAN SEE IT IN YOUR FACE, BROTHER. YOU THINK THIS IS A BAD IDEA.
IT'S *NOT.* SHADOWCLAN'S GROWING *LARGER*, WITH ALL THE KITS BORN OVER THE PAST FEW SEASONS...
...SO MUCH THAT OUR HUNTING GROUNDS WON'T SUPPORT US FOR LONG.
BUT ONCE WE DRIVE OUT WINDCLAN AND TAKE *THEIR* HUNTING GROUNDS? THEN WE'LL HAVE *PLENTY* OF PREY.
IT'S JUST – DRIVING WINDCLAN OUT *COMPLETELY?*
THERE HAVE *ALWAYS* BEEN FOUR CLANS IN THE FOREST, AND... I DON'T MEAN TO SOUND CRUEL, BUT...
...RAGGEDSTAR WAS KILLED IN *BATTLE*. IT'S SAD, BUT IT *HAPPENS.*
THIS *CAN'T* BE STARCLAN'S WILL.
YOU'RE WRONG.
WINDCLAN'S GOING TO GET WHAT THEY DESERVE.

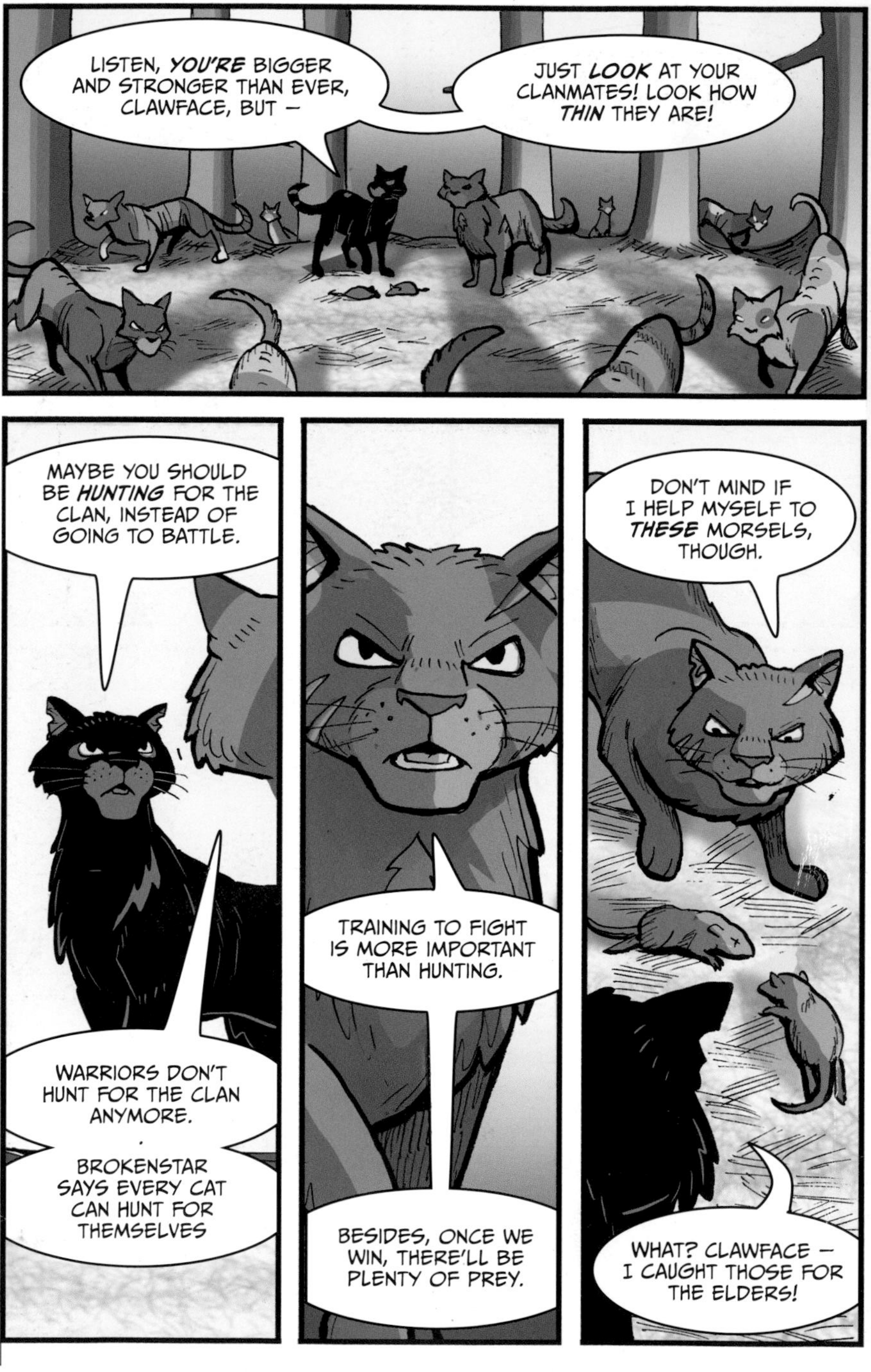
LISTEN, YOU'RE BIGGER AND STRONGER THAN EVER, CLAWFACE, BUT –
JUST LOOK AT YOUR CLANMATES! LOOK HOW THIN THEY ARE!
MAYBE YOU SHOULD BE HUNTING FOR THE CLAN, INSTEAD OF GOING TO BATTLE.
WARRIORS DON'T HUNT FOR THE CLAN ANYMORE.
BROKENSTAR SAYS EVERY CAT CAN HUNT FOR THEMSELVES
TRAINING TO FIGHT IS MORE IMPORTANT THAN HUNTING.
BESIDES, ONCE WE WIN, THERE'LL BE PLENTY OF PREY.
DON'T MIND IF I HELP MYSELF TO THESE MORSELS, THOUGH.
WHAT? CLAWFACE – I CAUGHT THOSE FOR THE ELDERS!

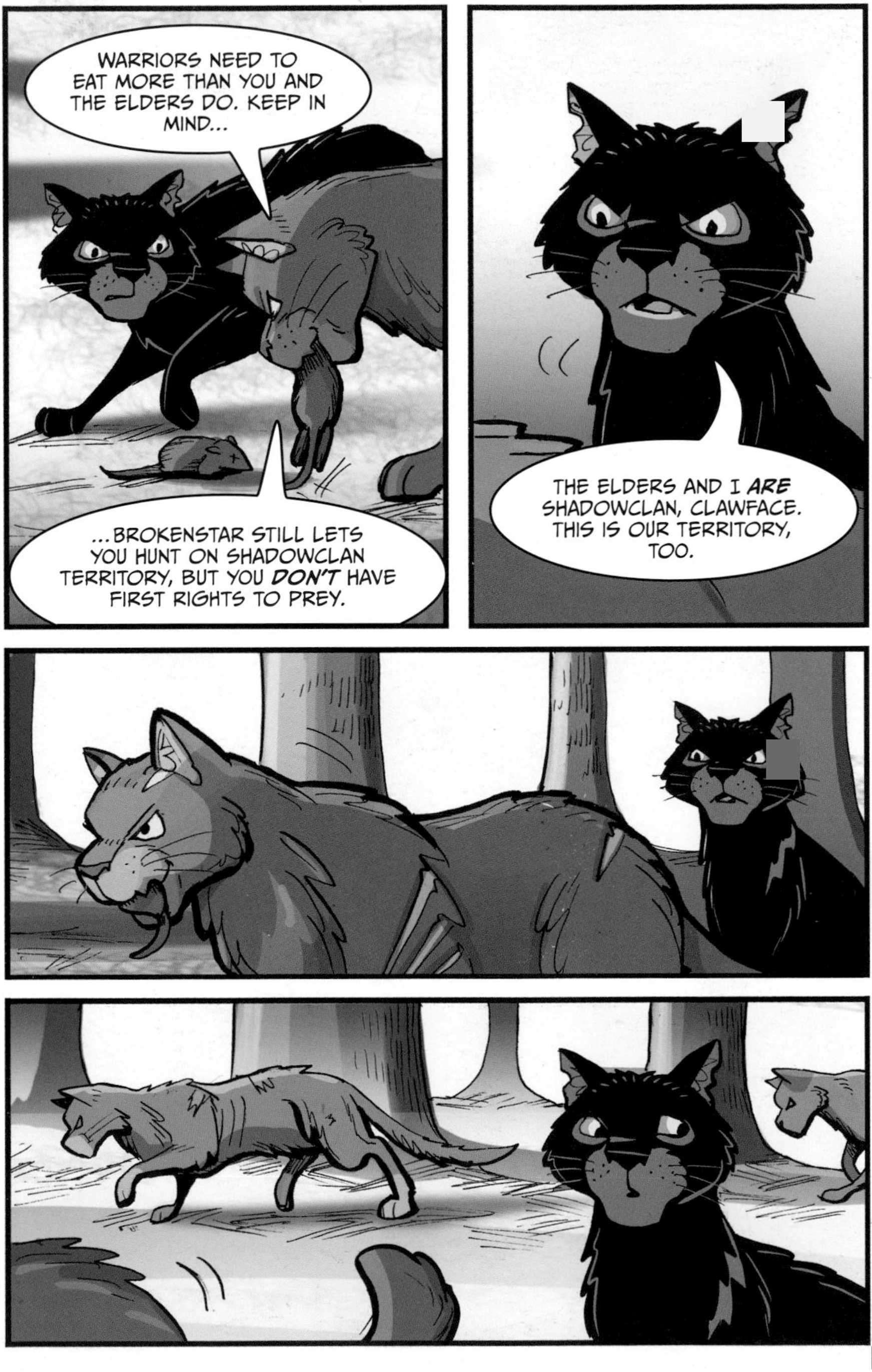
WARRIORS NEED TO EAT MORE THAN YOU AND THE ELDERS DO. KEEP IN MIND...
...BROKENSTAR STILL LETS YOU HUNT ON SHADOWCLAN TERRITORY, BUT YOU DON'T HAVE FIRST RIGHTS TO PREY.
THE ELDERS AND I ARE SHADOWCLAN, CLAWFACE. THIS IS OUR TERRITORY, TOO.

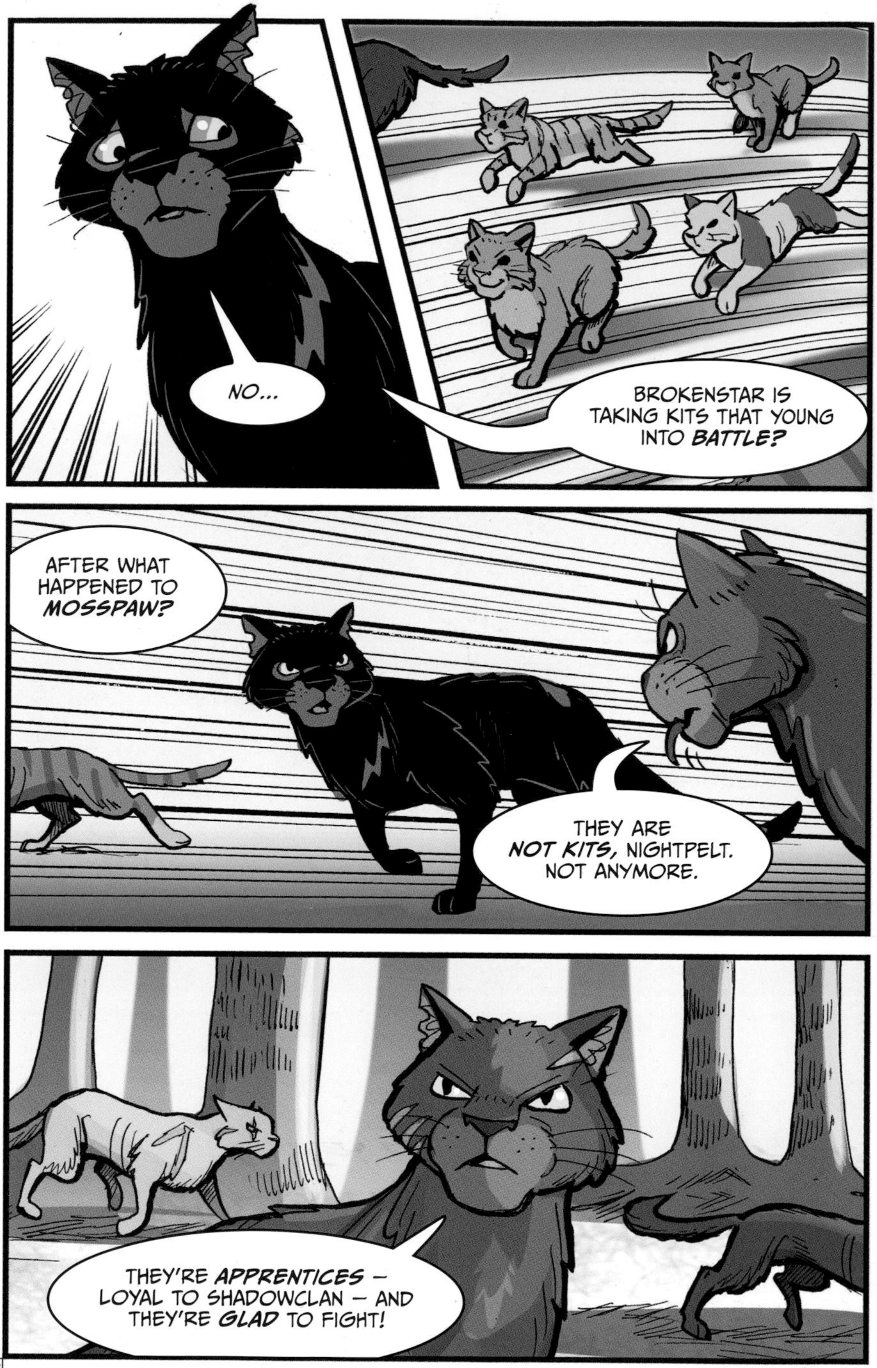
NO...
BROKENSTAR IS TAKING KITS THAT YOUNG INTO BATTLE?
AFTER WHAT HAPPENED TO MOSSPAW?
THEY ARE NOT KITS, NIGHTPELT. NOT ANYMORE.
THEY'RE APPRENTICES – LOYAL TO SHADOWCLAN – AND THEY'RE GLAD TO FIGHT!

WHY CAN'T CLAWFACE SEE THAT THIS IS *WRONG?*
SHADOWCLAN'S CATS ARE *POWERFUL.* MORE POWERFUL THAN THE OTHER CLANS!
OUR APPRENTICES ARE READY TO FIGHT WHEN OTHER KITS ARE STILL USELESS BALLS OF FLUFF IN THE NURSERY.
CLAWFACE! ARE WE *GOING?* WE NEED TO HURRY, OR THEY'LL LEAVE US BEHIND! I DON'T WANT TO GET LEFT BEHIND!
YOU CAN'T DO *THIS!* LEAD A KIT THIS TINY INTO *BATTLE?* HE'LL BE KILLED!
IT'D BE AN *HONOR* TO DIE FOR SHADOWCLAN!
COME ON, APPRENTICE.
AS YOU SAID, LET'S CATCH UP.

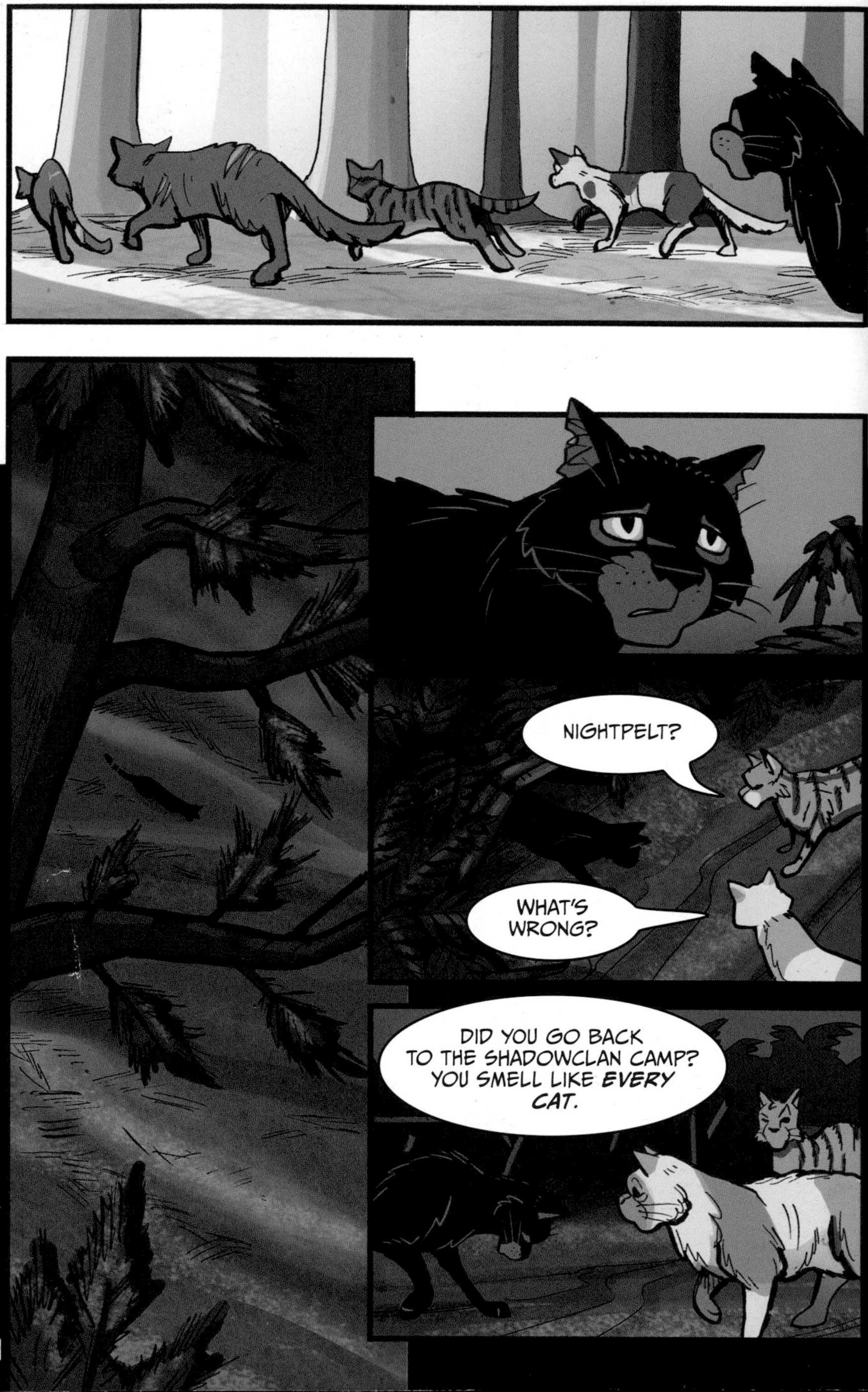
NIGHTPELT?
WHAT'S WRONG?
DID YOU GO BACK TO THE SHADOWCLAN CAMP? YOU SMELL LIKE *EVERY* CAT.

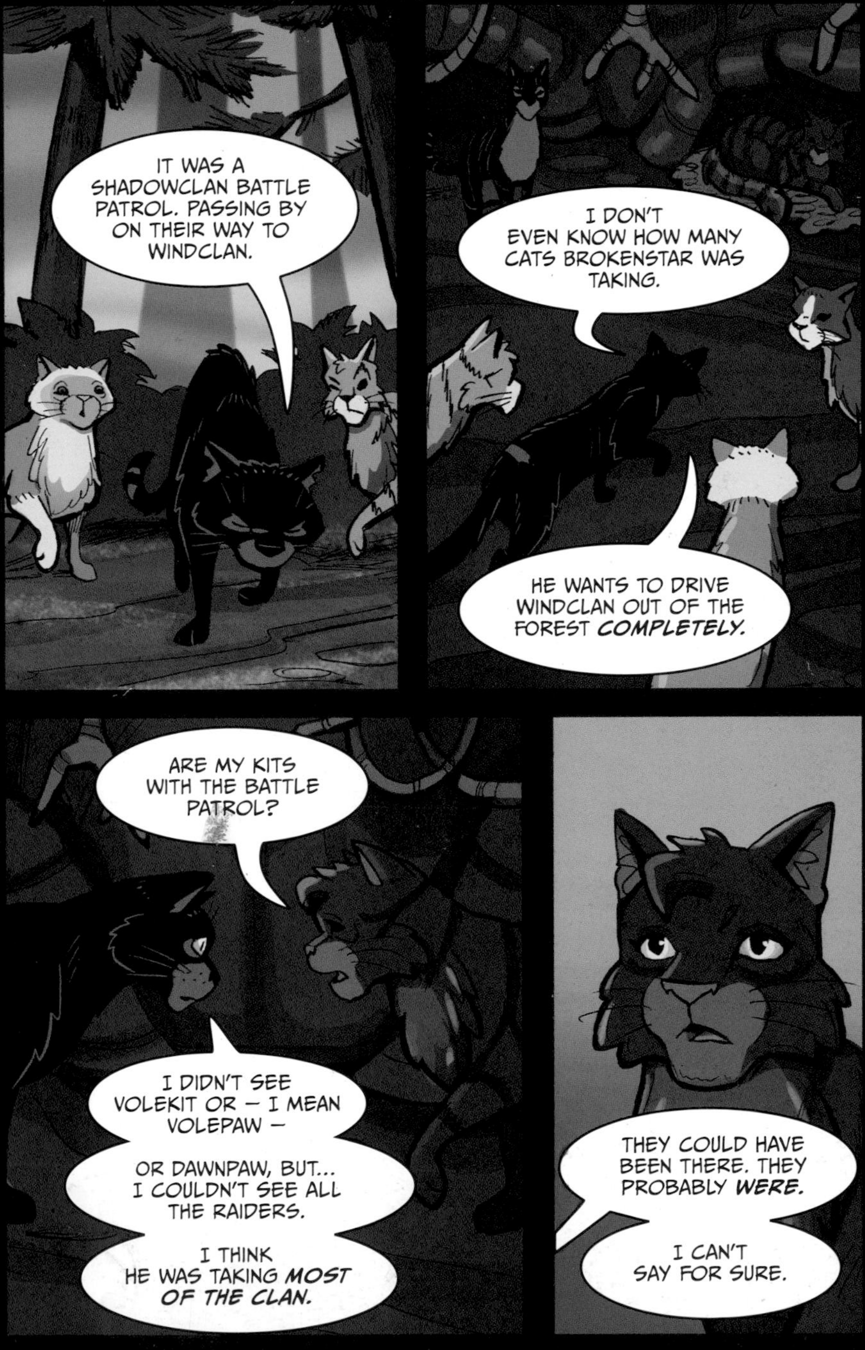
IT WAS A SHADOWCLAN BATTLE PATROL. PASSING BY ON THEIR WAY TO WINDCLAN.
I DON'T EVEN KNOW HOW MANY CATS BROKENSTAR WAS TAKING.
HE WANTS TO DRIVE WINDCLAN OUT OF THE FOREST *COMPLETELY.*
ARE MY KITS WITH THE BATTLE PATROL?
I DIDN'T SEE VOLEKIT OR – I MEAN VOLEPAW –
OR DAWNPAW, BUT... I COULDN'T SEE ALL THE RAIDERS.
I THINK HE WAS TAKING *MOST OF THE CLAN.*
THEY COULD HAVE BEEN THERE. THEY PROBABLY *WERE.*
I CAN'T SAY FOR SURE.

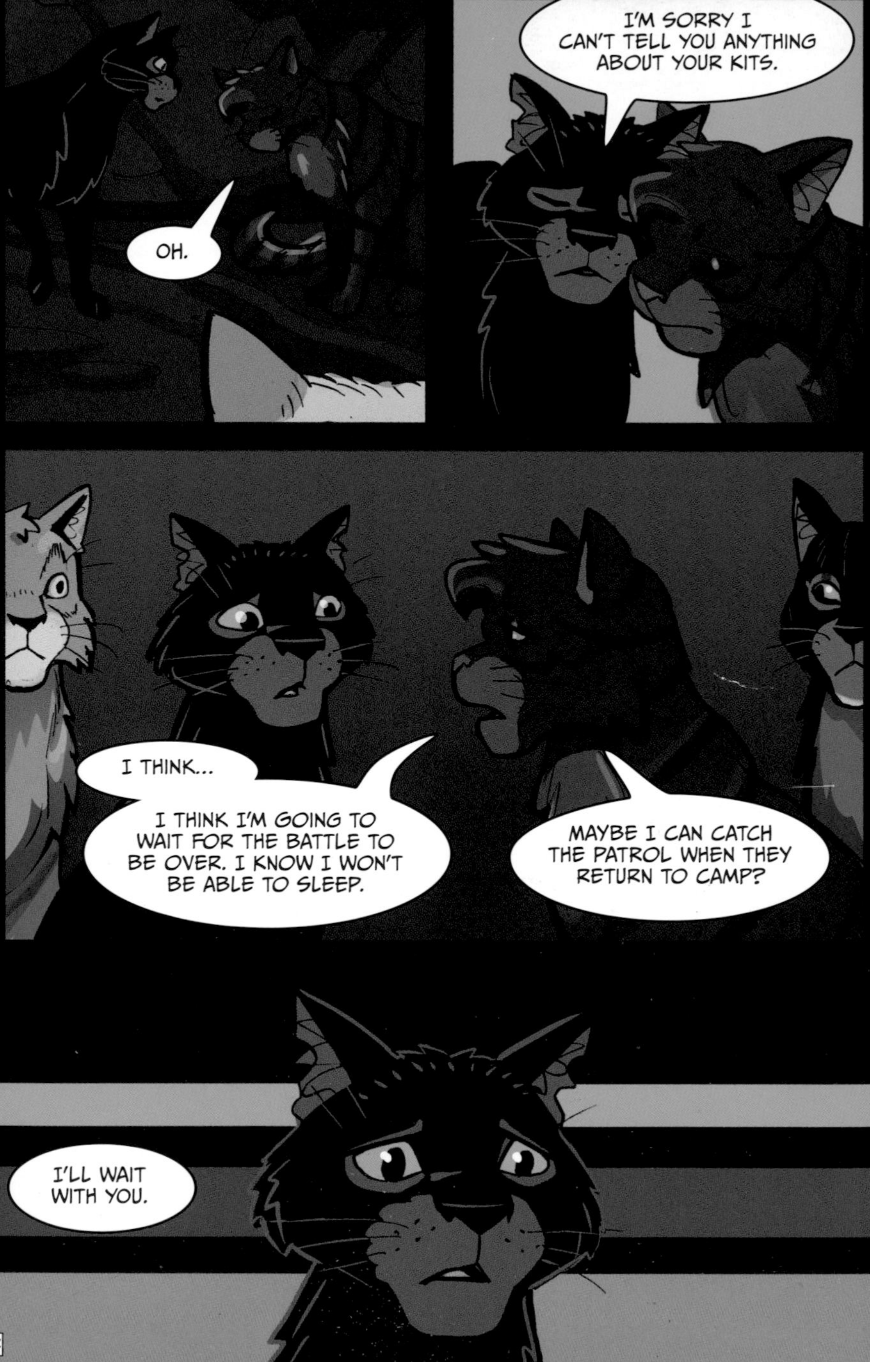
OH.
I'M SORRY I CAN'T TELL YOU ANYTHING ABOUT YOUR KITS.
I THINK...
I THINK I'M GOING TO WAIT FOR THE BATTLE TO BE OVER. I KNOW I WON'T BE ABLE TO SLEEP.
MAYBE I CAN CATCH THE PATROL WHEN THEY RETURN TO CAMP?
I'LL WAIT WITH YOU.

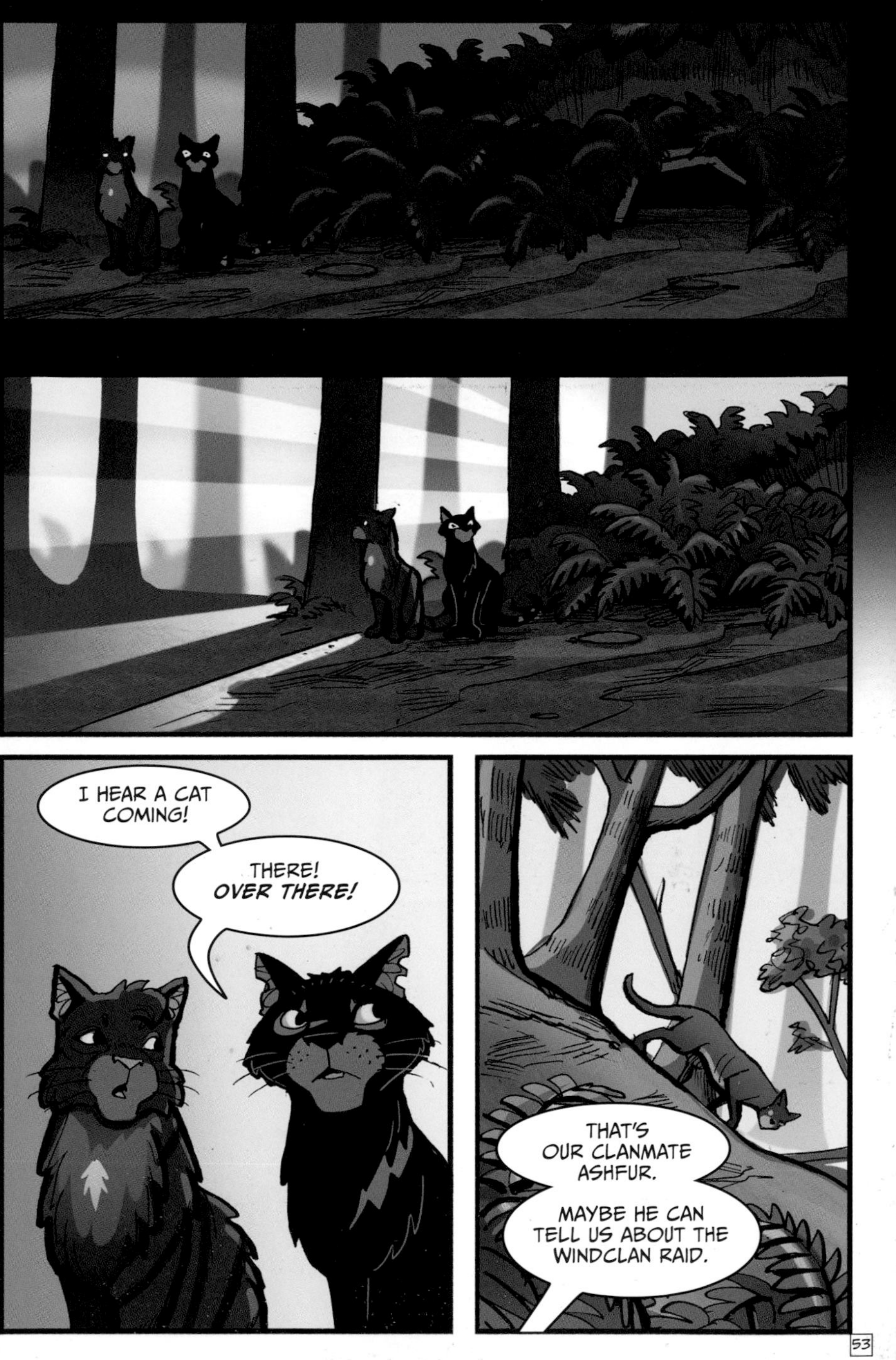
I HEAR A CAT COMING!
THERE! OVER THERE!
THAT'S OUR CLANMATE ASHFUR.
MAYBE HE CAN TELL US ABOUT THE WINDCLAN RAID.

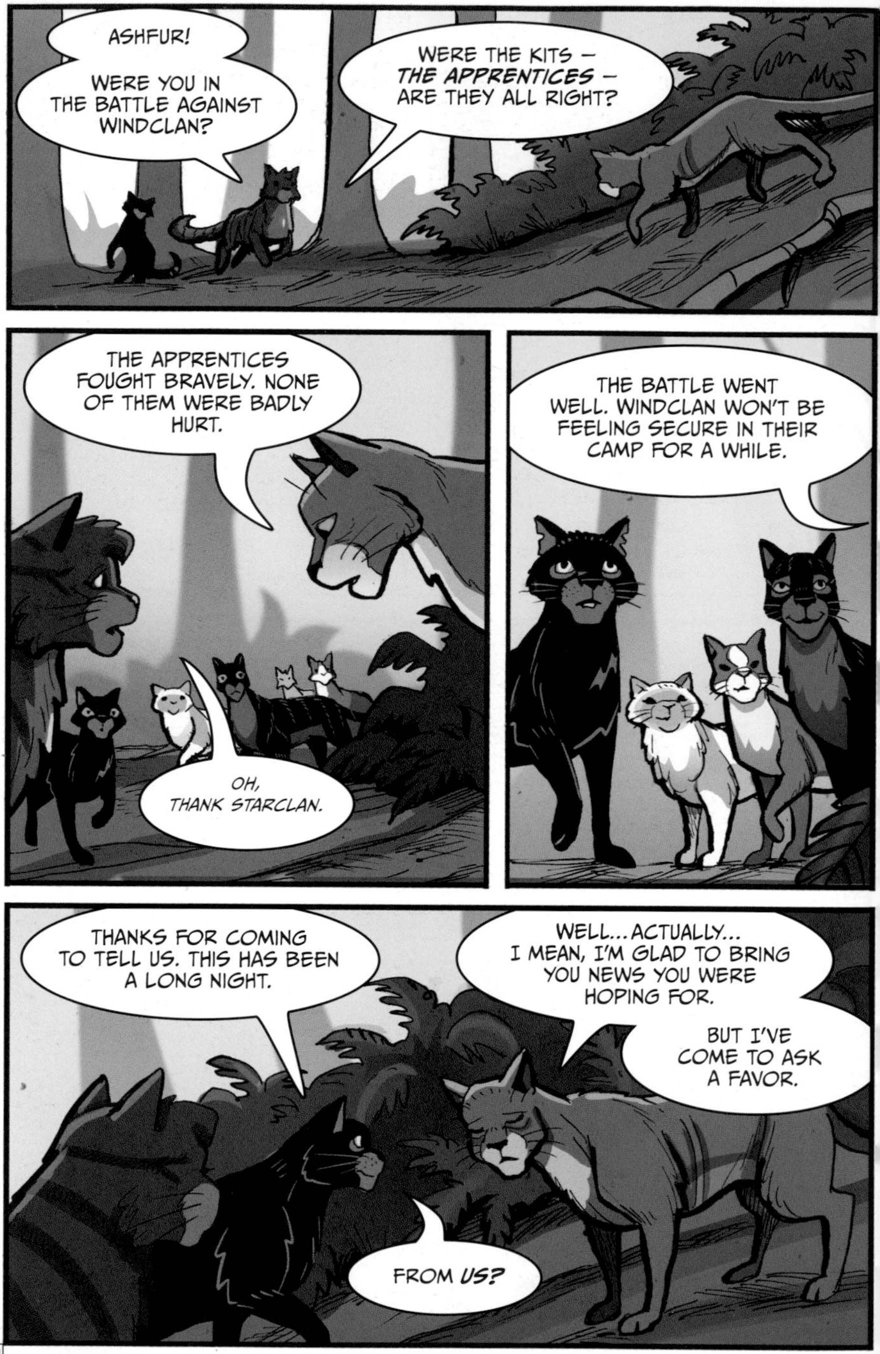
ASHFUR!
WERE YOU IN THE BATTLE AGAINST WINDCLAN?
WERE THE KITS — *THE APPRENTICES* — ARE THEY ALL RIGHT?
THE APPRENTICES FOUGHT BRAVELY. NONE OF THEM WERE BADLY HURT.
OH, THANK STARCLAN.
THE BATTLE WENT WELL. WINDCLAN WON'T BE FEELING SECURE IN THEIR CAMP FOR A WHILE.
THANKS FOR COMING TO TELL US. THIS HAS BEEN A LONG NIGHT.
WELL... ACTUALLY... I MEAN, I'M GLAD TO BRING YOU NEWS YOU WERE HOPING FOR.
BUT I'VE COME TO ASK A FAVOR.
FROM *US?*

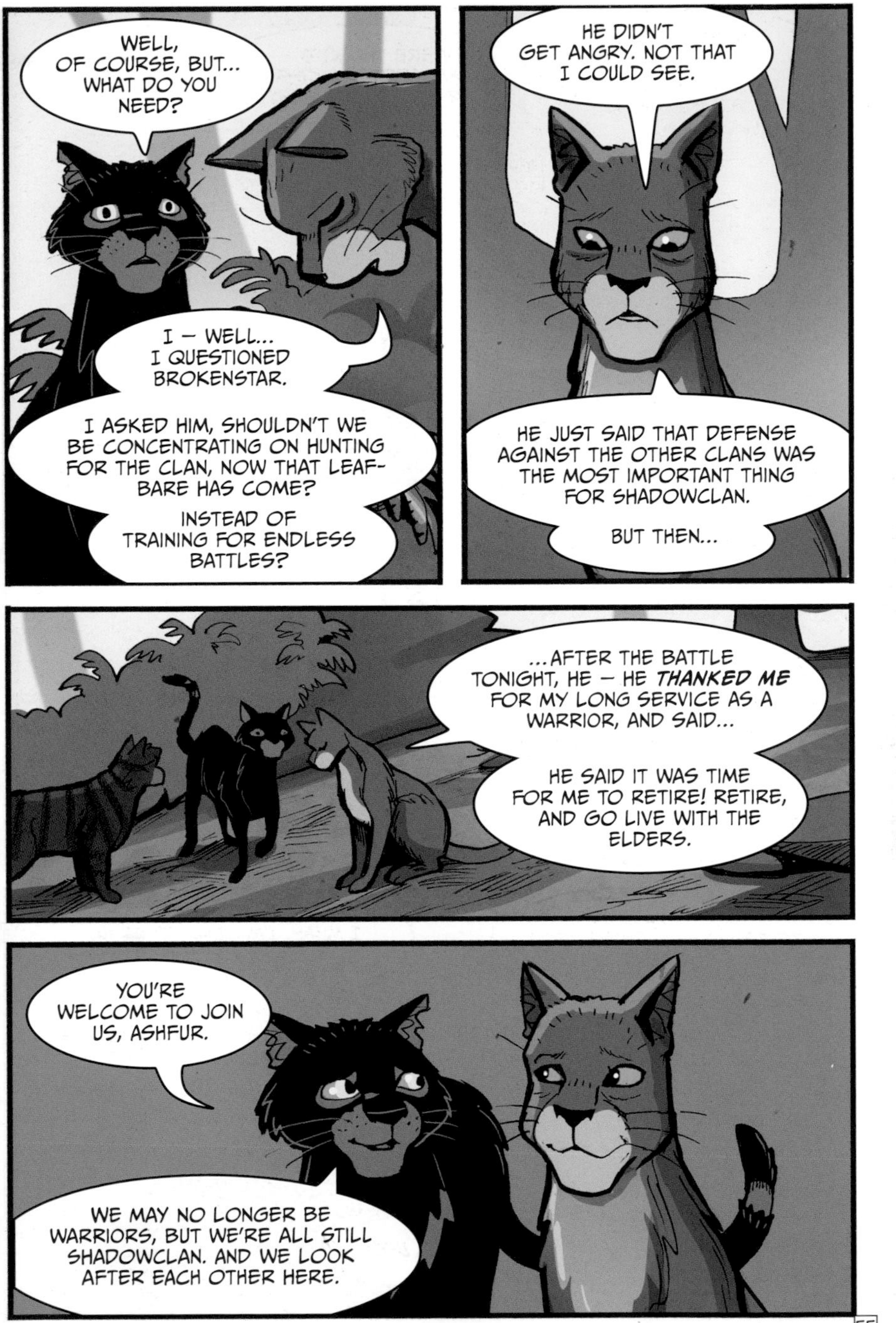
WELL, OF COURSE, BUT... WHAT DO YOU NEED?
I — WELL... I QUESTIONED BROKENSTAR.
I ASKED HIM, SHOULDN'T WE BE CONCENTRATING ON HUNTING FOR THE CLAN, NOW THAT LEAF-BARE HAS COME?
INSTEAD OF TRAINING FOR ENDLESS BATTLES?
HE DIDN'T GET ANGRY. NOT THAT I COULD SEE.
HE JUST SAID THAT DEFENSE AGAINST THE OTHER CLANS WAS THE MOST IMPORTANT THING FOR SHADOWCLAN.
BUT THEN...
...AFTER THE BATTLE TONIGHT, HE — HE *THANKED ME* FOR MY LONG SERVICE AS A WARRIOR, AND SAID...
HE SAID IT WAS TIME FOR ME TO RETIRE! RETIRE, AND GO LIVE WITH THE ELDERS.
YOU'RE WELCOME TO JOIN US, ASHFUR.
WE MAY NO LONGER BE WARRIORS, BUT WE'RE ALL STILL SHADOWCLAN. AND WE LOOK AFTER EACH OTHER HERE.

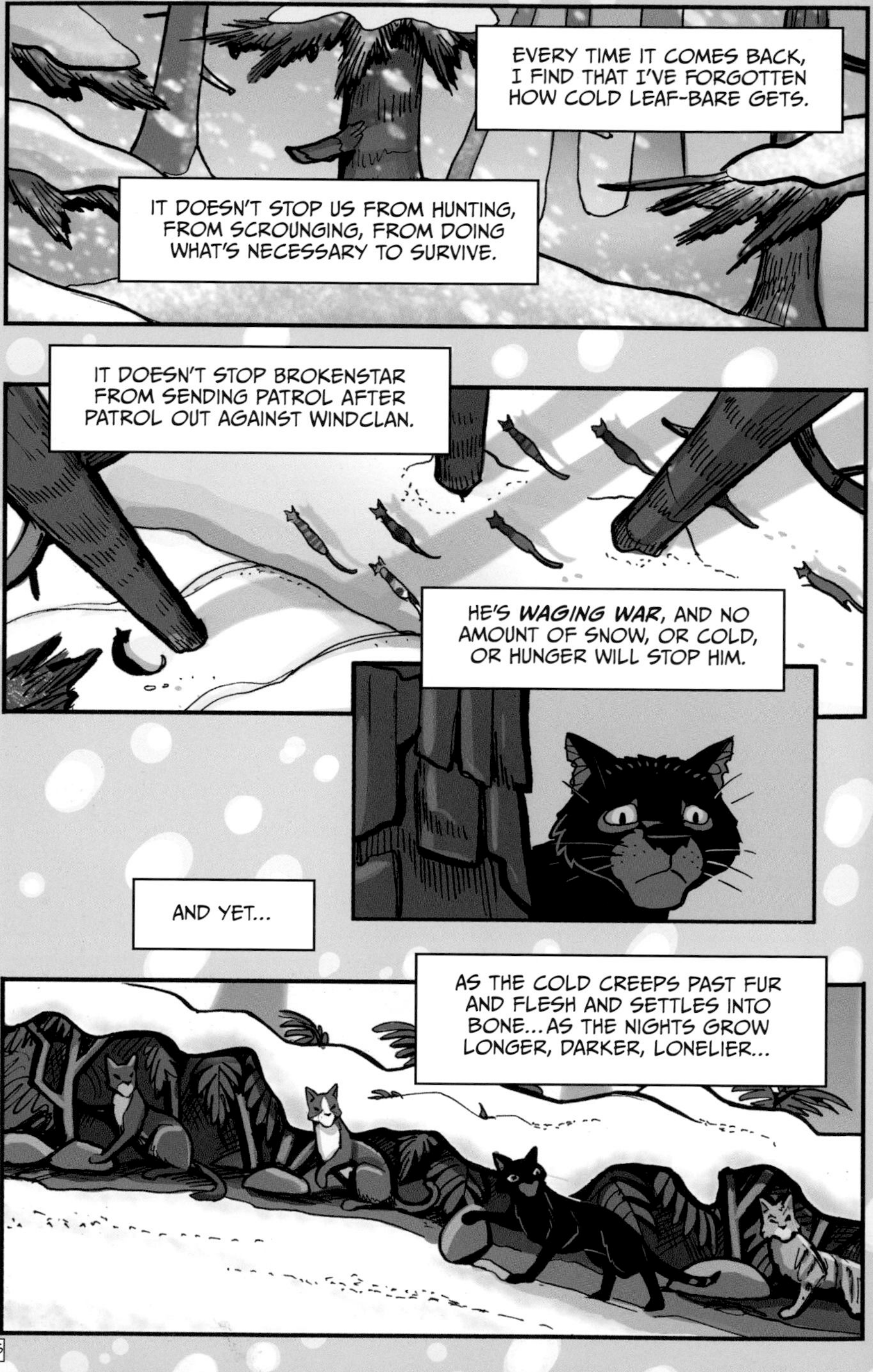
EVERY TIME IT COMES BACK, I FIND THAT I'VE FORGOTTEN HOW COLD LEAF-BARE GETS.
IT DOESN'T STOP US FROM HUNTING, FROM SCROUNGING, FROM DOING WHAT'S NECESSARY TO SURVIVE.
IT DOESN'T STOP BROKENSTAR FROM SENDING PATROL AFTER PATROL OUT AGAINST WINDCLAN.
HE'S ***WAGING WAR***, AND NO AMOUNT OF SNOW, OR COLD, OR HUNGER WILL STOP HIM.
AND YET...
AS THE COLD CREEPS PAST FUR AND FLESH AND SETTLES INTO BONE...AS THE NIGHTS GROW LONGER, DARKER, LONELIER...

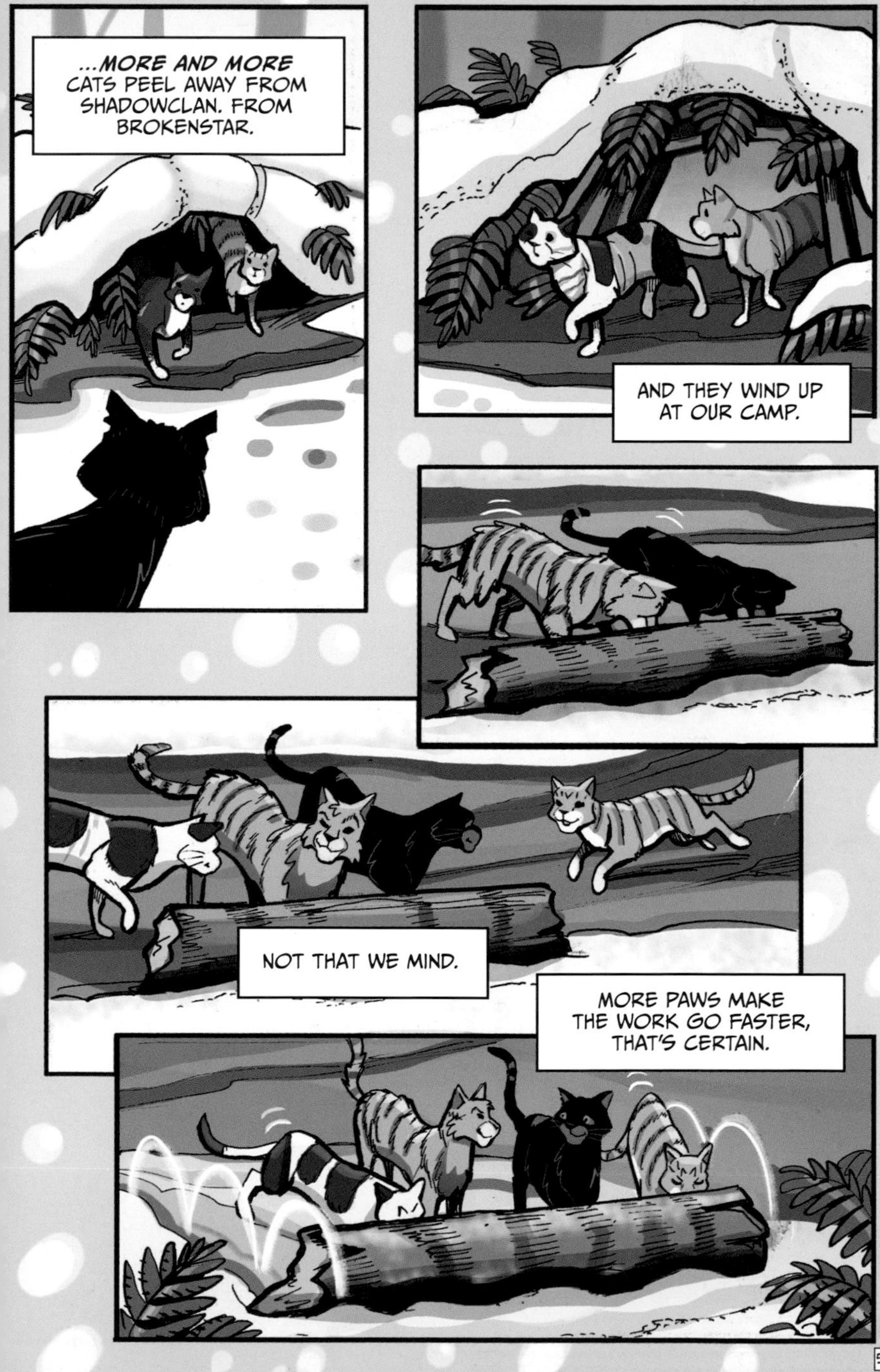
...MORE AND MORE CATS PEEL AWAY FROM SHADOWCLAN. FROM BROKENSTAR.
AND THEY WIND UP AT OUR CAMP.
NOT THAT WE MIND.
MORE PAWS MAKE THE WORK GO FASTER, THAT'S CERTAIN.

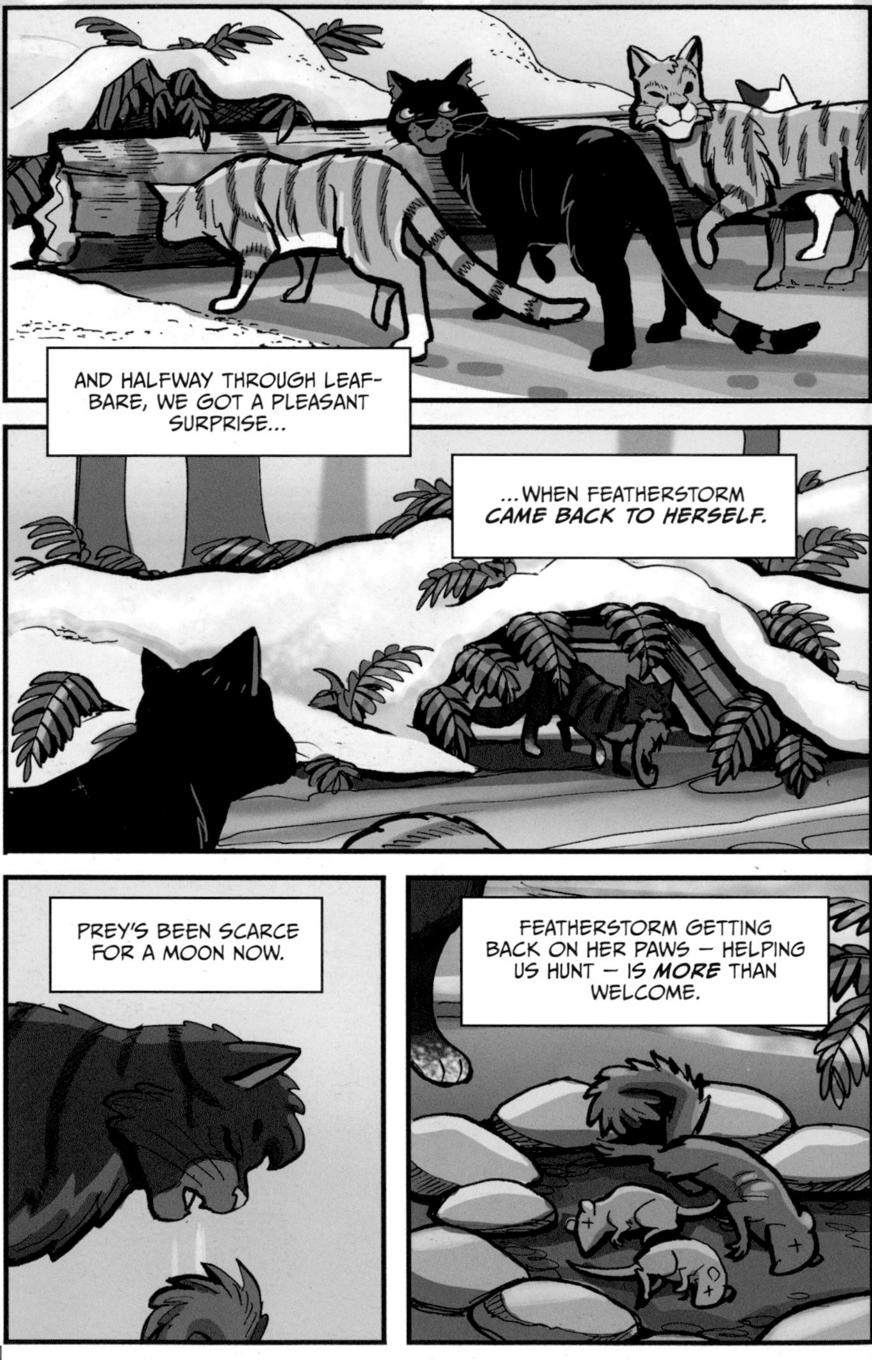
AND HALFWAY THROUGH LEAF-BARE, WE GOT A PLEASANT SURPRISE...
...WHEN FEATHERSTORM *CAME BACK TO HERSELF.*
PREY'S BEEN SCARCE FOR A MOON NOW.
FEATHERSTORM GETTING BACK ON HER PAWS — HELPING US HUNT — IS ***MORE*** THAN WELCOME.

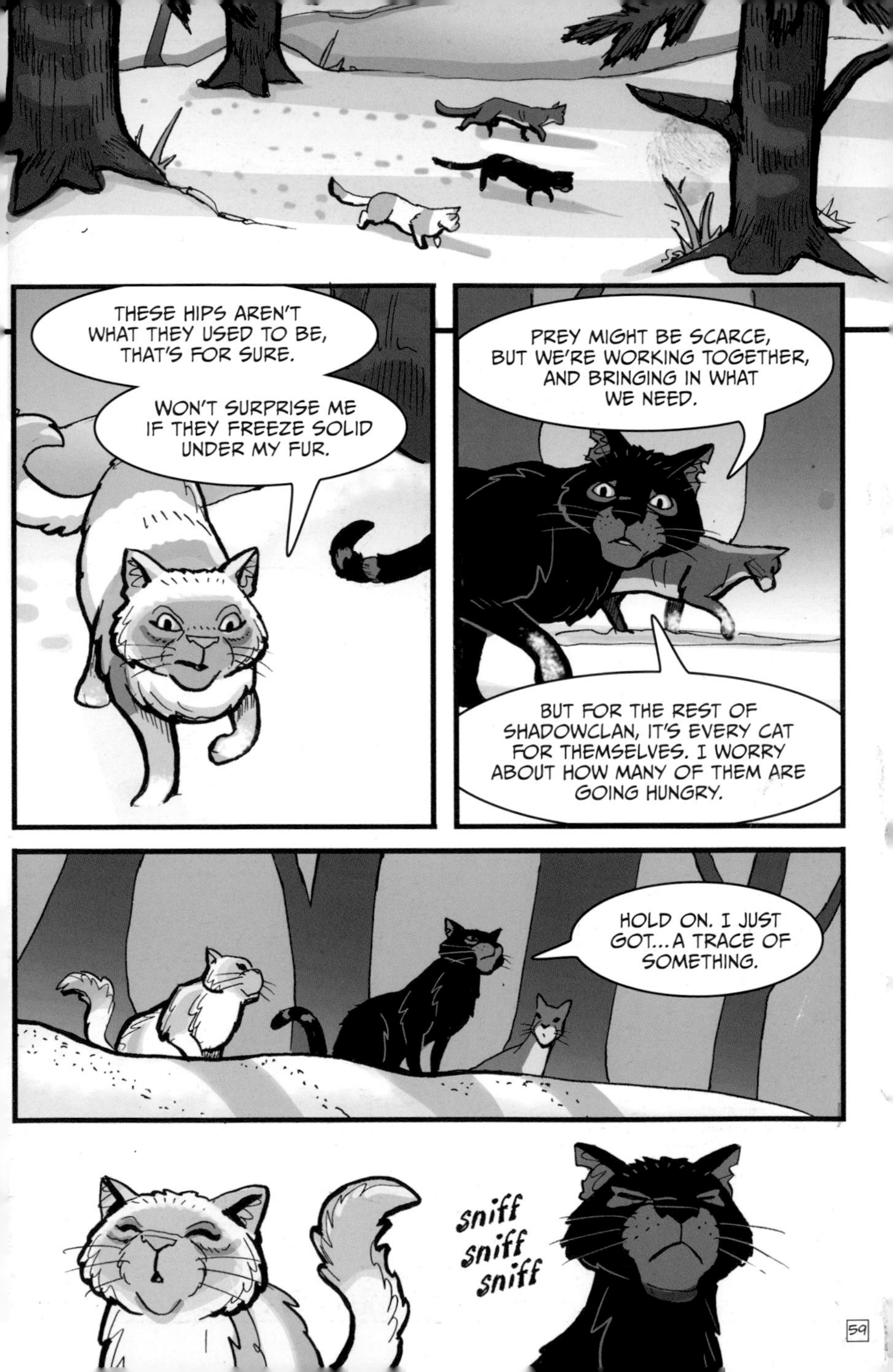
THESE HIPS AREN'T WHAT THEY USED TO BE, THAT'S FOR SURE.
WON'T SURPRISE ME IF THEY FREEZE SOLID UNDER MY FUR.
PREY MIGHT BE SCARCE, BUT WE'RE WORKING TOGETHER, AND BRINGING IN WHAT WE NEED.
BUT FOR THE REST OF SHADOWCLAN, IT'S EVERY CAT FOR THEMSELVES. I WORRY ABOUT HOW MANY OF THEM ARE GOING HUNGRY.
HOLD ON. I JUST GOT...A TRACE OF SOMETHING.
sniff
sniff
sniff

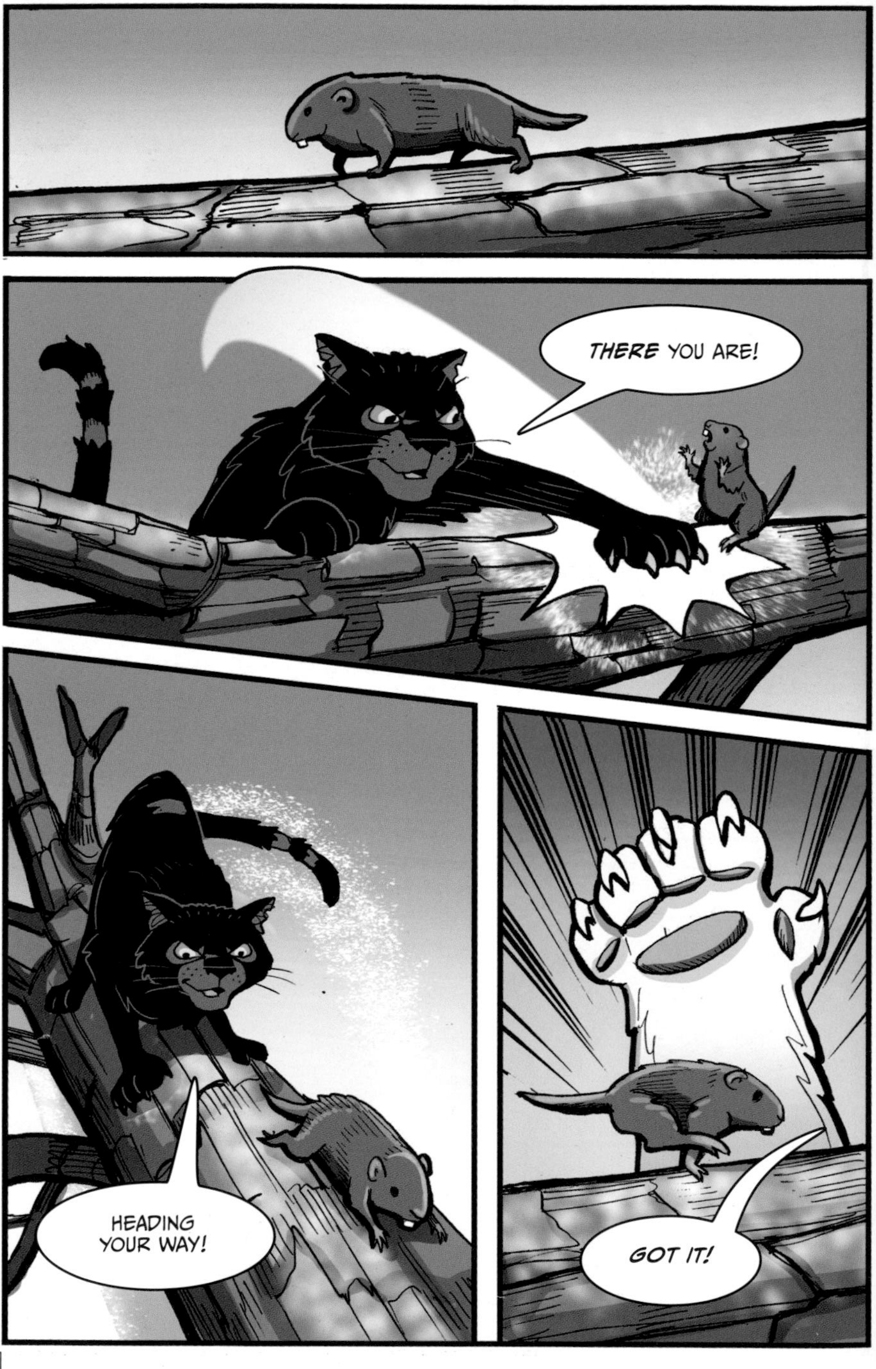
THERE YOU ARE!
HEADING YOUR WAY!
GOT IT!

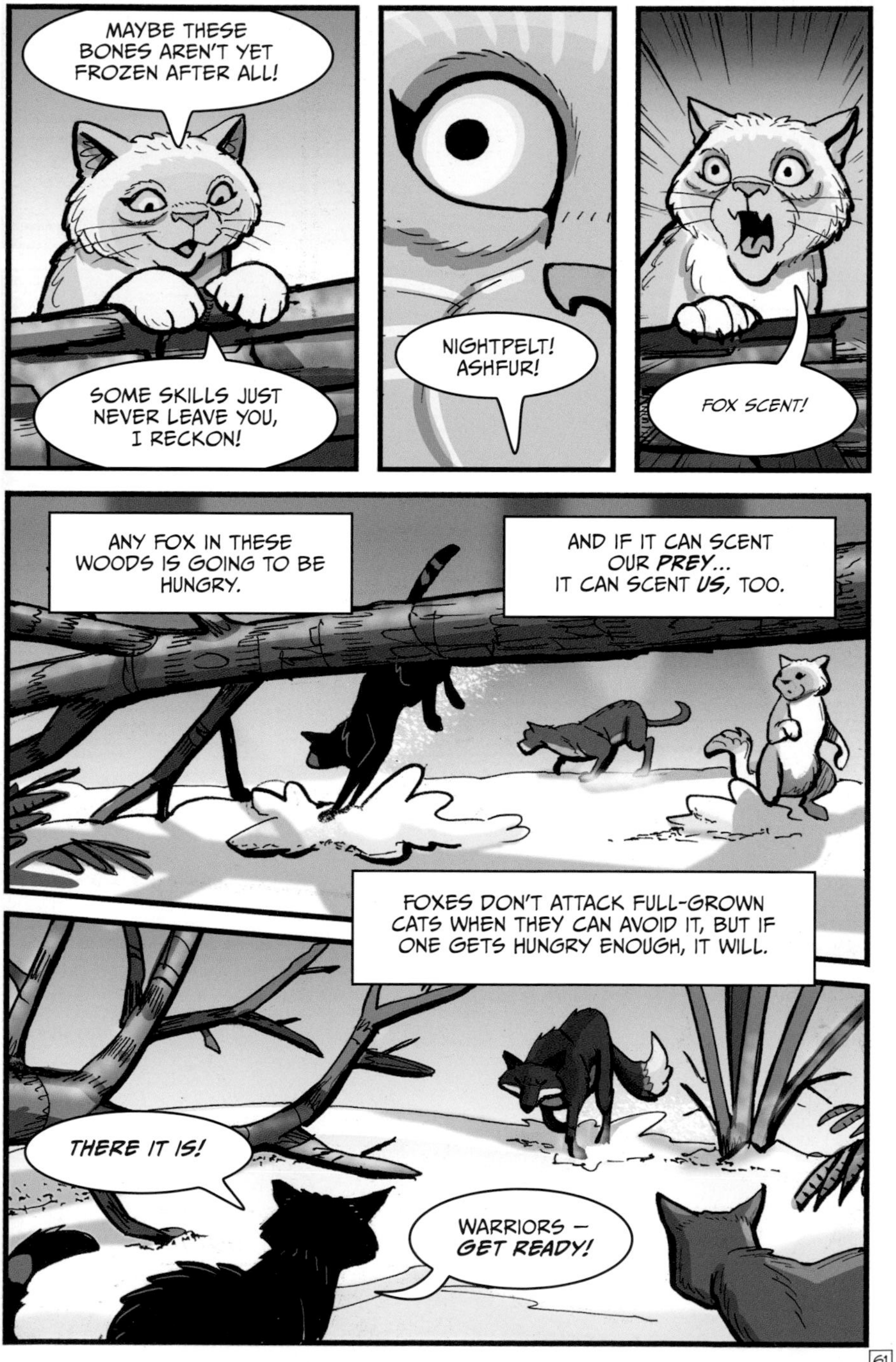
MAYBE THESE BONES AREN'T YET FROZEN AFTER ALL!
SOME SKILLS JUST NEVER LEAVE YOU, I RECKON!
NIGHTPELT! ASHFUR!
FOX SCENT!
ANY FOX IN THESE WOODS IS GOING TO BE HUNGRY.
AND IF IT CAN SCENT OUR PREY... IT CAN SCENT US, TOO.
FOXES DON'T ATTACK FULL-GROWN CATS WHEN THEY CAN AVOID IT, BUT IF ONE GETS HUNGRY ENOUGH, IT WILL.
THERE IT IS!
WARRIORS — GET READY!

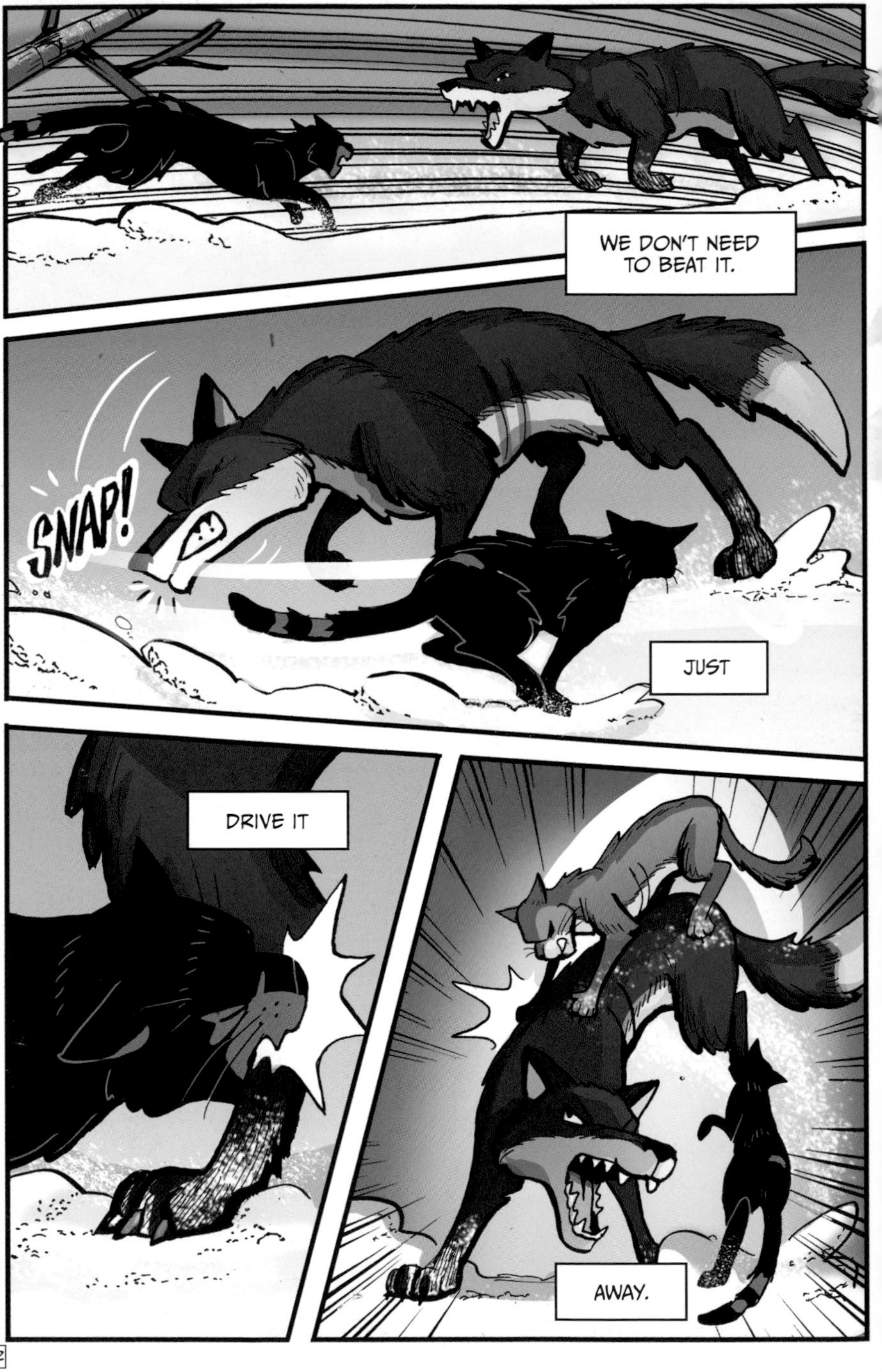
WE DON'T NEED TO BEAT IT.
SNAP!
JUST
DRIVE IT
AWAY.

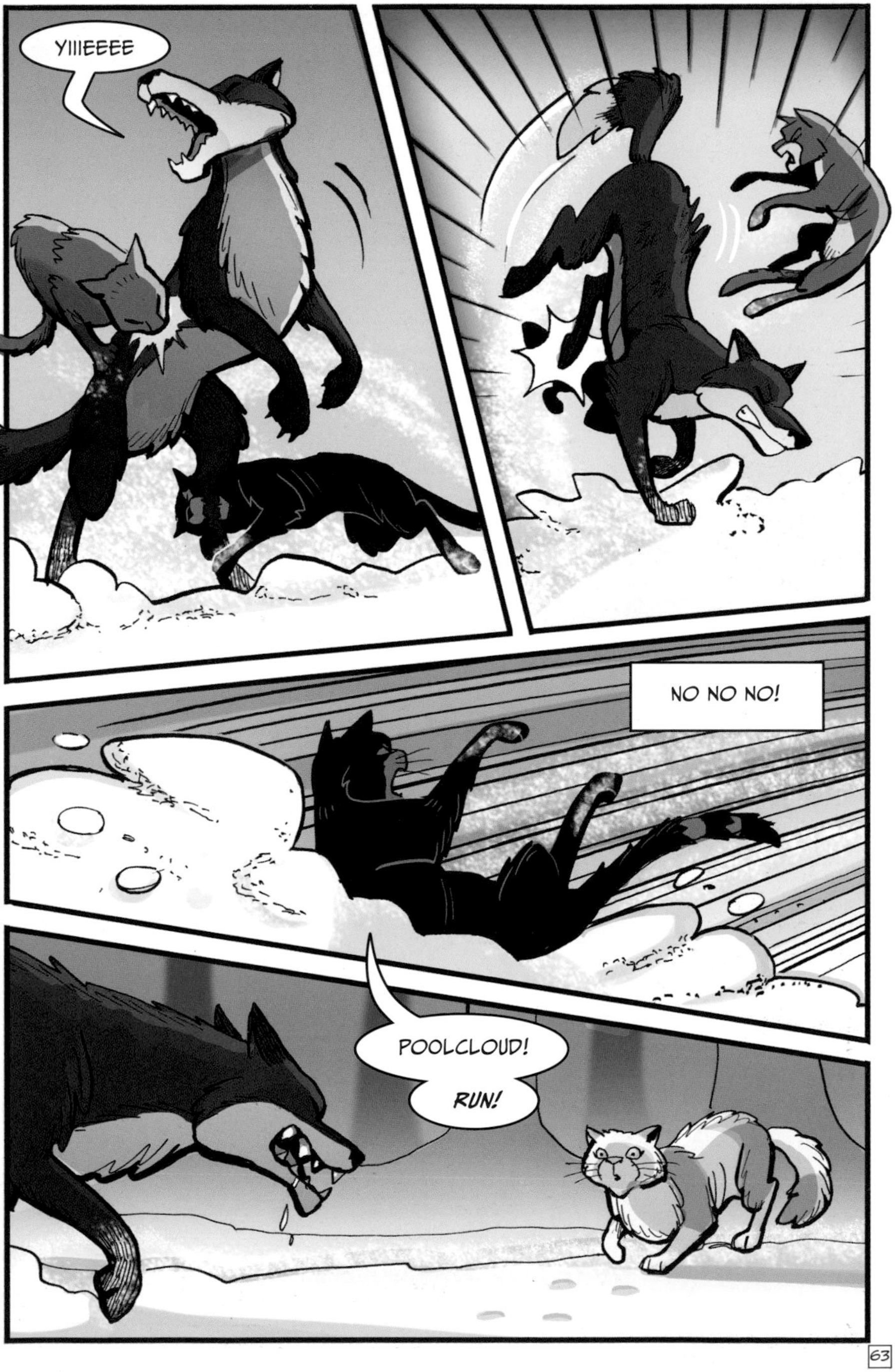
YIIIEEEE
NO NO NO!
POOLCLOUD!
RUN!

RRRHHHEE***EEEE***RRRH!

NO, NO, STARCLAN, PLEASE, NO —

WHOMP

WHOMP

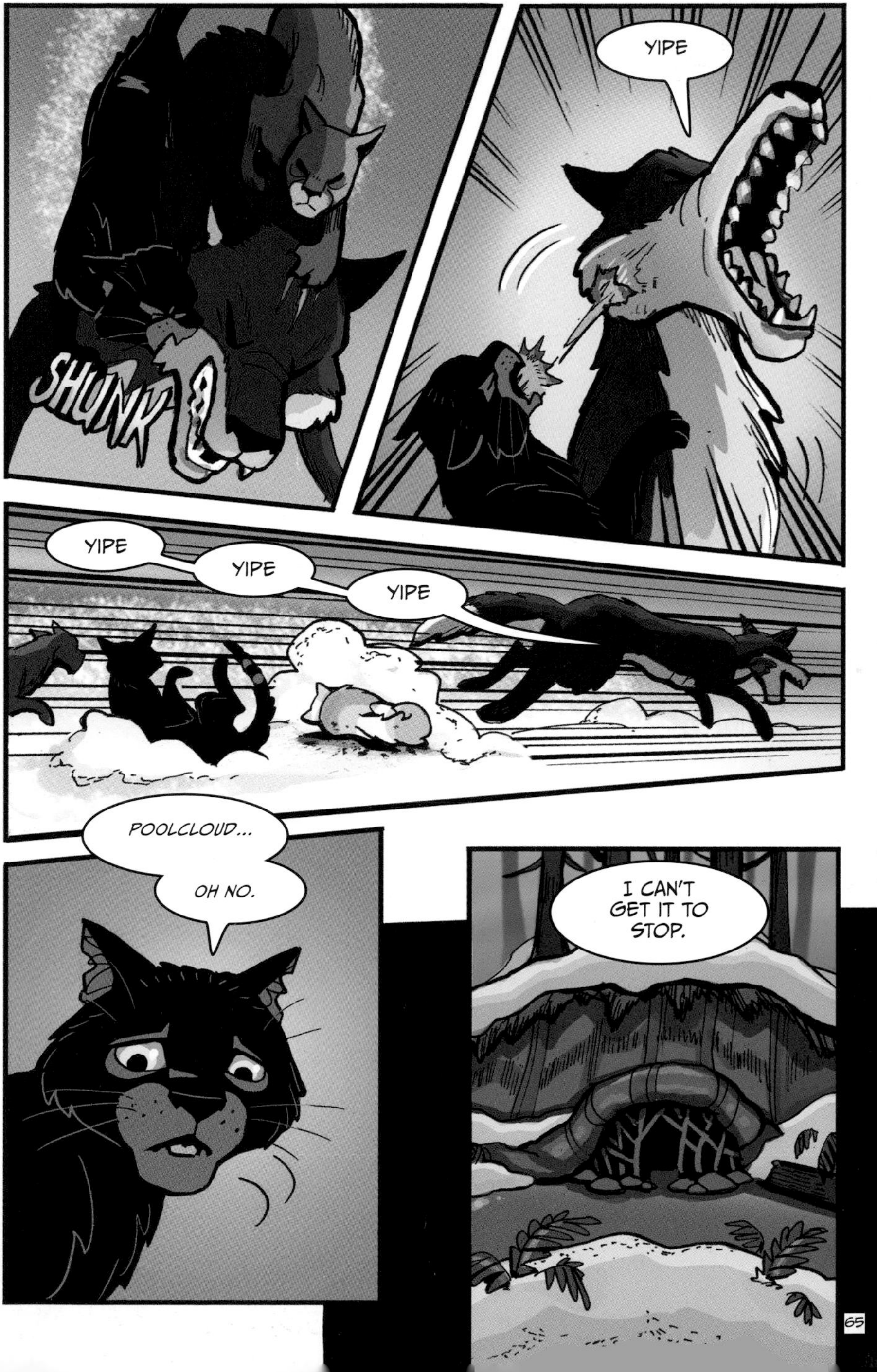
SHUNK
YIPE
YIPE
YIPE
YIPE
POOLCLOUD...
OH NO.
I CAN'T GET IT TO STOP.

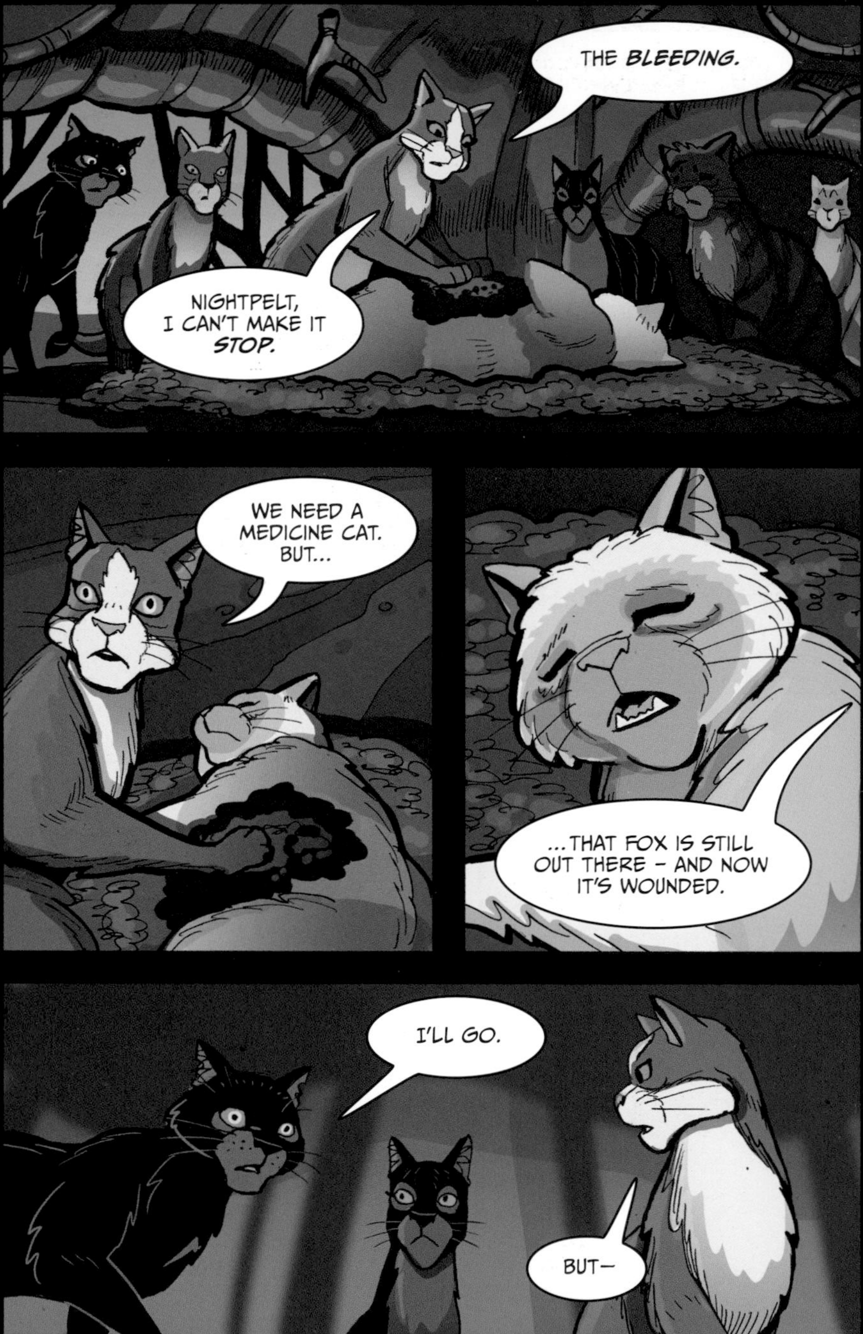
THE BLEEDING.
NIGHTPELT, I CAN'T MAKE IT STOP.
WE NEED A MEDICINE CAT. BUT...
...THAT FOX IS STILL OUT THERE – AND NOW IT'S WOUNDED.
I'LL GO.
BUT–

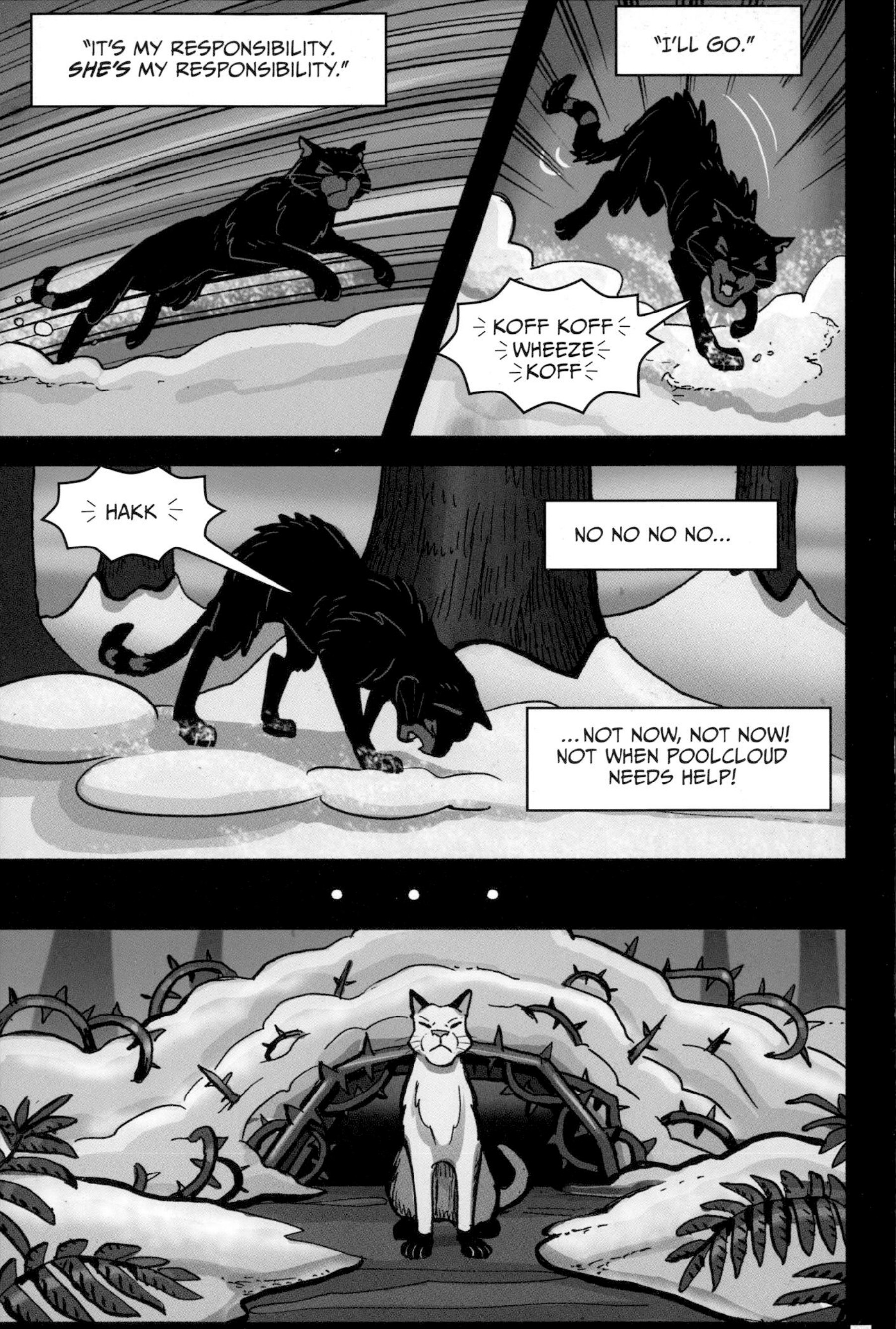
"IT'S MY RESPONSIBILITY. SHE'S MY RESPONSIBILITY."
"I'LL GO."
KOFF KOFF WHEEZE KOFF
HAKK
NO NO NO NO...
...NOT NOW, NOT NOW! NOT WHEN POOLCLOUD NEEDS HELP!

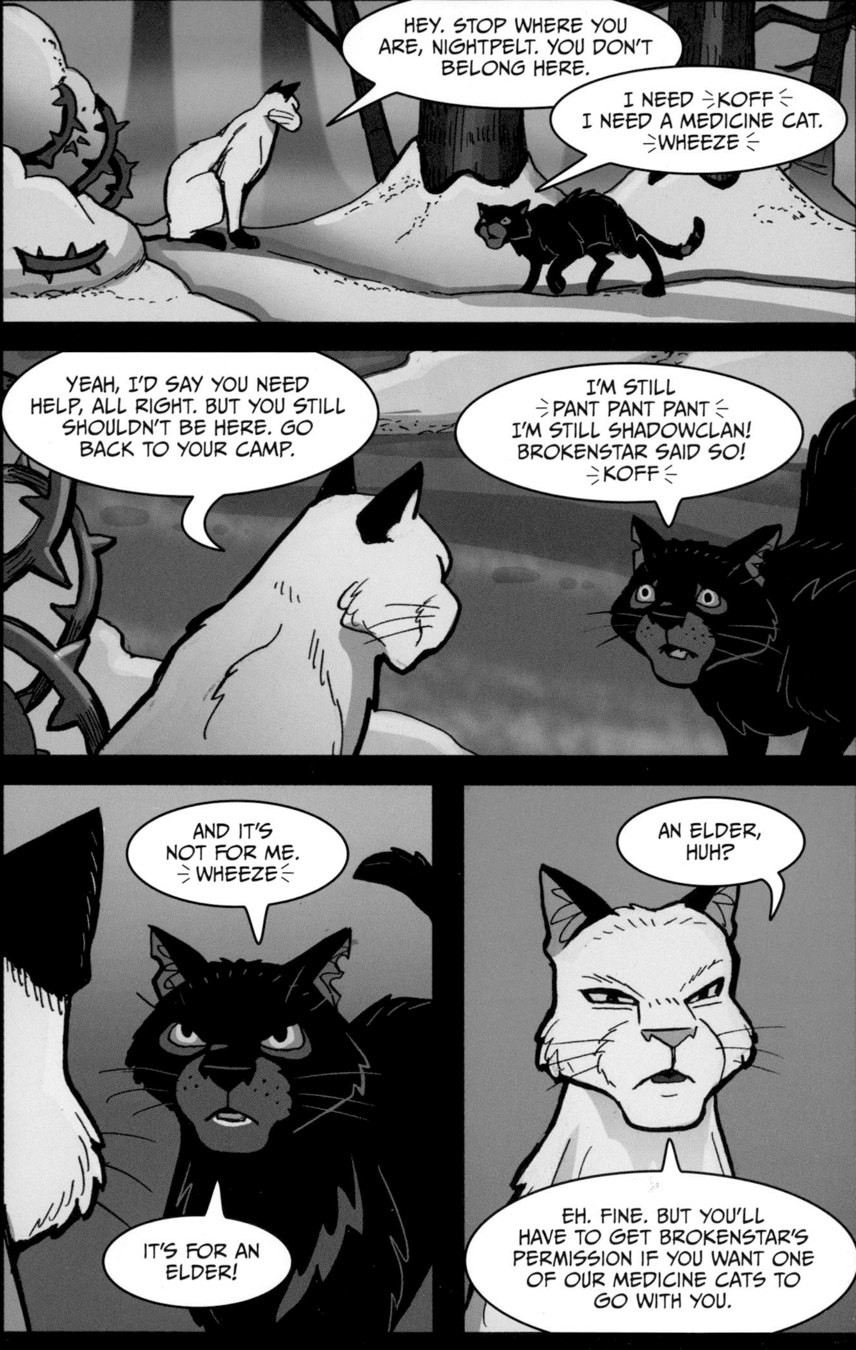
HEY. STOP WHERE YOU ARE, NIGHTPELT. YOU DON'T BELONG HERE.
I NEED ⩶KOFF⩵ I NEED A MEDICINE CAT. ⩶WHEEZE⩵
YEAH, I'D SAY YOU NEED HELP, ALL RIGHT. BUT YOU STILL SHOULDN'T BE HERE. GO BACK TO YOUR CAMP.
I'M STILL ⩶PANT PANT PANT⩵ I'M STILL SHADOWCLAN! BROKENSTAR SAID SO! ⩶KOFF⩵
AND IT'S NOT FOR ME. ⩶WHEEZE⩵
IT'S FOR AN ELDER!
AN ELDER, HUH?
EH. FINE. BUT YOU'LL HAVE TO GET BROKENSTAR'S PERMISSION IF YOU WANT ONE OF OUR MEDICINE CATS TO GO WITH YOU.

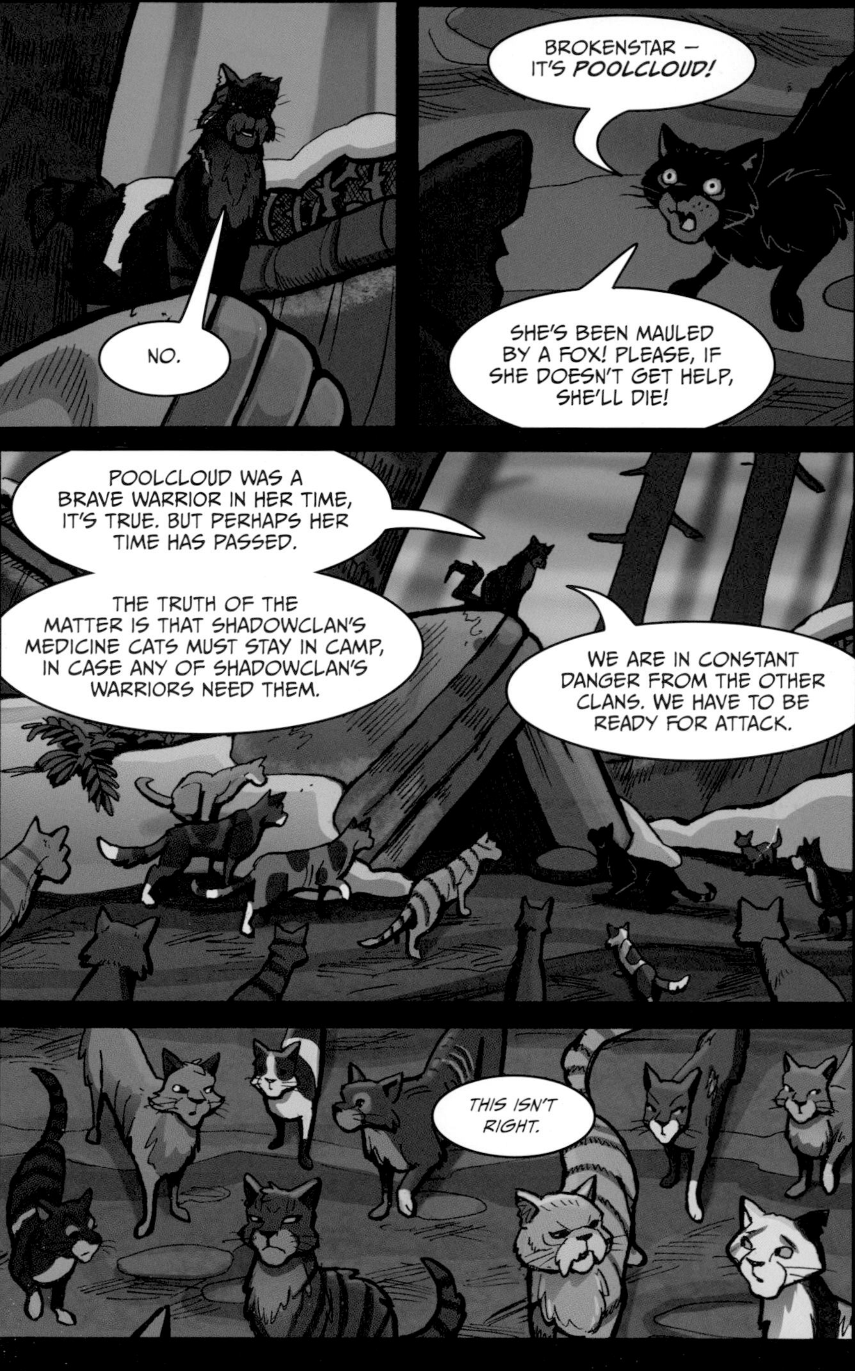
NO.
BROKENSTAR — IT'S *POOLCLOUD!*
SHE'S BEEN MAULED BY A FOX! PLEASE, IF SHE DOESN'T GET HELP, SHE'LL DIE!
POOLCLOUD WAS A BRAVE WARRIOR IN HER TIME, IT'S TRUE. BUT PERHAPS HER TIME HAS PASSED.
THE TRUTH OF THE MATTER IS THAT SHADOWCLAN'S MEDICINE CATS MUST STAY IN CAMP, IN CASE ANY OF SHADOWCLAN'S WARRIORS NEED THEM.
WE ARE IN CONSTANT DANGER FROM THE OTHER CLANS. WE HAVE TO BE READY FOR ATTACK.
THIS ISN'T RIGHT.

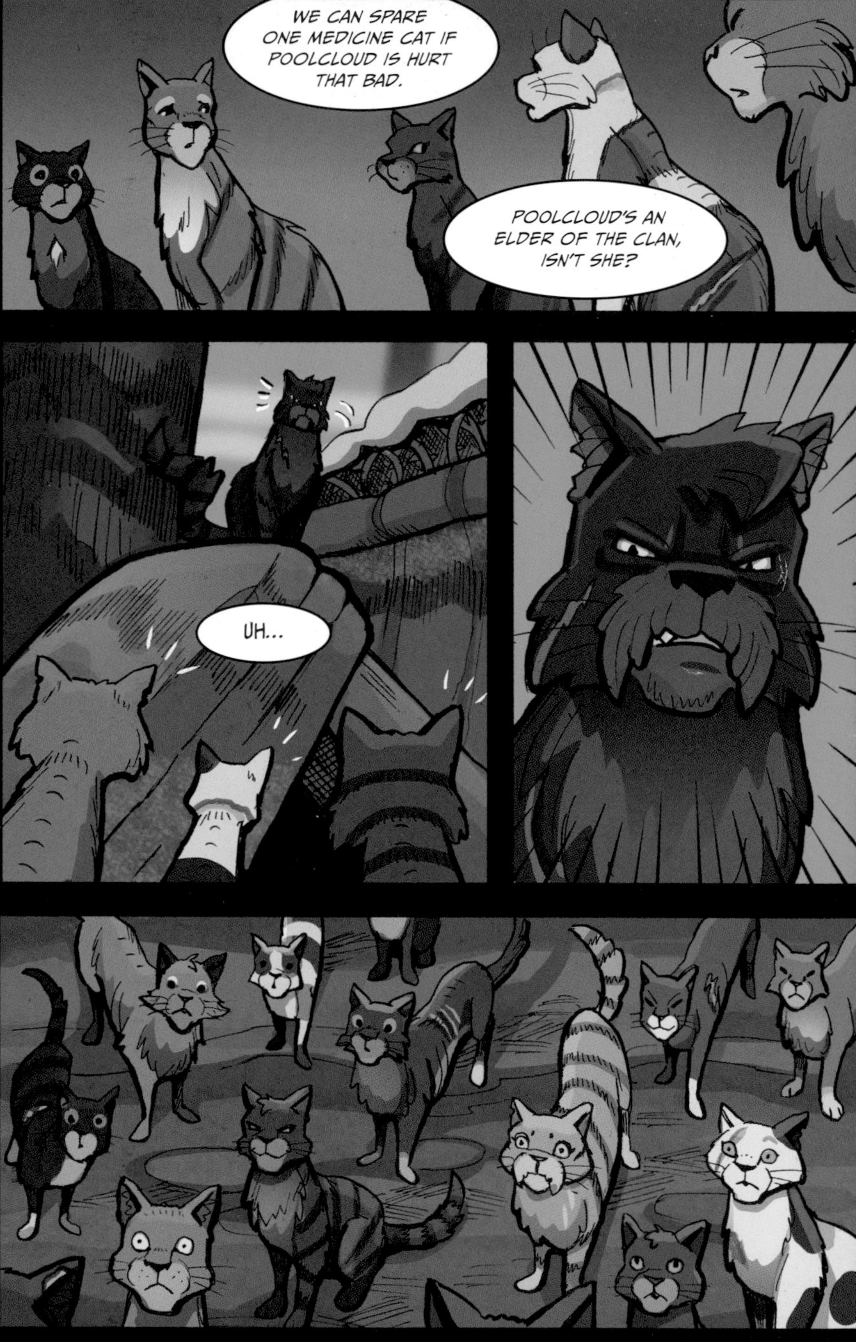
WE CAN SPARE ONE MEDICINE CAT IF POOLCLOUD IS HURT THAT BAD.
POOLCLOUD'S AN ELDER OF THE CLAN, ISN'T SHE?
UH...

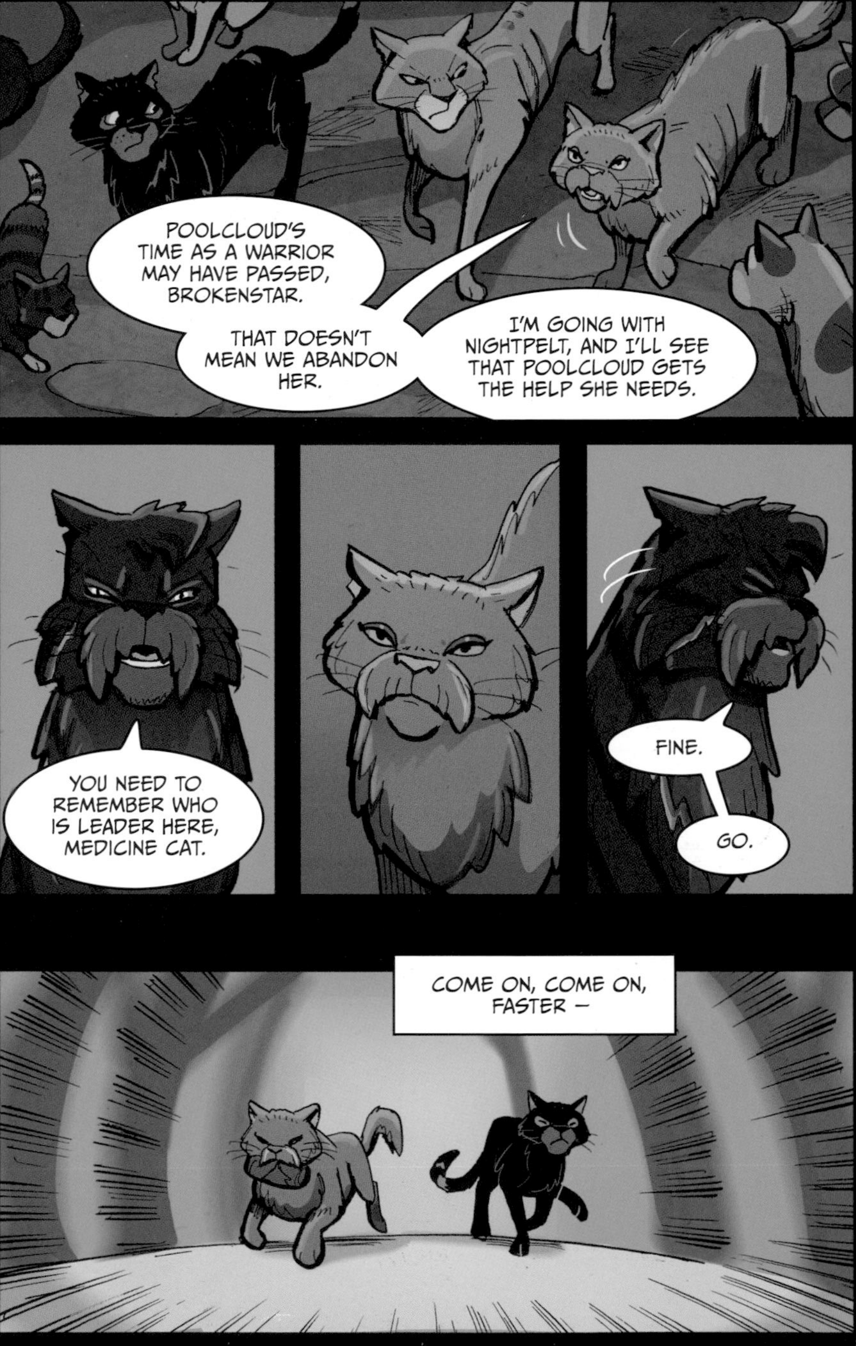
POOLCLOUD'S TIME AS A WARRIOR MAY HAVE PASSED, BROKENSTAR.
THAT DOESN'T MEAN WE ABANDON HER.
I'M GOING WITH NIGHTPELT, AND I'LL SEE THAT POOLCLOUD GETS THE HELP SHE NEEDS.
YOU NEED TO REMEMBER WHO IS LEADER HERE, MEDICINE CAT.
FINE.
GO.
COME ON, COME ON, FASTER –

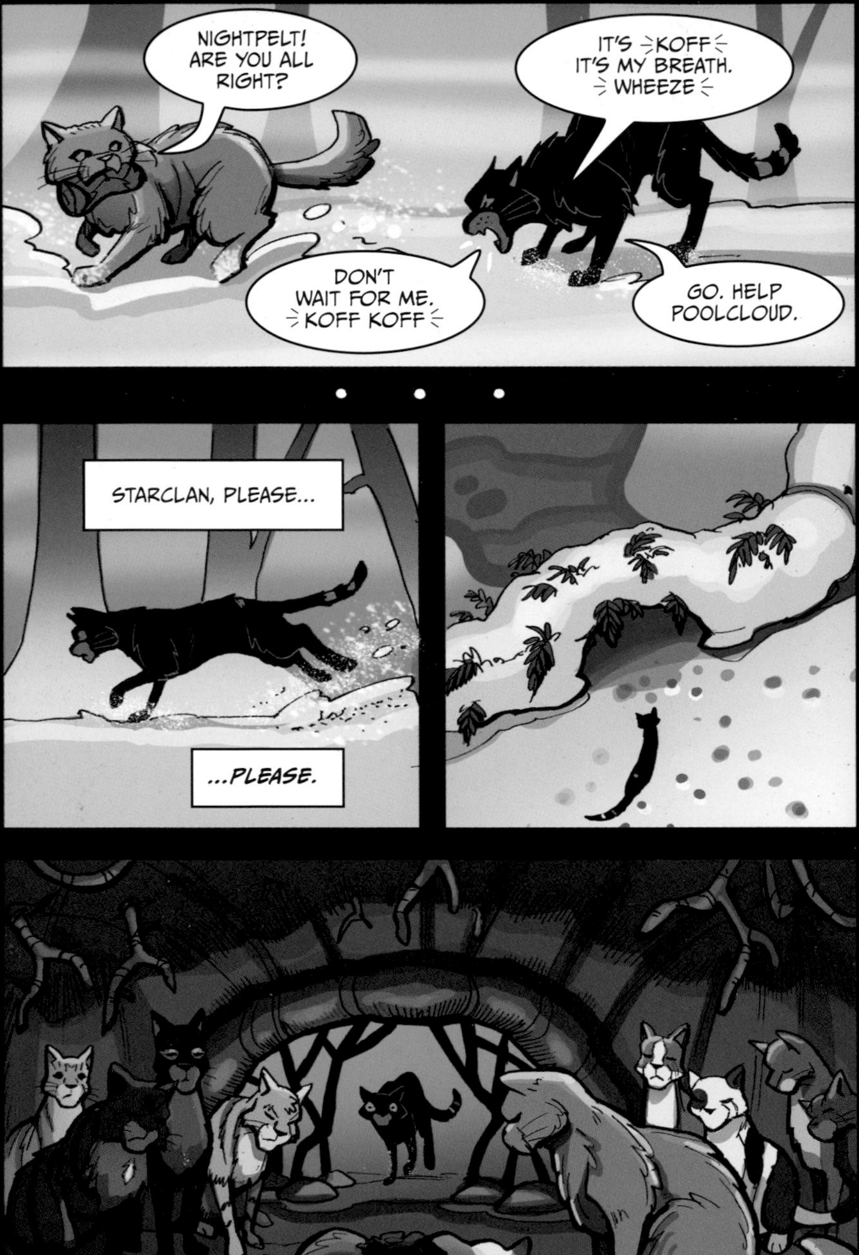
NIGHTPELT! ARE YOU ALL RIGHT?
IT'S KOFF IT'S MY BREATH. WHEEZE
DON'T WAIT FOR ME. KOFF KOFF
GO. HELP POOLCLOUD.
STARCLAN, PLEASE...
...PLEASE.

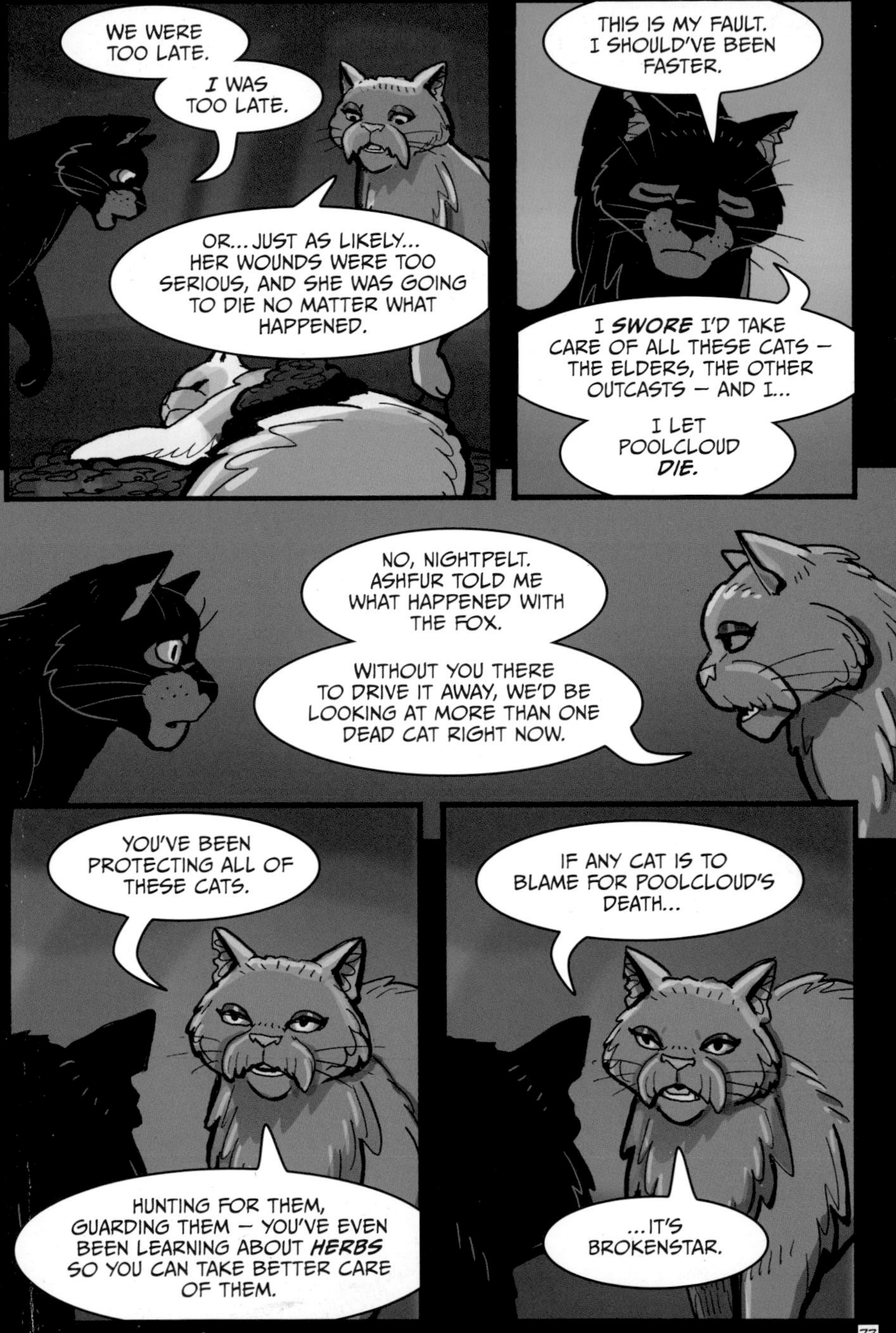
WE WERE TOO LATE.
I WAS TOO LATE.
OR... JUST AS LIKELY... HER WOUNDS WERE TOO SERIOUS, AND SHE WAS GOING TO DIE NO MATTER WHAT HAPPENED.
THIS IS MY FAULT. I SHOULD'VE BEEN FASTER.
I ***SWORE*** I'D TAKE CARE OF ALL THESE CATS — THE ELDERS, THE OTHER OUTCASTS — AND I...
I LET POOLCLOUD ***DIE.***
NO, NIGHTPELT. ASHFUR TOLD ME WHAT HAPPENED WITH THE FOX.
WITHOUT YOU THERE TO DRIVE IT AWAY, WE'D BE LOOKING AT MORE THAN ONE DEAD CAT RIGHT NOW.
YOU'VE BEEN PROTECTING ALL OF THESE CATS.
HUNTING FOR THEM, GUARDING THEM — YOU'VE EVEN BEEN LEARNING ABOUT ***HERBS*** SO YOU CAN TAKE BETTER CARE OF THEM.
IF ANY CAT IS TO BLAME FOR POOLCLOUD'S DEATH...
...IT'S BROKENSTAR.

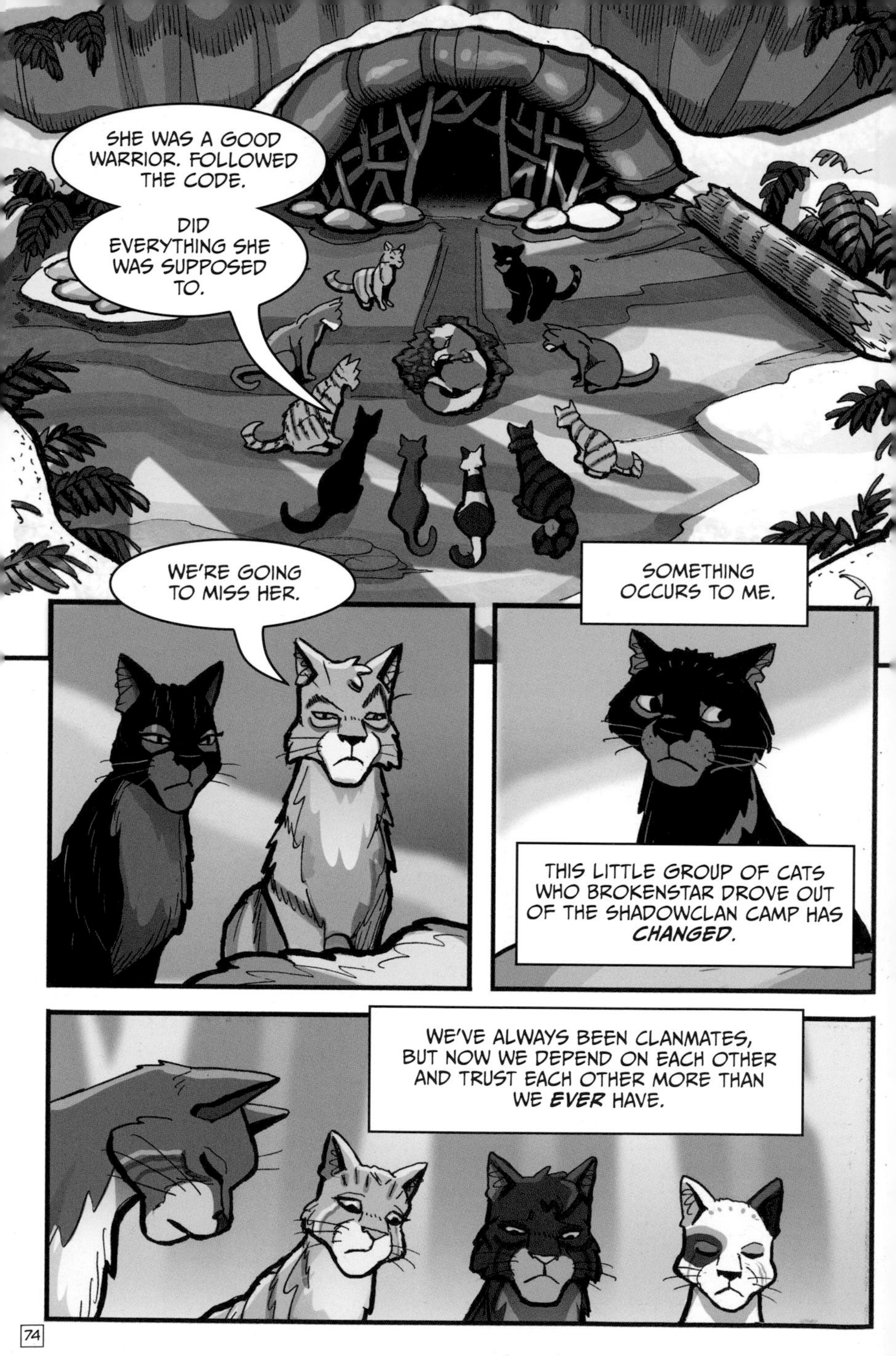
SHE WAS A GOOD WARRIOR. FOLLOWED THE CODE.
DID EVERYTHING SHE WAS SUPPOSED TO.
WE'RE GOING TO MISS HER.
SOMETHING OCCURS TO ME.
THIS LITTLE GROUP OF CATS WHO BROKENSTAR DROVE OUT OF THE SHADOWCLAN CAMP HAS *CHANGED.*
WE'VE ALWAYS BEEN CLANMATES, BUT NOW WE DEPEND ON EACH OTHER AND TRUST EACH OTHER MORE THAN WE *EVER* HAVE.

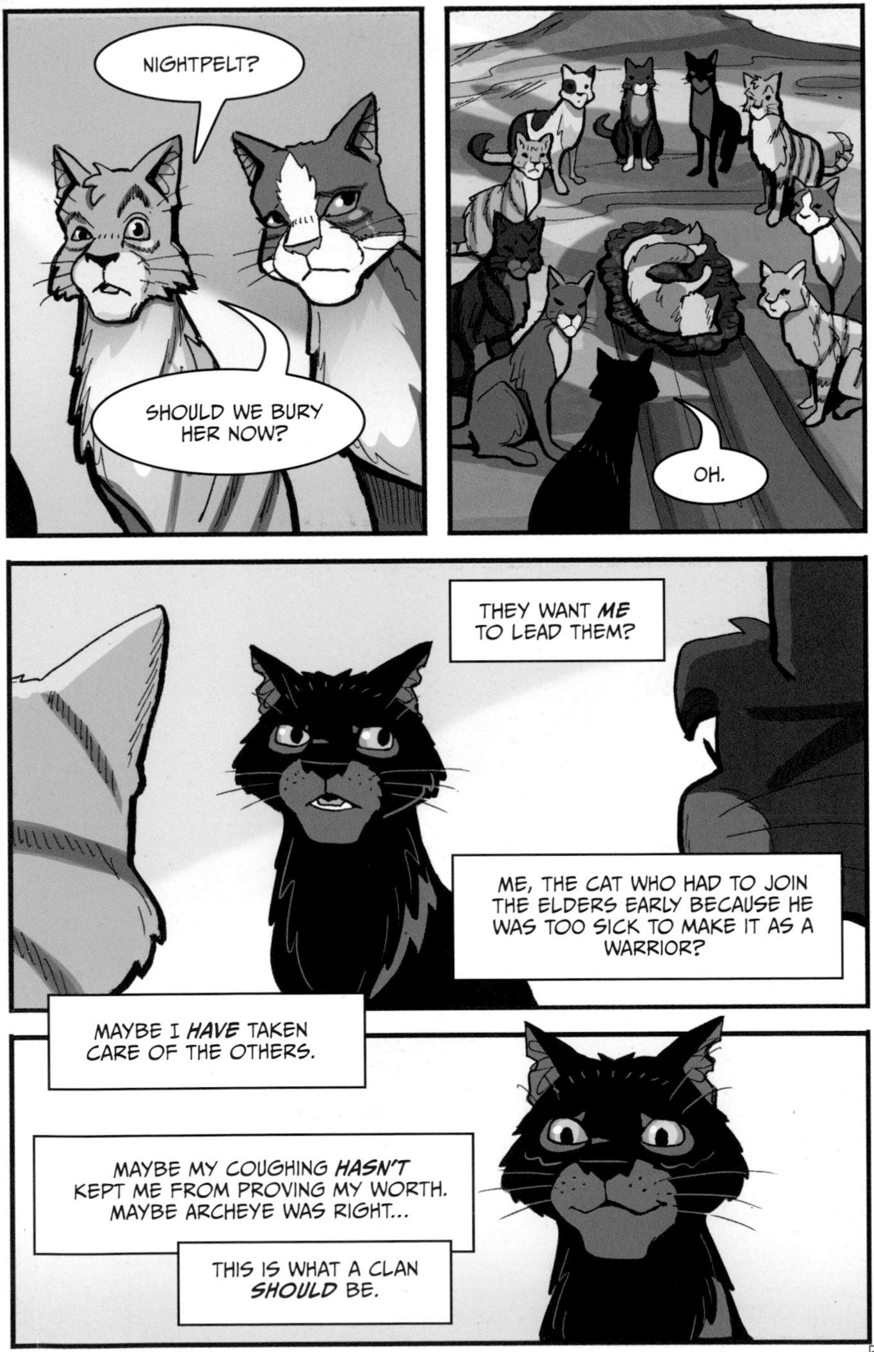
NIGHTPELT?
SHOULD WE BURY HER NOW?
OH.
THEY WANT ***ME*** TO LEAD THEM?
ME, THE CAT WHO HAD TO JOIN THE ELDERS EARLY BECAUSE HE WAS TOO SICK TO MAKE IT AS A WARRIOR?
MAYBE I ***HAVE*** TAKEN CARE OF THE OTHERS.
MAYBE MY COUGHING ***HASN'T*** KEPT ME FROM PROVING MY WORTH. MAYBE ARCHEYE WAS RIGHT...
THIS IS WHAT A CLAN ***SHOULD*** BE.

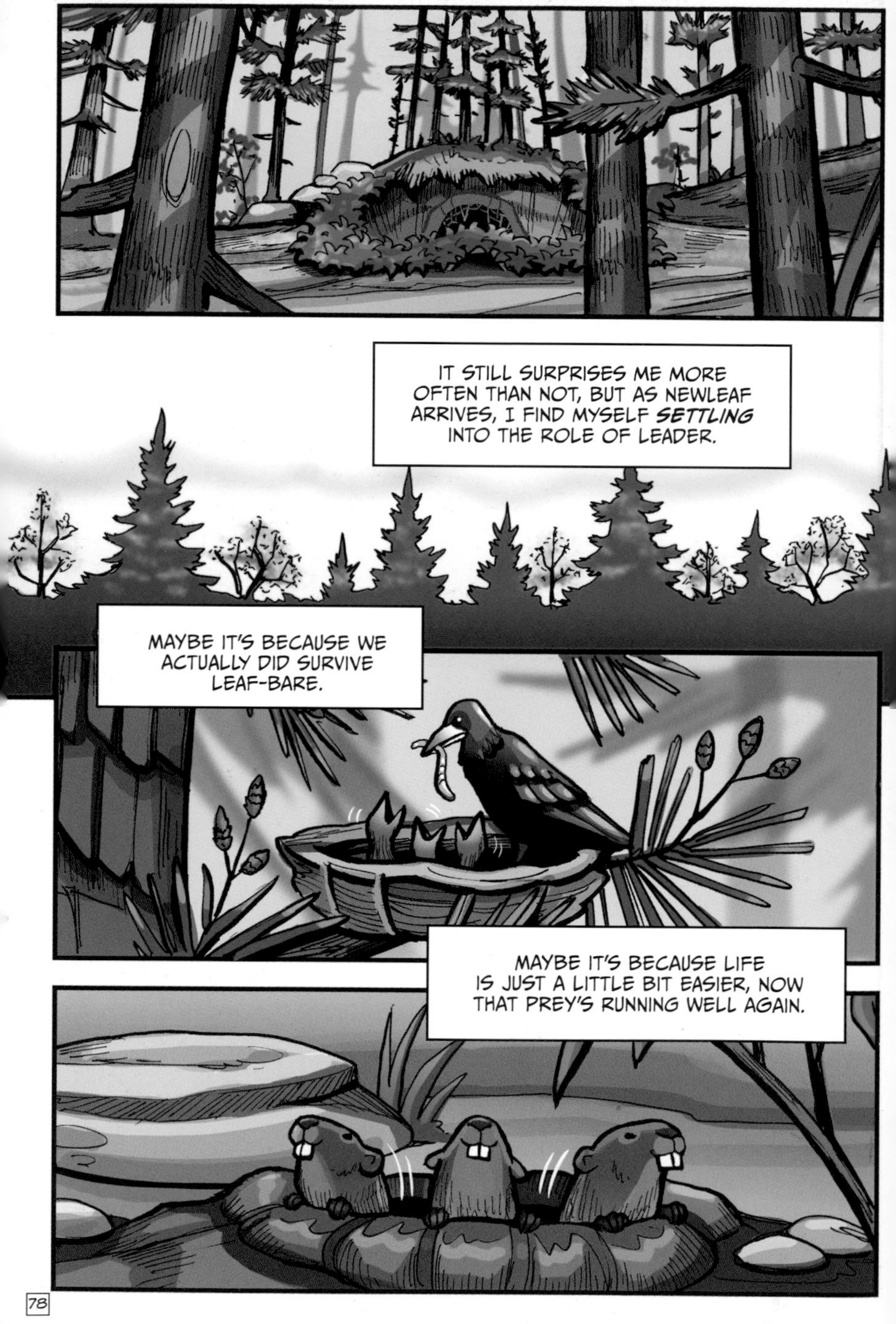
IT STILL SURPRISES ME MORE OFTEN THAN NOT, BUT AS NEWLEAF ARRIVES, I FIND MYSELF *SETTLING* INTO THE ROLE OF LEADER.
MAYBE IT'S BECAUSE WE ACTUALLY DID SURVIVE LEAF-BARE.
MAYBE IT'S BECAUSE LIFE IS JUST A LITTLE BIT EASIER, NOW THAT PREY'S RUNNING WELL AGAIN.

AND WITHOUT A STATE OF CONSTANT CRISIS, I CAN CONCENTRATE ON THE SMALLER THINGS...

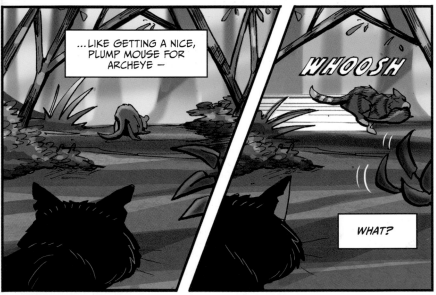

...LIKE GETTING A NICE, PLUMP MOUSE FOR ARCHEYE —

WHOOSH

WHAT?

DID YOU SEE? DID YOU SEE ME?

THAT MOUSE NEVER EVEN KNEW YOU WERE THERE!

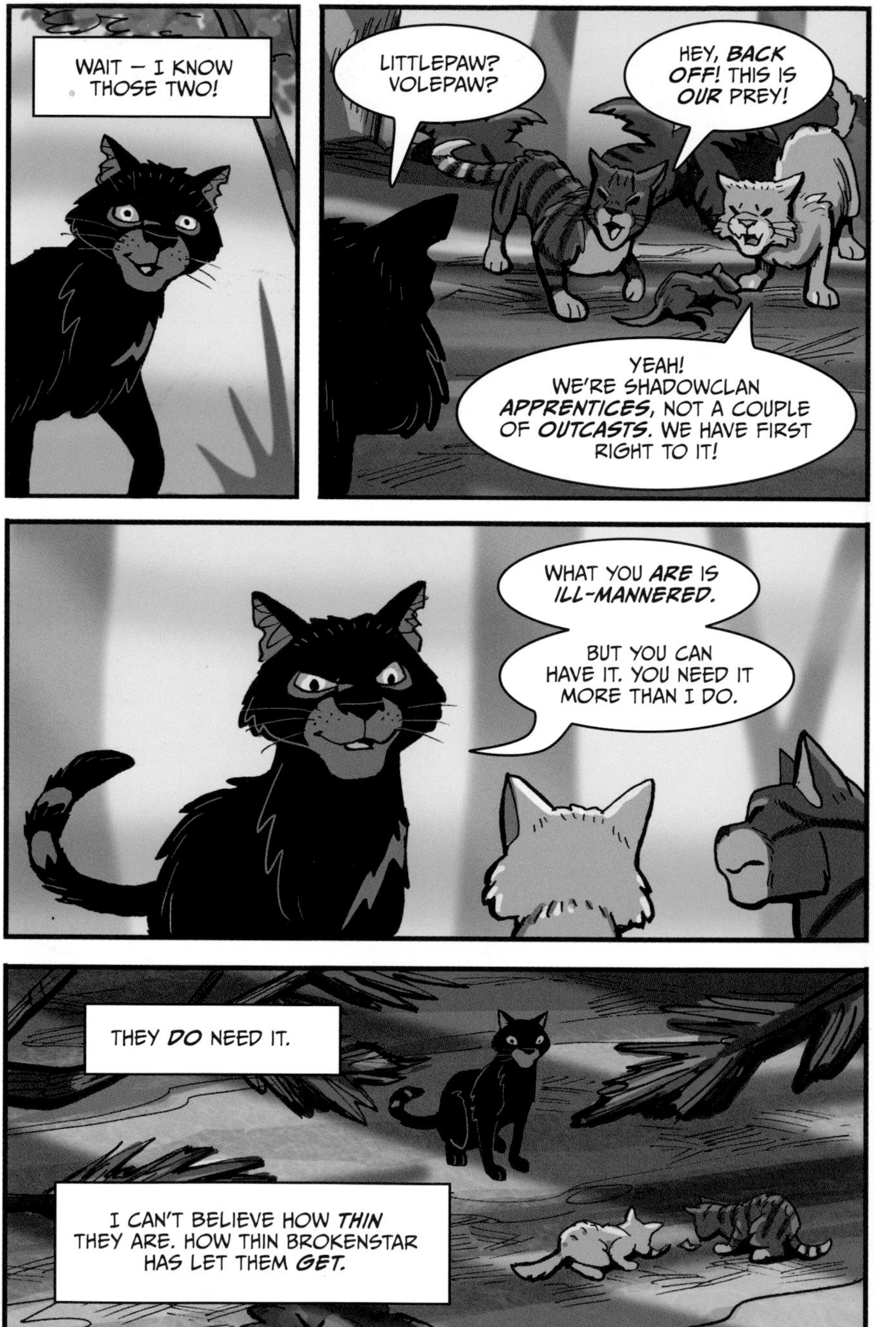

WAIT — I KNOW THOSE TWO!
LITTLEPAW? VOLEPAW?
HEY, *BACK OFF*! THIS IS *OUR* PREY!
YEAH! WE'RE SHADOWCLAN *APPRENTICES*, NOT A COUPLE OF *OUTCASTS*. WE HAVE FIRST RIGHT TO IT!
WHAT YOU *ARE* IS *ILL-MANNERED.*
BUT YOU CAN HAVE IT. YOU NEED IT MORE THAN I DO.
THEY *DO* NEED IT.
I CAN'T BELIEVE HOW *THIN* THEY ARE. HOW THIN BROKENSTAR HAS LET THEM *GET.*

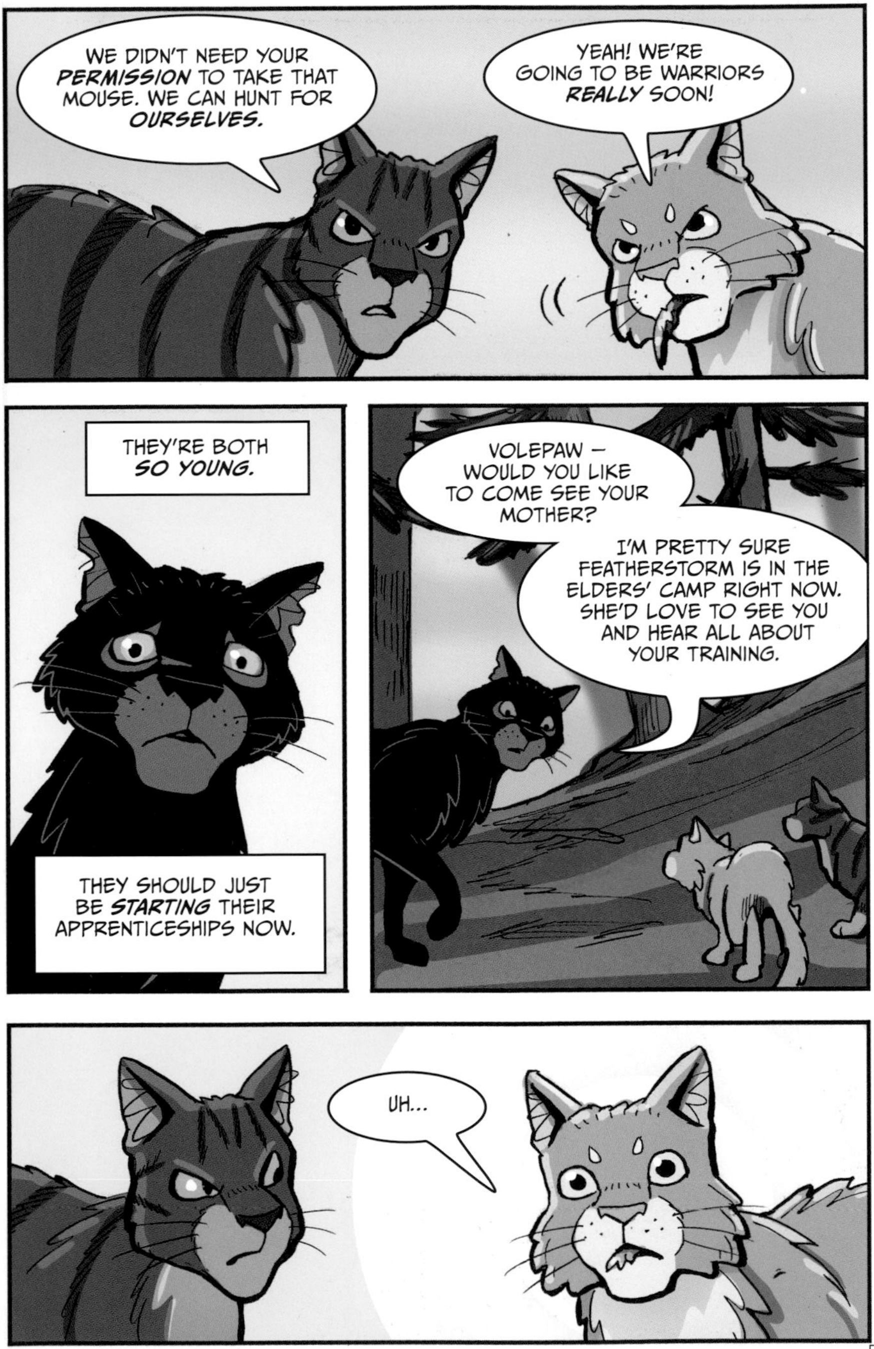
WE DIDN'T NEED YOUR *PERMISSION* TO TAKE THAT MOUSE. WE CAN HUNT FOR *OURSELVES.*
YEAH! WE'RE GOING TO BE WARRIORS *REALLY* SOON!
THEY'RE BOTH *SO YOUNG.*
THEY SHOULD JUST BE *STARTING* THEIR APPRENTICESHIPS NOW.
VOLEPAW — WOULD YOU LIKE TO COME SEE YOUR MOTHER?
I'M PRETTY SURE FEATHERSTORM IS IN THE ELDERS' CAMP RIGHT NOW. SHE'D LOVE TO SEE YOU AND HEAR ALL ABOUT YOUR TRAINING.
UH...

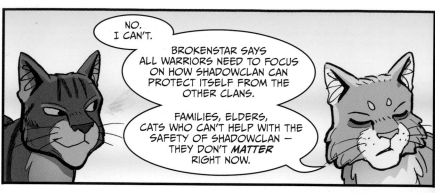

NO. I CAN'T.

BROKENSTAR SAYS ALL WARRIORS NEED TO FOCUS ON HOW SHADOWCLAN CAN PROTECT ITSELF FROM THE OTHER CLANS.

FAMILIES, ELDERS, CATS WHO CAN'T HELP WITH THE SAFETY OF SHADOWCLAN — THEY DON'T *MATTER* RIGHT NOW.

ARE YOU SURE YOU DON'T WANT TO JUST *SEE* YOUR MOTHER?

SHE'S *VERY* CLOSE BY.

SERIOUSLY?

WE NEED TO *GO!*

OUR MENTORS ARE PROBABLY ALREADY WAITING AT THE CARRIONPLACE!

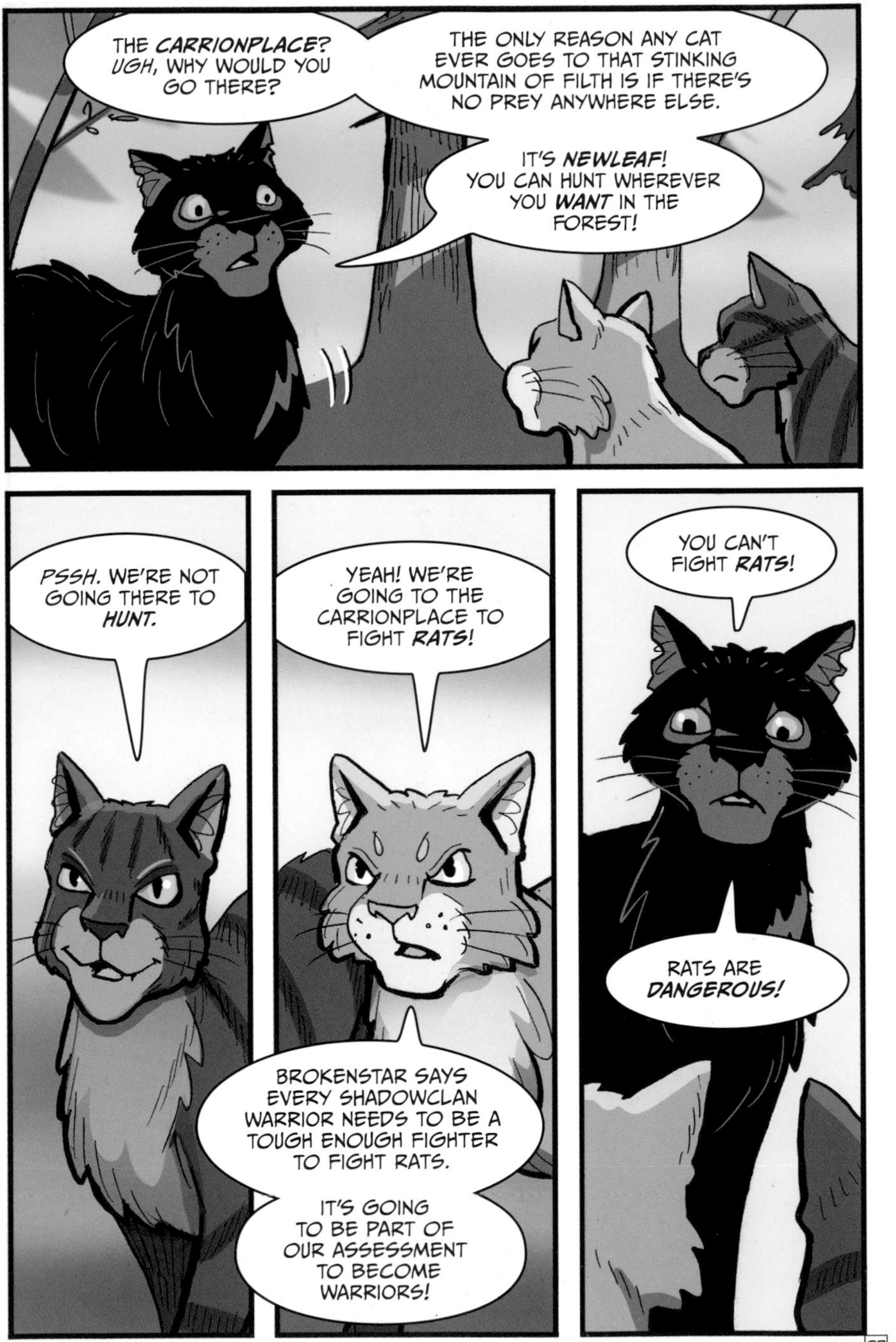
THE *CARRIONPLACE?* *UGH*, WHY WOULD YOU GO THERE?
THE ONLY REASON ANY CAT EVER GOES TO THAT STINKING MOUNTAIN OF FILTH IS IF THERE'S NO PREY ANYWHERE ELSE.
IT'S ***NEWLEAF!*** YOU CAN HUNT WHEREVER YOU ***WANT*** IN THE FOREST!
PSSH. WE'RE NOT GOING THERE TO ***HUNT.***
YEAH! WE'RE GOING TO THE CARRIONPLACE TO FIGHT ***RATS!***
BROKENSTAR SAYS EVERY SHADOWCLAN WARRIOR NEEDS TO BE A TOUGH ENOUGH FIGHTER TO FIGHT RATS.
IT'S GOING TO BE PART OF OUR ASSESSMENT TO BECOME WARRIORS!
YOU CAN'T FIGHT ***RATS!***
RATS ARE ***DANGEROUS!***

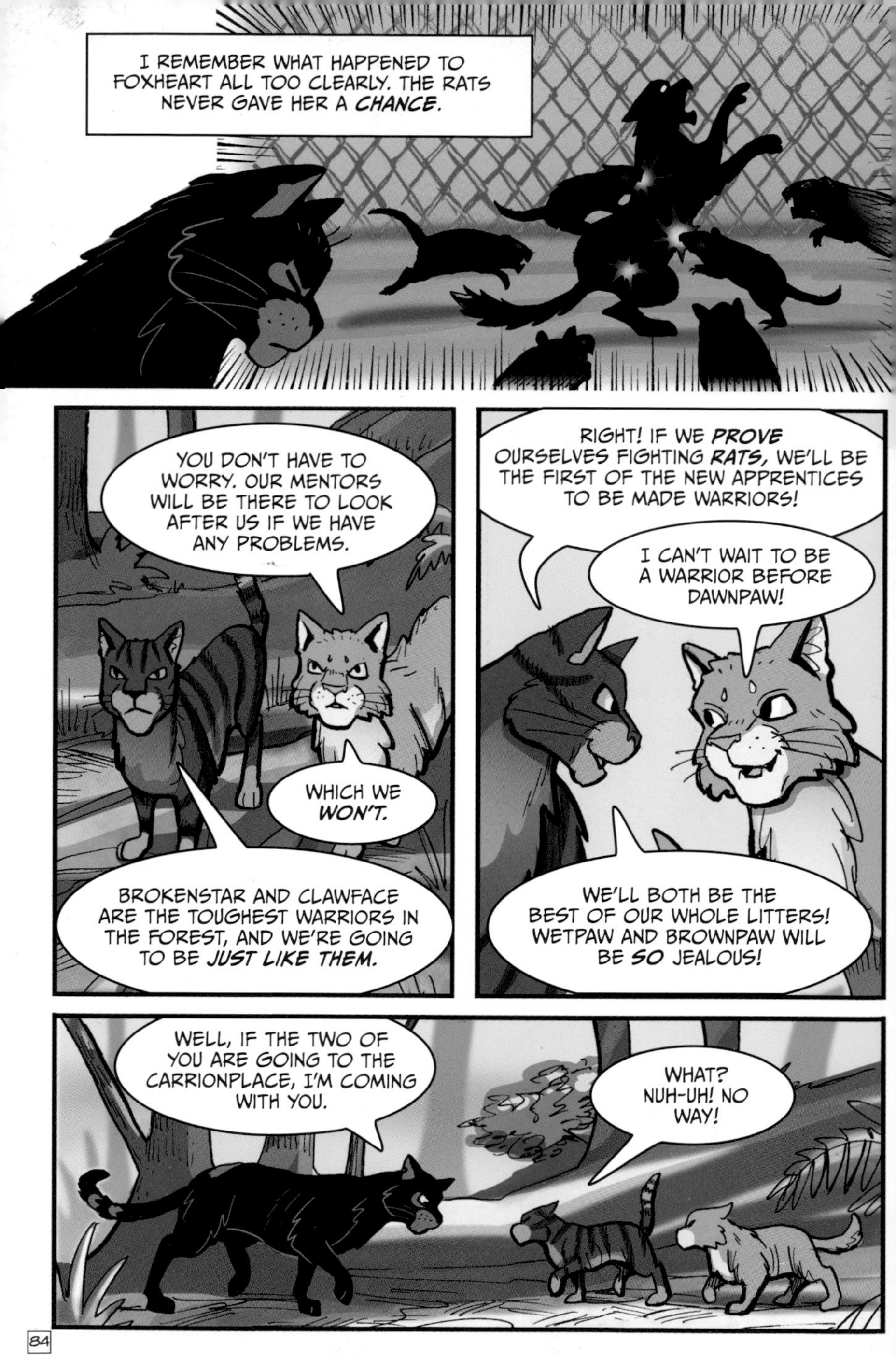
I REMEMBER WHAT HAPPENED TO FOXHEART ALL TOO CLEARLY. THE RATS NEVER GAVE HER A *CHANCE*.
YOU DON'T HAVE TO WORRY. OUR MENTORS WILL BE THERE TO LOOK AFTER US IF WE HAVE ANY PROBLEMS.
WHICH WE *WON'T*.
BROKENSTAR AND CLAWFACE ARE THE TOUGHEST WARRIORS IN THE FOREST, AND WE'RE GOING TO BE *JUST LIKE THEM*.
RIGHT! IF WE *PROVE* OURSELVES FIGHTING *RATS*, WE'LL BE THE FIRST OF THE NEW APPRENTICES TO BE MADE WARRIORS!
I CAN'T WAIT TO BE A WARRIOR BEFORE DAWNPAW!
WE'LL BOTH BE THE BEST OF OUR WHOLE LITTERS! WETPAW AND BROWNPAW WILL BE *SO* JEALOUS!
WELL, IF THE TWO OF YOU ARE GOING TO THE CARRIONPLACE, I'M COMING WITH YOU.
WHAT? NUH-UH! NO WAY!

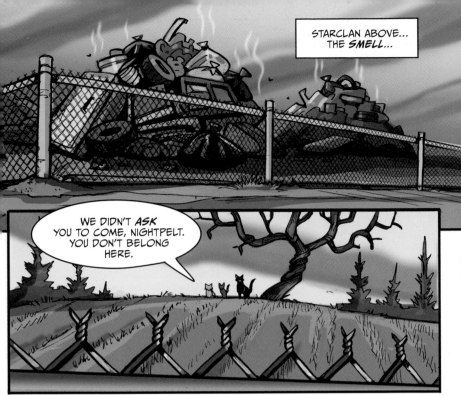

STARCLAN ABOVE... THE *SMELL*...

WE DIDN'T *ASK* YOU TO COME, NIGHTPELT. YOU DON'T BELONG HERE.

NO CAT BELONGS HERE.

YOU'RE LATE, APPRENTICES!

SORRY, BROKENSTAR!

YEAH, SORRY!

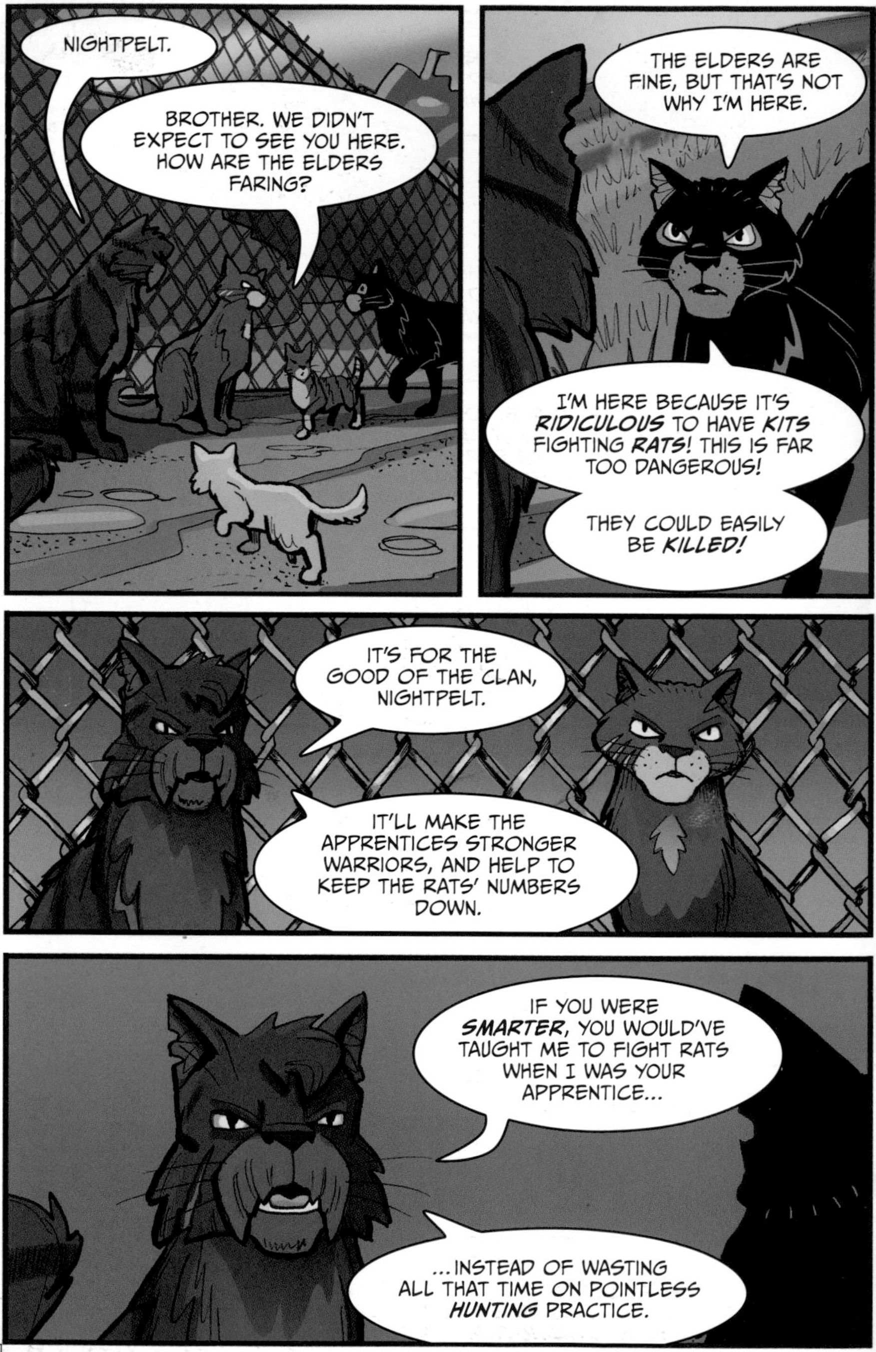
NIGHTPELT.
BROTHER. WE DIDN'T EXPECT TO SEE YOU HERE. HOW ARE THE ELDERS FARING?
THE ELDERS ARE FINE, BUT THAT'S NOT WHY I'M HERE.
I'M HERE BECAUSE IT'S *RIDICULOUS* TO HAVE *KITS* FIGHTING *RATS*! THIS IS FAR TOO DANGEROUS!
THEY COULD EASILY BE *KILLED!*
IT'S FOR THE GOOD OF THE CLAN, NIGHTPELT.
IT'LL MAKE THE APPRENTICES STRONGER WARRIORS, AND HELP TO KEEP THE RATS' NUMBERS DOWN.
IF YOU WERE *SMARTER*, YOU WOULD'VE TAUGHT ME TO FIGHT RATS WHEN I WAS YOUR APPRENTICE...
...INSTEAD OF WASTING ALL THAT TIME ON POINTLESS *HUNTING* PRACTICE.

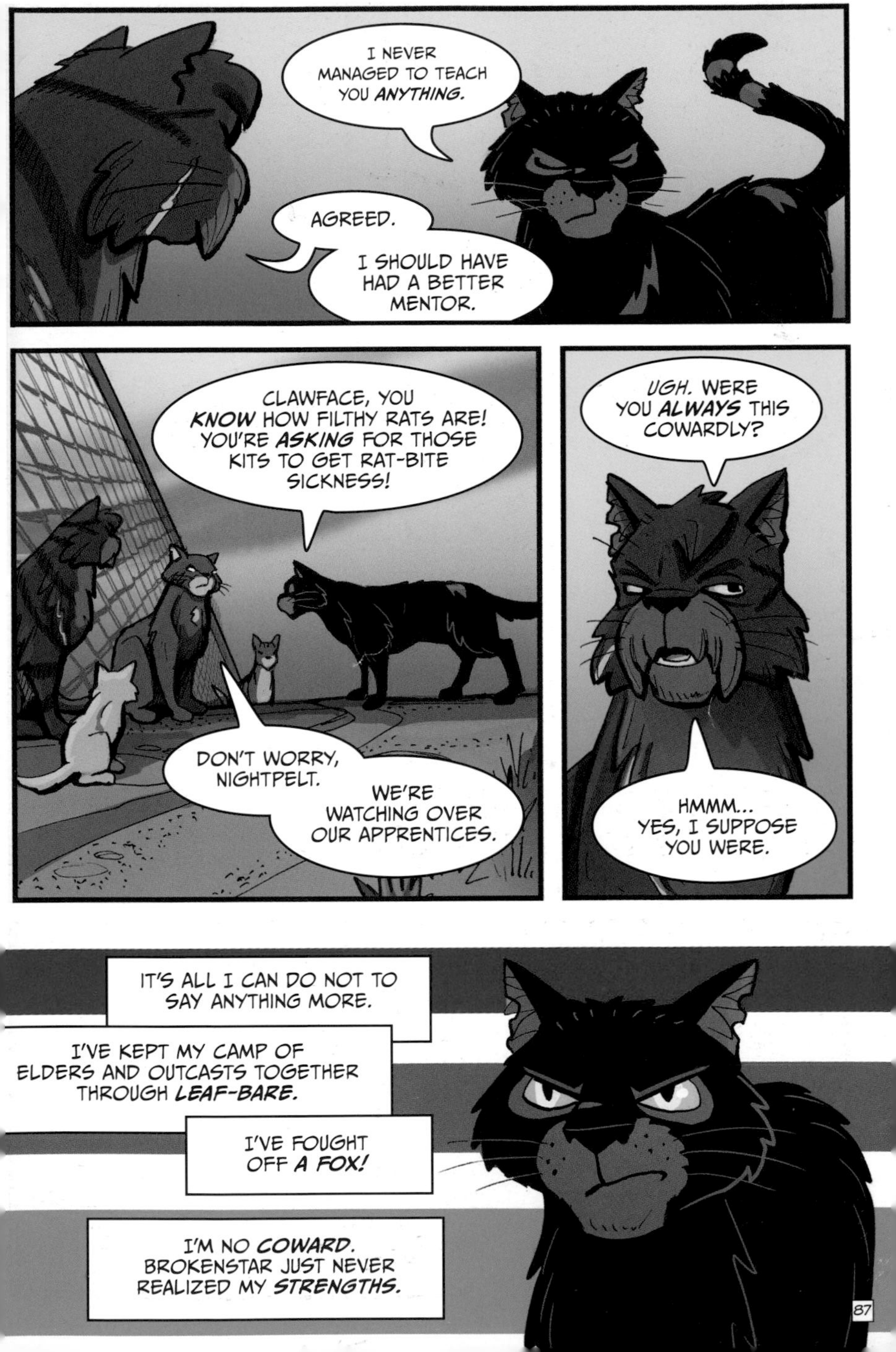
I NEVER MANAGED TO TEACH YOU *ANYTHING.*
AGREED.
I SHOULD HAVE HAD A BETTER MENTOR.
CLAWFACE, YOU *KNOW* HOW FILTHY RATS ARE! YOU'RE *ASKING* FOR THOSE KITS TO GET RAT-BITE SICKNESS!
DON'T WORRY, NIGHTPELT.
WE'RE WATCHING OVER OUR APPRENTICES.
UGH. WERE YOU *ALWAYS* THIS COWARDLY?
HMMM... YES, I SUPPOSE YOU WERE.
IT'S ALL I CAN DO NOT TO SAY ANYTHING MORE.
I'VE KEPT MY CAMP OF ELDERS AND OUTCASTS TOGETHER THROUGH *LEAF-BARE.*
I'VE FOUGHT OFF *A FOX!*
I'M NO *COWARD.* BROKENSTAR JUST NEVER REALIZED MY *STRENGTHS.*

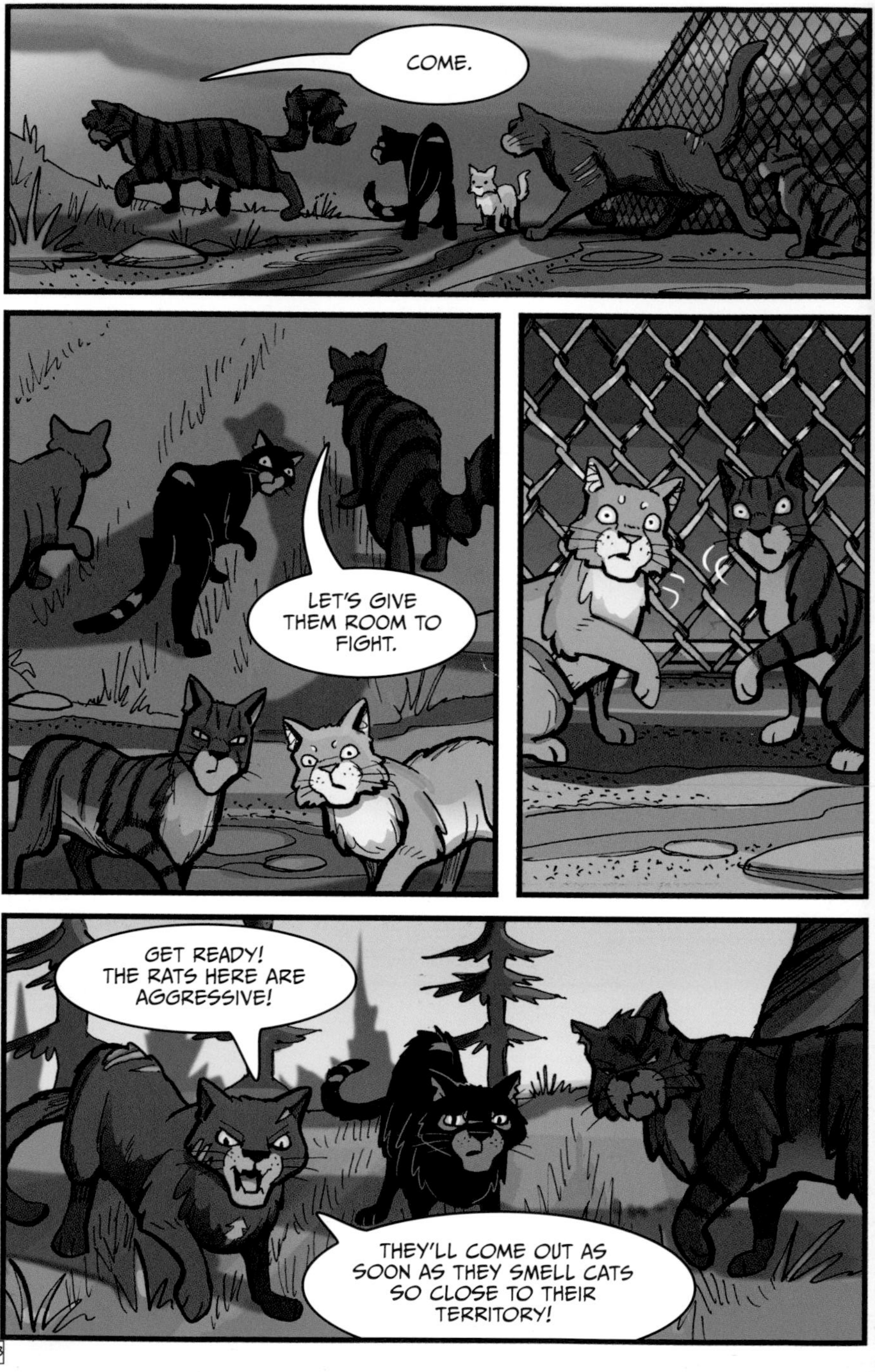
COME.
LET'S GIVE THEM ROOM TO FIGHT.
GET READY! THE RATS HERE ARE AGGRESSIVE!
THEY'LL COME OUT AS SOON AS THEY SMELL CATS SO CLOSE TO THEIR TERRITORY!

DON'T WORRY.

WE'LL STEP IN IF TOO MANY RATS TURN UP.

RUSTLE RUSTLE

Sniff Sniff

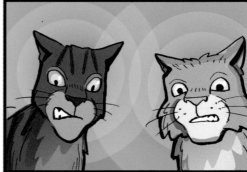

HSSSSS

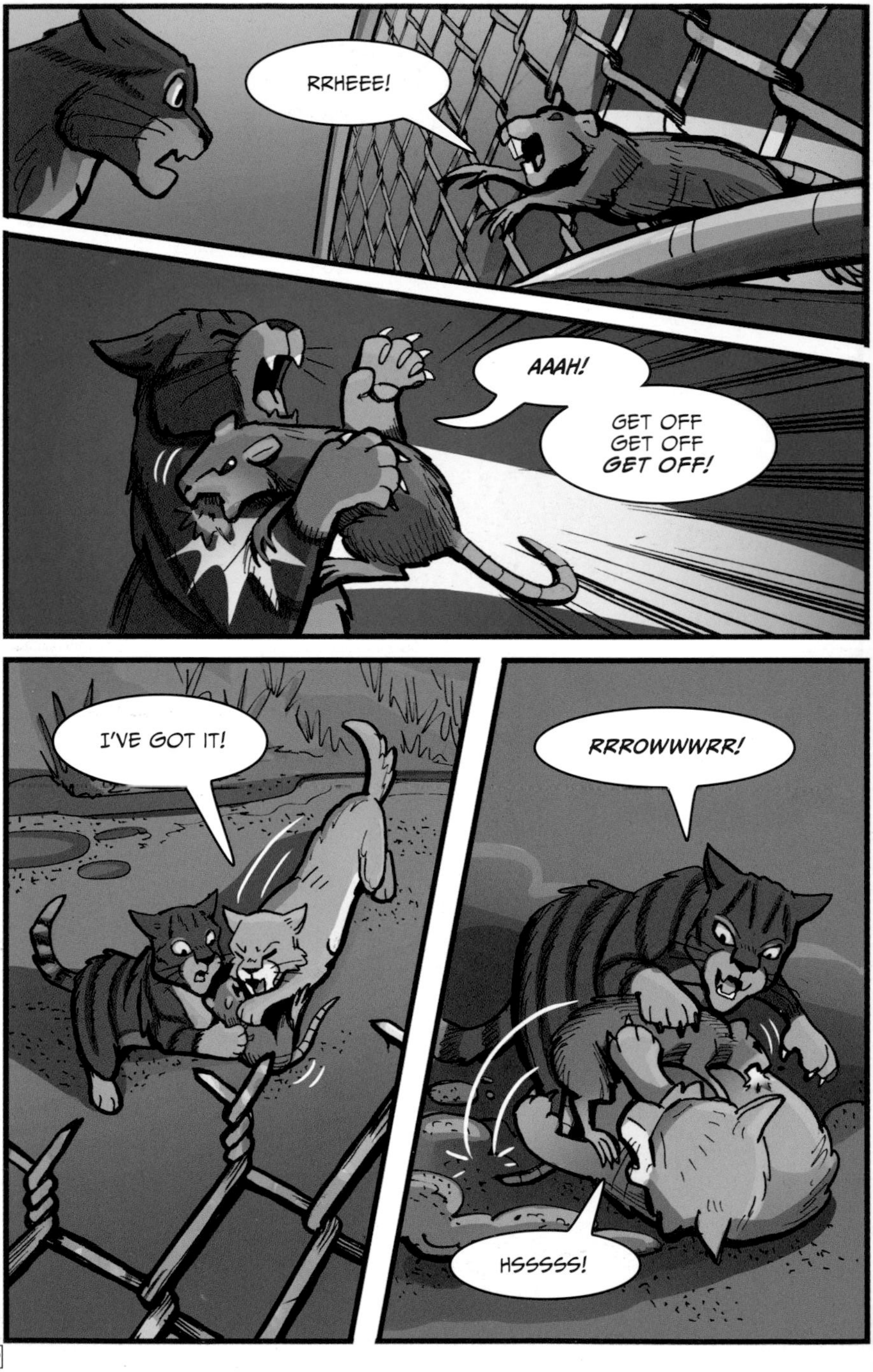
RRHEEE!
AAAH!
GET OFF
GET OFF
GET OFF!
I'VE GOT IT!
RRROWWWRR!
HSSSSS!

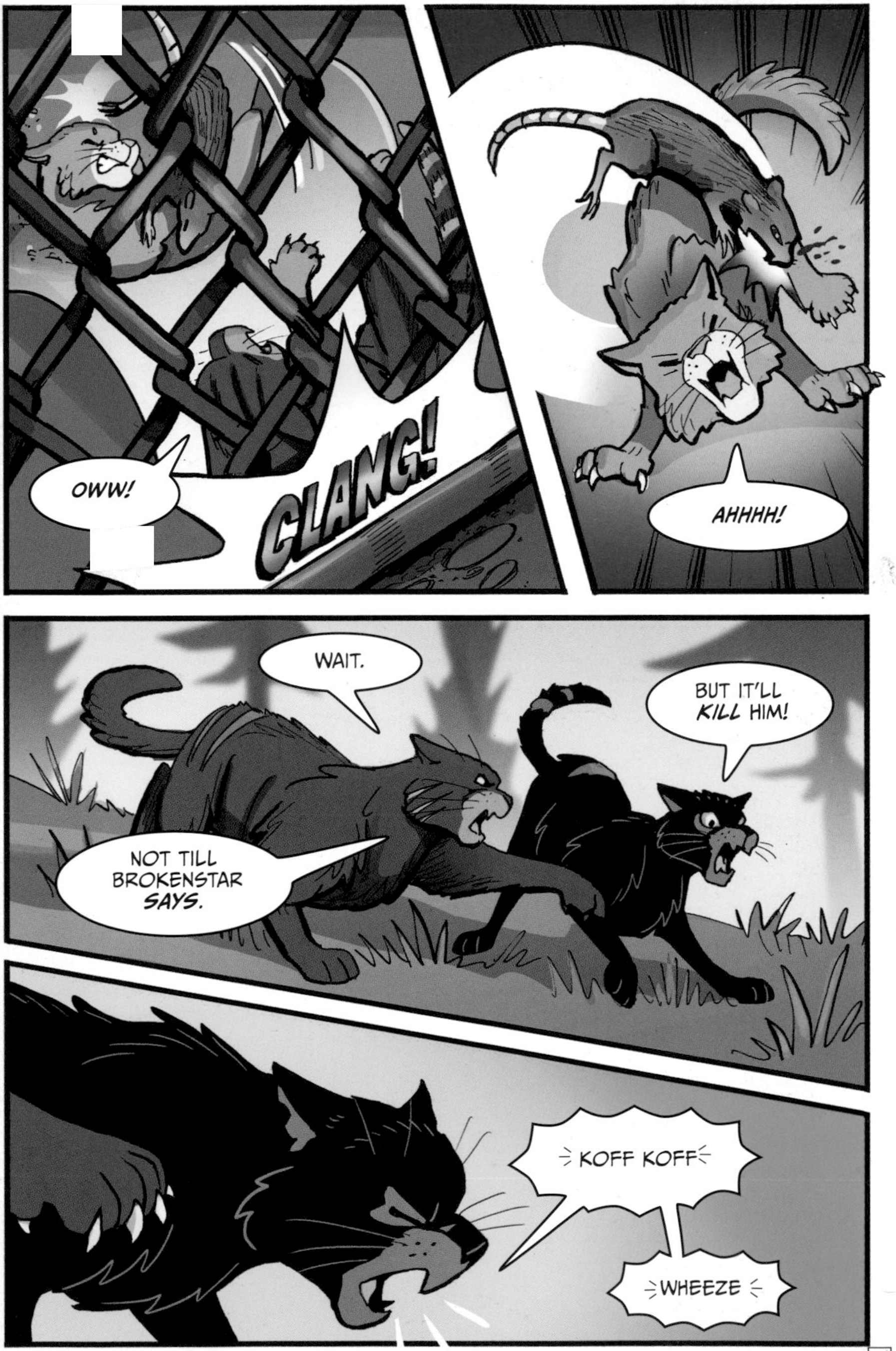

OWW!
CLANG!
AHHHH!
WAIT.
BUT IT'LL KILL HIM!
NOT TILL BROKENSTAR SAYS.
KOFF KOFF
WHEEZE

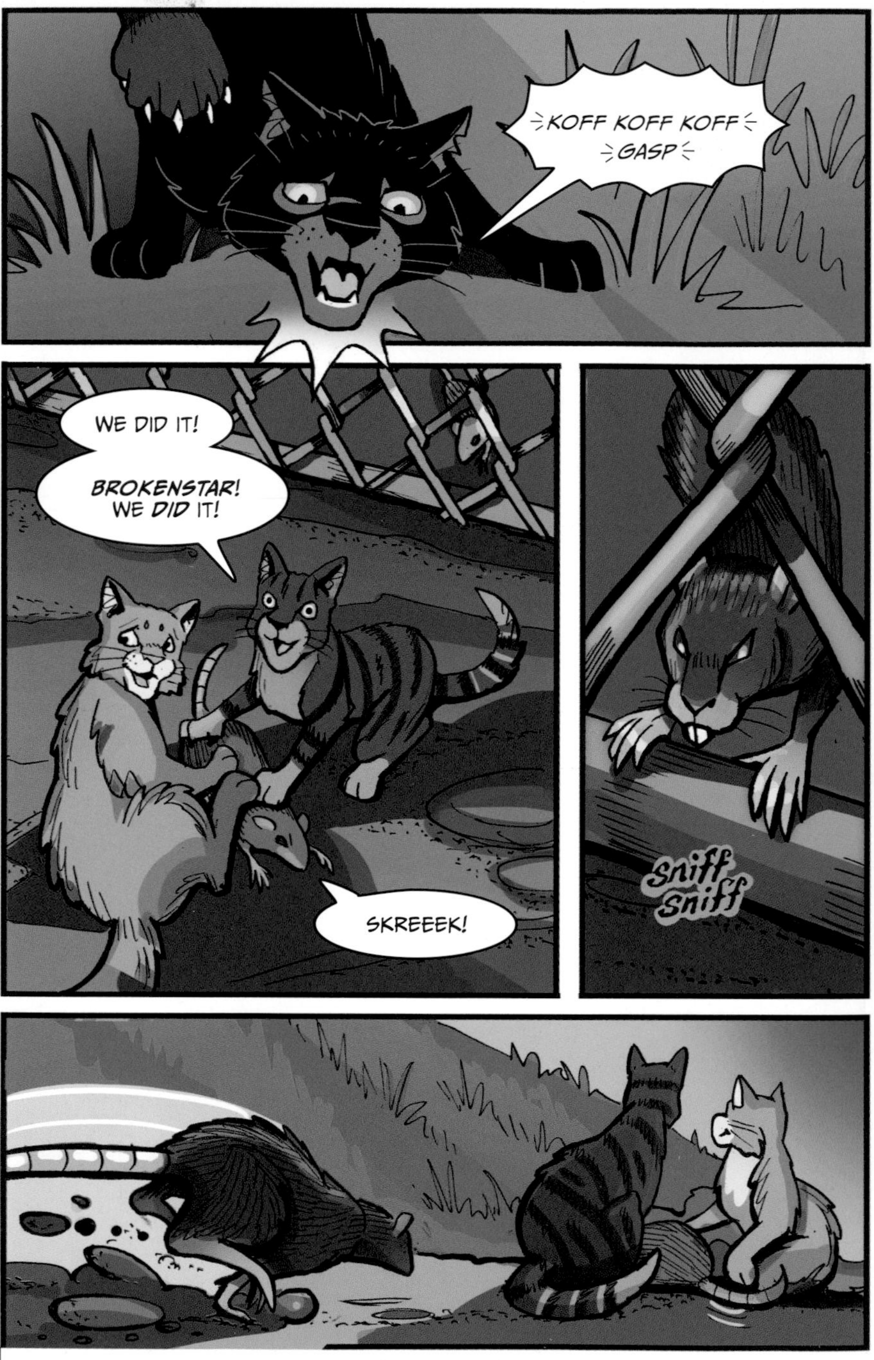
KOFF KOFF KOFF
GASP
WE DID IT!
BROKENSTAR! WE *DID* IT!
SKREEEK!
Sniff Sniff

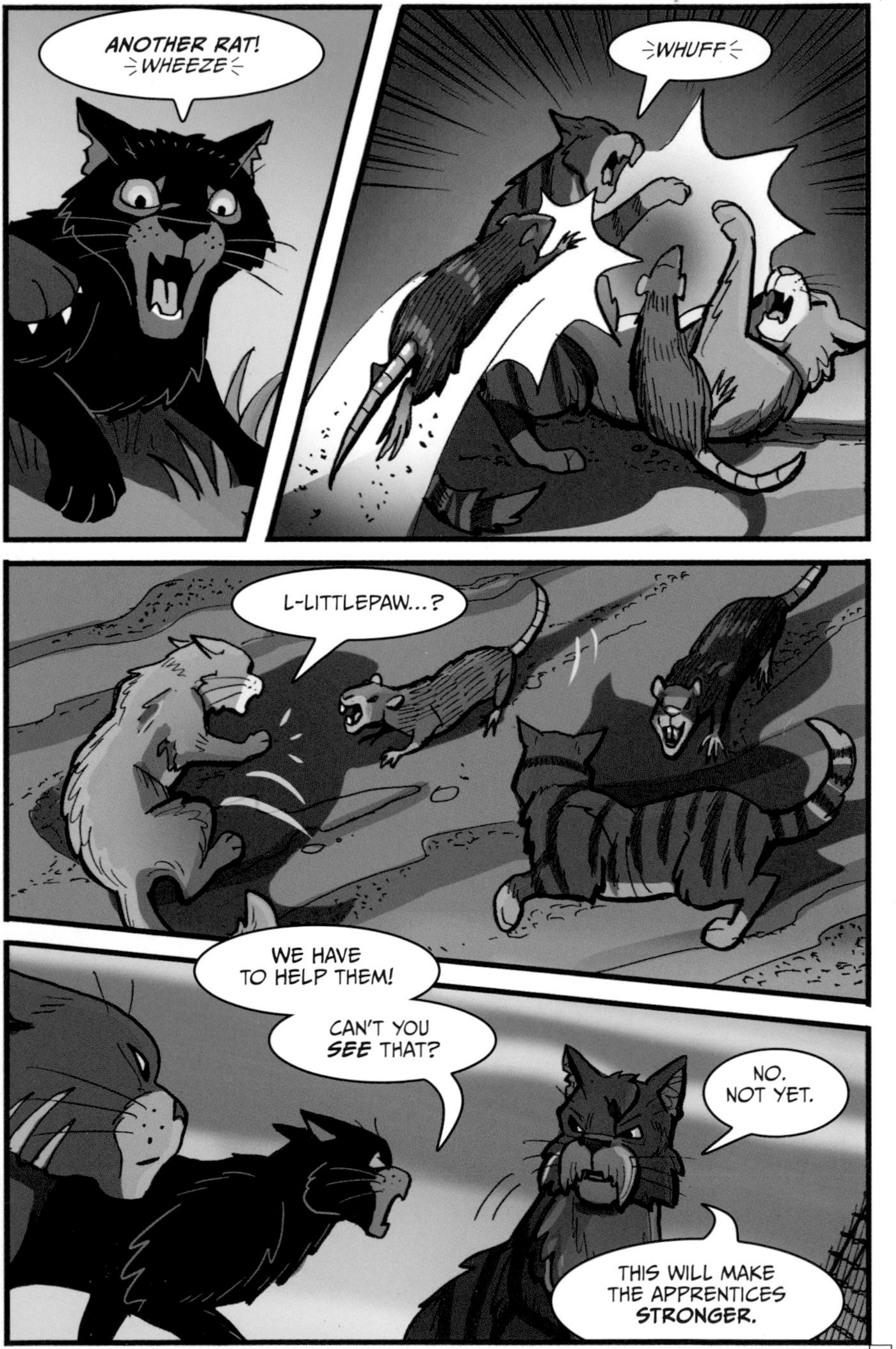
ANOTHER RAT!
WHEEZE
WHUFF
L-LITTLEPAW...?
WE HAVE TO HELP THEM!
CAN'T YOU SEE THAT?
NO. NOT YET.
THIS WILL MAKE THE APPRENTICES STRONGER.

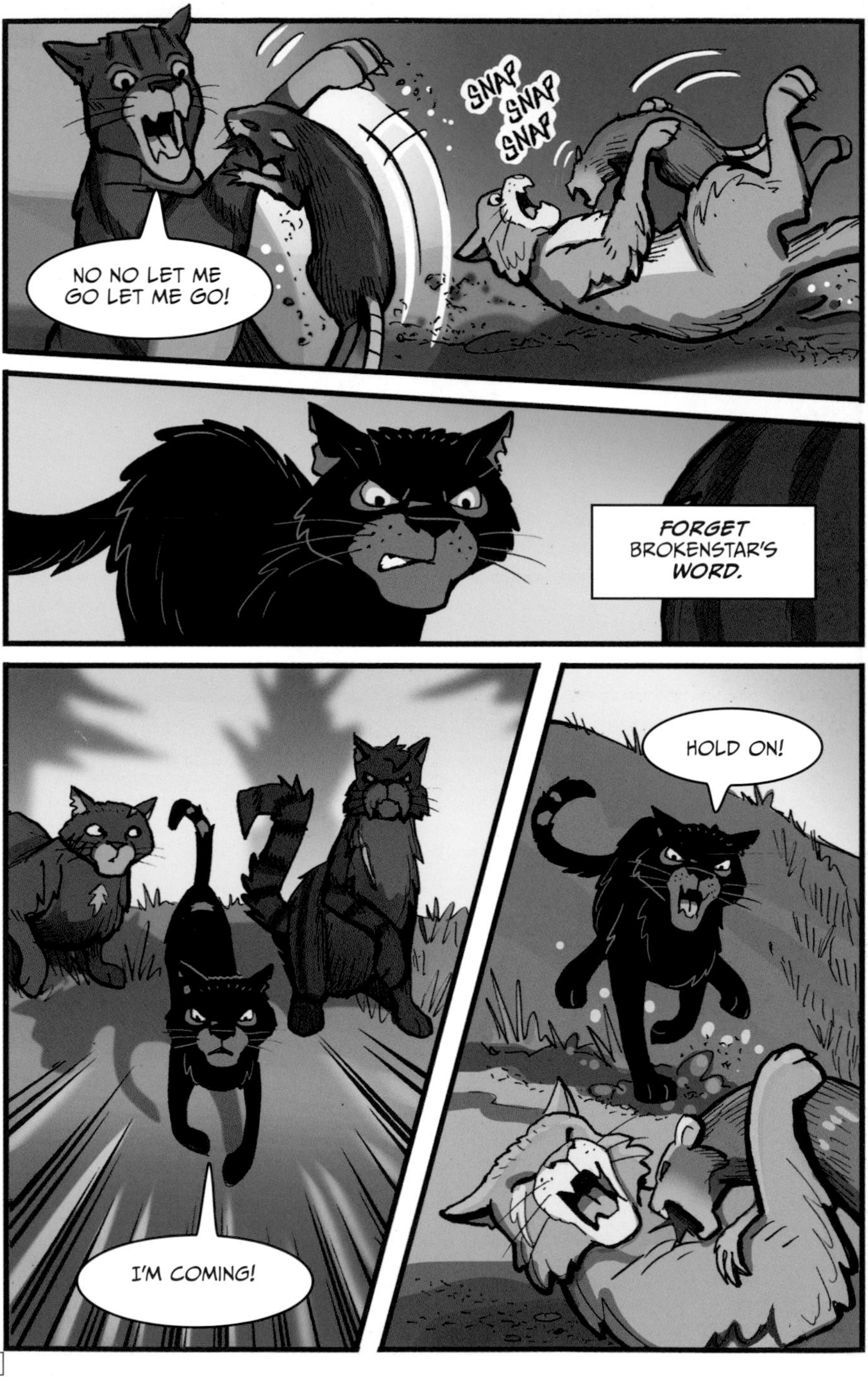
NO NO LET ME GO LET ME GO!
SNAP SNAP SNAP
FORGET BROKENSTAR'S WORD.
I'M COMING!
HOLD ON!

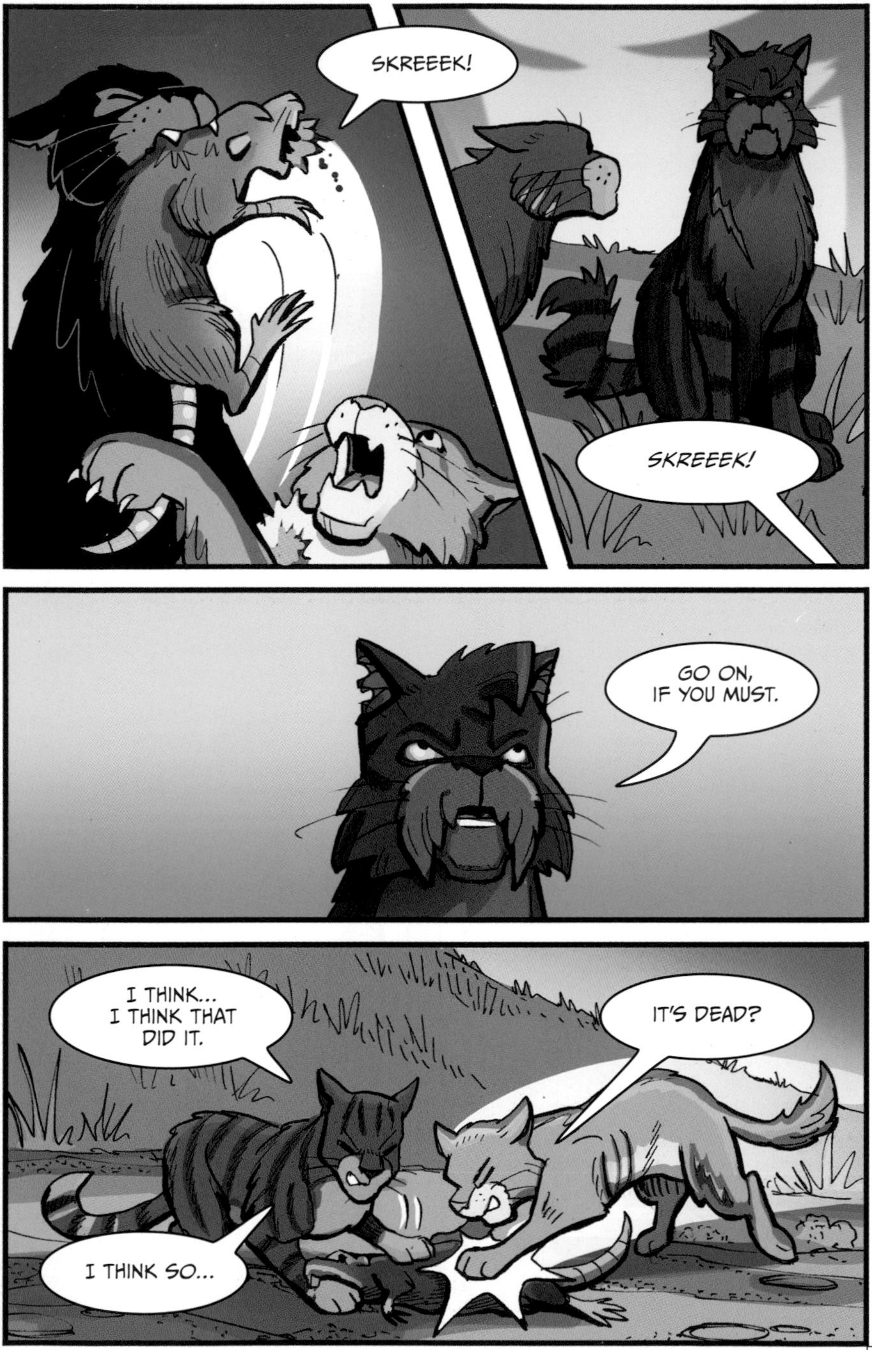
SKREEEK!
SKREEEK!
GO ON, IF YOU MUST.
I THINK... I THINK THAT DID IT.
IT'S DEAD?
I THINK SO...

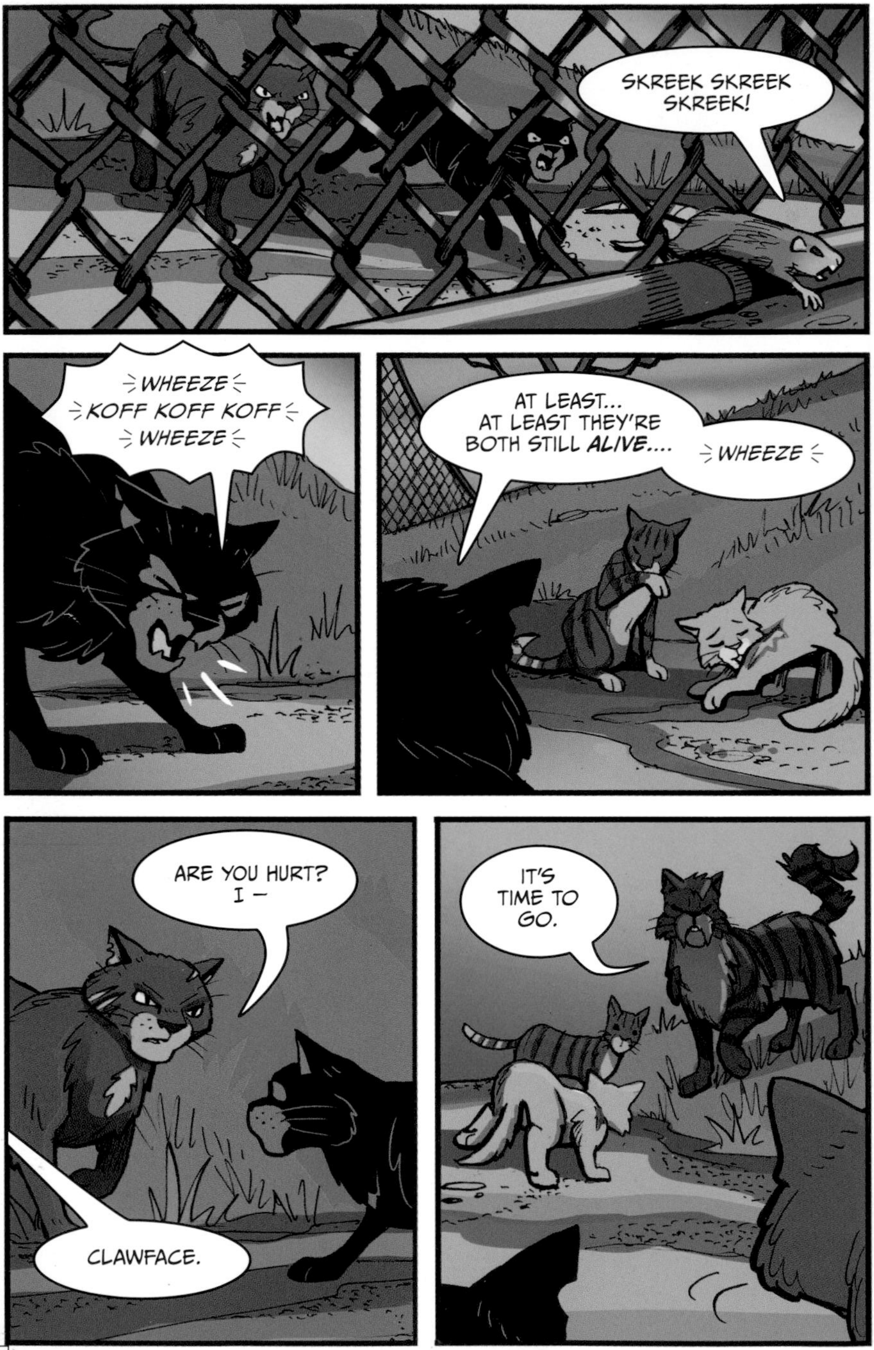

SKREEK SKREEK SKREEK!
WHEEZE KOFF KOFF KOFF WHEEZE
AT LEAST... AT LEAST THEY'RE BOTH STILL ***ALIVE***....
WHEEZE
ARE YOU HURT? I —
CLAWFACE.
IT'S TIME TO GO.

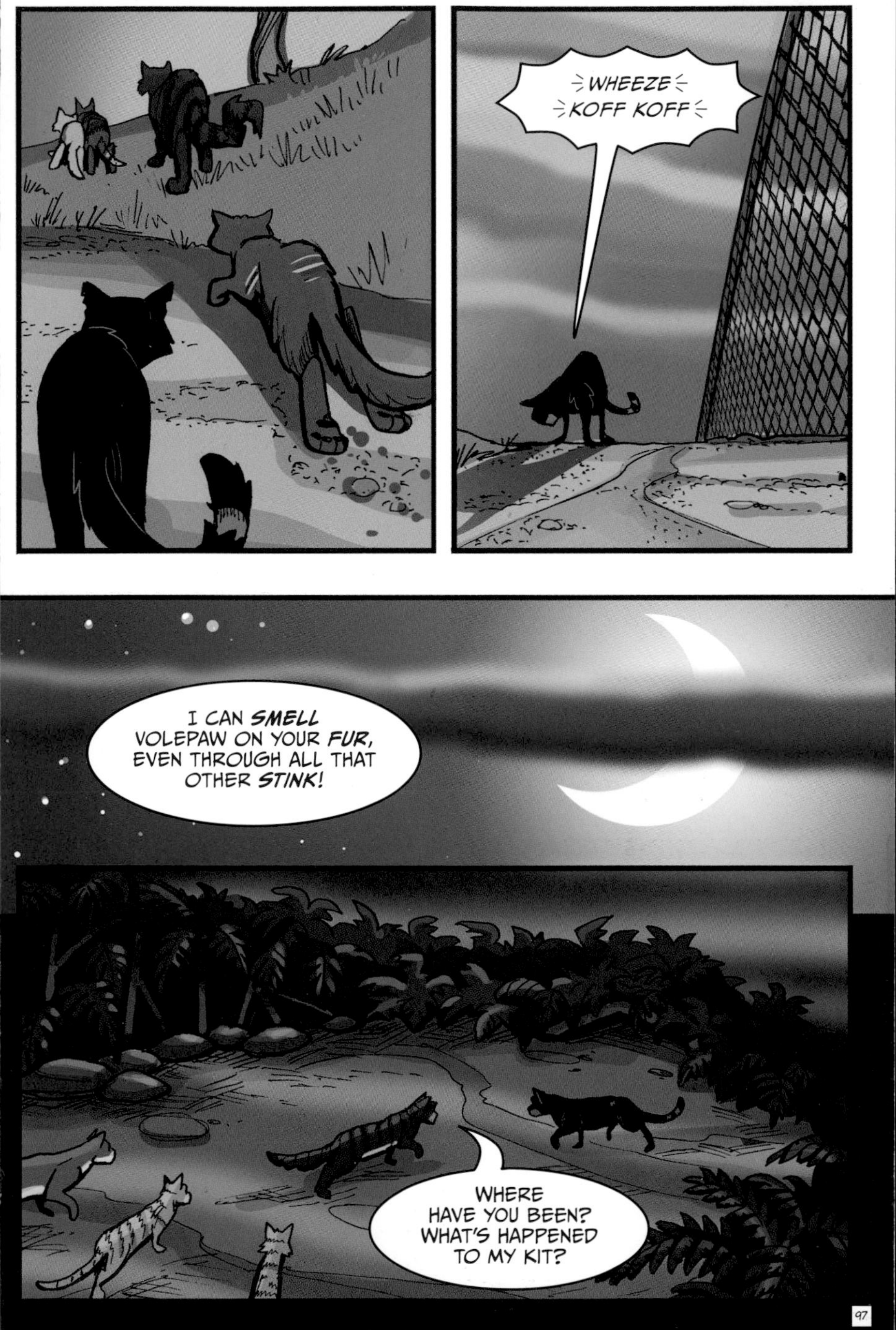
WHEEZE
KOFF KOFF
I CAN SMELL VOLEPAW ON YOUR FUR, EVEN THROUGH ALL THAT OTHER STINK!
WHERE HAVE YOU BEEN? WHAT'S HAPPENED TO MY KIT?

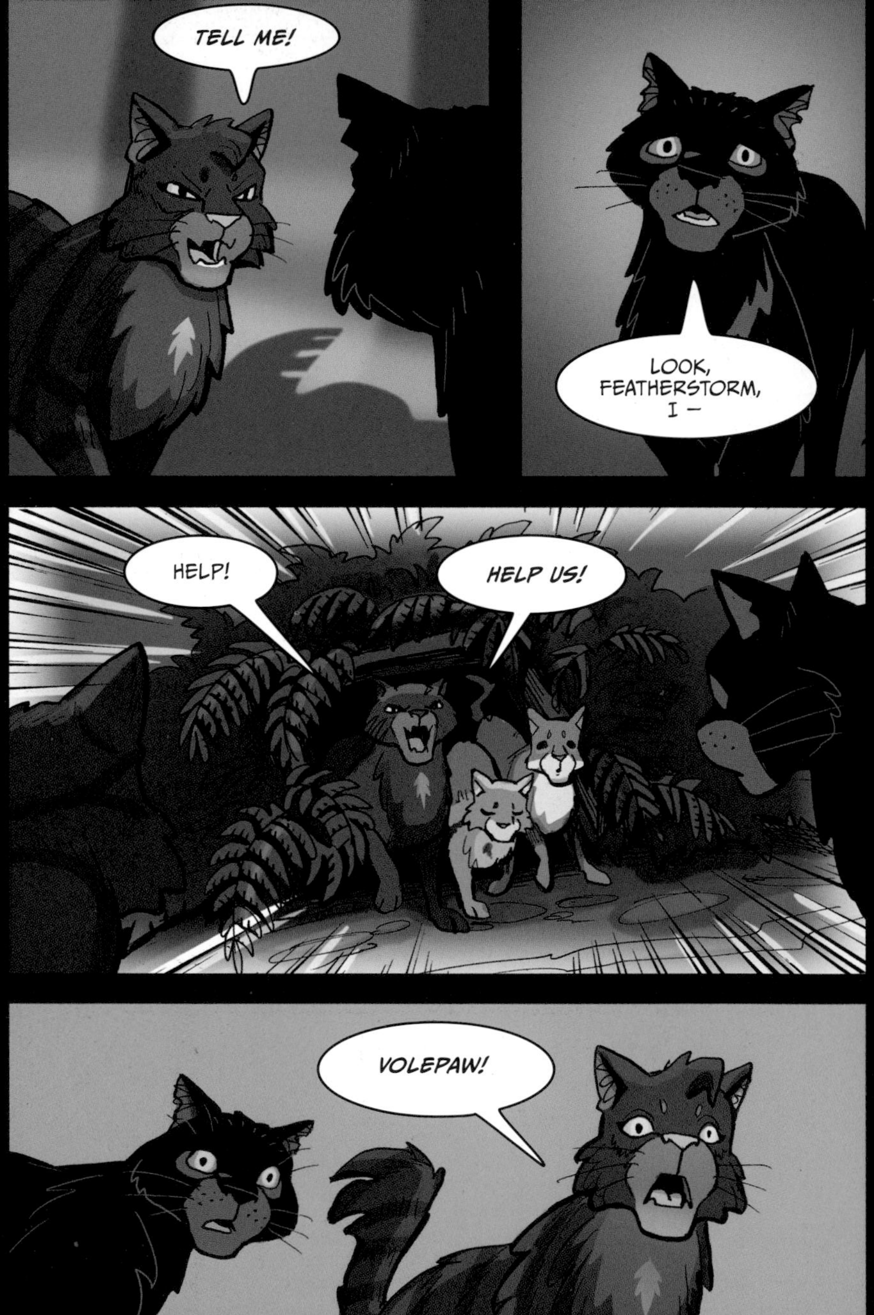
TELL ME!
LOOK, FEATHERSTORM, I –
HELP!
HELP US!
VOLEPAW!

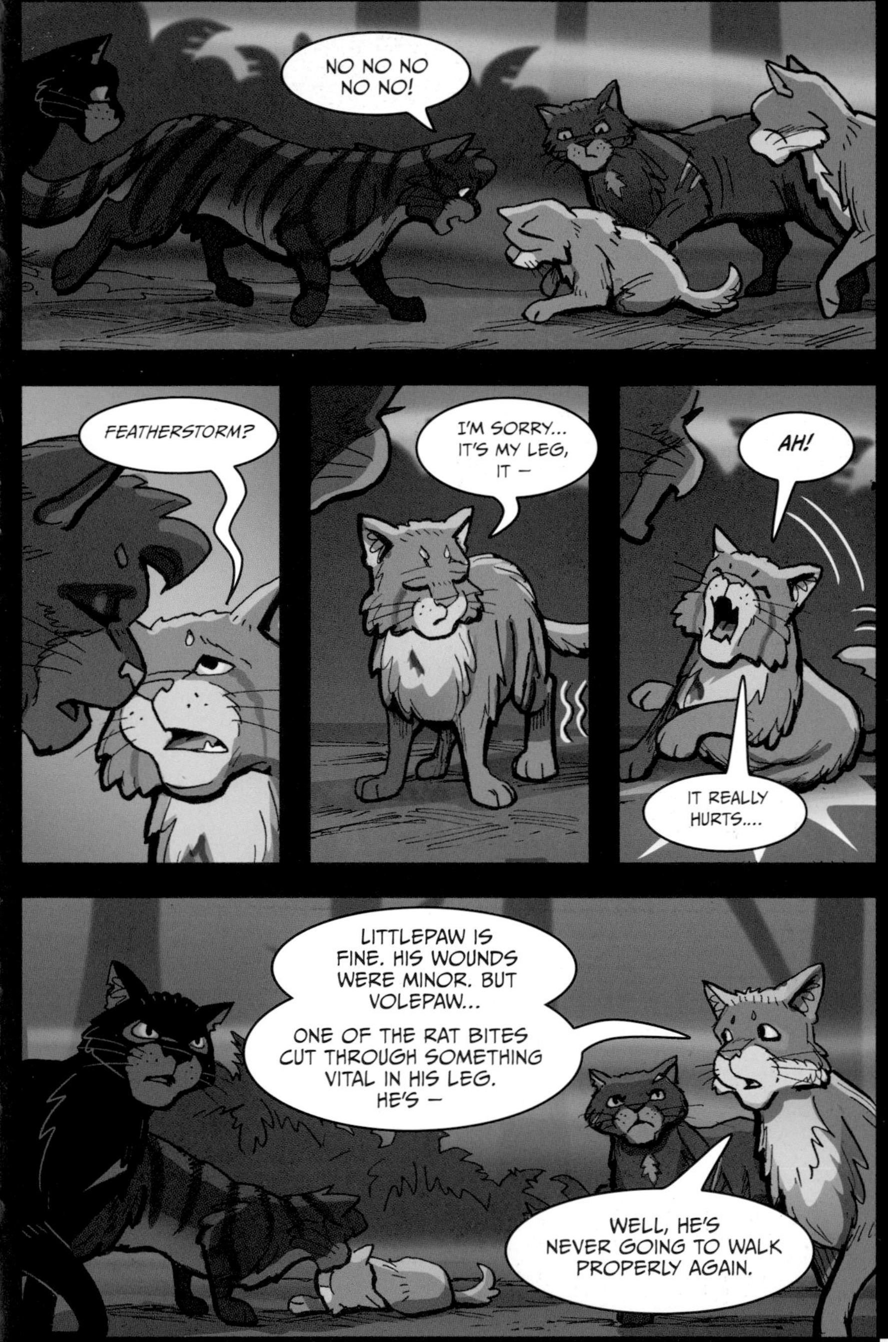
NO NO NO NO NO!
FEATHERSTORM?
I'M SORRY... IT'S MY LEG, IT –
AH!
IT REALLY HURTS....
LITTLEPAW IS FINE. HIS WOUNDS WERE MINOR. BUT VOLEPAW...
ONE OF THE RAT BITES CUT THROUGH SOMETHING VITAL IN HIS LEG. HE'S –
WELL, HE'S NEVER GOING TO WALK PROPERLY AGAIN.

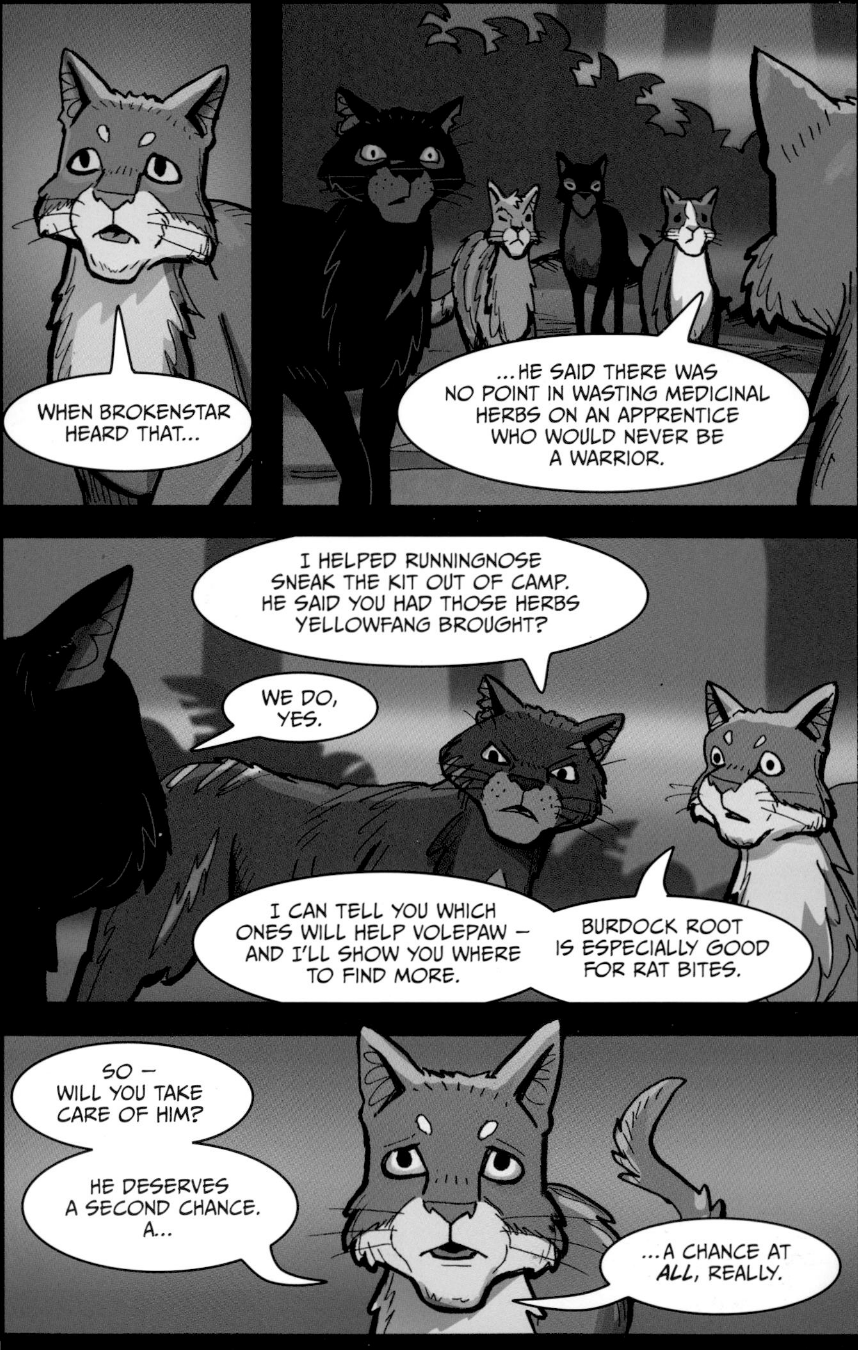
WHEN BROKENSTAR HEARD THAT...
...HE SAID THERE WAS NO POINT IN WASTING MEDICINAL HERBS ON AN APPRENTICE WHO WOULD NEVER BE A WARRIOR.
I HELPED RUNNINGNOSE SNEAK THE KIT OUT OF CAMP. HE SAID YOU HAD THOSE HERBS YELLOWFANG BROUGHT?
WE DO, YES.
I CAN TELL YOU WHICH ONES WILL HELP VOLEPAW – AND I'LL SHOW YOU WHERE TO FIND MORE.
BURDOCK ROOT IS ESPECIALLY GOOD FOR RAT BITES.
SO – WILL YOU TAKE CARE OF HIM?
HE DESERVES A SECOND CHANCE. A...
...A CHANCE AT *ALL*, REALLY.

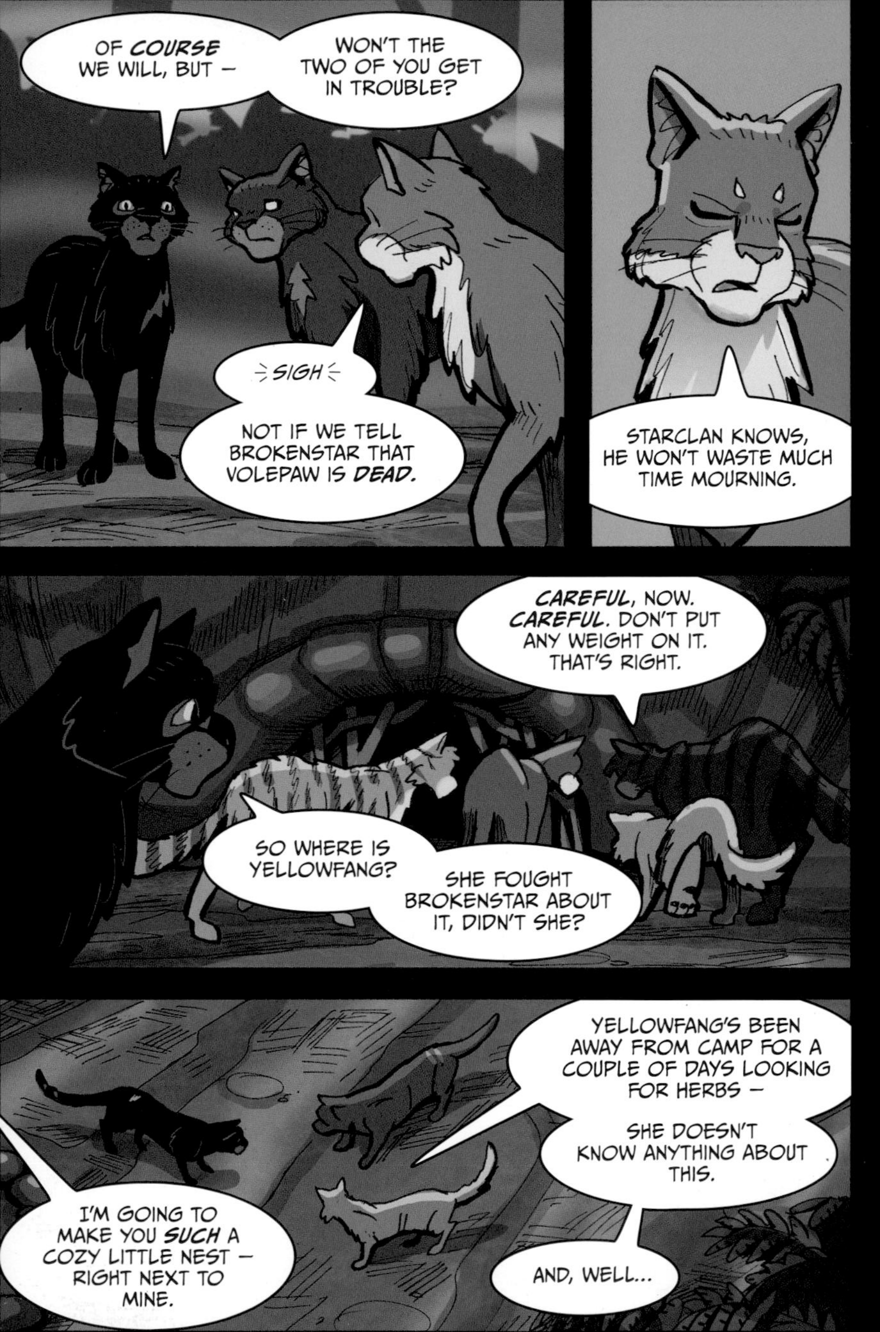
OF COURSE WE WILL, BUT –
WON'T THE TWO OF YOU GET IN TROUBLE?
SIGH
NOT IF WE TELL BROKENSTAR THAT VOLEPAW IS DEAD.
STARCLAN KNOWS, HE WON'T WASTE MUCH TIME MOURNING.
CAREFUL, NOW. CAREFUL. DON'T PUT ANY WEIGHT ON IT. THAT'S RIGHT.
SO WHERE IS YELLOWFANG?
SHE FOUGHT BROKENSTAR ABOUT IT, DIDN'T SHE?
YELLOWFANG'S BEEN AWAY FROM CAMP FOR A COUPLE OF DAYS LOOKING FOR HERBS –
SHE DOESN'T KNOW ANYTHING ABOUT THIS.
AND, WELL...
I'M GOING TO MAKE YOU SUCH A COZY LITTLE NEST – RIGHT NEXT TO MINE.

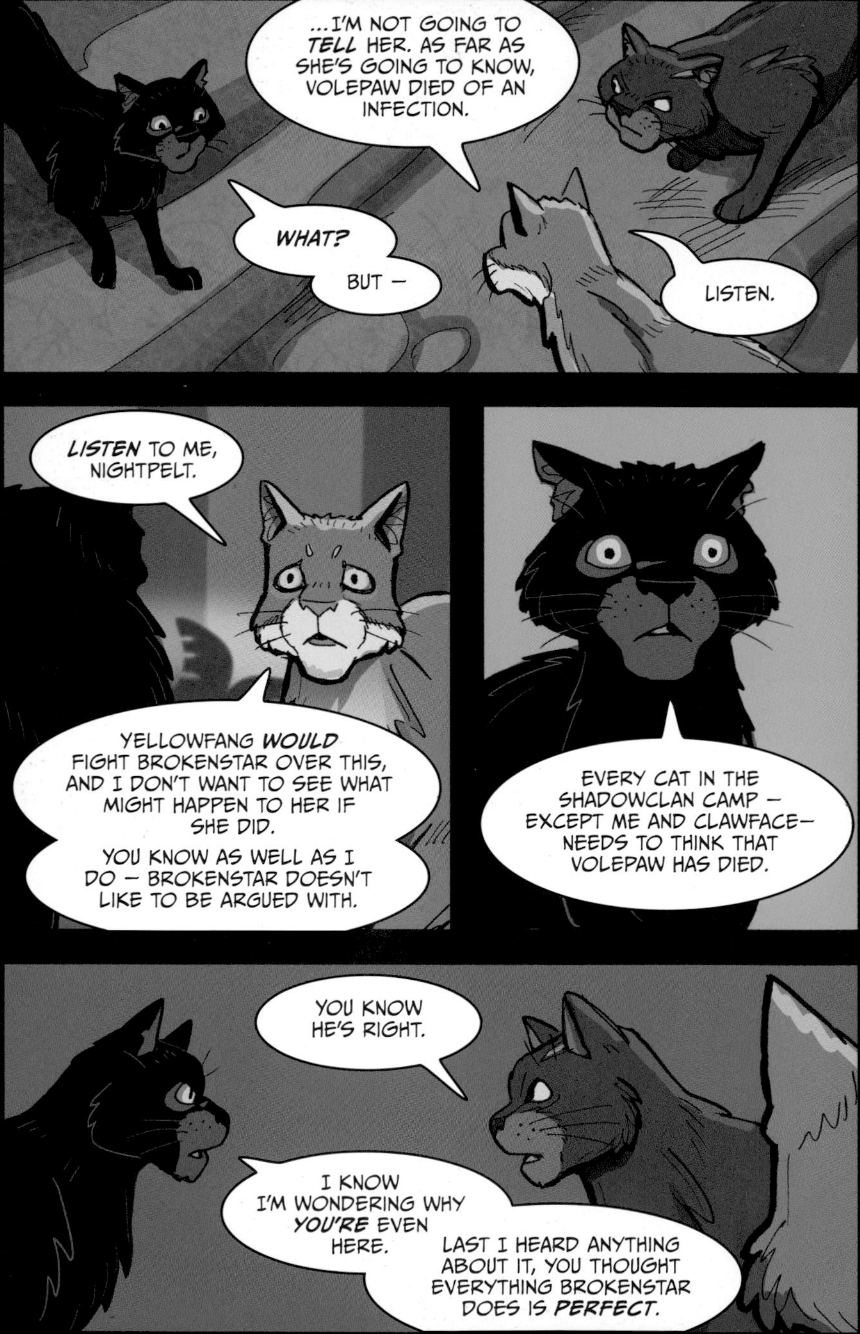
...I'M NOT GOING TO TELL HER. AS FAR AS SHE'S GOING TO KNOW, VOLEPAW DIED OF AN INFECTION.
WHAT?
BUT —
LISTEN.
LISTEN TO ME, NIGHTPELT.
YELLOWFANG WOULD FIGHT BROKENSTAR OVER THIS, AND I DON'T WANT TO SEE WHAT MIGHT HAPPEN TO HER IF SHE DID.
YOU KNOW AS WELL AS I DO — BROKENSTAR DOESN'T LIKE TO BE ARGUED WITH.
EVERY CAT IN THE SHADOWCLAN CAMP — EXCEPT ME AND CLAWFACE— NEEDS TO THINK THAT VOLEPAW HAS DIED.
YOU KNOW HE'S RIGHT.
I KNOW I'M WONDERING WHY YOU'RE EVEN HERE.
LAST I HEARD ANYTHING ABOUT IT, YOU THOUGHT EVERYTHING BROKENSTAR DOES IS PERFECT.

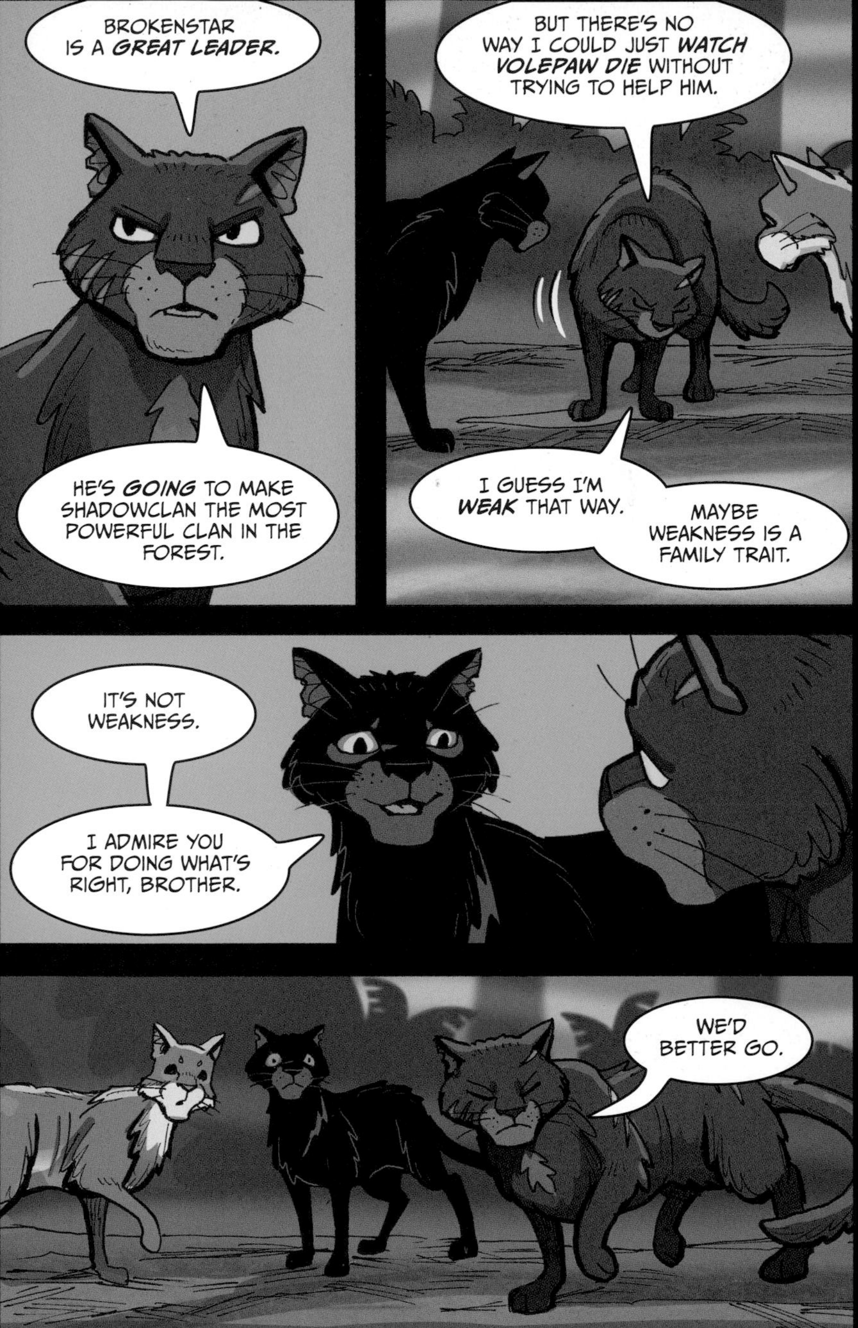
BROKENSTAR IS A GREAT LEADER.
HE'S GOING TO MAKE SHADOWCLAN THE MOST POWERFUL CLAN IN THE FOREST.
BUT THERE'S NO WAY I COULD JUST WATCH VOLEPAW DIE WITHOUT TRYING TO HELP HIM.
I GUESS I'M WEAK THAT WAY.
MAYBE WEAKNESS IS A FAMILY TRAIT.
IT'S NOT WEAKNESS.
I ADMIRE YOU FOR DOING WHAT'S RIGHT, BROTHER.
WE'D BETTER GO.

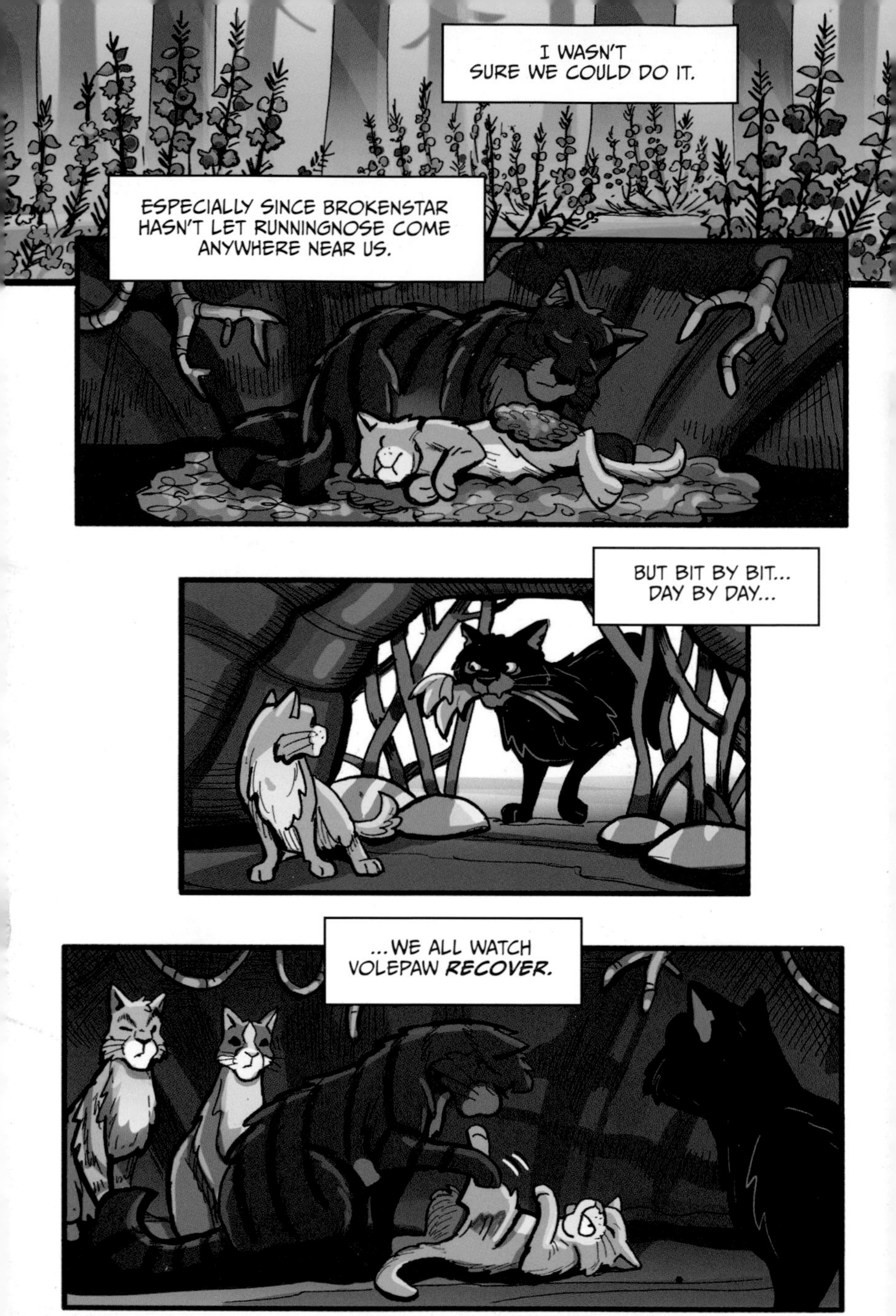
I WASN'T SURE WE COULD DO IT.
ESPECIALLY SINCE BROKENSTAR HASN'T LET RUNNINGNOSE COME ANYWHERE NEAR US.
BUT BIT BY BIT... DAY BY DAY...
...WE ALL WATCH VOLEPAW *RECOVER.*

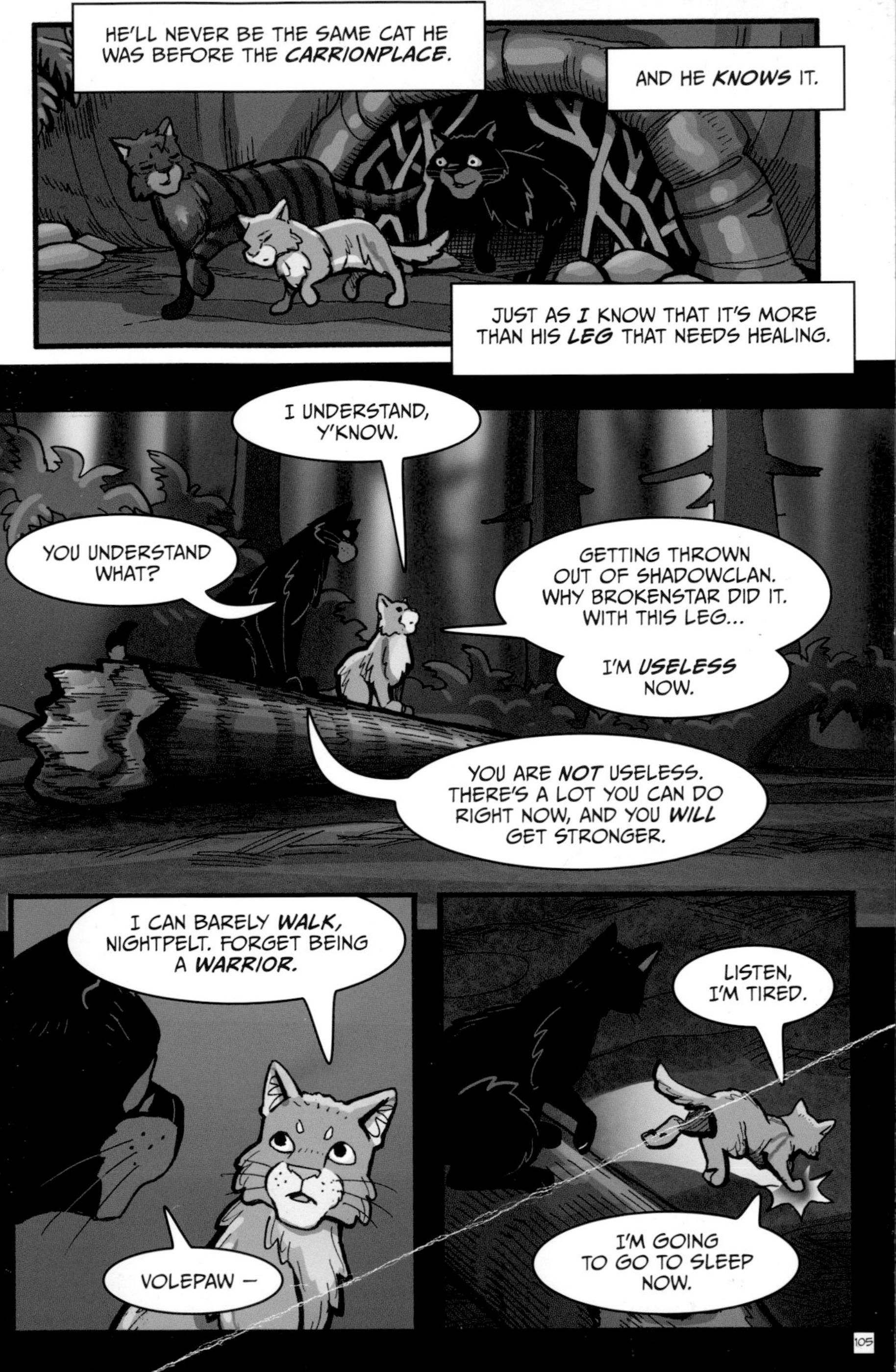
HE'LL NEVER BE THE SAME CAT HE WAS BEFORE THE *CARRIONPLACE*.
AND HE *KNOWS* IT.
JUST AS *I* KNOW THAT IT'S MORE THAN HIS *LEG* THAT NEEDS HEALING.
I UNDERSTAND, Y'KNOW.
YOU UNDERSTAND WHAT?
GETTING THROWN OUT OF SHADOWCLAN. WHY BROKENSTAR DID IT. WITH THIS LEG...
I'M *USELESS* NOW.
YOU ARE *NOT* USELESS. THERE'S A LOT YOU CAN DO RIGHT NOW, AND YOU *WILL* GET STRONGER.
I CAN BARELY *WALK*, NIGHTPELT. FORGET BEING A *WARRIOR.*
VOLEPAW –
LISTEN, I'M TIRED.
I'M GOING TO GO TO SLEEP NOW.

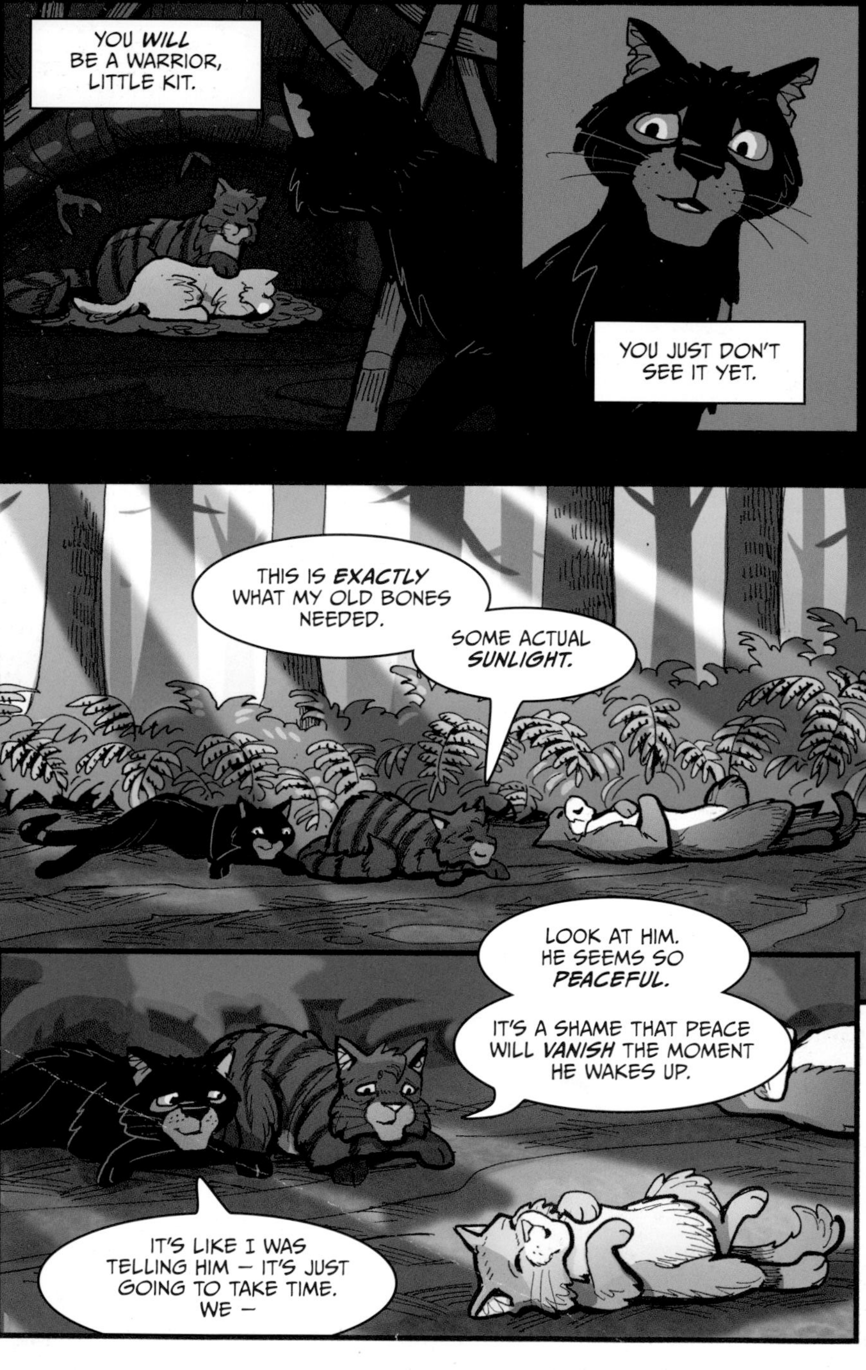
YOU *WILL* BE A WARRIOR, LITTLE KIT.
YOU JUST DON'T SEE IT YET.
THIS IS *EXACTLY* WHAT MY OLD BONES NEEDED.
SOME ACTUAL *SUNLIGHT.*
LOOK AT HIM. HE SEEMS SO *PEACEFUL.*
IT'S A SHAME THAT PEACE WILL *VANISH* THE MOMENT HE WAKES UP.
IT'S LIKE I WAS TELLING HIM — IT'S JUST GOING TO TAKE TIME. WE —

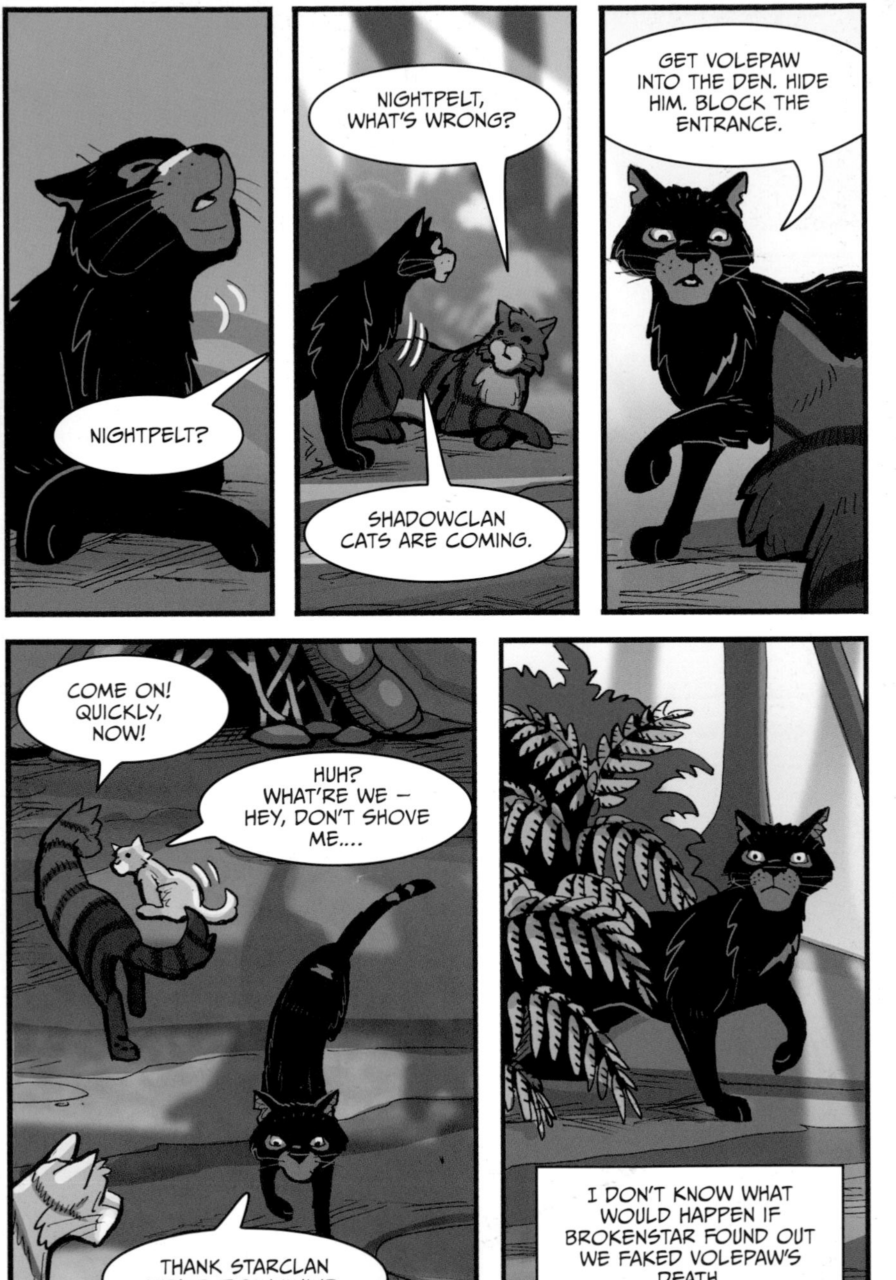
NIGHTPELT?
NIGHTPELT, WHAT'S WRONG?
SHADOWCLAN CATS ARE COMING.
GET VOLEPAW INTO THE DEN. HIDE HIM. BLOCK THE ENTRANCE.
COME ON! QUICKLY, NOW!
HUH? WHAT'RE WE – HEY, DON'T SHOVE ME....
THANK STARCLAN WE'RE *DOWNWIND.*
I DON'T KNOW WHAT WOULD HAPPEN IF BROKENSTAR FOUND OUT WE FAKED VOLEPAW'S DEATH.

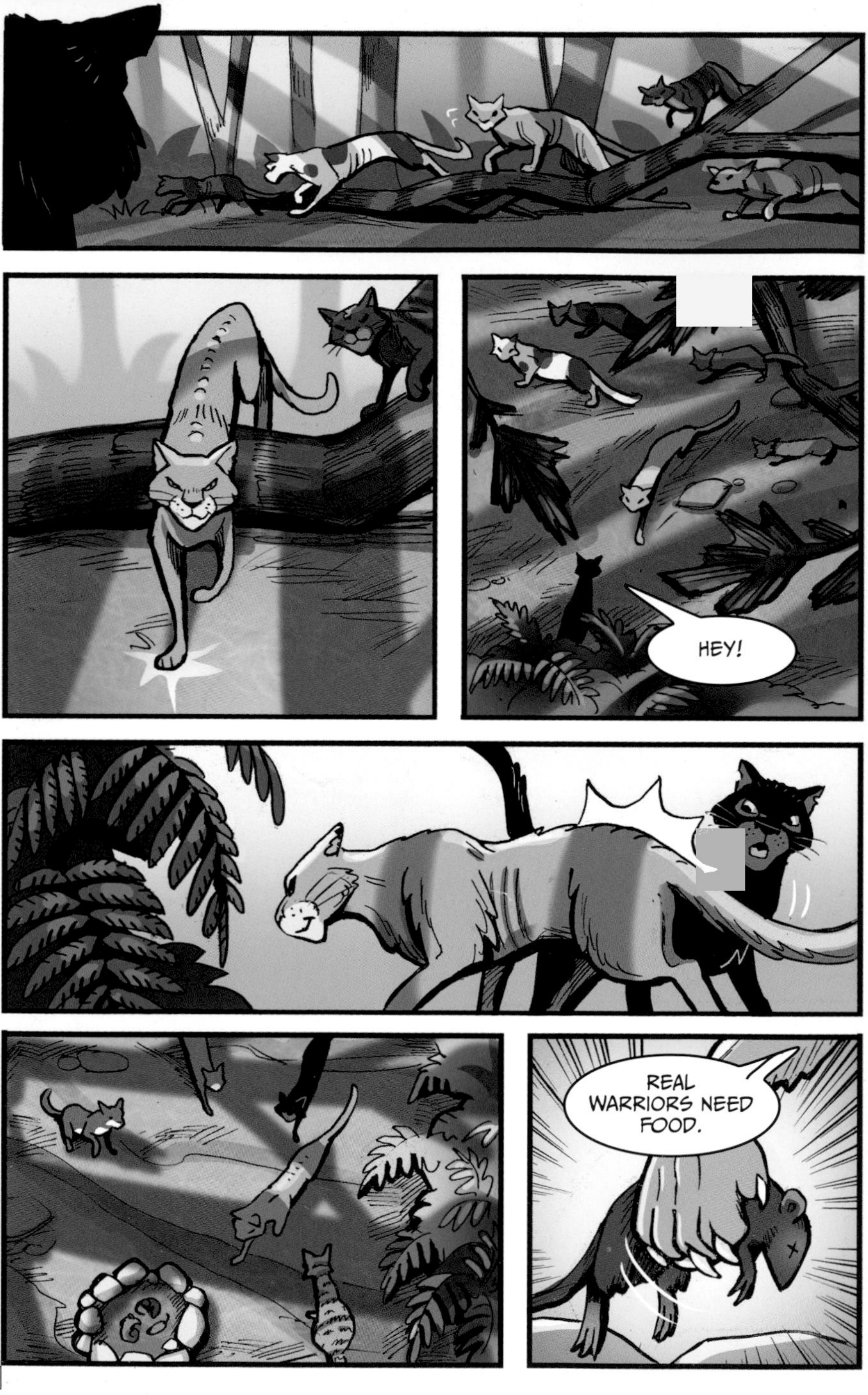
HEY!
REAL WARRIORS NEED FOOD.

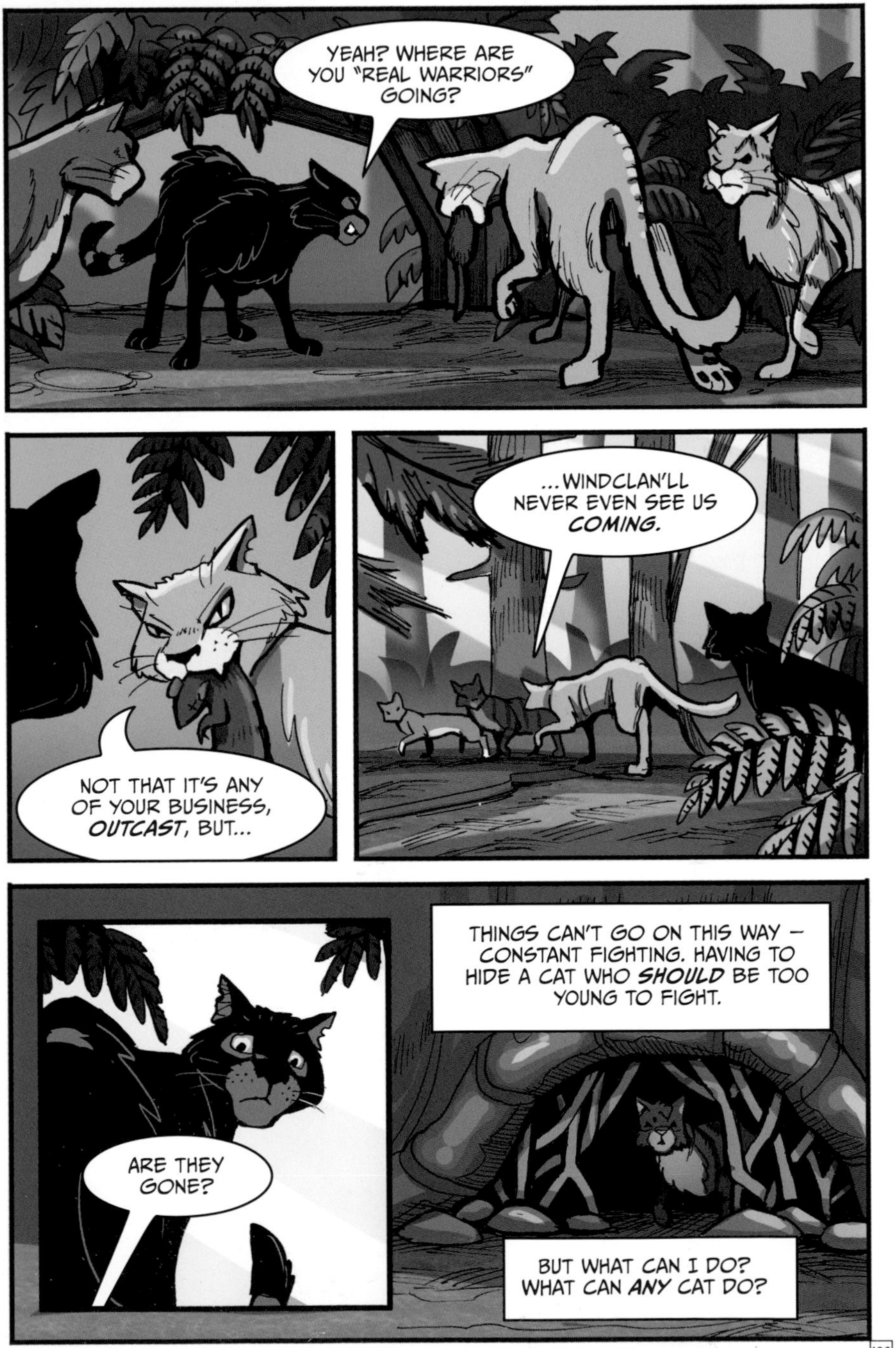
YEAH? WHERE ARE YOU "REAL WARRIORS" GOING?
NOT THAT IT'S ANY OF YOUR BUSINESS, *OUTCAST*, BUT...
...WINDCLAN'LL NEVER EVEN SEE US *COMING.*
ARE THEY GONE?
THINGS CAN'T GO ON THIS WAY – CONSTANT FIGHTING. HAVING TO HIDE A CAT WHO *SHOULD* BE TOO YOUNG TO FIGHT.
BUT WHAT CAN I DO? WHAT CAN *ANY* CAT DO?

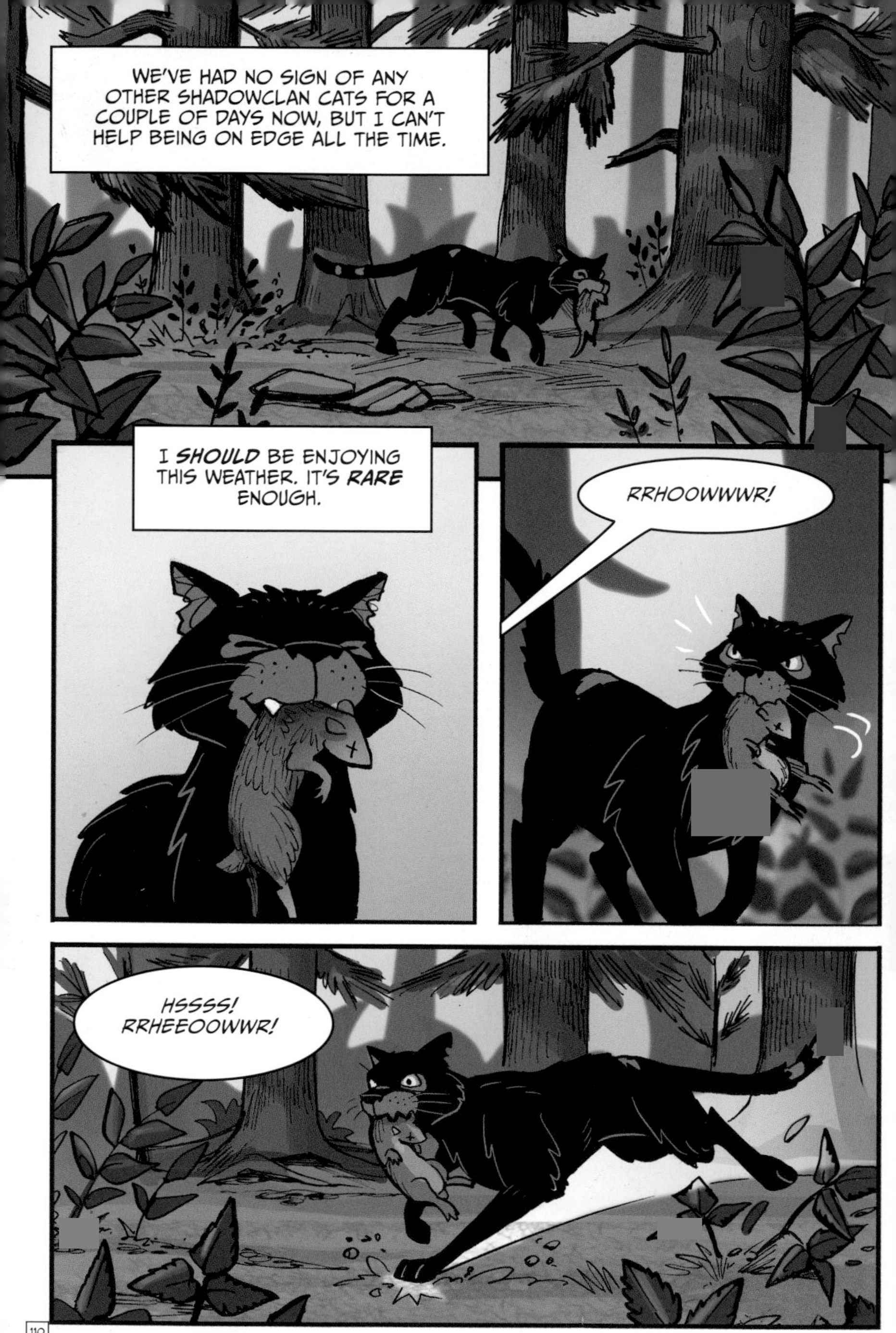
WE'VE HAD NO SIGN OF ANY OTHER SHADOWCLAN CATS FOR A COUPLE OF DAYS NOW, BUT I CAN'T HELP BEING ON EDGE ALL THE TIME.
I *SHOULD* BE ENJOYING THIS WEATHER. IT'S *RARE* ENOUGH.
RRHOOWWWR!
HSSSS! RRHEEOOWWR!

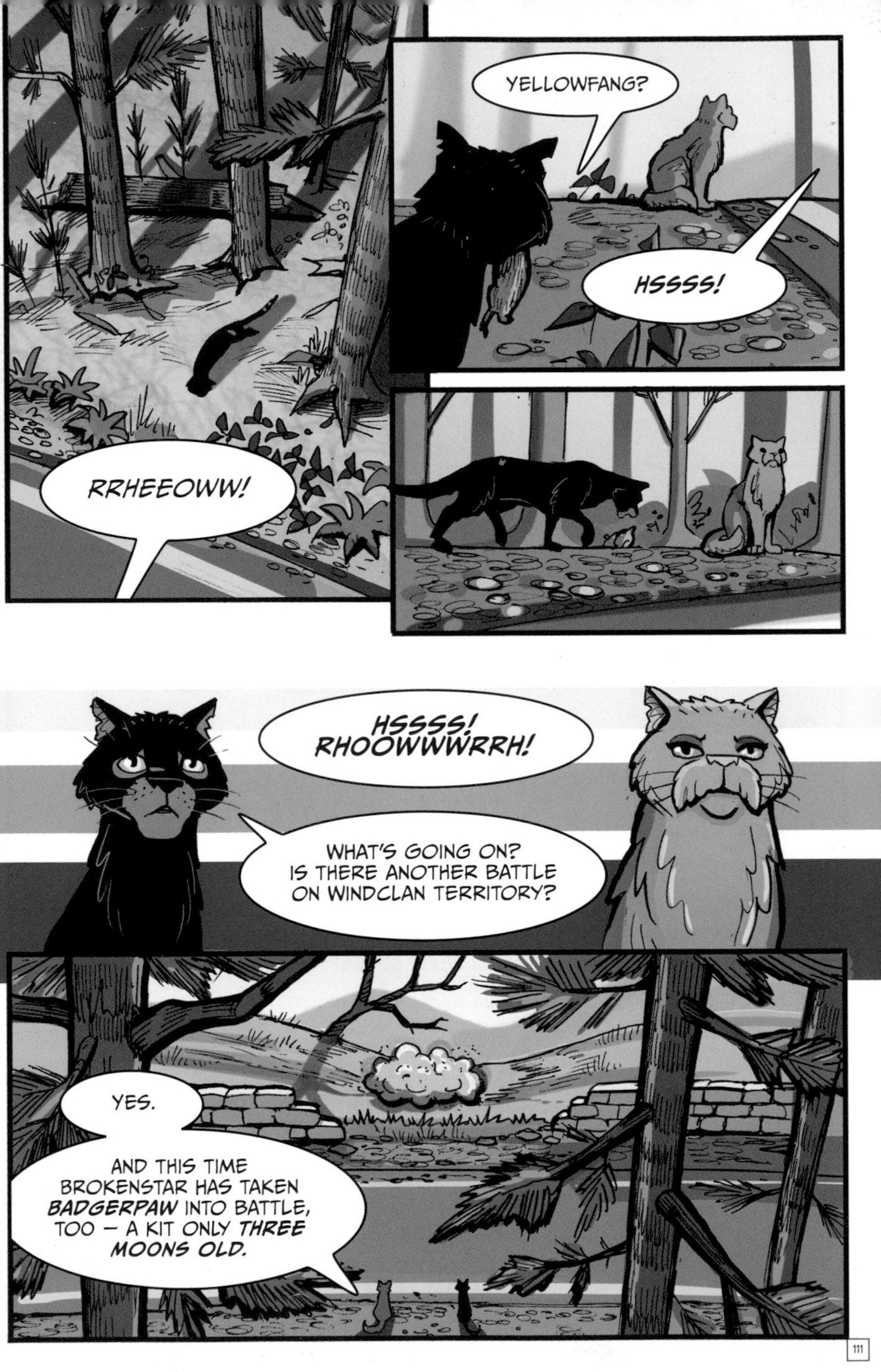
RRHEEOWW!
YELLOWFANG?
HSSSS!
HSSSS! RHOOWWWRRH!
WHAT'S GOING ON? IS THERE ANOTHER BATTLE ON WINDCLAN TERRITORY?
YES.
AND THIS TIME BROKENSTAR HAS TAKEN BADGERPAW INTO BATTLE, TOO — A KIT ONLY THREE MOONS OLD.

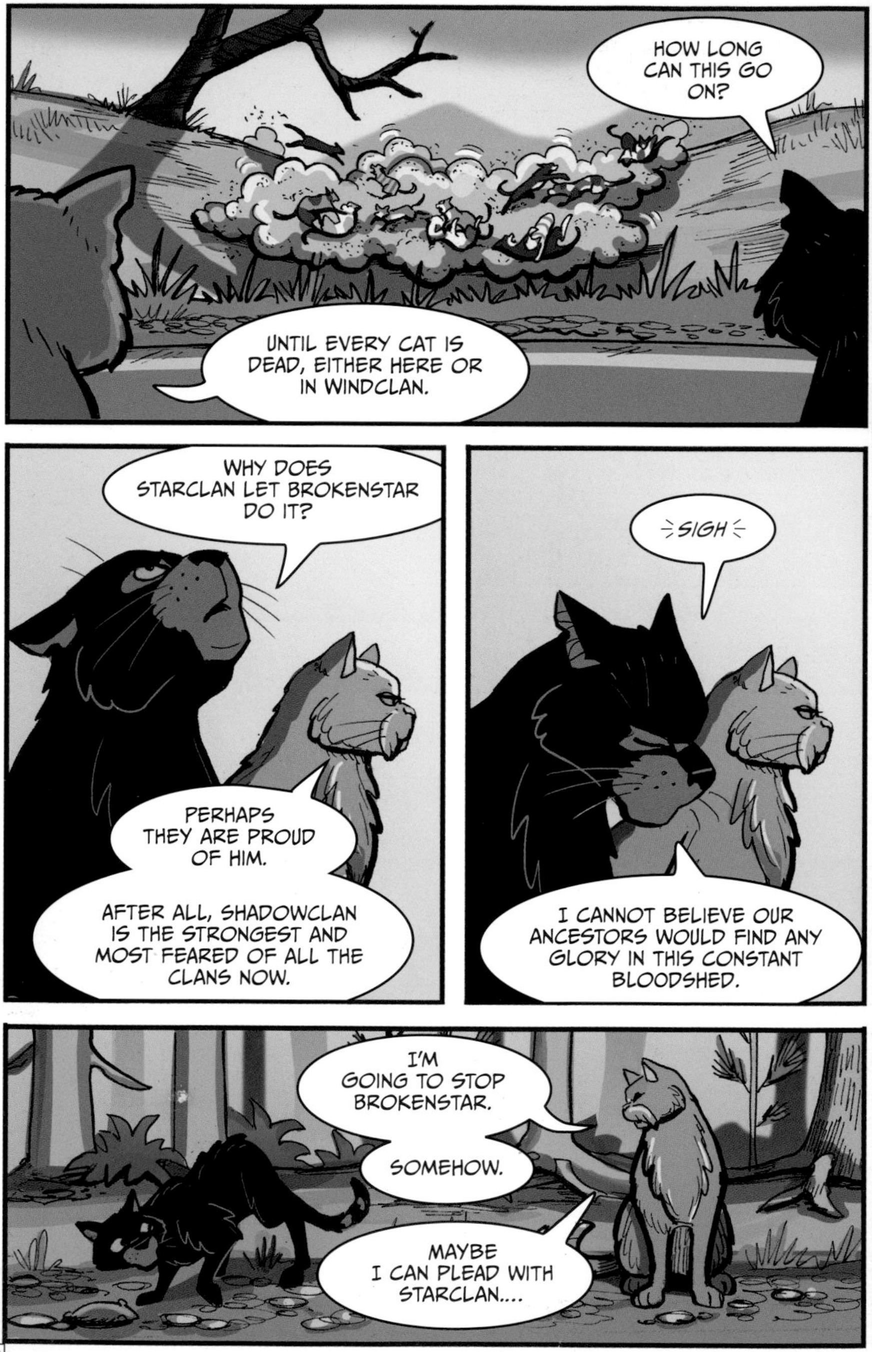
HOW LONG CAN THIS GO ON?
UNTIL EVERY CAT IS DEAD, EITHER HERE OR IN WINDCLAN.
WHY DOES STARCLAN LET BROKENSTAR DO IT?
PERHAPS THEY ARE PROUD OF HIM.
AFTER ALL, SHADOWCLAN IS THE STRONGEST AND MOST FEARED OF ALL THE CLANS NOW.
SIGH
I CANNOT BELIEVE OUR ANCESTORS WOULD FIND ANY GLORY IN THIS CONSTANT BLOODSHED.
I'M GOING TO STOP BROKENSTAR.
SOMEHOW.
MAYBE I CAN PLEAD WITH STARCLAN....

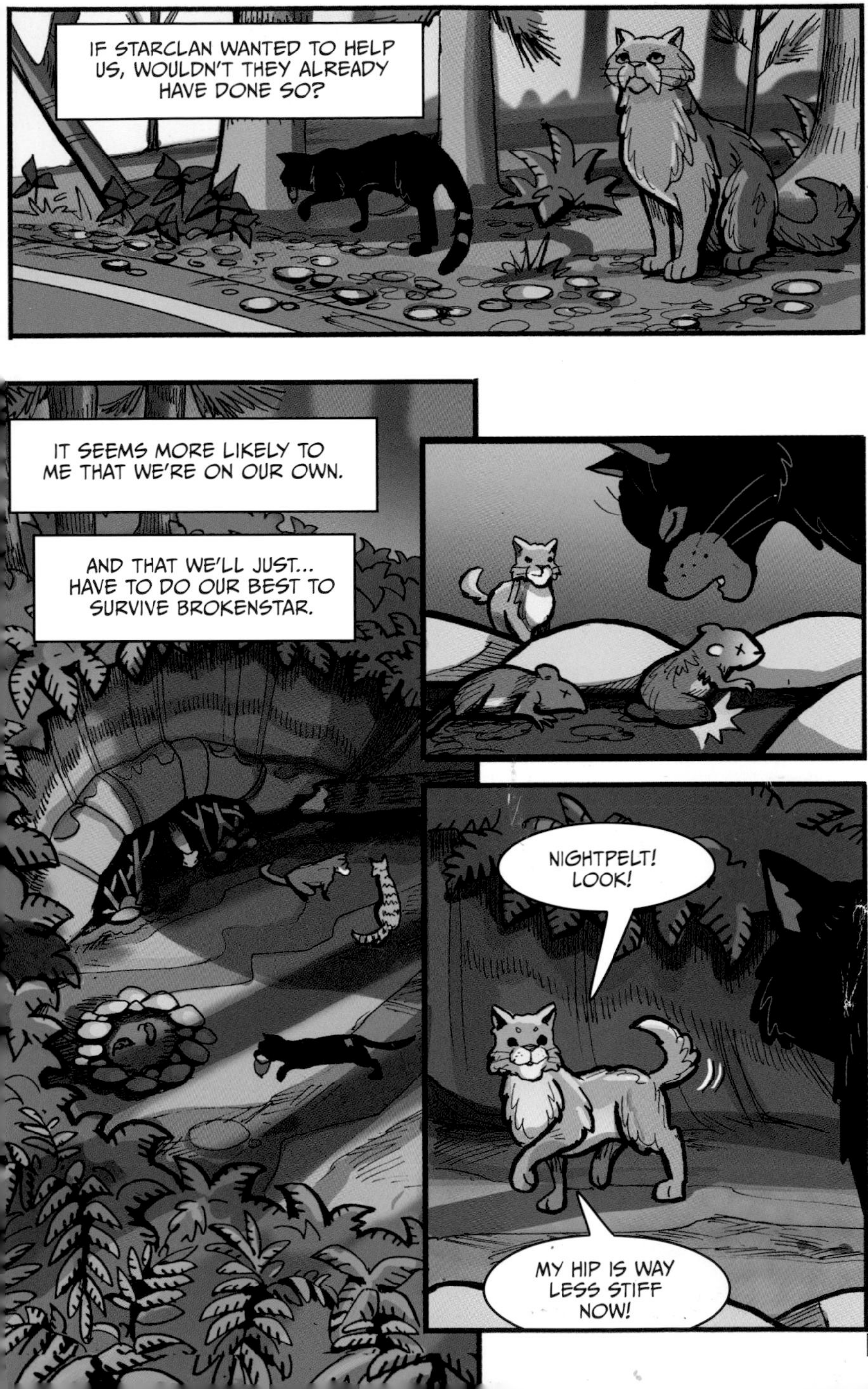
IF STARCLAN WANTED TO HELP US, WOULDN'T THEY ALREADY HAVE DONE SO?
IT SEEMS MORE LIKELY TO ME THAT WE'RE ON OUR OWN.
AND THAT WE'LL JUST... HAVE TO DO OUR BEST TO SURVIVE BROKENSTAR.
NIGHTPELT! LOOK!
MY HIP IS WAY LESS STIFF NOW!

YOU'RE MAKING *EXCELLENT* PROGRESS, VOLEPAW. WE'RE ALL *VERY* PROUD OF YOU.

AND YOU SHOULD BE PROUD OF *YOURSELF.*

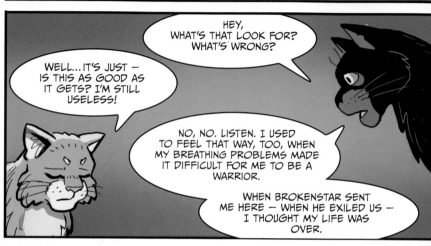

HEY, WHAT'S THAT LOOK FOR? WHAT'S WRONG?

WELL...IT'S JUST — IS THIS AS GOOD AS IT GETS? I'M STILL USELESS!

NO, NO. LISTEN. I USED TO FEEL THAT WAY, TOO, WHEN MY BREATHING PROBLEMS MADE IT DIFFICULT FOR ME TO BE A WARRIOR.

WHEN BROKENSTAR SENT ME HERE — WHEN HE EXILED US — I THOUGHT MY LIFE WAS OVER.

IT WASN'T JUST ME, EITHER.

THE ELDERS, LIKE ARCHEYE AND HOLLYFLOWER, THOUGHT THEY WERE TOO OLD TO BE OF USE TO SHADOWCLAN.

BUT LOOK AT HOW ALL THE CATS HERE HAVE WORKED TOGETHER!

WE ALL HAVE SOMETHING TO CONTRIBUTE. WE ALL TAKE CARE OF EACH OTHER.

THIS IS WHAT A CLAN *SHOULD* BE.

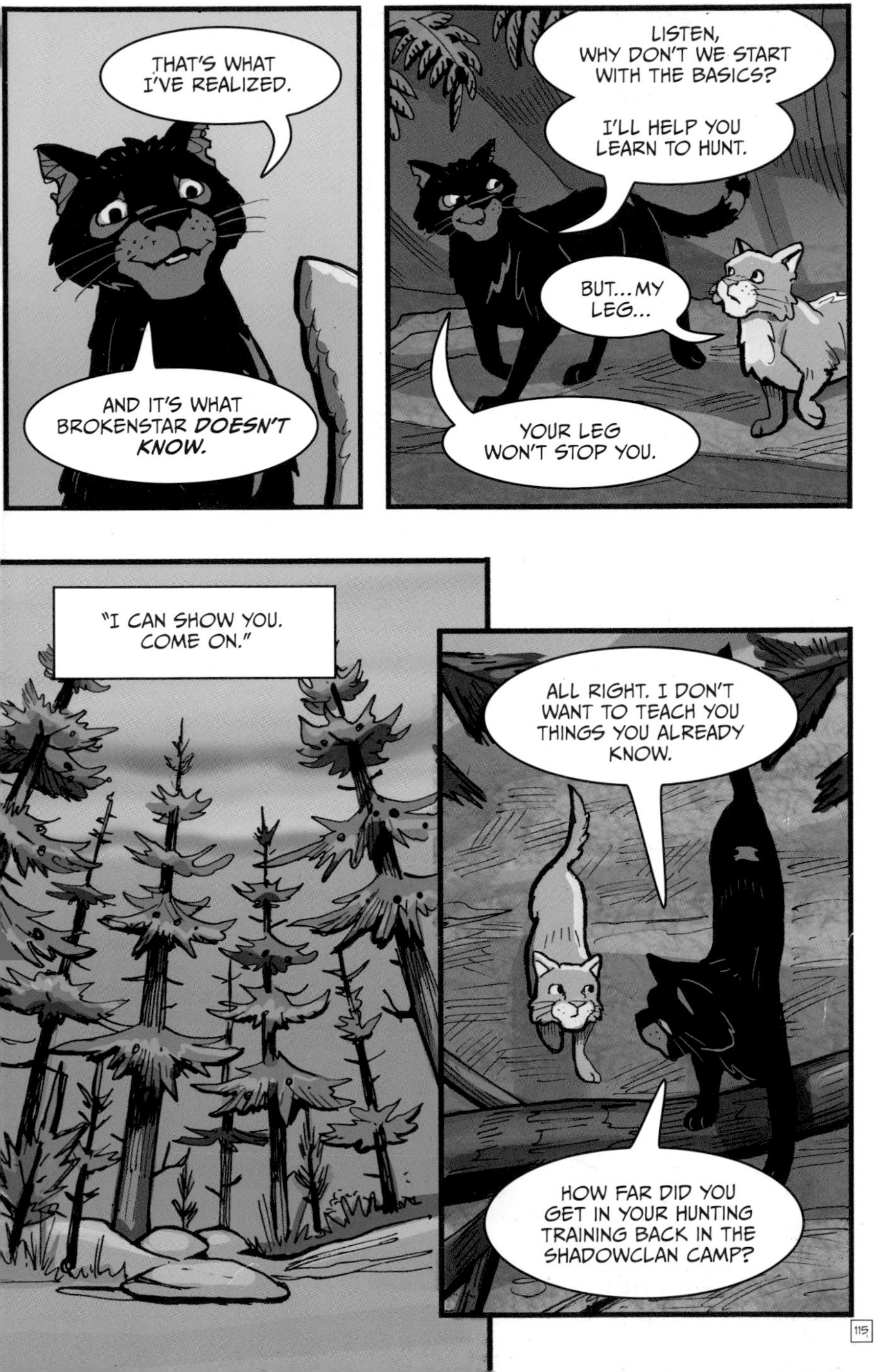
THAT'S WHAT I'VE REALIZED.
AND IT'S WHAT BROKENSTAR ***DOESN'T KNOW.***
LISTEN, WHY DON'T WE START WITH THE BASICS?
I'LL HELP YOU LEARN TO HUNT.
BUT... MY LEG...
YOUR LEG WON'T STOP YOU.
"I CAN SHOW YOU. COME ON."
ALL RIGHT. I DON'T WANT TO TEACH YOU THINGS YOU ALREADY KNOW.
HOW FAR DID YOU GET IN YOUR HUNTING TRAINING BACK IN THE SHADOWCLAN CAMP?

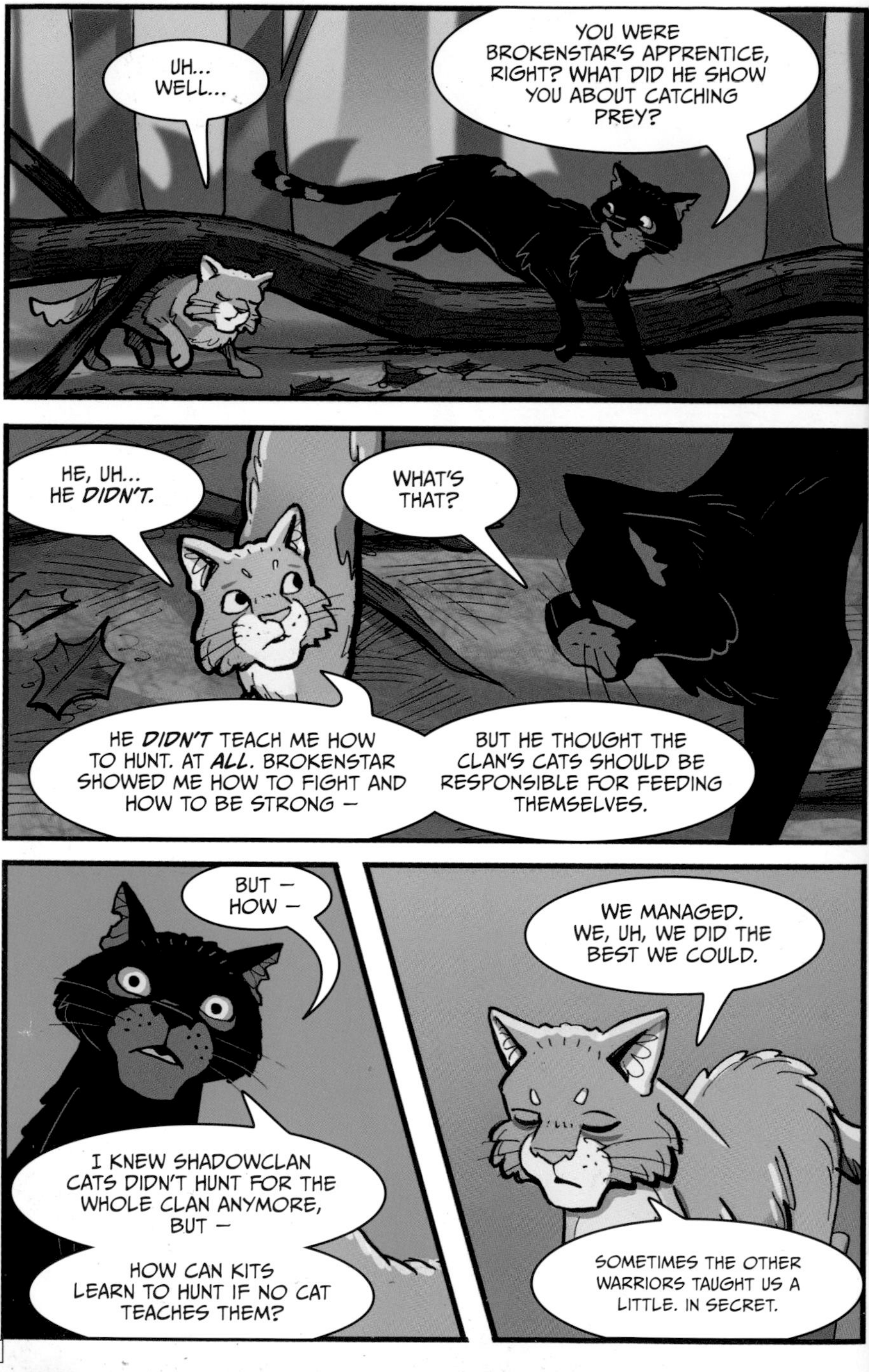
UH... WELL...
YOU WERE BROKENSTAR'S APPRENTICE, RIGHT? WHAT DID HE SHOW YOU ABOUT CATCHING PREY?
HE, UH... HE *DIDN'T.*
WHAT'S THAT?
HE *DIDN'T* TEACH ME HOW TO HUNT. AT *ALL.* BROKENSTAR SHOWED ME HOW TO FIGHT AND HOW TO BE STRONG —
BUT HE THOUGHT THE CLAN'S CATS SHOULD BE RESPONSIBLE FOR FEEDING THEMSELVES.
BUT — HOW —
I KNEW SHADOWCLAN CATS DIDN'T HUNT FOR THE WHOLE CLAN ANYMORE, BUT —
HOW CAN KITS LEARN TO HUNT IF NO CAT TEACHES THEM?
WE MANAGED. WE, UH, WE DID THE BEST WE COULD.
SOMETIMES THE OTHER WARRIORS TAUGHT US A LITTLE. IN SECRET.

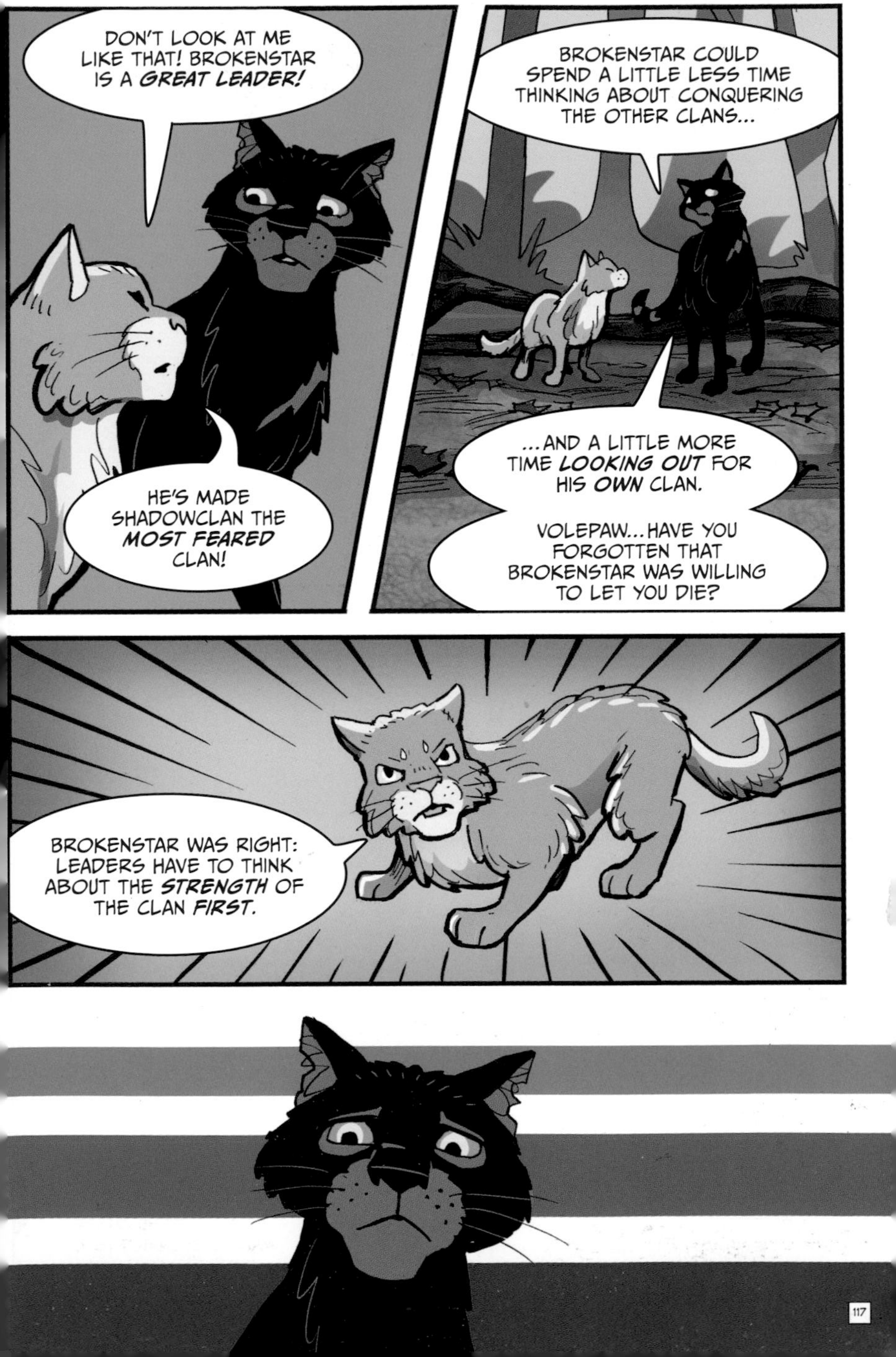
DON'T LOOK AT ME LIKE THAT! BROKENSTAR IS A *GREAT LEADER!*
HE'S MADE SHADOWCLAN THE *MOST FEARED* CLAN!
BROKENSTAR COULD SPEND A LITTLE LESS TIME THINKING ABOUT CONQUERING THE OTHER CLANS...
...AND A LITTLE MORE TIME *LOOKING OUT* FOR HIS *OWN* CLAN.
VOLEPAW...HAVE YOU FORGOTTEN THAT BROKENSTAR WAS WILLING TO LET YOU DIE?
BROKENSTAR WAS RIGHT: LEADERS HAVE TO THINK ABOUT THE *STRENGTH* OF THE CLAN *FIRST*.

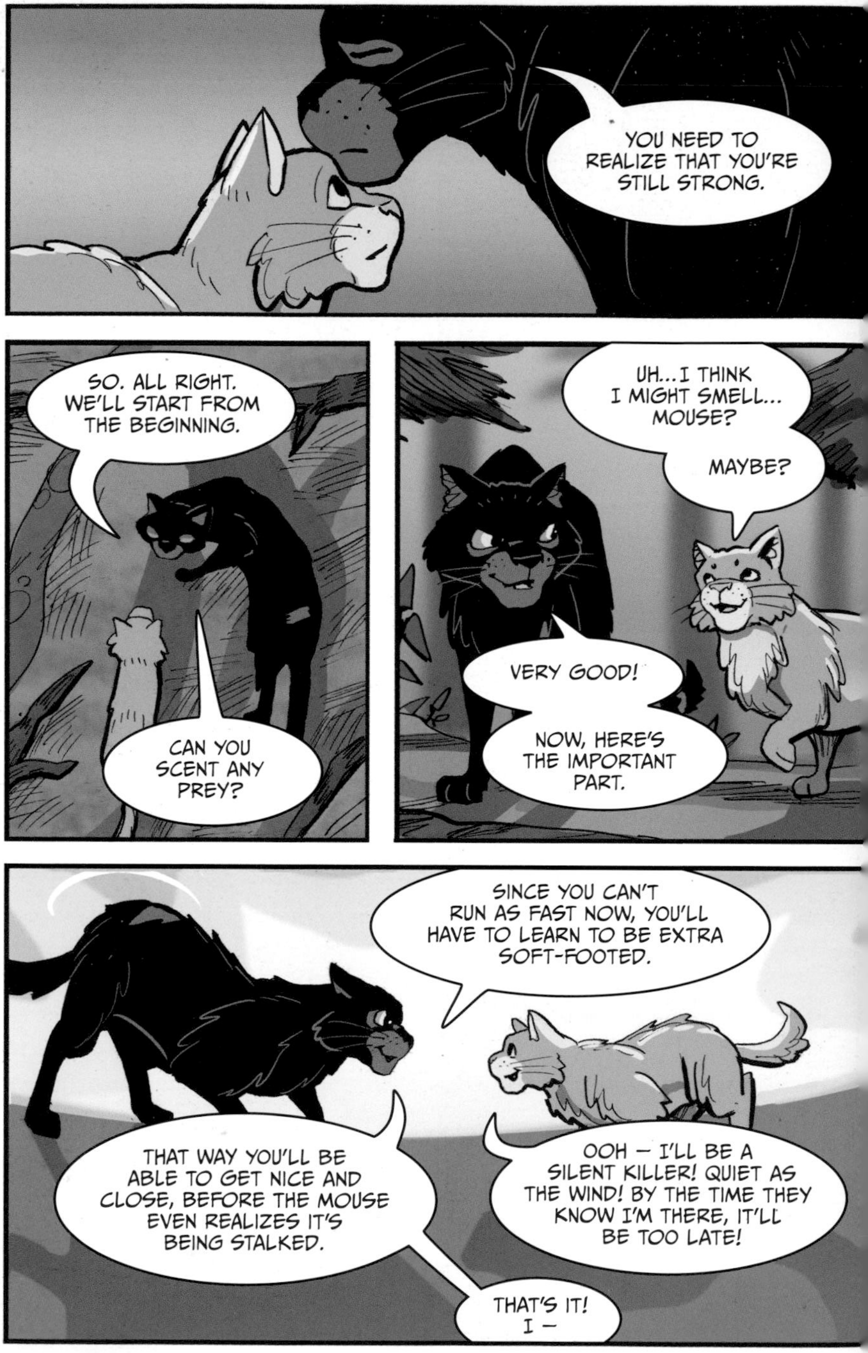
YOU NEED TO REALIZE THAT YOU'RE STILL STRONG.
SO. ALL RIGHT. WE'LL START FROM THE BEGINNING.
CAN YOU SCENT ANY PREY?
UH...I THINK I MIGHT SMELL... MOUSE?
MAYBE?
VERY GOOD!
NOW, HERE'S THE IMPORTANT PART.
SINCE YOU CAN'T RUN AS FAST NOW, YOU'LL HAVE TO LEARN TO BE EXTRA SOFT-FOOTED.
THAT WAY YOU'LL BE ABLE TO GET NICE AND CLOSE, BEFORE THE MOUSE EVEN REALIZES IT'S BEING STALKED.
OOH — I'LL BE A SILENT KILLER! QUIET AS THE WIND! BY THE TIME THEY KNOW I'M THERE, IT'LL BE TOO LATE!
THAT'S IT! I —

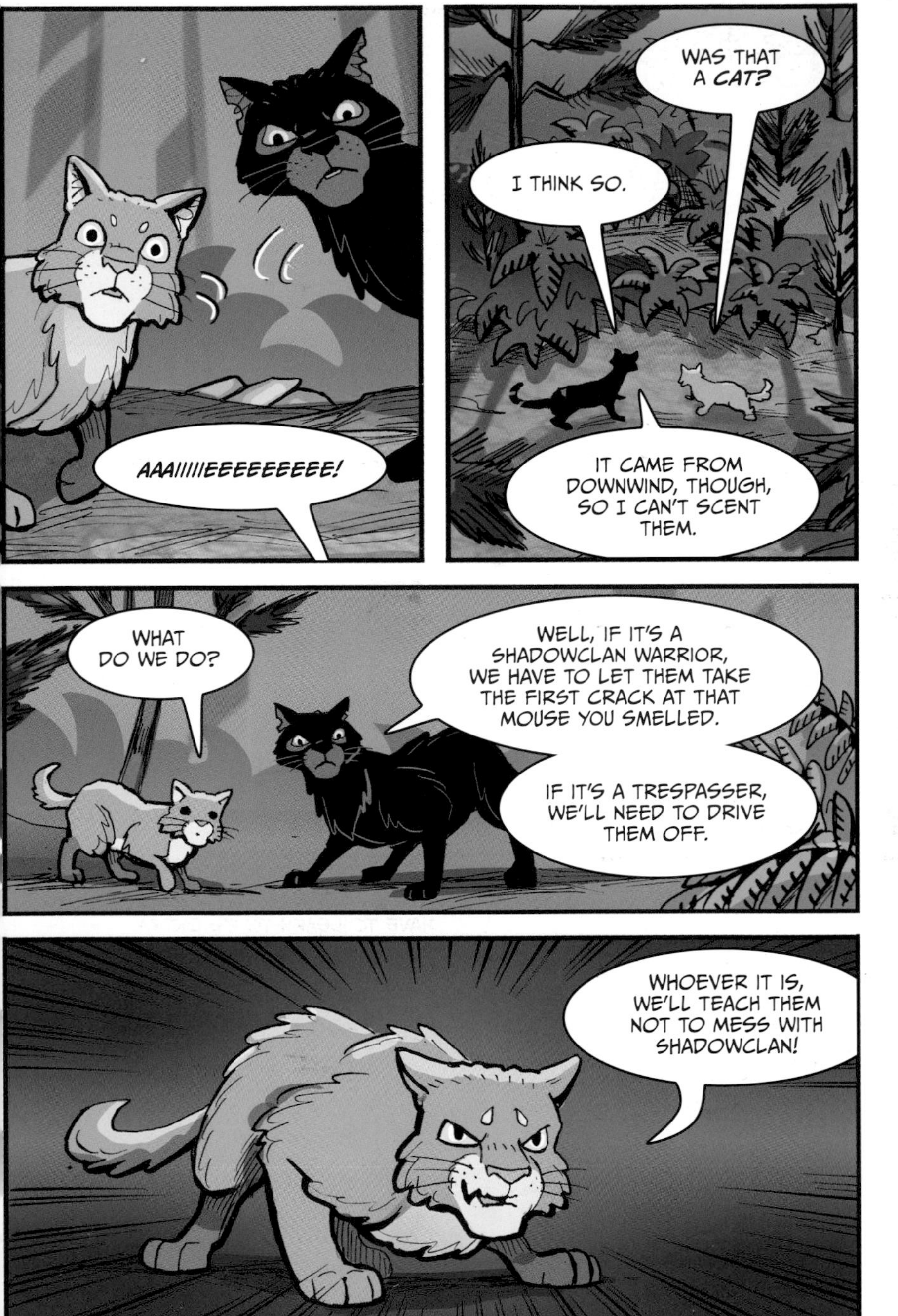
AAAIIIIIEEEEEEEEE!
WAS THAT A CAT?
I THINK SO.
IT CAME FROM DOWNWIND, THOUGH, SO I CAN'T SCENT THEM.
WHAT DO WE DO?
WELL, IF IT'S A SHADOWCLAN WARRIOR, WE HAVE TO LET THEM TAKE THE FIRST CRACK AT THAT MOUSE YOU SMELLED.
IF IT'S A TRESPASSER, WE'LL NEED TO DRIVE THEM OFF.
WHOEVER IT IS, WE'LL TEACH THEM NOT TO MESS WITH SHADOWCLAN!

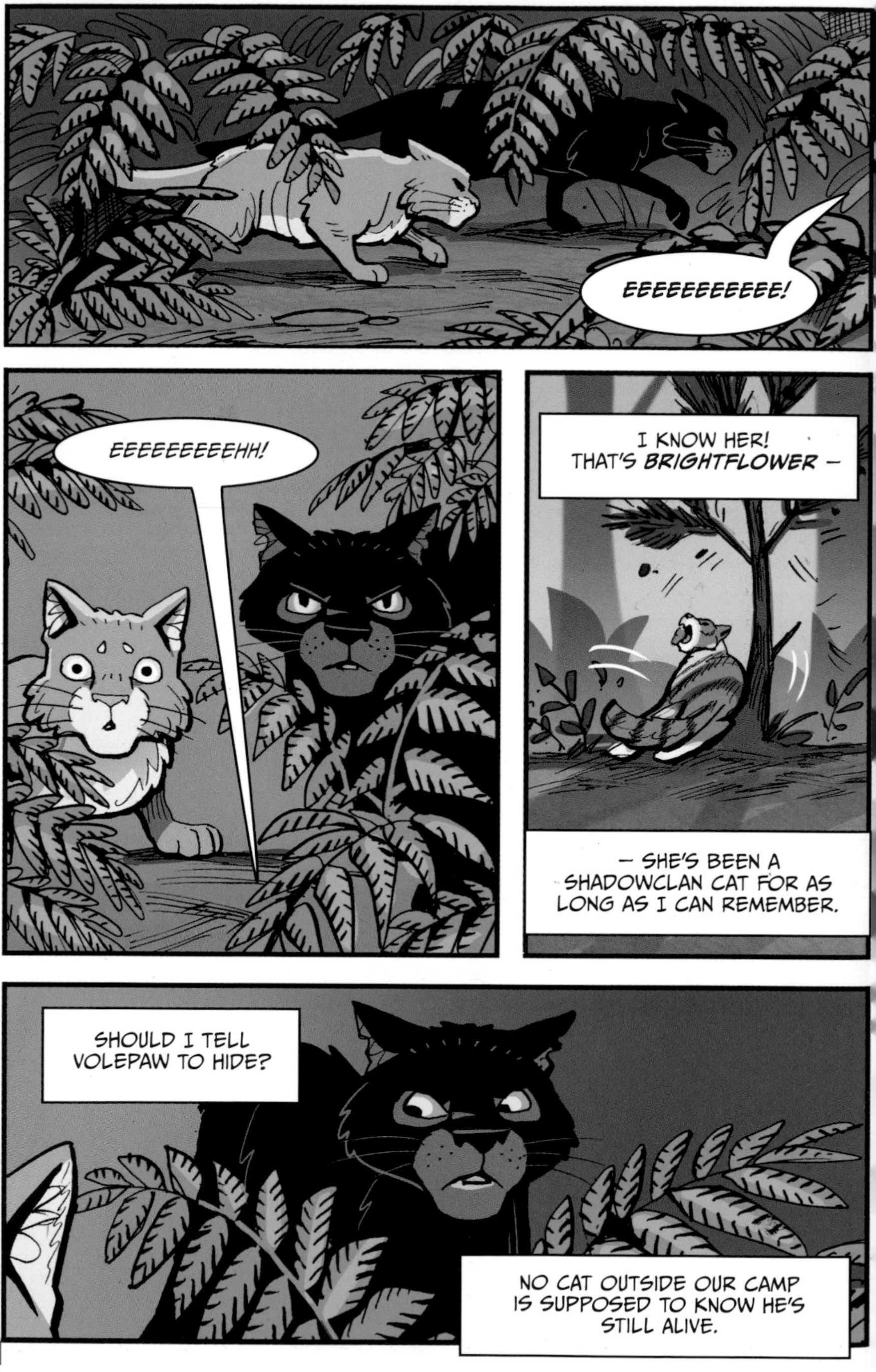
EEEEEEEEEEE!
EEEEEEEEEEHH!
I KNOW HER! THAT'S *BRIGHTFLOWER* –
– SHE'S BEEN A SHADOWCLAN CAT FOR AS LONG AS I CAN REMEMBER.
SHOULD I TELL VOLEPAW TO HIDE?
NO CAT OUTSIDE OUR CAMP IS SUPPOSED TO KNOW HE'S STILL ALIVE.

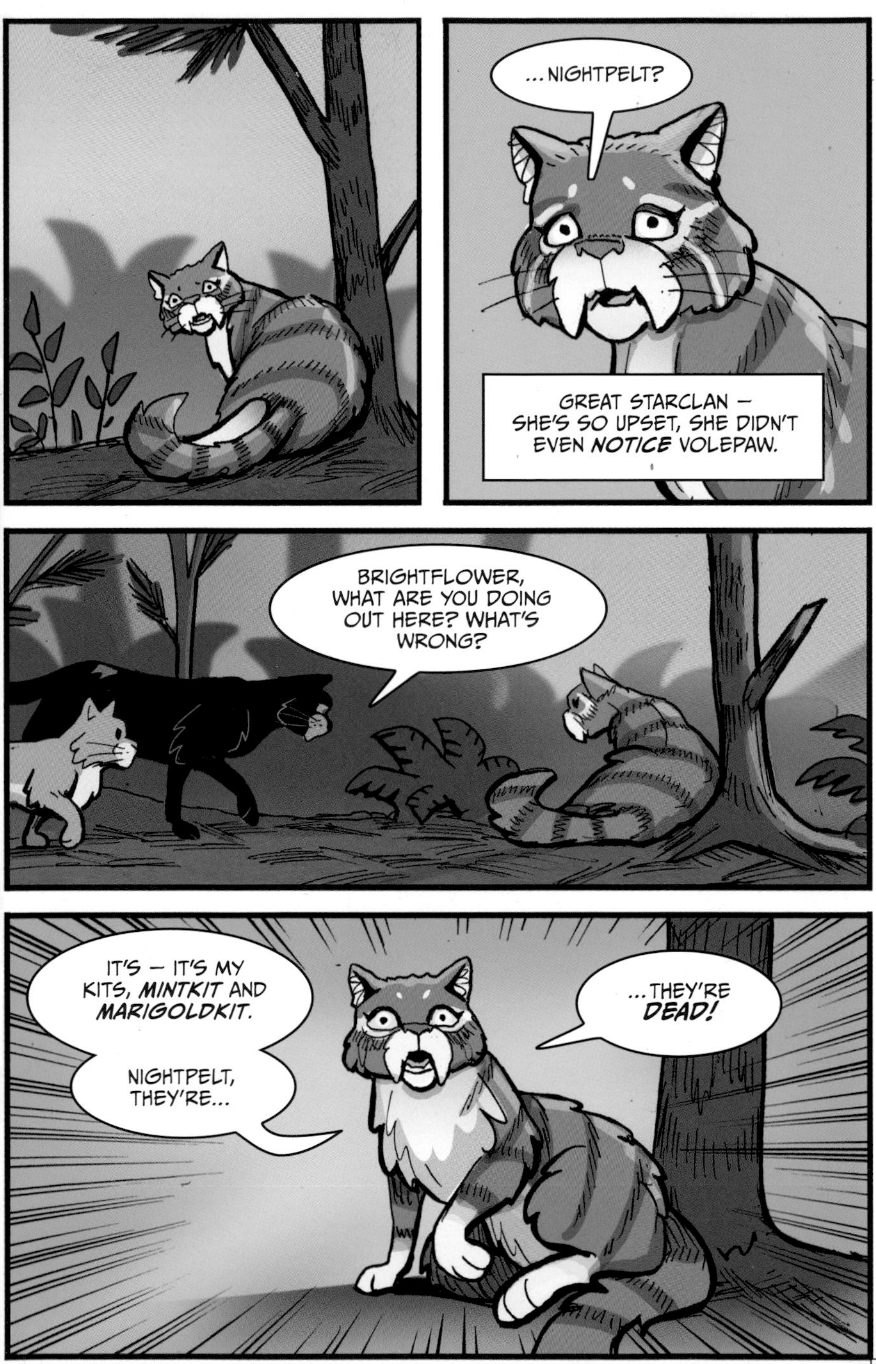
...NIGHTPELT?
GREAT STARCLAN — SHE'S SO UPSET, SHE DIDN'T EVEN *NOTICE* VOLEPAW.
BRIGHTFLOWER, WHAT ARE YOU DOING OUT HERE? WHAT'S WRONG?
IT'S — IT'S MY KITS, *MINTKIT* AND *MARIGOLDKIT*.
NIGHTPELT, THEY'RE...
...THEY'RE *DEAD!*

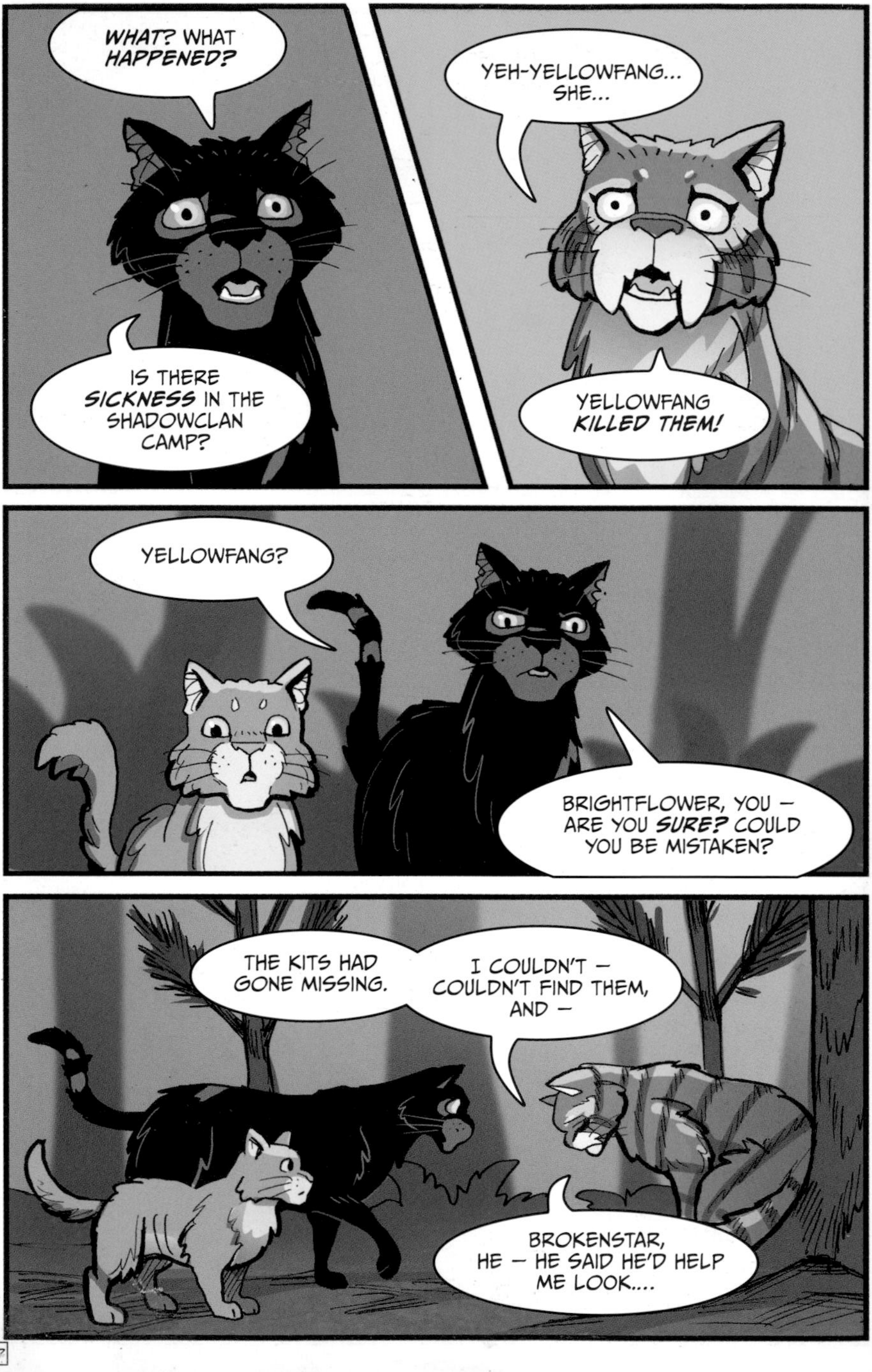
WHAT? WHAT HAPPENED?
IS THERE SICKNESS IN THE SHADOWCLAN CAMP?
YEH-YELLOWFANG... SHE...
YELLOWFANG KILLED THEM!
YELLOWFANG?
BRIGHTFLOWER, YOU — ARE YOU SURE? COULD YOU BE MISTAKEN?
THE KITS HAD GONE MISSING.
I COULDN'T — COULDN'T FIND THEM, AND —
BROKENSTAR, HE — HE SAID HE'D HELP ME LOOK....

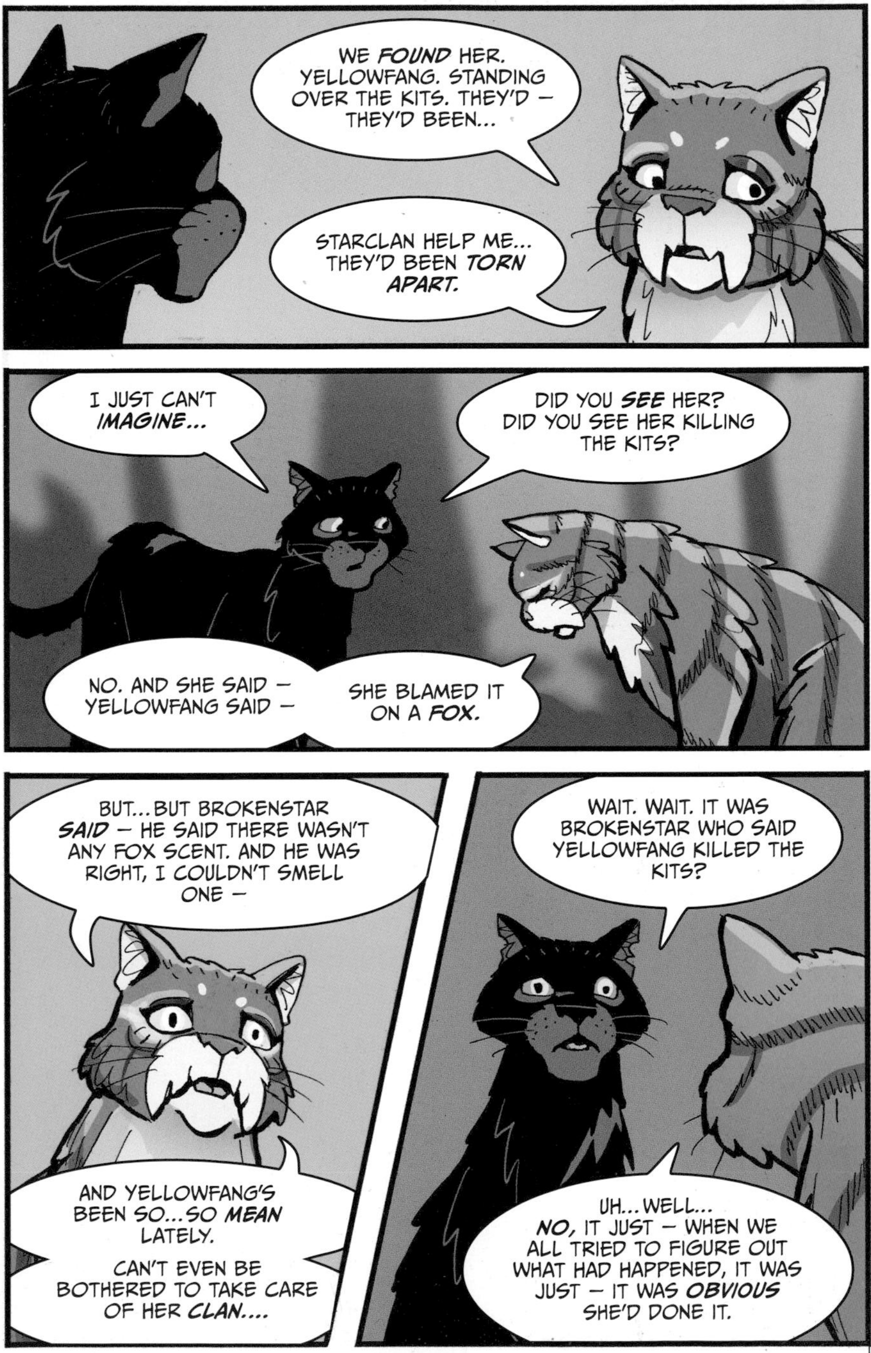
WE *FOUND* HER. YELLOWFANG. STANDING OVER THE KITS. THEY'D — THEY'D BEEN...
STARCLAN HELP ME... THEY'D BEEN *TORN APART.*
I JUST CAN'T *IMAGINE...*
DID YOU *SEE* HER? DID YOU SEE HER KILLING THE KITS?
NO. AND SHE SAID — YELLOWFANG SAID —
SHE BLAMED IT ON A *FOX.*
BUT...BUT BROKENSTAR *SAID* — HE SAID THERE WASN'T ANY FOX SCENT. AND HE WAS RIGHT, I COULDN'T SMELL ONE —
AND YELLOWFANG'S BEEN SO...SO *MEAN* LATELY.
CAN'T EVEN BE BOTHERED TO TAKE CARE OF HER *CLAN....*
WAIT. WAIT. IT WAS BROKENSTAR WHO SAID YELLOWFANG KILLED THE KITS?
UH...WELL... *NO,* IT JUST — WHEN WE ALL TRIED TO FIGURE OUT WHAT HAD HAPPENED, IT WAS JUST — IT WAS *OBVIOUS* SHE'D DONE IT.

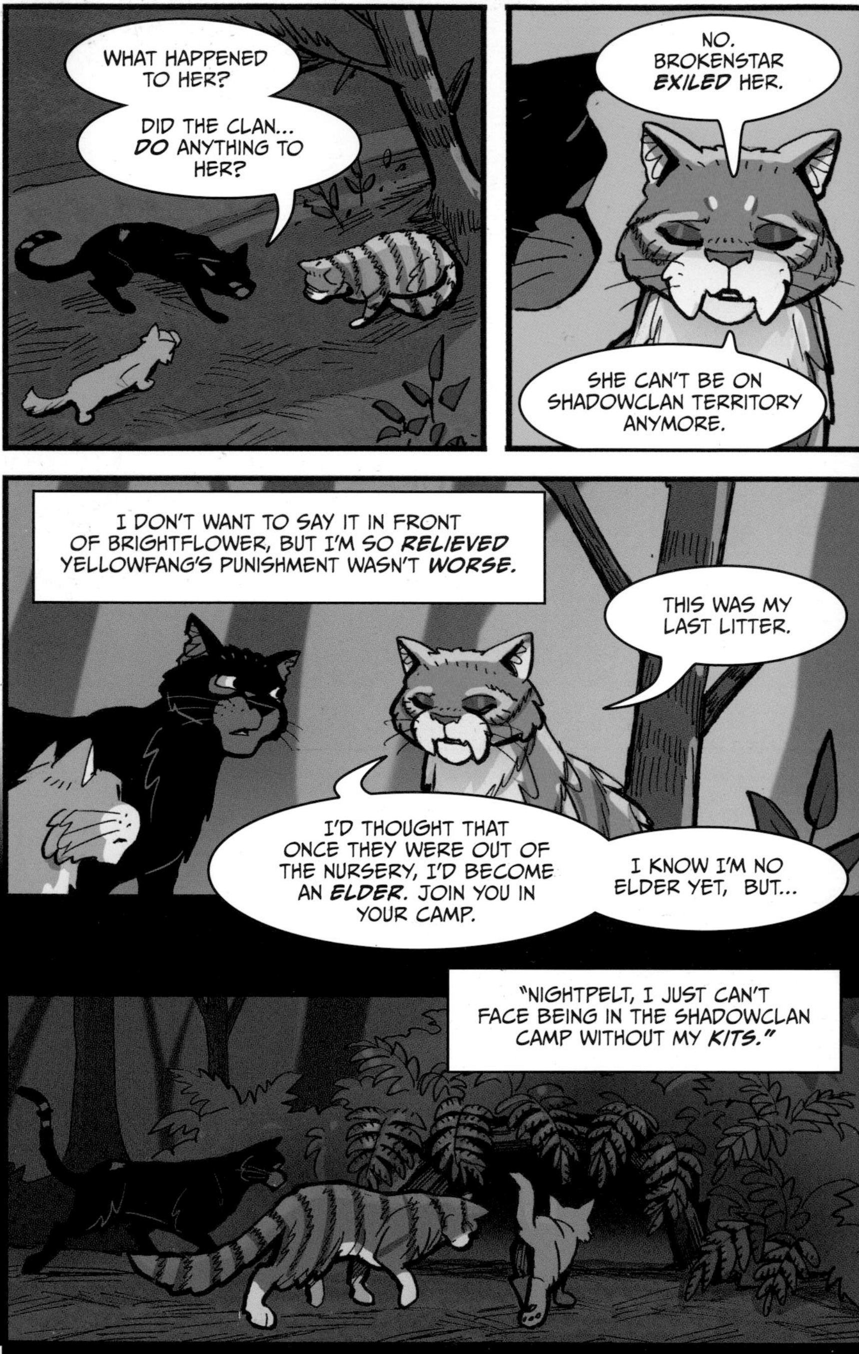
WHAT HAPPENED TO HER?
DID THE CLAN... DO ANYTHING TO HER?
NO. BROKENSTAR EXILED HER.
SHE CAN'T BE ON SHADOWCLAN TERRITORY ANYMORE.
I DON'T WANT TO SAY IT IN FRONT OF BRIGHTFLOWER, BUT I'M SO RELIEVED YELLOWFANG'S PUNISHMENT WASN'T WORSE.
THIS WAS MY LAST LITTER.
I'D THOUGHT THAT ONCE THEY WERE OUT OF THE NURSERY, I'D BECOME AN ELDER. JOIN YOU IN YOUR CAMP.
I KNOW I'M NO ELDER YET, BUT...
"NIGHTPELT, I JUST CAN'T FACE BEING IN THE SHADOWCLAN CAMP WITHOUT MY KITS."

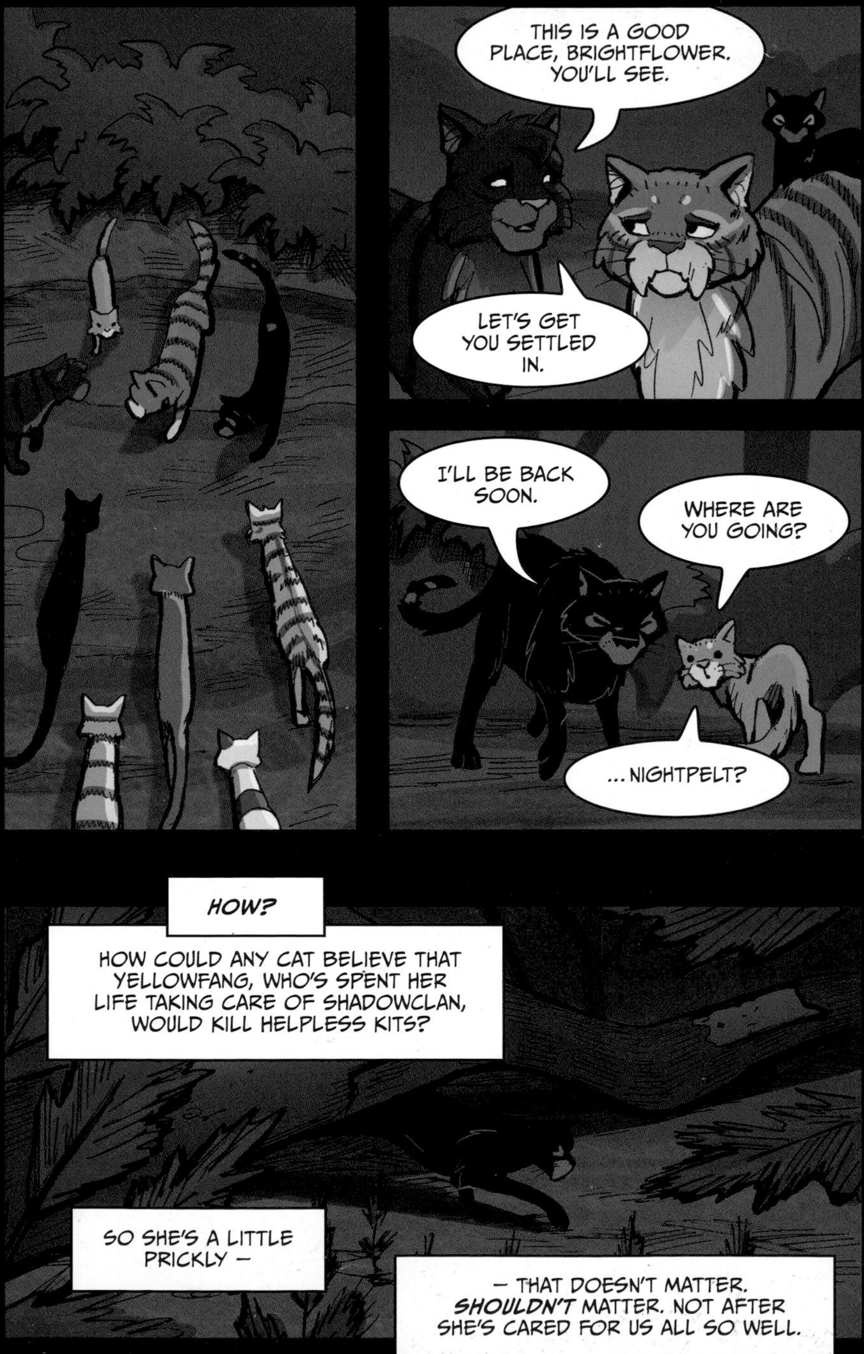
THIS IS A GOOD PLACE, BRIGHTFLOWER. YOU'LL SEE.
LET'S GET YOU SETTLED IN.
I'LL BE BACK SOON.
WHERE ARE YOU GOING?
... NIGHTPELT?
HOW?
HOW COULD ANY CAT BELIEVE THAT YELLOWFANG, WHO'S SPENT HER LIFE TAKING CARE OF SHADOWCLAN, WOULD KILL HELPLESS KITS?
SO SHE'S A LITTLE PRICKLY –
– THAT DOESN'T MATTER. *SHOULDN'T* MATTER. NOT AFTER SHE'S CARED FOR US ALL SO WELL.

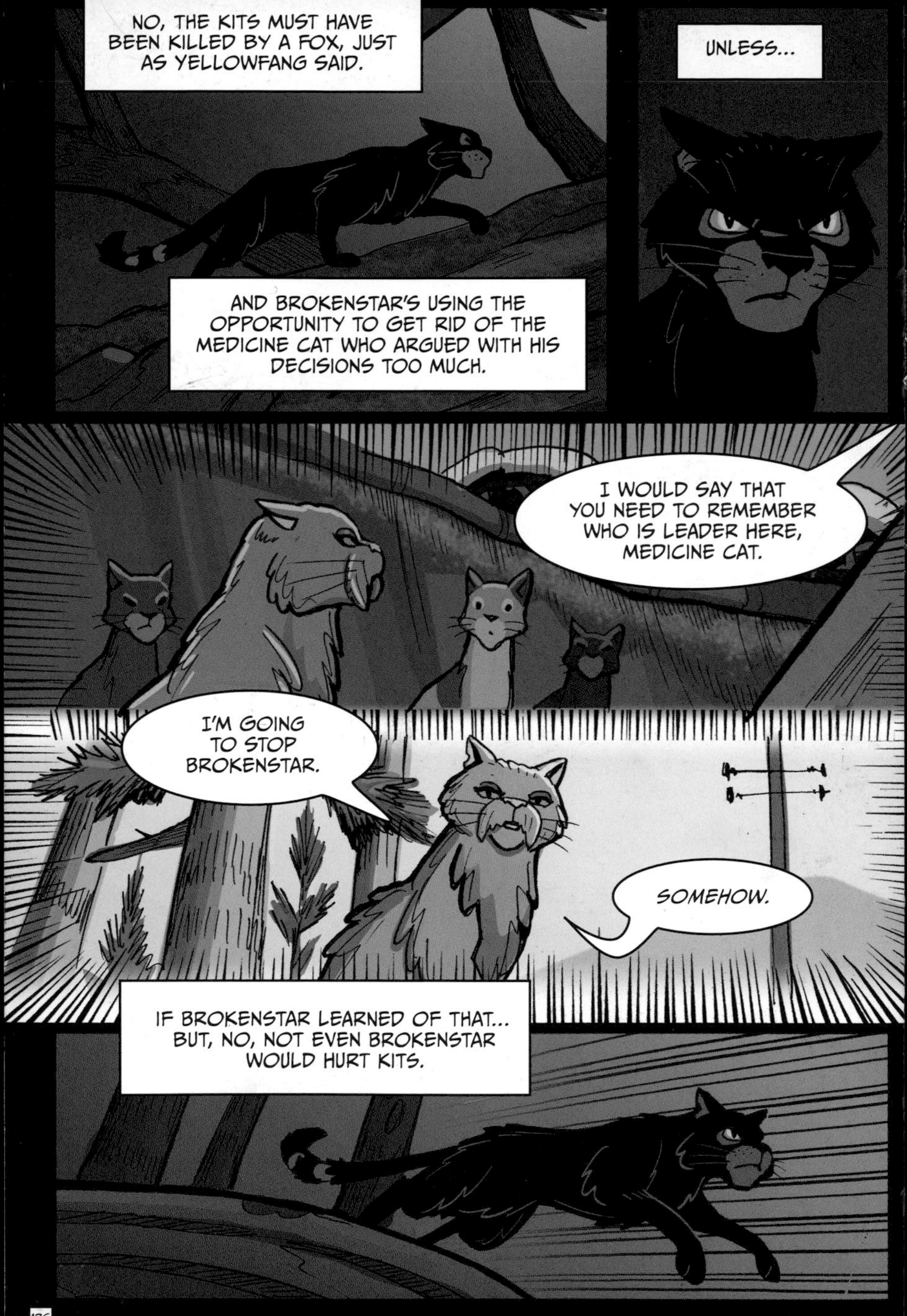
NO, THE KITS MUST HAVE BEEN KILLED BY A FOX, JUST AS YELLOWFANG SAID.
AND BROKENSTAR'S USING THE OPPORTUNITY TO GET RID OF THE MEDICINE CAT WHO ARGUED WITH HIS DECISIONS TOO MUCH.
UNLESS...
I WOULD SAY THAT YOU NEED TO REMEMBER WHO IS LEADER HERE, MEDICINE CAT.
I'M GOING TO STOP BROKENSTAR.
SOMEHOW.
IF BROKENSTAR LEARNED OF THAT... BUT, NO, NOT EVEN BROKENSTAR WOULD HURT KITS.

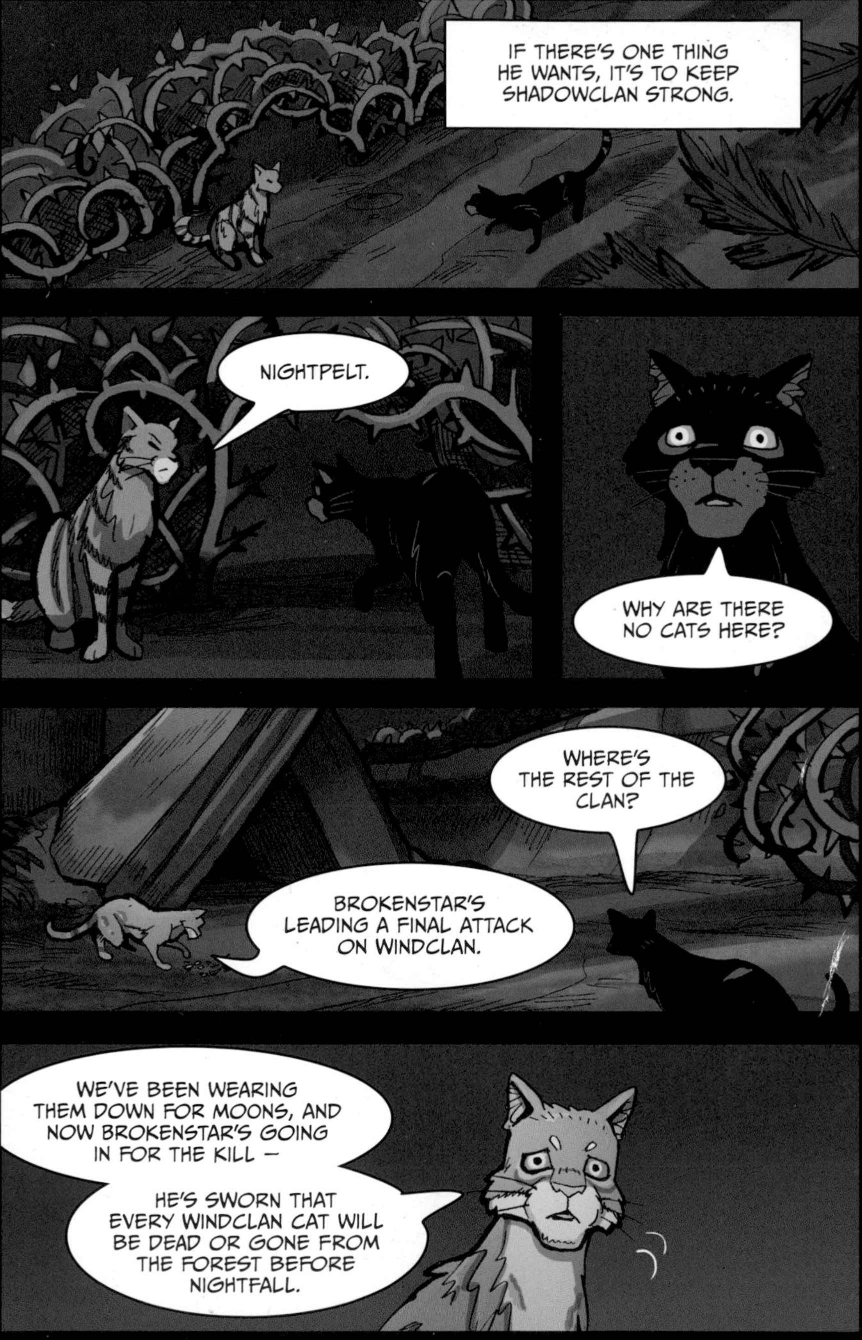
IF THERE'S ONE THING HE WANTS, IT'S TO KEEP SHADOWCLAN STRONG.
NIGHTPELT.
WHY ARE THERE NO CATS HERE?
WHERE'S THE REST OF THE CLAN?
BROKENSTAR'S LEADING A FINAL ATTACK ON WINDCLAN.
WE'VE BEEN WEARING THEM DOWN FOR MOONS, AND NOW BROKENSTAR'S GOING IN FOR THE KILL —
HE'S SWORN THAT EVERY WINDCLAN CAT WILL BE DEAD OR GONE FROM THE FOREST BEFORE NIGHTFALL.

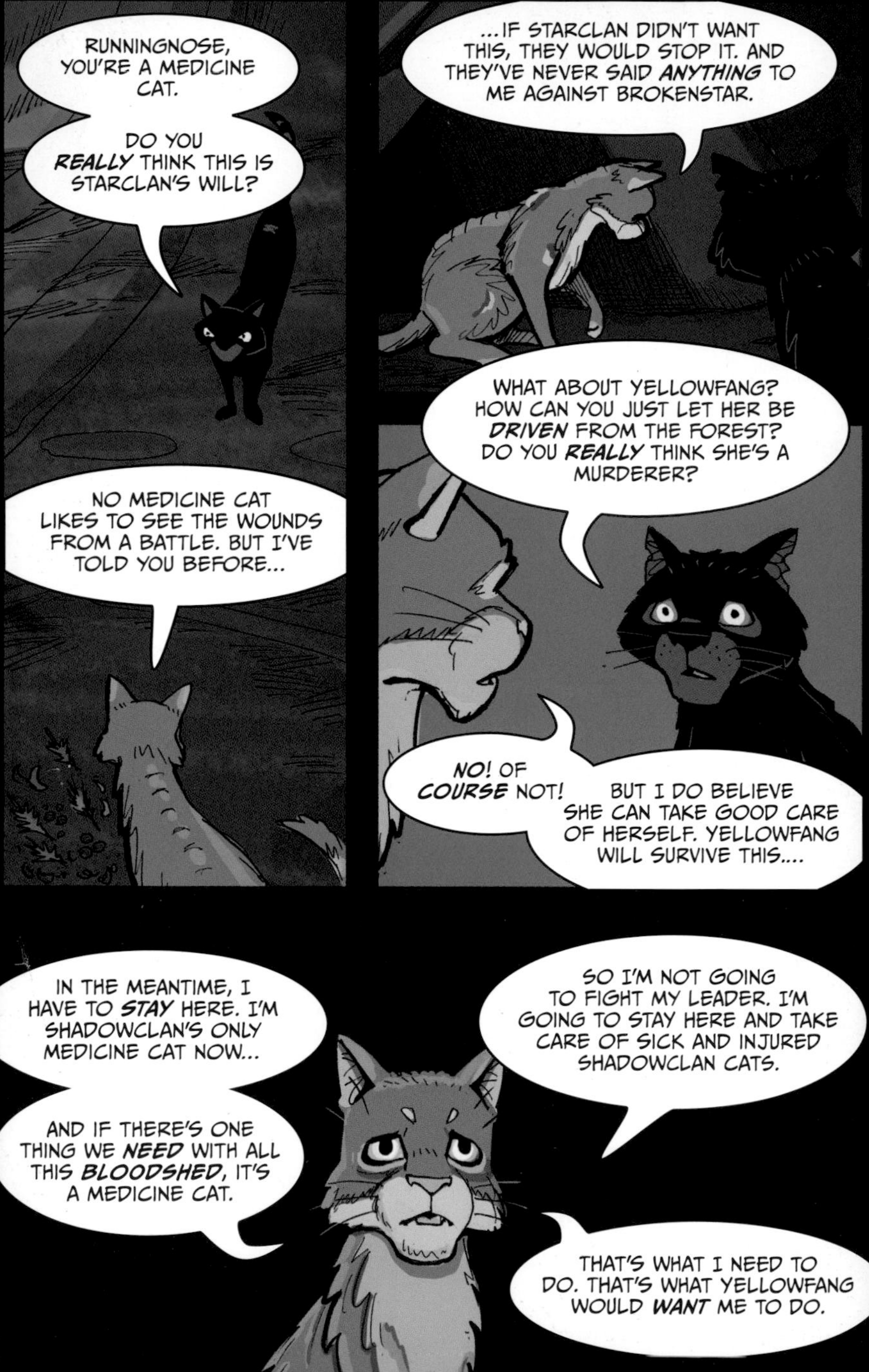
RUNNINGNOSE, YOU'RE A MEDICINE CAT.
DO YOU REALLY THINK THIS IS STARCLAN'S WILL?
NO MEDICINE CAT LIKES TO SEE THE WOUNDS FROM A BATTLE. BUT I'VE TOLD YOU BEFORE...
...IF STARCLAN DIDN'T WANT THIS, THEY WOULD STOP IT. AND THEY'VE NEVER SAID ANYTHING TO ME AGAINST BROKENSTAR.
WHAT ABOUT YELLOWFANG? HOW CAN YOU JUST LET HER BE DRIVEN FROM THE FOREST? DO YOU REALLY THINK SHE'S A MURDERER?
NO! OF COURSE NOT!
BUT I DO BELIEVE SHE CAN TAKE GOOD CARE OF HERSELF. YELLOWFANG WILL SURVIVE THIS....
IN THE MEANTIME, I HAVE TO STAY HERE. I'M SHADOWCLAN'S ONLY MEDICINE CAT NOW...
AND IF THERE'S ONE THING WE NEED WITH ALL THIS BLOODSHED, IT'S A MEDICINE CAT.
SO I'M NOT GOING TO FIGHT MY LEADER. I'M GOING TO STAY HERE AND TAKE CARE OF SICK AND INJURED SHADOWCLAN CATS.
THAT'S WHAT I NEED TO DO. THAT'S WHAT YELLOWFANG WOULD WANT ME TO DO.

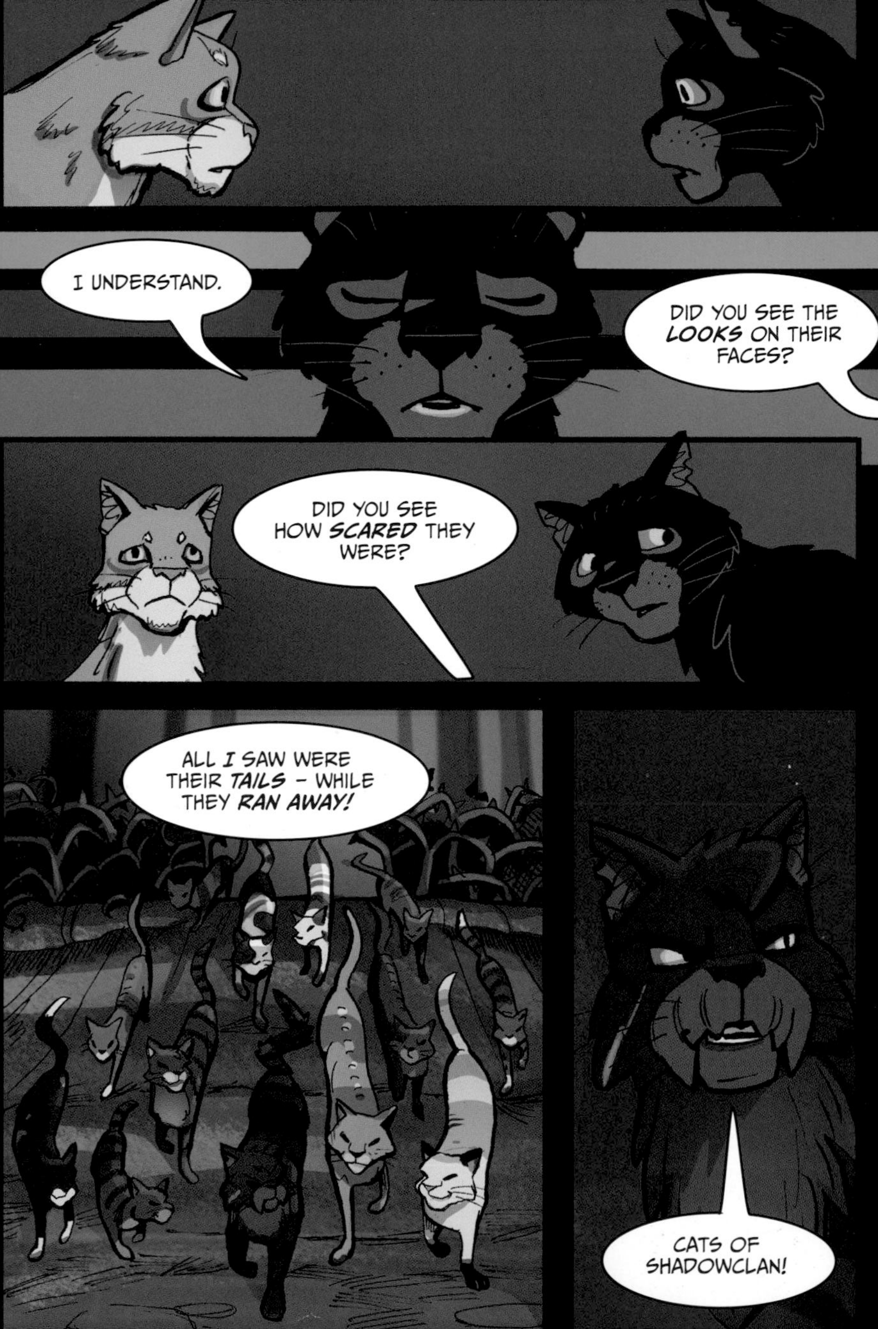
I UNDERSTAND.
DID YOU SEE THE LOOKS ON THEIR FACES?
DID YOU SEE HOW SCARED THEY WERE?
ALL I SAW WERE THEIR TAILS - WHILE THEY RAN AWAY!
CATS OF SHADOWCLAN!

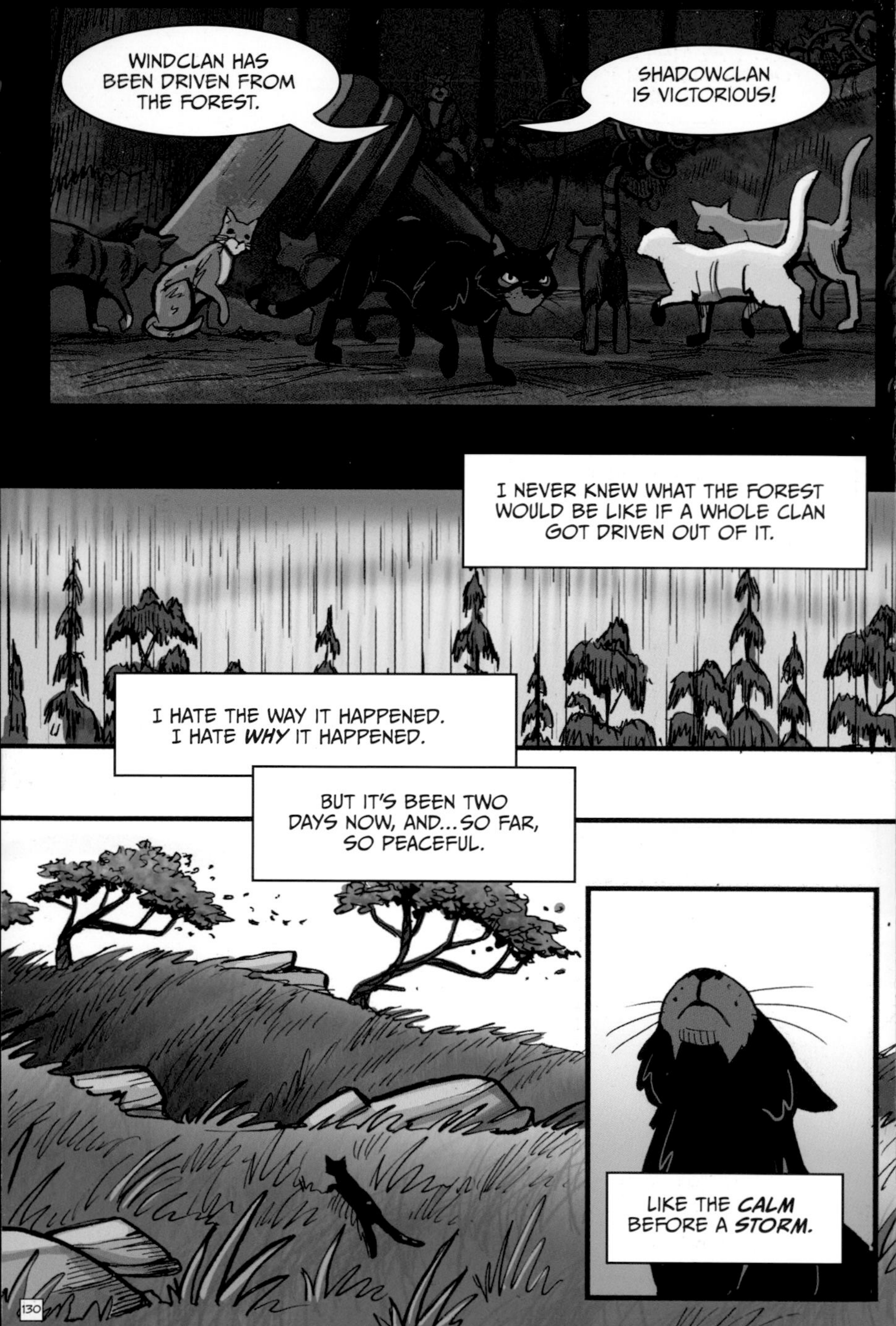
WINDCLAN HAS BEEN DRIVEN FROM THE FOREST.
SHADOWCLAN IS VICTORIOUS!
I NEVER KNEW WHAT THE FOREST WOULD BE LIKE IF A WHOLE CLAN GOT DRIVEN OUT OF IT.
I HATE THE WAY IT HAPPENED. I HATE *WHY* IT HAPPENED.
BUT IT'S BEEN TWO DAYS NOW, AND...SO FAR, SO PEACEFUL.
LIKE THE *CALM* BEFORE A *STORM.*

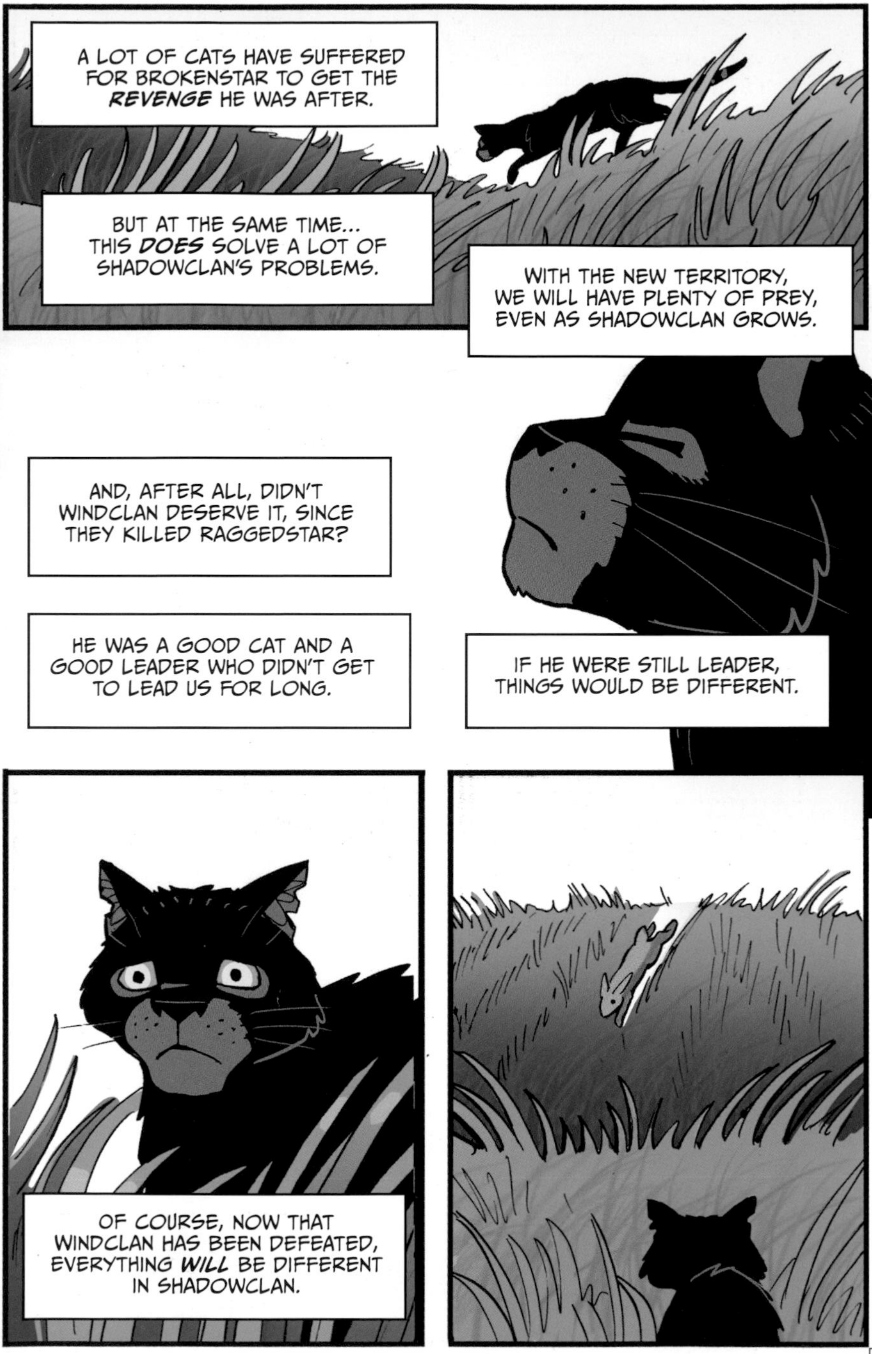
A LOT OF CATS HAVE SUFFERED FOR BROKENSTAR TO GET THE ***REVENGE*** HE WAS AFTER.
BUT AT THE SAME TIME... THIS ***DOES*** SOLVE A LOT OF SHADOWCLAN'S PROBLEMS.
WITH THE NEW TERRITORY, WE WILL HAVE PLENTY OF PREY, EVEN AS SHADOWCLAN GROWS.
AND, AFTER ALL, DIDN'T WINDCLAN DESERVE IT, SINCE THEY KILLED RAGGEDSTAR?
HE WAS A GOOD CAT AND A GOOD LEADER WHO DIDN'T GET TO LEAD US FOR LONG.
IF HE WERE STILL LEADER, THINGS WOULD BE DIFFERENT.
OF COURSE, NOW THAT WINDCLAN HAS BEEN DEFEATED, EVERYTHING ***WILL*** BE DIFFERENT IN SHADOWCLAN.

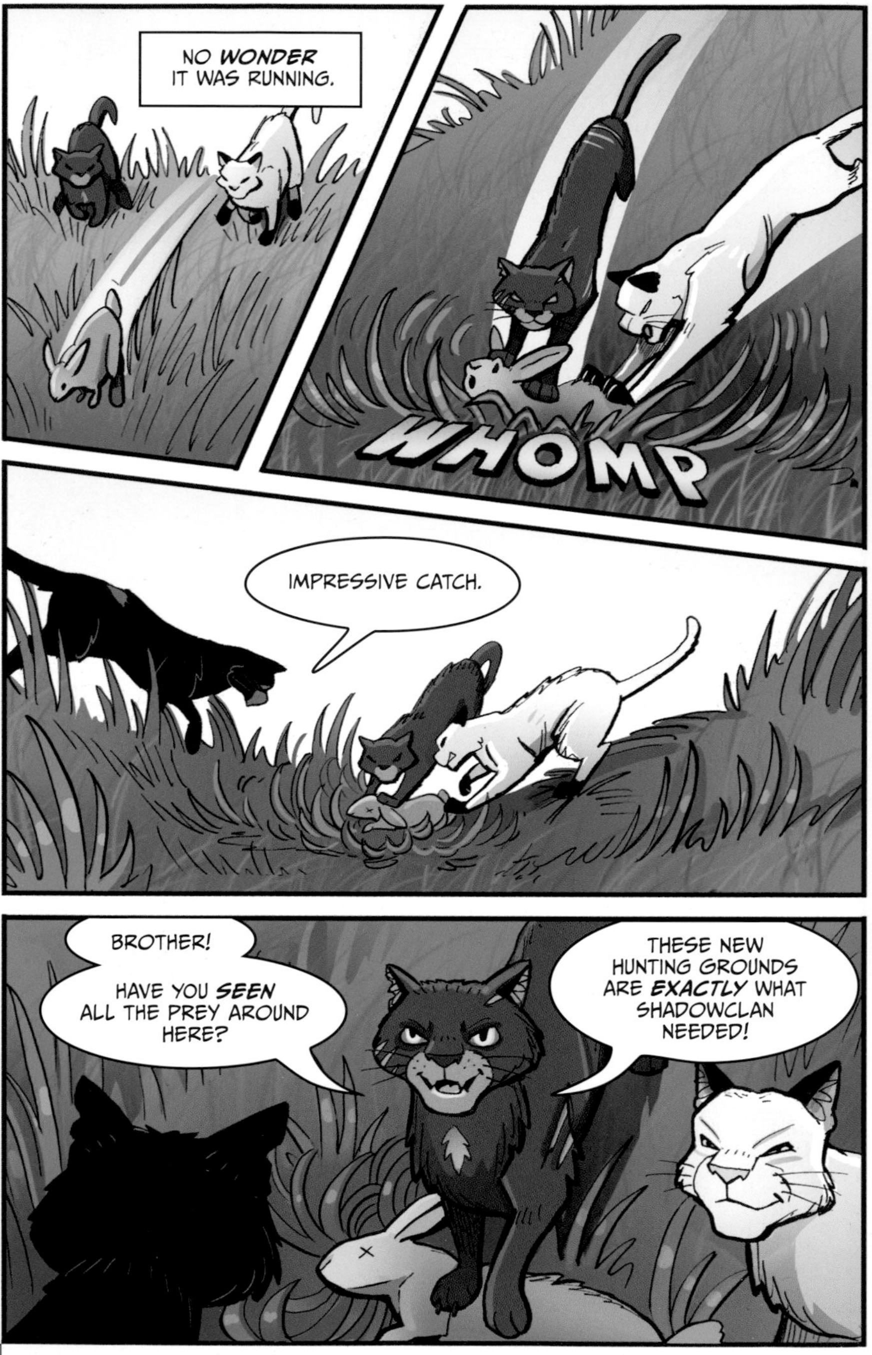
NO WONDER IT WAS RUNNING.
WHOMP
IMPRESSIVE CATCH.
BROTHER!
HAVE YOU SEEN ALL THE PREY AROUND HERE?
THESE NEW HUNTING GROUNDS ARE EXACTLY WHAT SHADOWCLAN NEEDED!

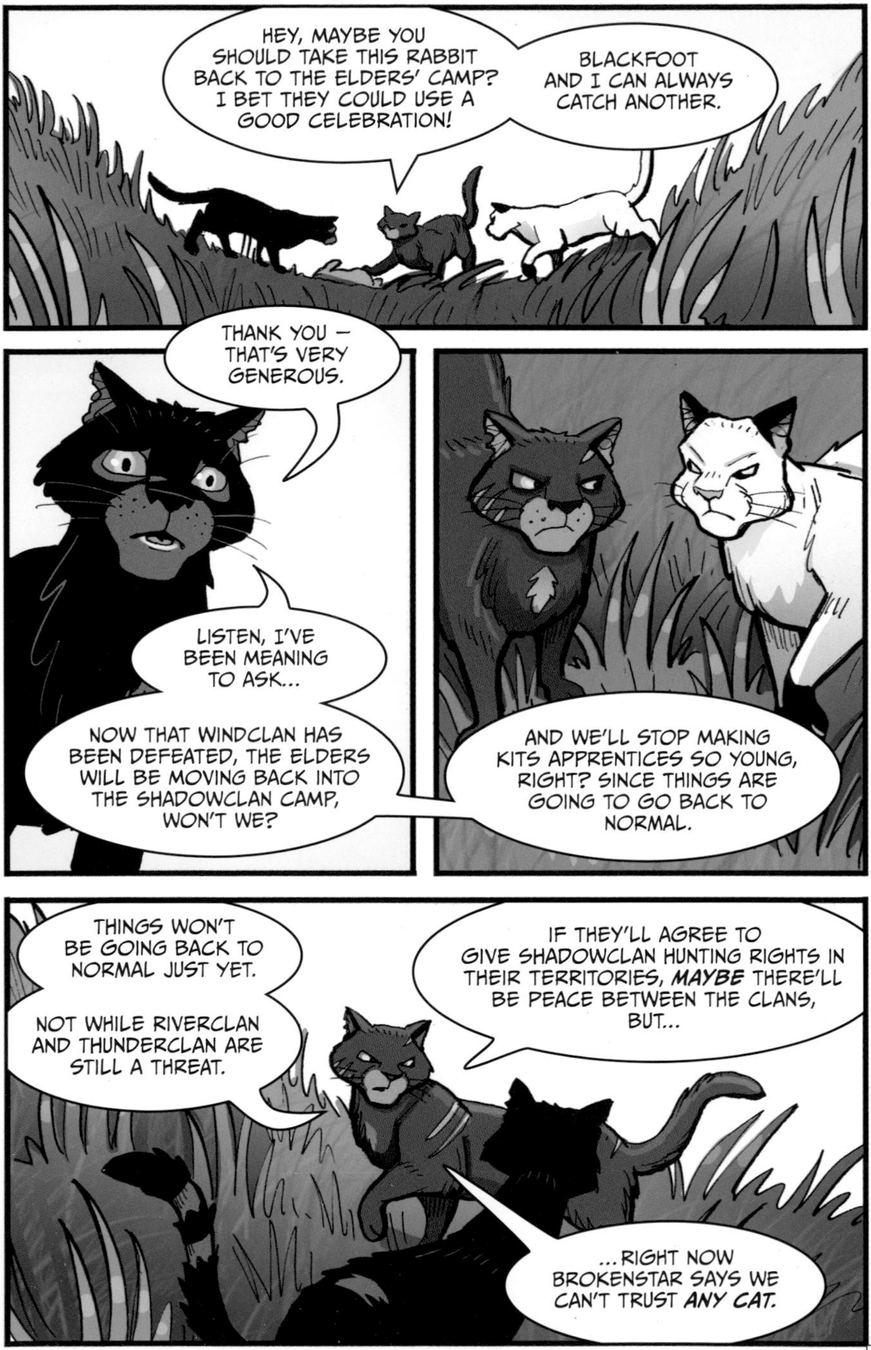
HEY, MAYBE YOU SHOULD TAKE THIS RABBIT BACK TO THE ELDERS' CAMP? I BET THEY COULD USE A GOOD CELEBRATION!
BLACKFOOT AND I CAN ALWAYS CATCH ANOTHER.
THANK YOU — THAT'S VERY GENEROUS.
LISTEN, I'VE BEEN MEANING TO ASK...
NOW THAT WINDCLAN HAS BEEN DEFEATED, THE ELDERS WILL BE MOVING BACK INTO THE SHADOWCLAN CAMP, WON'T WE?
AND WE'LL STOP MAKING KITS APPRENTICES SO YOUNG, RIGHT? SINCE THINGS ARE GOING TO GO BACK TO NORMAL.
THINGS WON'T BE GOING BACK TO NORMAL JUST YET.
NOT WHILE RIVERCLAN AND THUNDERCLAN ARE STILL A THREAT.
IF THEY'LL AGREE TO GIVE SHADOWCLAN HUNTING RIGHTS IN THEIR TERRITORIES, MAYBE THERE'LL BE PEACE BETWEEN THE CLANS, BUT...
...RIGHT NOW BROKENSTAR SAYS WE CAN'T TRUST ANY CAT.

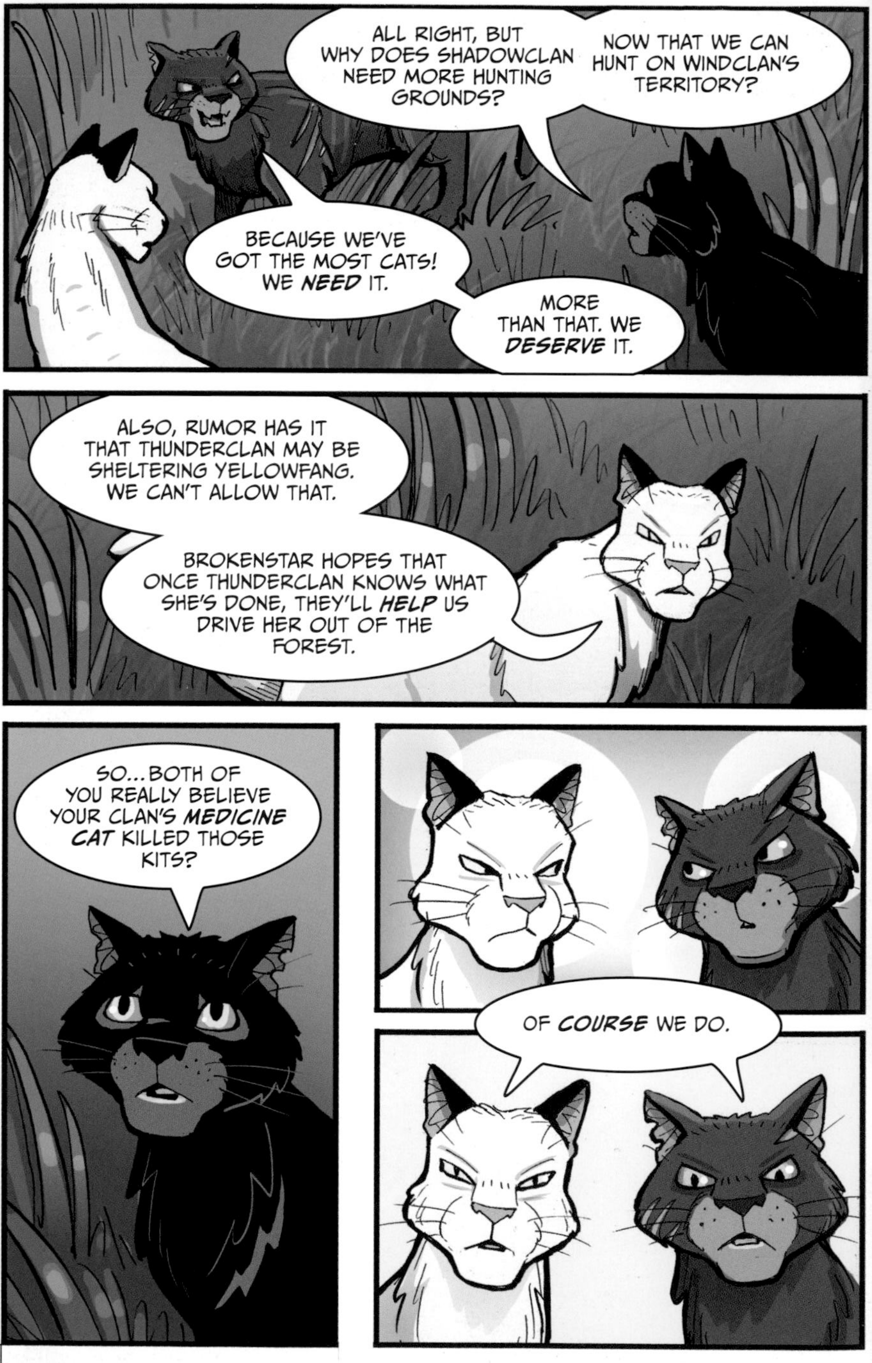
ALL RIGHT, BUT WHY DOES SHADOWCLAN NEED MORE HUNTING GROUNDS?
NOW THAT WE CAN HUNT ON WINDCLAN'S TERRITORY?
BECAUSE WE'VE GOT THE MOST CATS! WE *NEED* IT.
MORE THAN THAT. WE *DESERVE* IT.
ALSO, RUMOR HAS IT THAT THUNDERCLAN MAY BE SHELTERING YELLOWFANG. WE CAN'T ALLOW THAT.
BROKENSTAR HOPES THAT ONCE THUNDERCLAN KNOWS WHAT SHE'S DONE, THEY'LL *HELP* US DRIVE HER OUT OF THE FOREST.
SO...BOTH OF YOU REALLY BELIEVE YOUR CLAN'S *MEDICINE CAT* KILLED THOSE KITS?
OF *COURSE* WE DO.

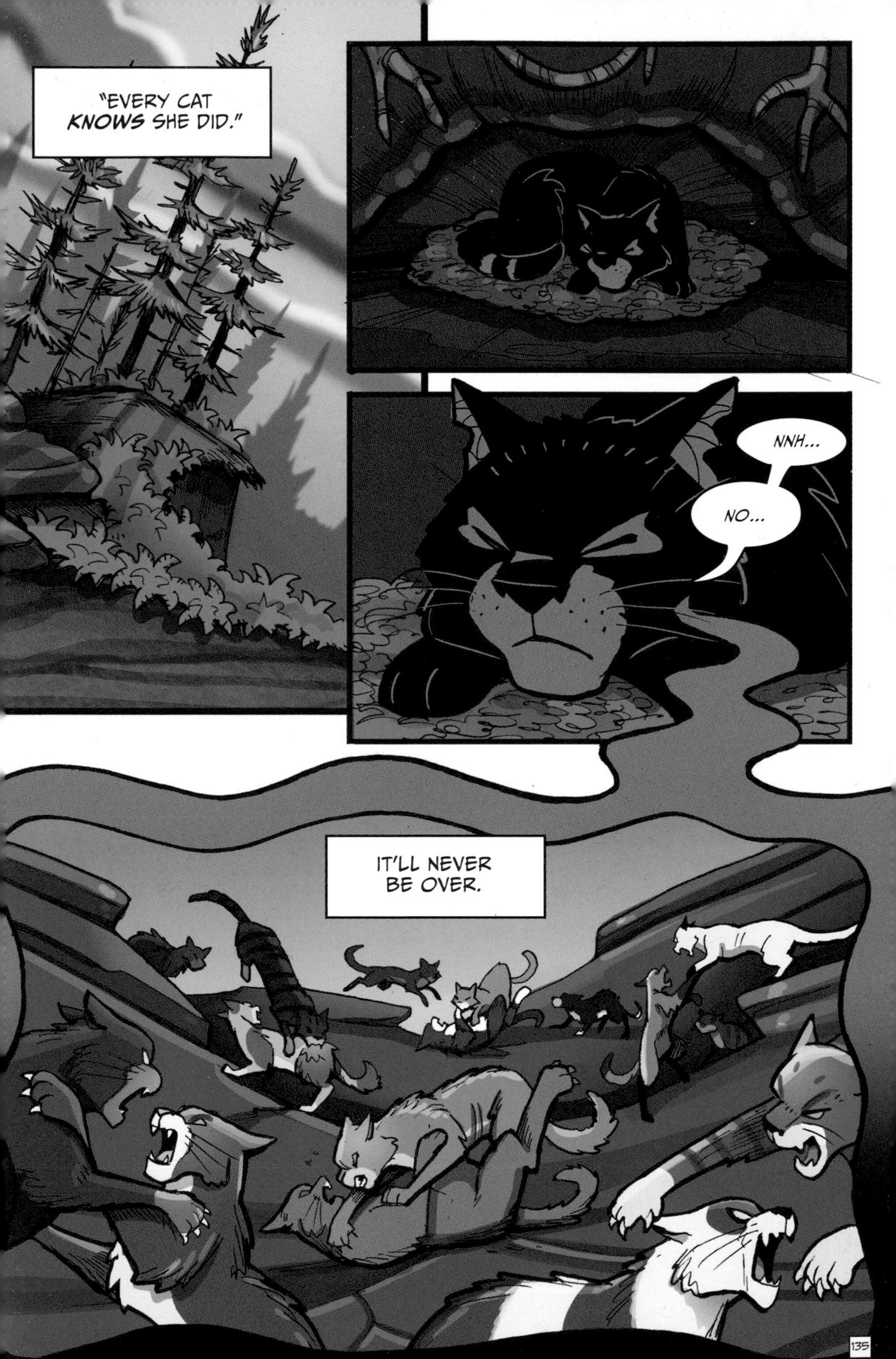
"EVERY CAT
KNOWS SHE DID."
NNH...
NO...
IT'LL NEVER
BE OVER.

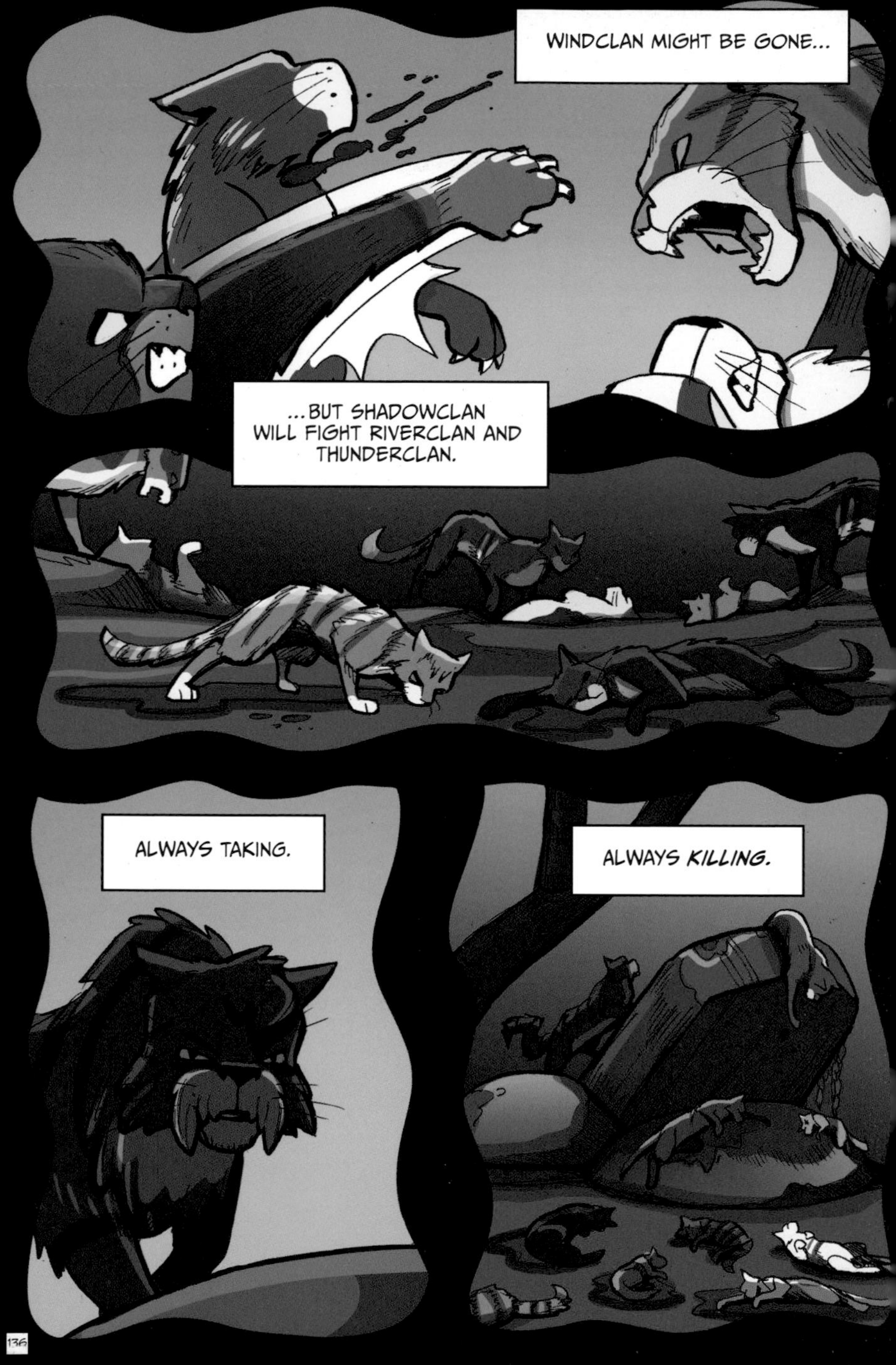
WINDCLAN MIGHT BE GONE...
...BUT SHADOWCLAN WILL FIGHT RIVERCLAN AND THUNDERCLAN.
ALWAYS TAKING.
ALWAYS *KILLING.*

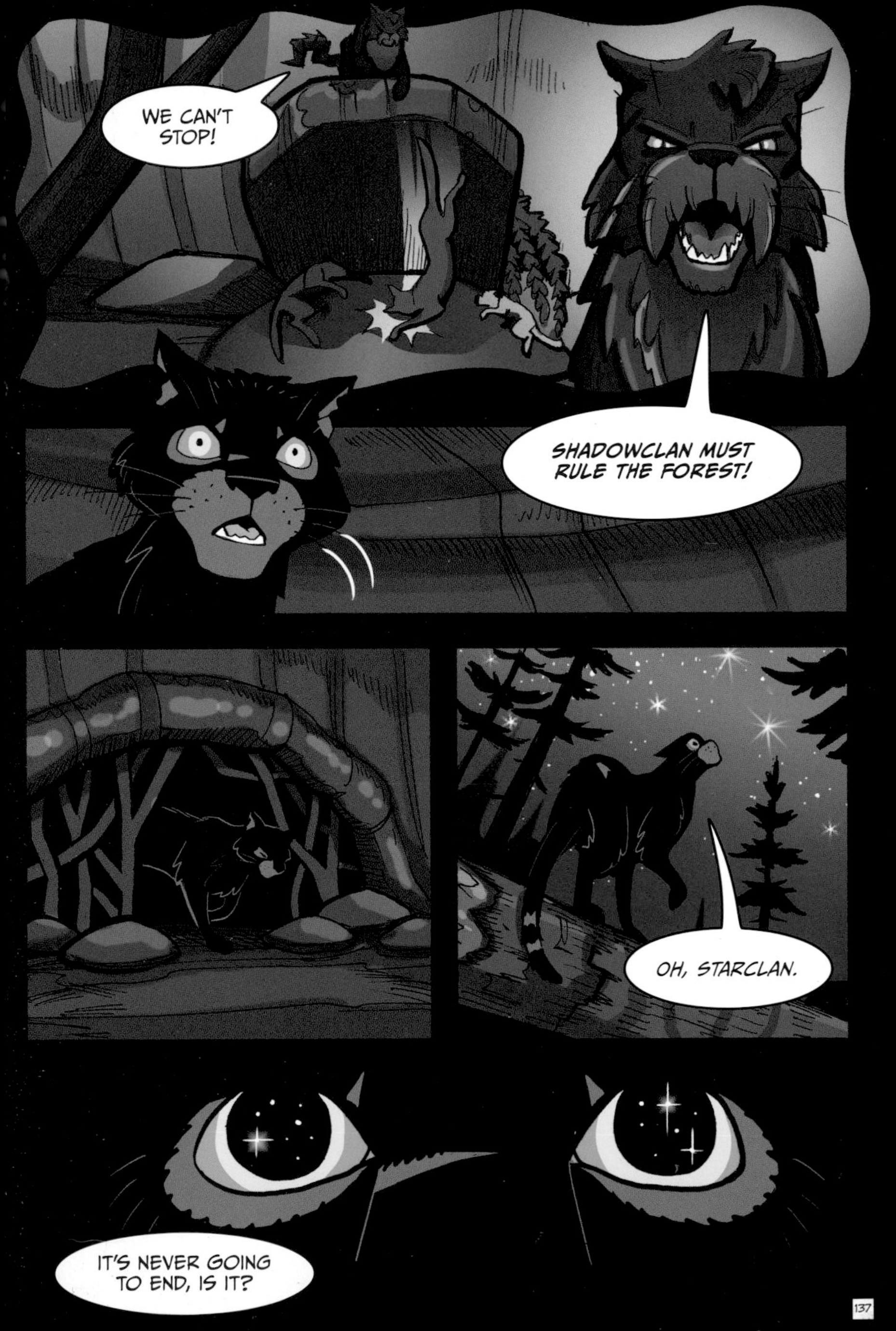
WE CAN'T STOP!
SHADOWCLAN MUST RULE THE FOREST!
OH, STARCLAN.
IT'S NEVER GOING TO END, IS IT?

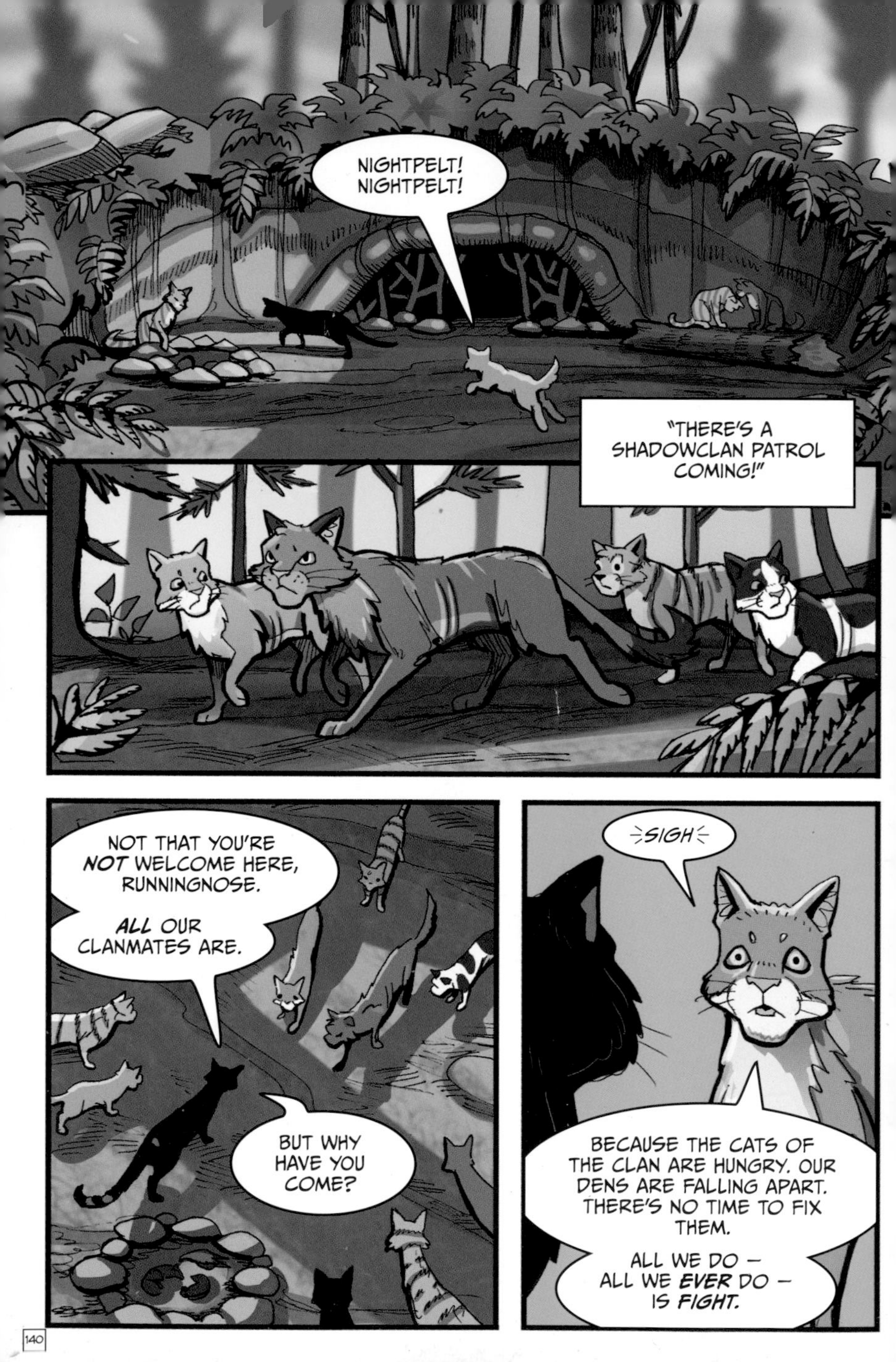
NIGHTPELT! NIGHTPELT!
"THERE'S A SHADOWCLAN PATROL COMING!"
NOT THAT YOU'RE *NOT* WELCOME HERE, RUNNINGNOSE.
ALL OUR CLANMATES ARE.
BUT WHY HAVE YOU COME?
SIGH
BECAUSE THE CATS OF THE CLAN ARE HUNGRY. OUR DENS ARE FALLING APART. THERE'S NO TIME TO FIX THEM.
ALL WE DO – ALL WE *EVER* DO – IS *FIGHT*.

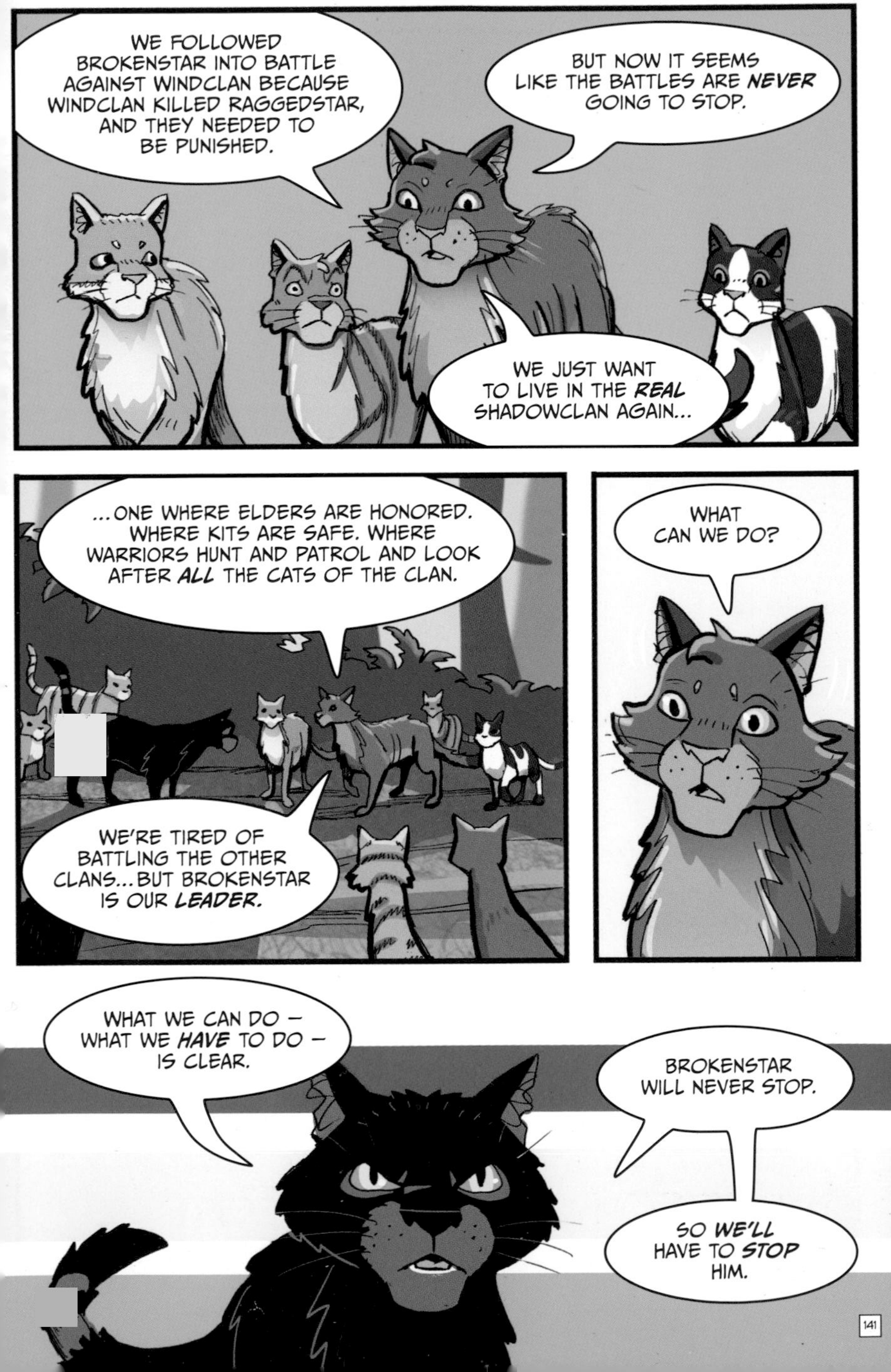

WE FOLLOWED BROKENSTAR INTO BATTLE AGAINST WINDCLAN BECAUSE WINDCLAN KILLED RAGGEDSTAR, AND THEY NEEDED TO BE PUNISHED.
BUT NOW IT SEEMS LIKE THE BATTLES ARE *NEVER* GOING TO STOP.
WE JUST WANT TO LIVE IN THE *REAL* SHADOWCLAN AGAIN...
...ONE WHERE ELDERS ARE HONORED. WHERE KITS ARE SAFE. WHERE WARRIORS HUNT AND PATROL AND LOOK AFTER *ALL* THE CATS OF THE CLAN.
WE'RE TIRED OF BATTLING THE OTHER CLANS...BUT BROKENSTAR IS OUR *LEADER.*
WHAT CAN WE DO?
WHAT WE CAN DO — WHAT WE *HAVE* TO DO — IS CLEAR.
BROKENSTAR WILL NEVER STOP.
SO *WE'LL* HAVE TO *STOP* HIM.

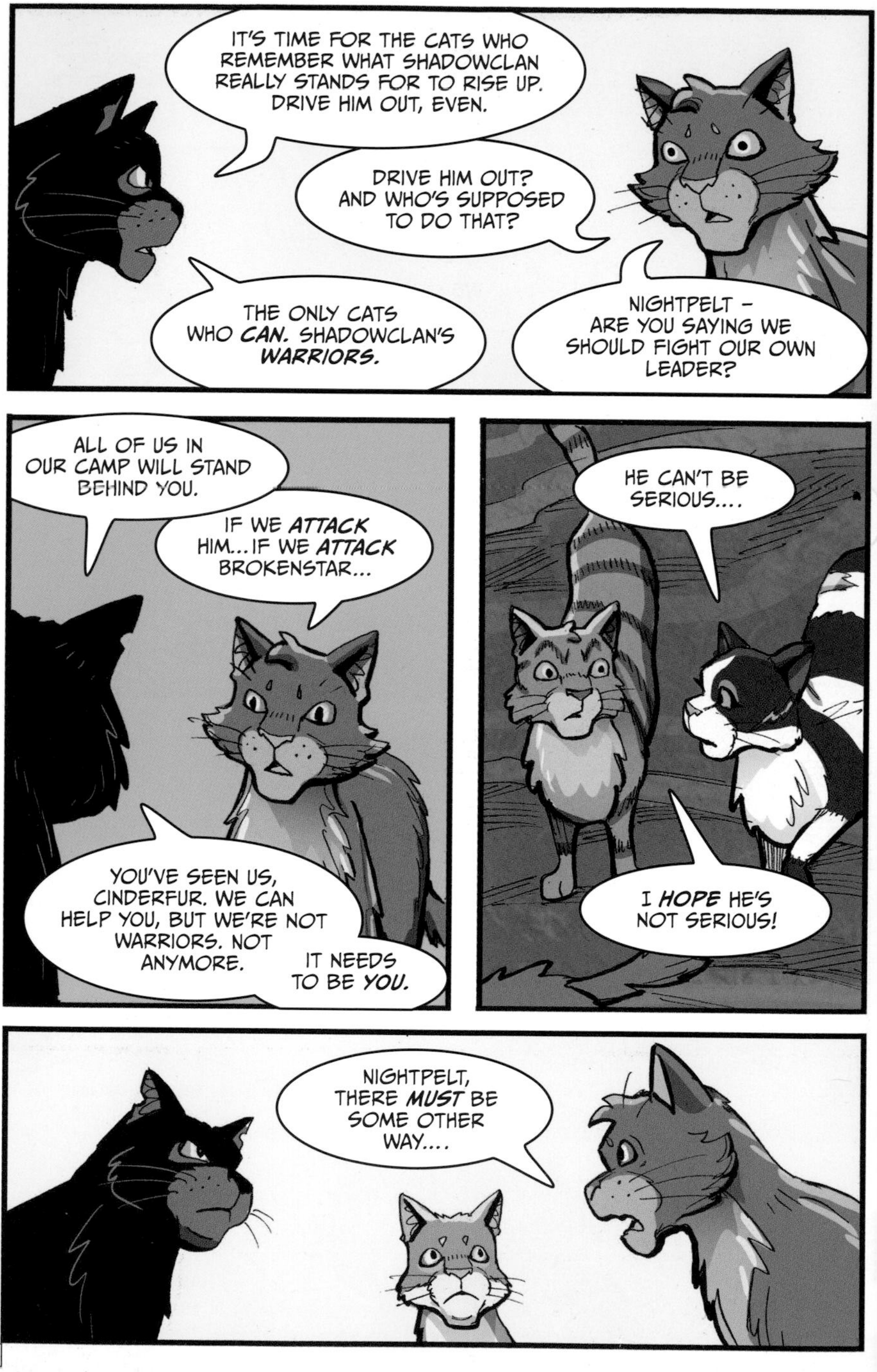
IT'S TIME FOR THE CATS WHO REMEMBER WHAT SHADOWCLAN REALLY STANDS FOR TO RISE UP. DRIVE HIM OUT, EVEN.
DRIVE HIM OUT? AND WHO'S SUPPOSED TO DO THAT?
THE ONLY CATS WHO *CAN.* SHADOWCLAN'S *WARRIORS.*
NIGHTPELT – ARE YOU SAYING WE SHOULD FIGHT OUR OWN LEADER?
ALL OF US IN OUR CAMP WILL STAND BEHIND YOU.
IF WE *ATTACK* HIM...IF WE *ATTACK* BROKENSTAR...
YOU'VE SEEN US, CINDERFUR. WE CAN HELP YOU, BUT WE'RE NOT WARRIORS. NOT ANYMORE.
IT NEEDS TO BE *YOU.*
HE CAN'T BE SERIOUS....
I *HOPE* HE'S NOT SERIOUS!
NIGHTPELT, THERE *MUST* BE SOME OTHER WAY....

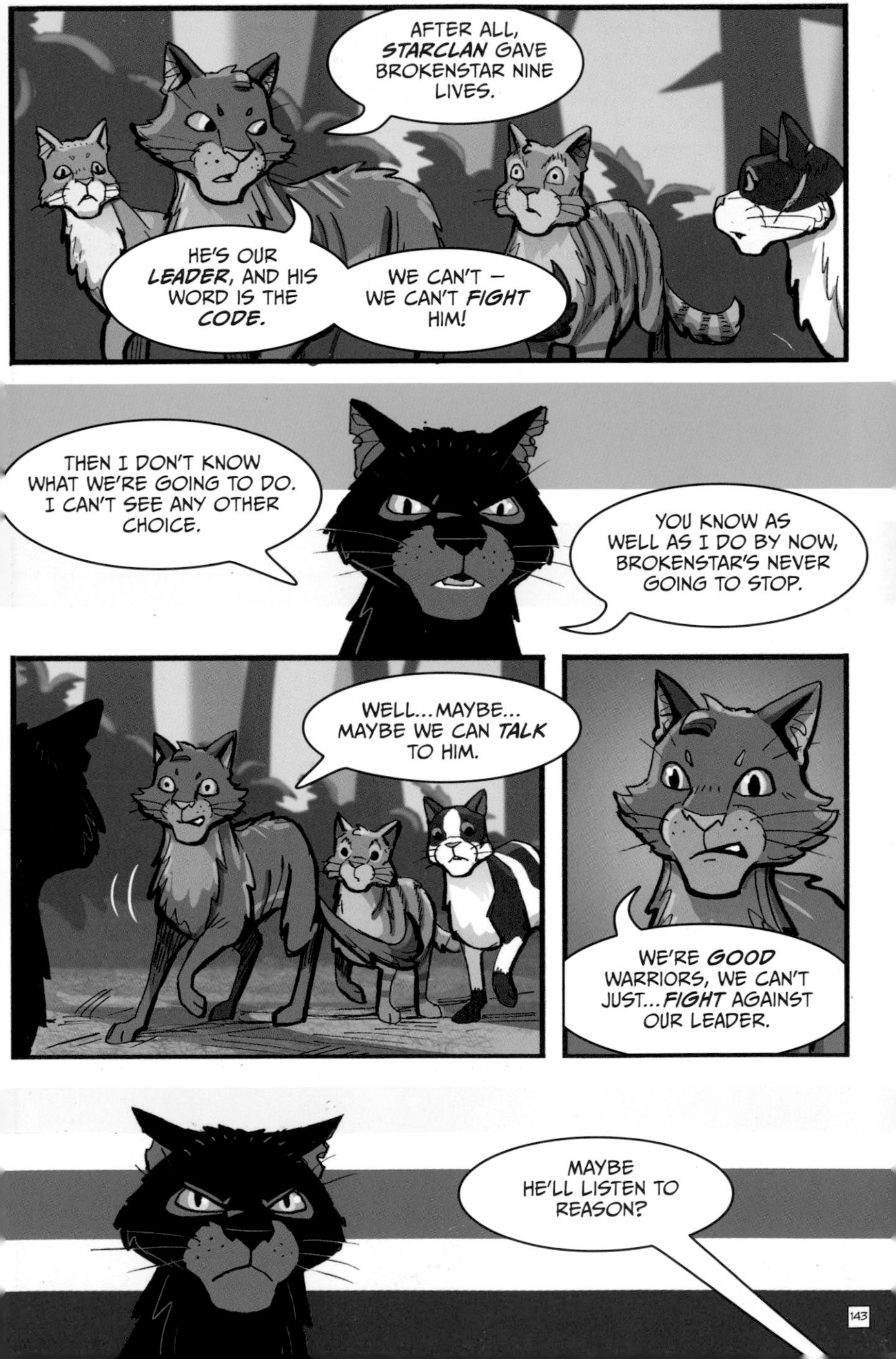
AFTER ALL, STARCLAN GAVE BROKENSTAR NINE LIVES.
HE'S OUR LEADER, AND HIS WORD IS THE CODE.
WE CAN'T — WE CAN'T FIGHT HIM!
THEN I DON'T KNOW WHAT WE'RE GOING TO DO. I CAN'T SEE ANY OTHER CHOICE.
YOU KNOW AS WELL AS I DO BY NOW, BROKENSTAR'S NEVER GOING TO STOP.
WELL...MAYBE... MAYBE WE CAN TALK TO HIM.
WE'RE GOOD WARRIORS, WE CAN'T JUST...FIGHT AGAINST OUR LEADER.
MAYBE HE'LL LISTEN TO REASON?

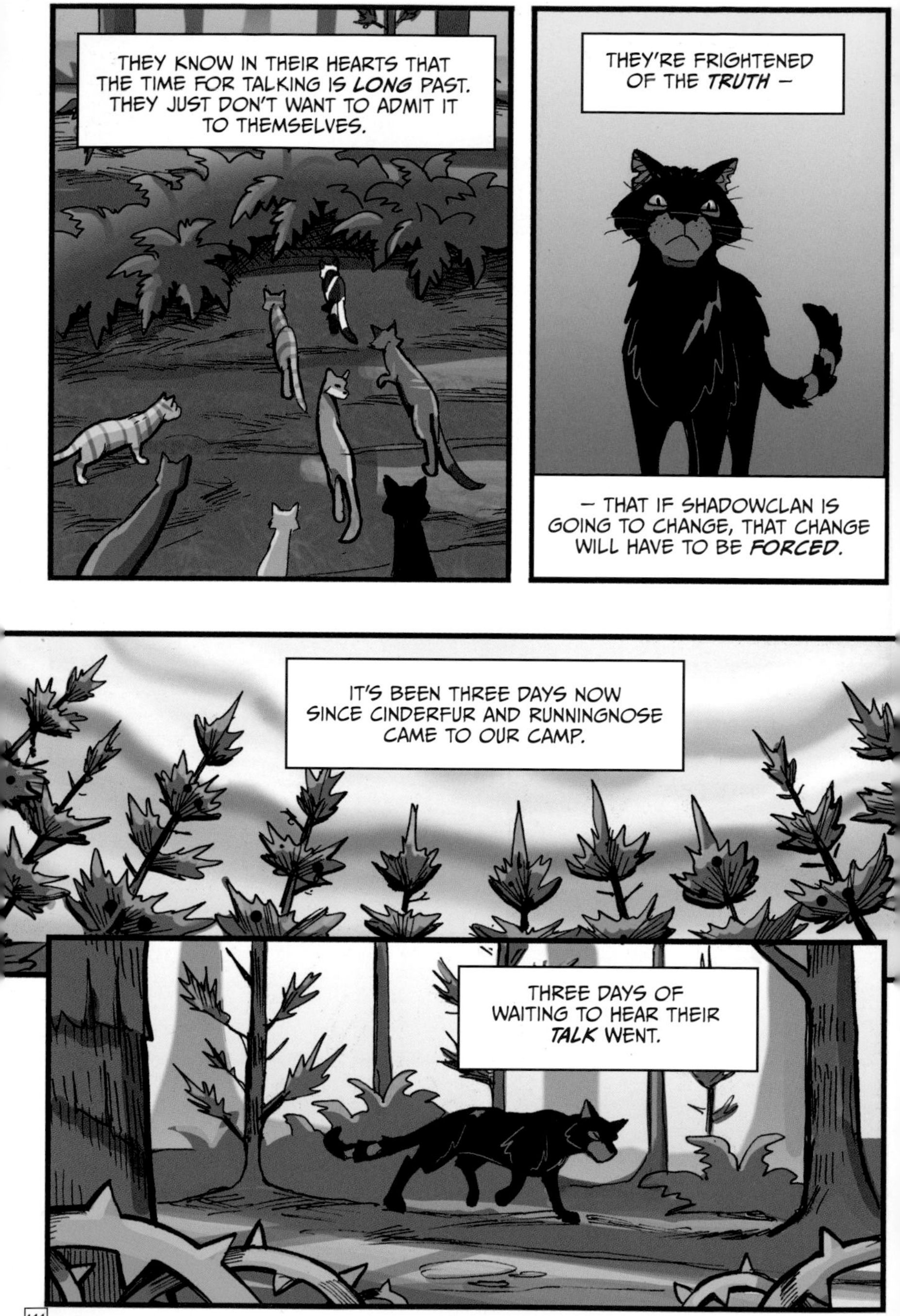
THEY KNOW IN THEIR HEARTS THAT THE TIME FOR TALKING IS *LONG* PAST. THEY JUST DON'T WANT TO ADMIT IT TO THEMSELVES.
THEY'RE FRIGHTENED OF THE *TRUTH* –
– THAT IF SHADOWCLAN IS GOING TO CHANGE, THAT CHANGE WILL HAVE TO BE *FORCED*.
IT'S BEEN THREE DAYS NOW SINCE CINDERFUR AND RUNNINGNOSE CAME TO OUR CAMP.
THREE DAYS OF WAITING TO HEAR THEIR *TALK* WENT.

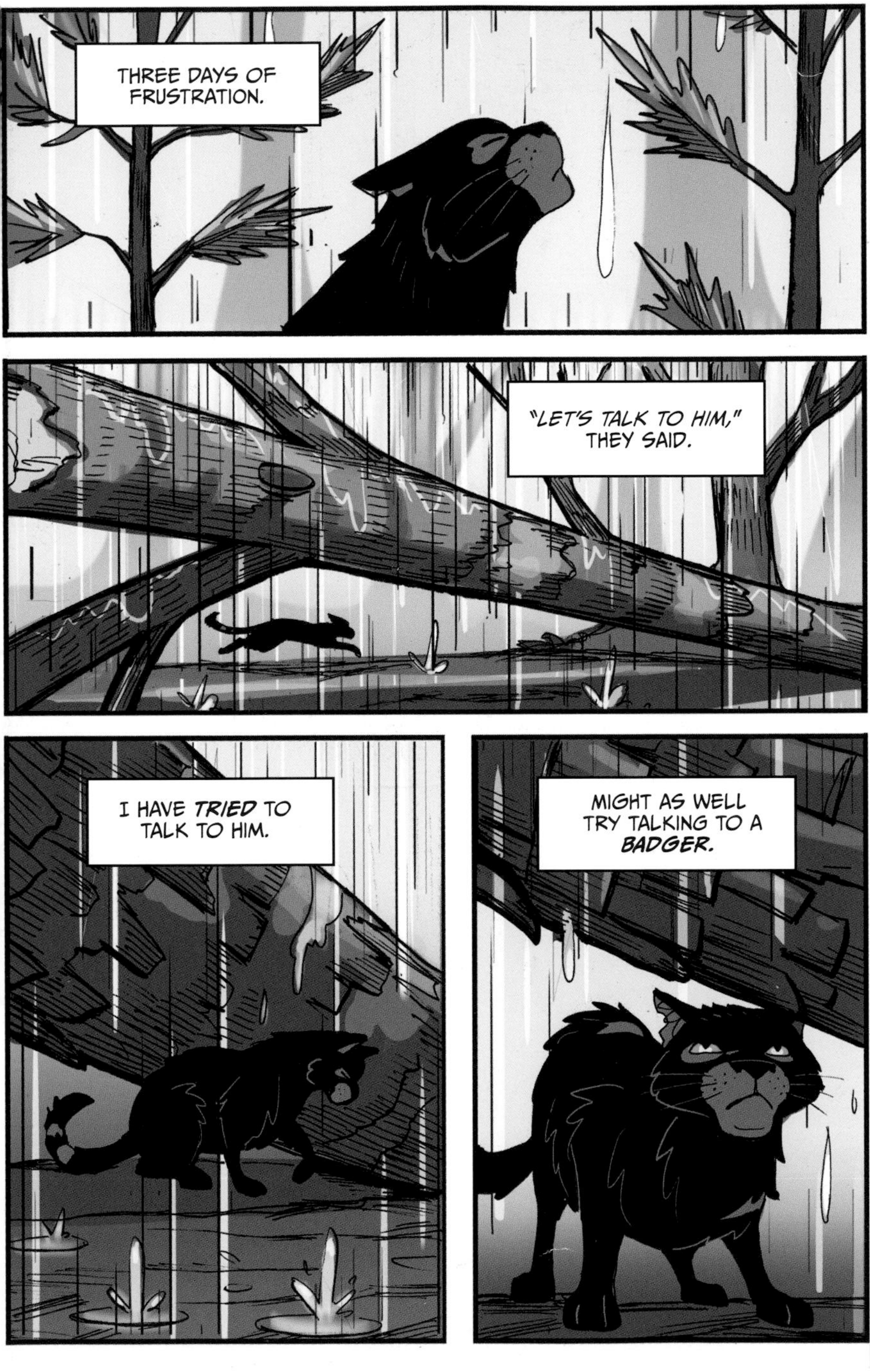
THREE DAYS OF FRUSTRATION.
"LET'S TALK TO HIM," THEY SAID.
I HAVE TRIED TO TALK TO HIM.
MIGHT AS WELL TRY TALKING TO A BADGER.

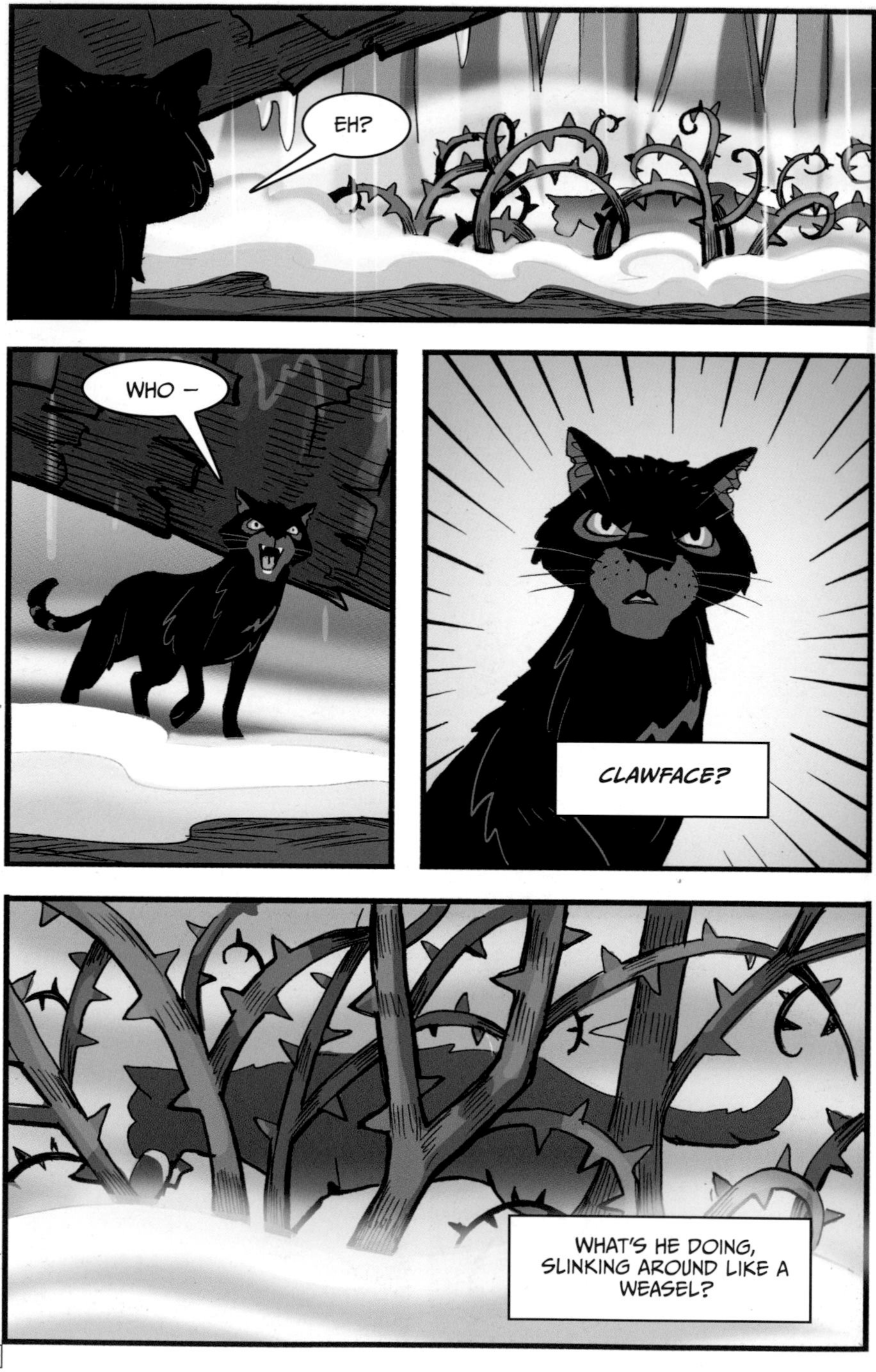
EH?
WHO –
CLAWFACE?
WHAT'S HE DOING, SLINKING AROUND LIKE A WEASEL?

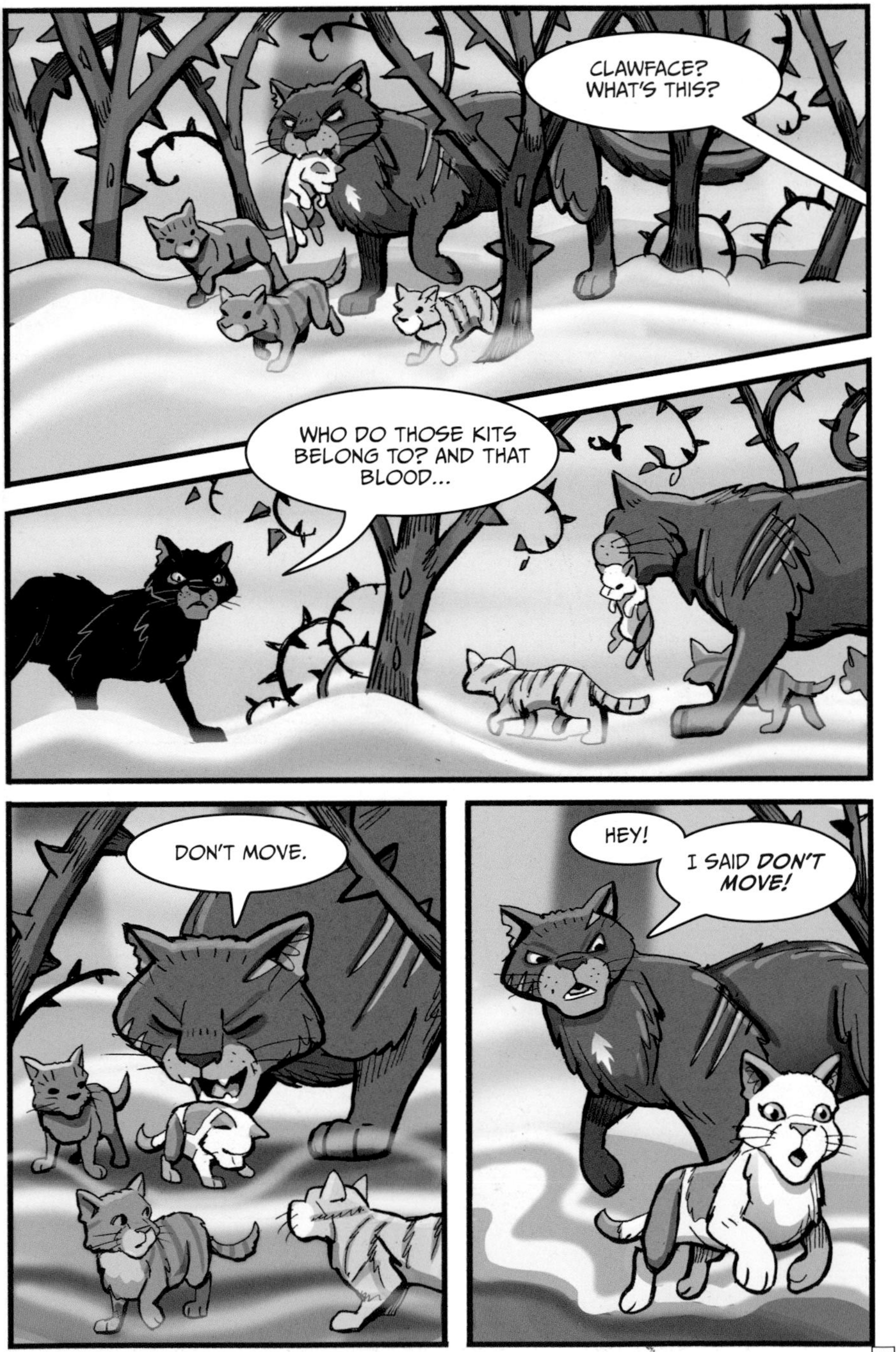
CLAWFACE? WHAT'S THIS?
WHO DO THOSE KITS BELONG TO? AND THAT BLOOD...
DON'T MOVE.
HEY!
I SAID *DON'T MOVE!*

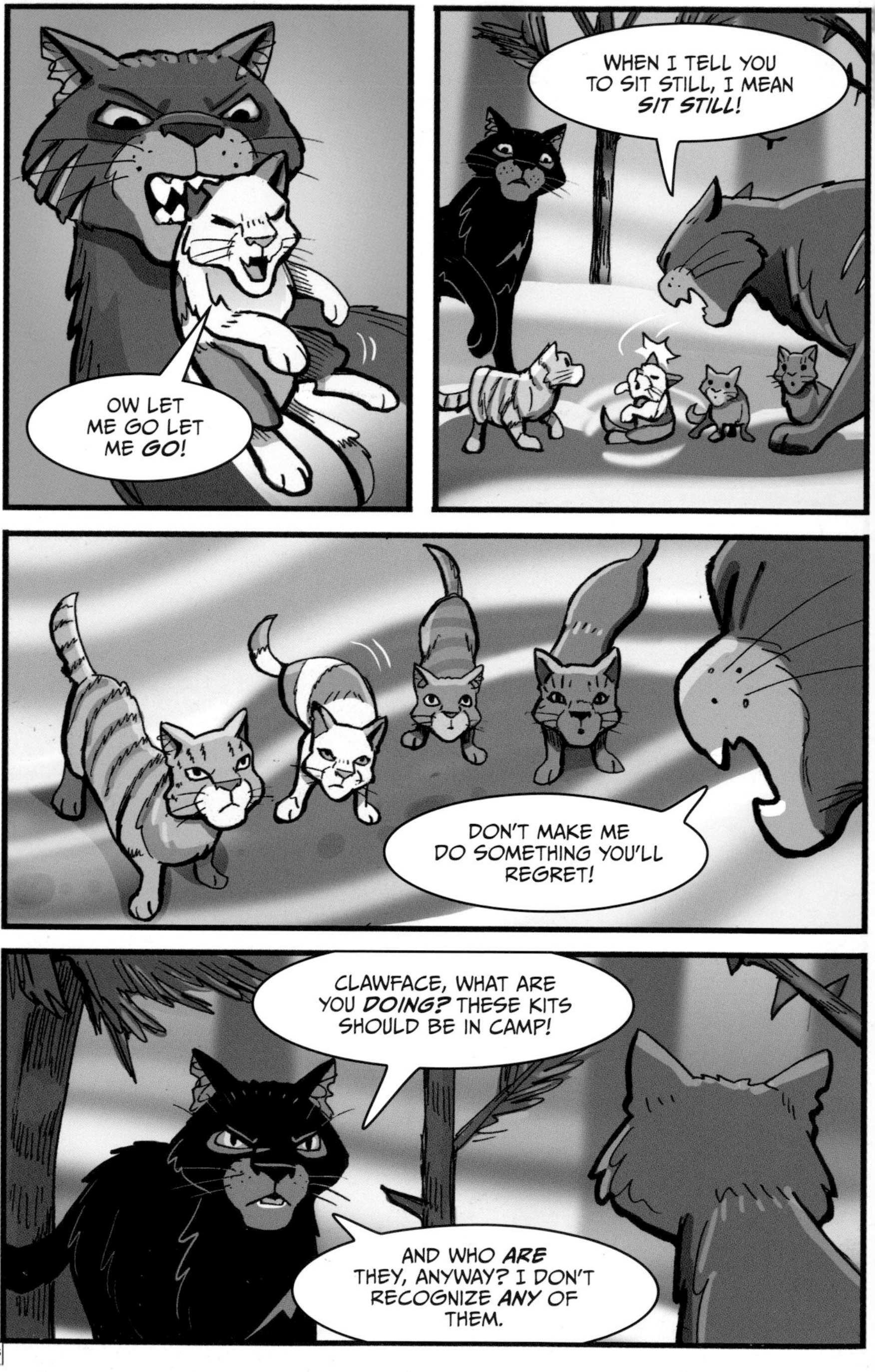
OW LET ME GO LET ME GO!
WHEN I TELL YOU TO SIT STILL, I MEAN SIT STILL!
DON'T MAKE ME DO SOMETHING YOU'LL REGRET!
CLAWFACE, WHAT ARE YOU DOING? THESE KITS SHOULD BE IN CAMP!
AND WHO ARE THEY, ANYWAY? I DON'T RECOGNIZE ANY OF THEM.

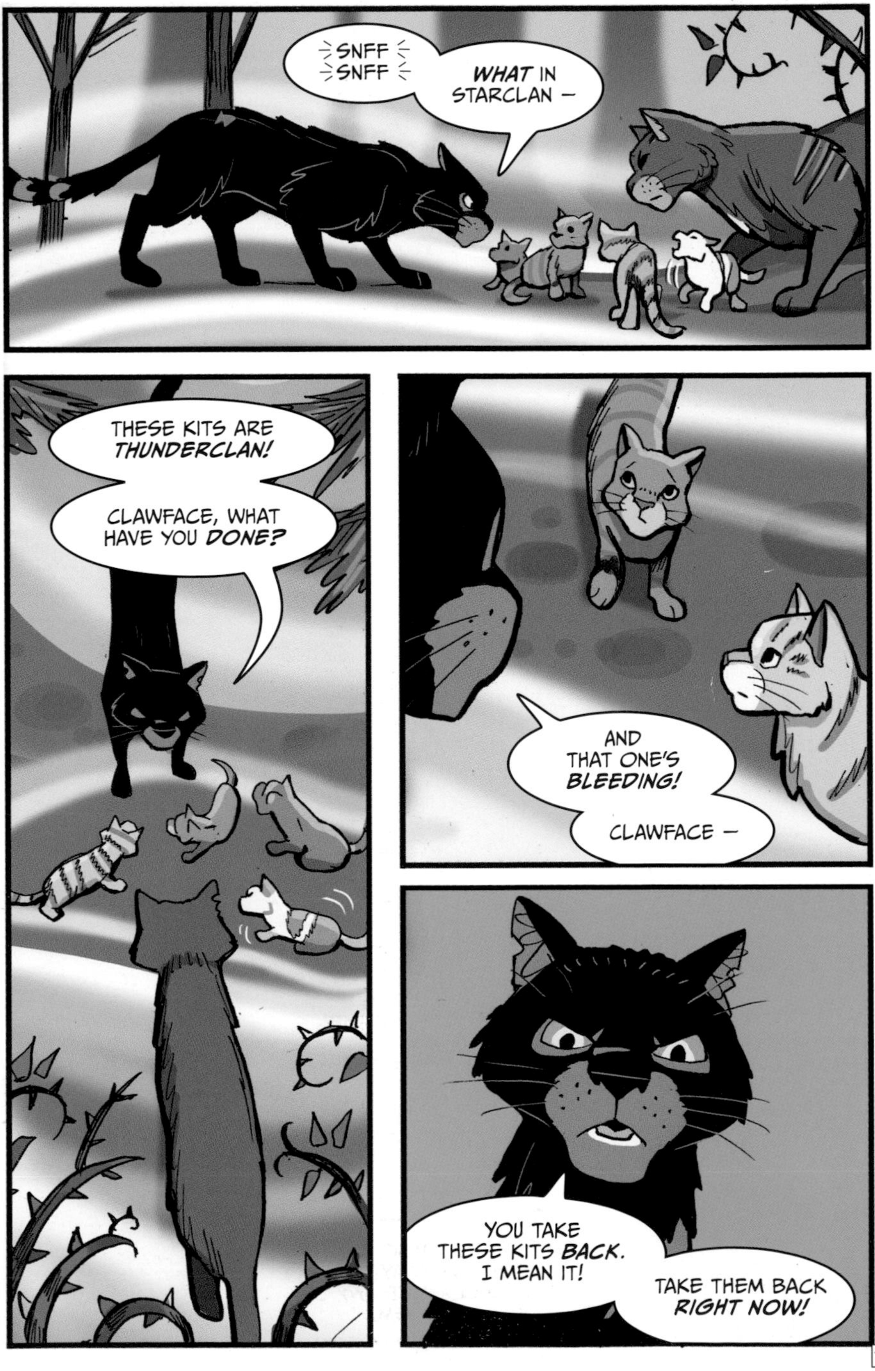
SNFF
SNFF
WHAT IN STARCLAN –
THESE KITS ARE THUNDERCLAN!
CLAWFACE, WHAT HAVE YOU DONE?
AND THAT ONE'S BLEEDING!
CLAWFACE –
YOU TAKE THESE KITS BACK. I MEAN IT!
TAKE THEM BACK RIGHT NOW!

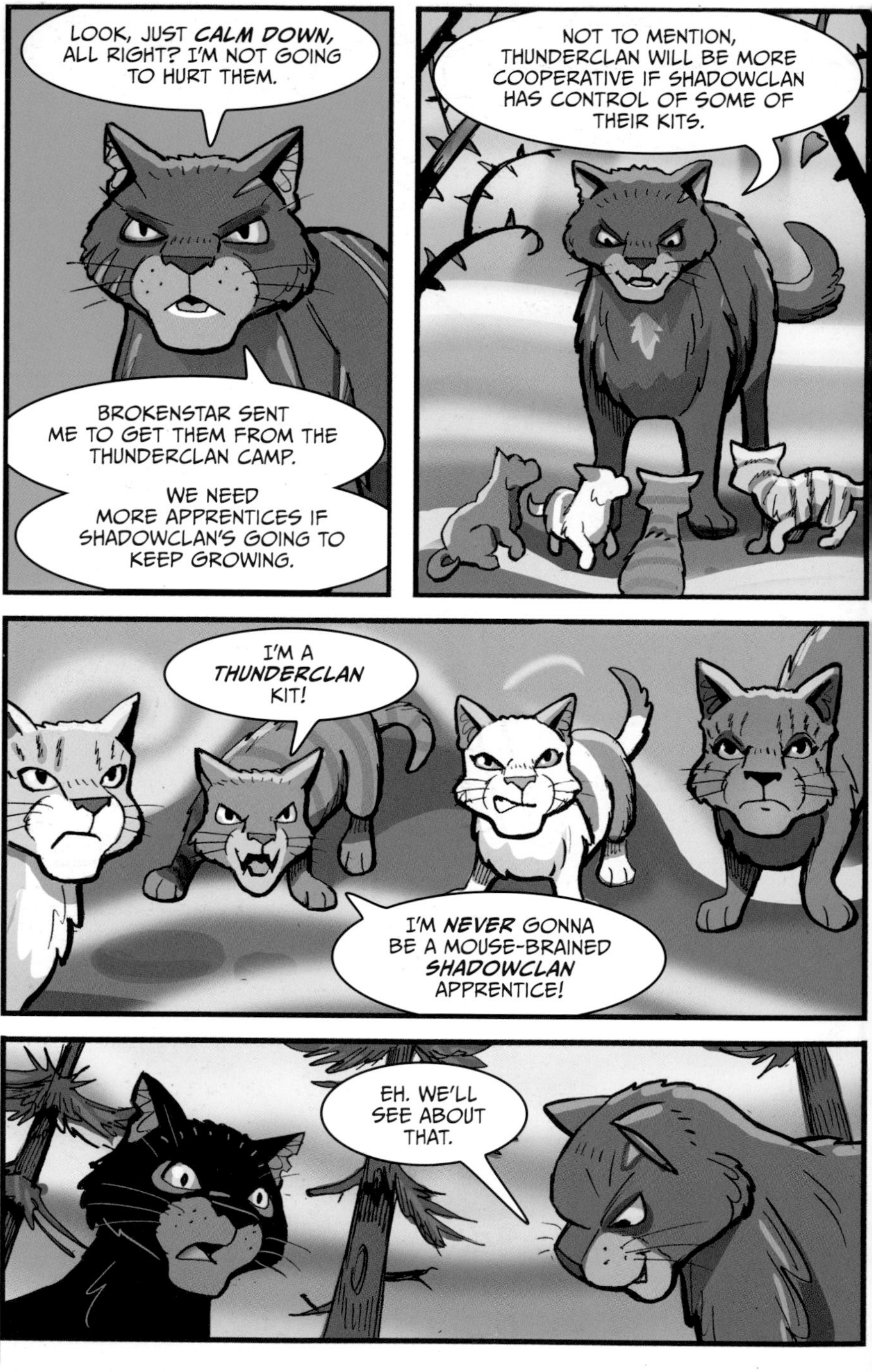
LOOK, JUST CALM DOWN, ALL RIGHT? I'M NOT GOING TO HURT THEM.
BROKENSTAR SENT ME TO GET THEM FROM THE THUNDERCLAN CAMP.
WE NEED MORE APPRENTICES IF SHADOWCLAN'S GOING TO KEEP GROWING.
NOT TO MENTION, THUNDERCLAN WILL BE MORE COOPERATIVE IF SHADOWCLAN HAS CONTROL OF SOME OF THEIR KITS.
I'M A THUNDERCLAN KIT!
I'M NEVER GONNA BE A MOUSE-BRAINED SHADOWCLAN APPRENTICE!
EH. WE'LL SEE ABOUT THAT.

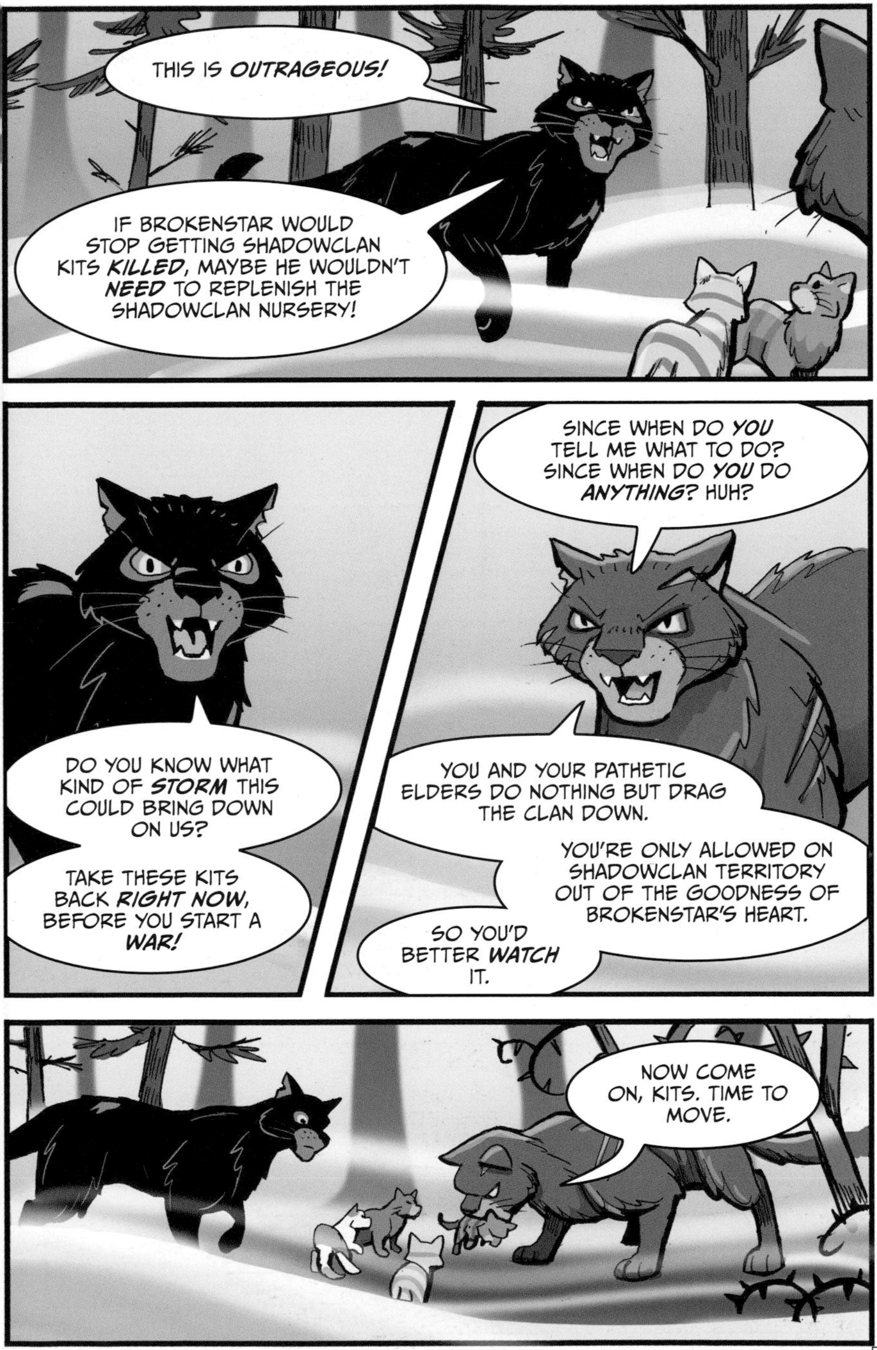
THIS IS OUTRAGEOUS!
IF BROKENSTAR WOULD STOP GETTING SHADOWCLAN KITS KILLED, MAYBE HE WOULDN'T NEED TO REPLENISH THE SHADOWCLAN NURSERY!
SINCE WHEN DO YOU TELL ME WHAT TO DO? SINCE WHEN DO YOU DO ANYTHING? HUH?
DO YOU KNOW WHAT KIND OF STORM THIS COULD BRING DOWN ON US?
TAKE THESE KITS BACK RIGHT NOW, BEFORE YOU START A WAR!
YOU AND YOUR PATHETIC ELDERS DO NOTHING BUT DRAG THE CLAN DOWN.
YOU'RE ONLY ALLOWED ON SHADOWCLAN TERRITORY OUT OF THE GOODNESS OF BROKENSTAR'S HEART.
SO YOU'D BETTER WATCH IT.
NOW COME ON, KITS. TIME TO MOVE.

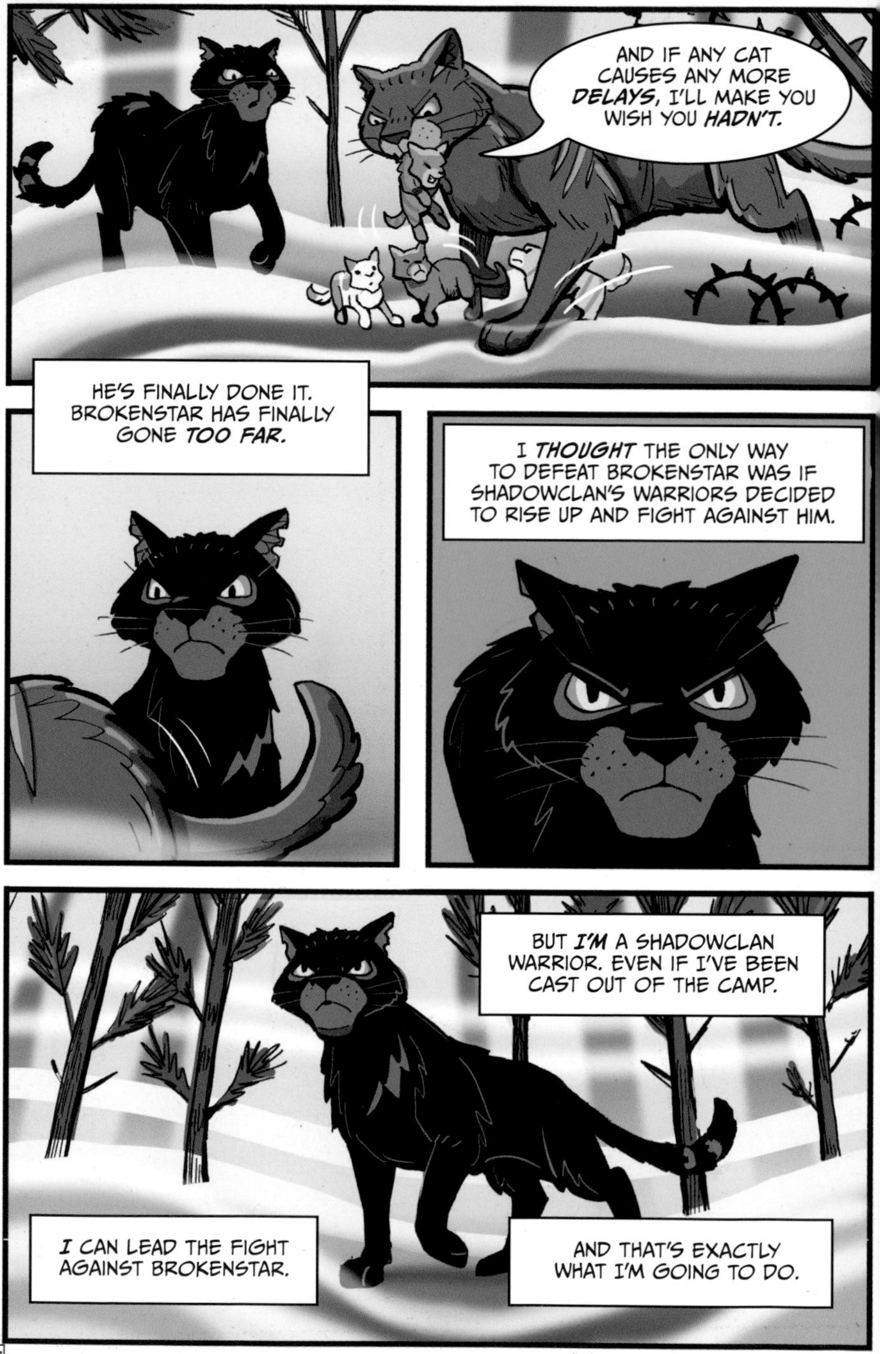
AND IF ANY CAT CAUSES ANY MORE *DELAYS,* I'LL MAKE YOU WISH YOU *HADN'T.*
HE'S FINALLY DONE IT. BROKENSTAR HAS FINALLY GONE *TOO FAR.*
I *THOUGHT* THE ONLY WAY TO DEFEAT BROKENSTAR WAS IF SHADOWCLAN'S WARRIORS DECIDED TO RISE UP AND FIGHT AGAINST HIM.
BUT *I'M* A SHADOWCLAN WARRIOR. EVEN IF I'VE BEEN CAST OUT OF THE CAMP.
I CAN LEAD THE FIGHT AGAINST BROKENSTAR.
AND THAT'S EXACTLY WHAT I'M GOING TO DO.

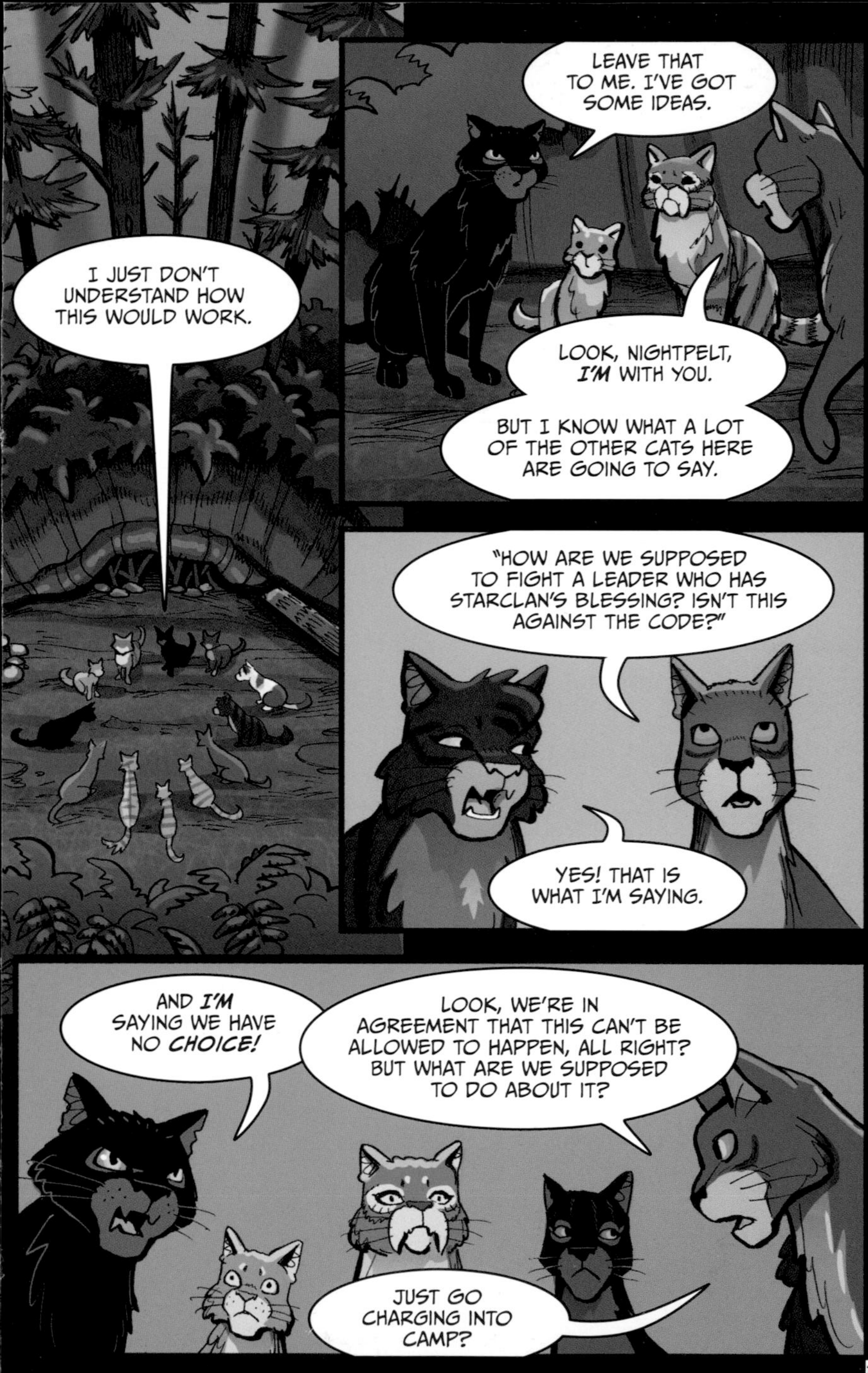
I JUST DON'T UNDERSTAND HOW THIS WOULD WORK.
LEAVE THAT TO ME. I'VE GOT SOME IDEAS.
LOOK, NIGHTPELT, *I'M* WITH YOU.
BUT I KNOW WHAT A LOT OF THE OTHER CATS HERE ARE GOING TO SAY.
"HOW ARE WE SUPPOSED TO FIGHT A LEADER WHO HAS STARCLAN'S BLESSING? ISN'T THIS AGAINST THE CODE?"
YES! THAT IS WHAT I'M SAYING.
AND *I'M* SAYING WE HAVE NO *CHOICE!*
LOOK, WE'RE IN AGREEMENT THAT THIS CAN'T BE ALLOWED TO HAPPEN, ALL RIGHT? BUT WHAT ARE WE SUPPOSED TO DO ABOUT IT?
JUST GO CHARGING INTO CAMP?

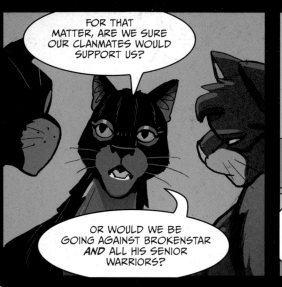

FOR THAT MATTER, ARE WE SURE OUR CLANMATES WOULD SUPPORT US?

OR WOULD WE BE GOING AGAINST BROKENSTAR *AND* ALL HIS SENIOR WARRIORS?

IT'S ONE THING TO SAY YOU'RE GOING TO OVERTHROW A LEADER, NIGHTPELT, BUT HOW DO YOU ACTUALLY *DO* IT? SPECIFICALLY?

NIGHTPELT!

CRASH

I NEED TO TALK TO YOU.

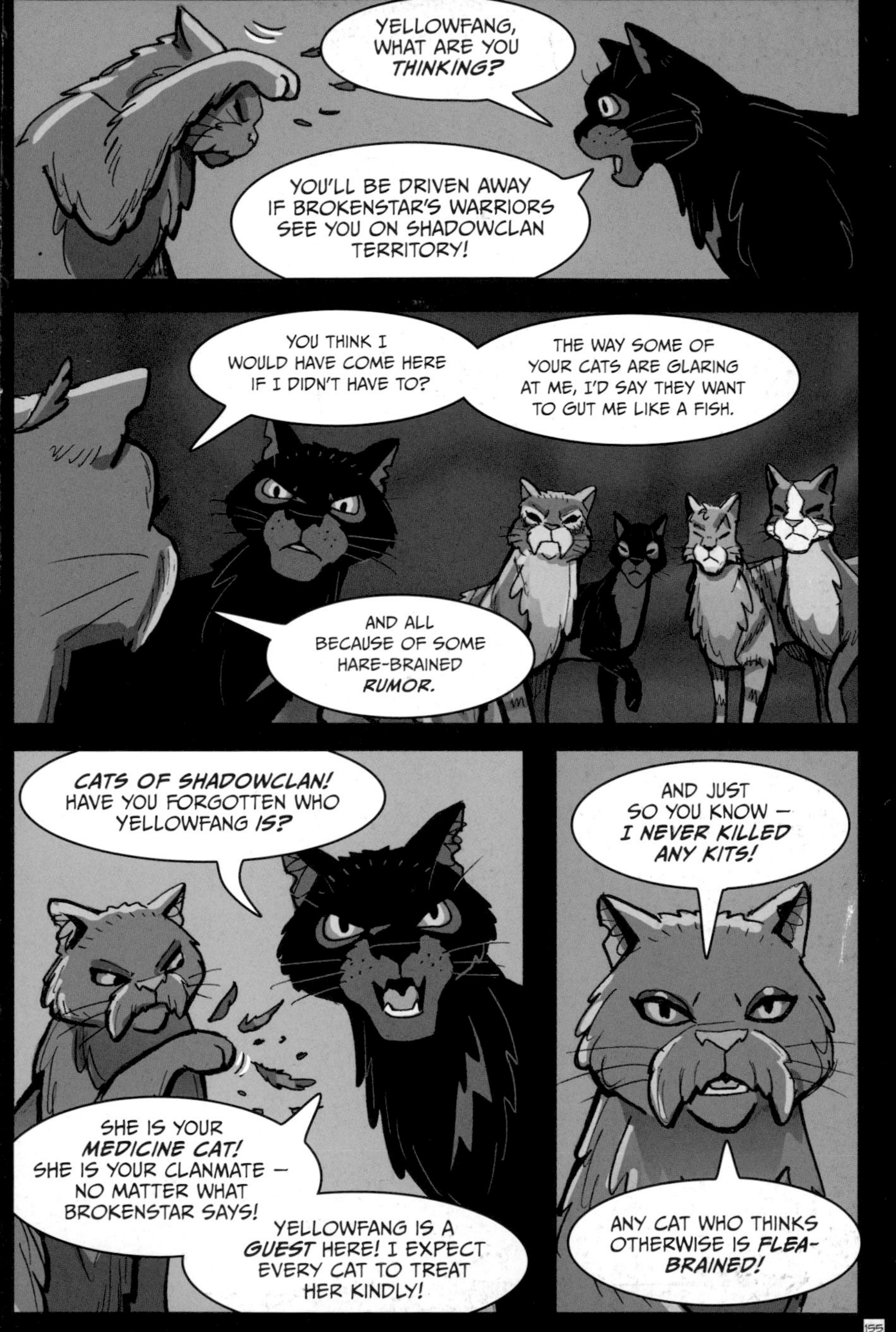
YELLOWFANG, WHAT ARE YOU *THINKING?*
YOU'LL BE DRIVEN AWAY IF BROKENSTAR'S WARRIORS SEE YOU ON SHADOWCLAN TERRITORY!
YOU THINK I WOULD HAVE COME HERE IF I DIDN'T HAVE TO?
THE WAY SOME OF YOUR CATS ARE GLARING AT ME, I'D SAY THEY WANT TO GUT ME LIKE A FISH.
AND ALL BECAUSE OF SOME HARE-BRAINED *RUMOR.*
CATS OF SHADOWCLAN! HAVE YOU FORGOTTEN WHO YELLOWFANG *IS?*
SHE IS YOUR *MEDICINE CAT!* SHE IS YOUR CLANMATE — NO MATTER WHAT BROKENSTAR SAYS!
YELLOWFANG IS A *GUEST* HERE! I EXPECT EVERY CAT TO TREAT HER KINDLY!
AND JUST SO YOU KNOW — *I NEVER KILLED ANY KITS!*
ANY CAT WHO THINKS OTHERWISE IS *FLEA-BRAINED!*

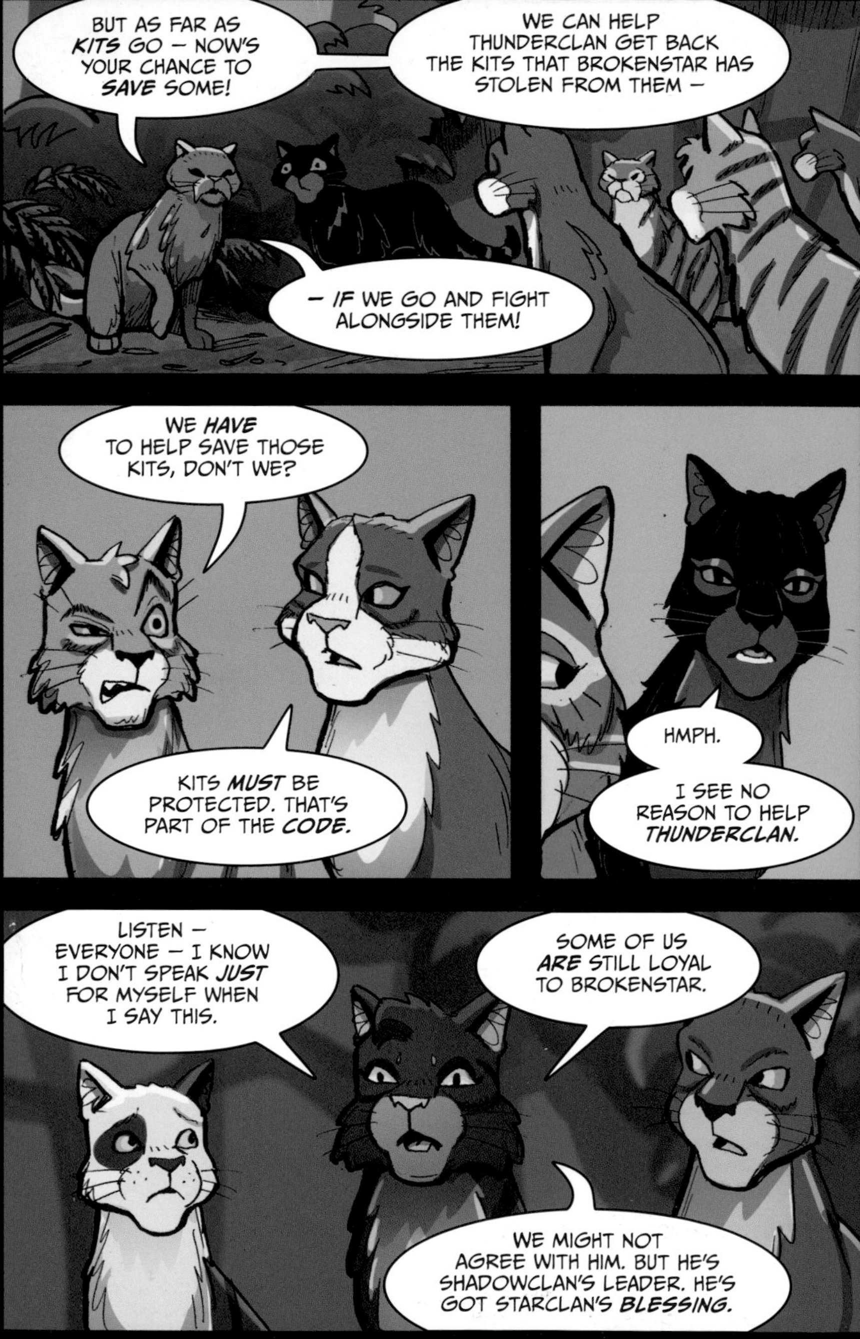

BUT AS FAR AS *KITS* GO — NOW'S YOUR CHANCE TO *SAVE* SOME!
WE CAN HELP THUNDERCLAN GET BACK THE KITS THAT BROKENSTAR HAS STOLEN FROM THEM —
— *IF* WE GO AND FIGHT ALONGSIDE THEM!
WE *HAVE* TO HELP SAVE THOSE KITS, DON'T WE?
KITS *MUST* BE PROTECTED. THAT'S PART OF THE *CODE.*
HMPH.
I SEE NO REASON TO HELP *THUNDERCLAN.*
LISTEN — EVERYONE — I KNOW I DON'T SPEAK *JUST* FOR MYSELF WHEN I SAY THIS.
SOME OF US *ARE* STILL LOYAL TO BROKENSTAR.
WE MIGHT NOT AGREE WITH HIM. BUT HE'S SHADOWCLAN'S LEADER. HE'S GOT STARCLAN'S *BLESSING.*

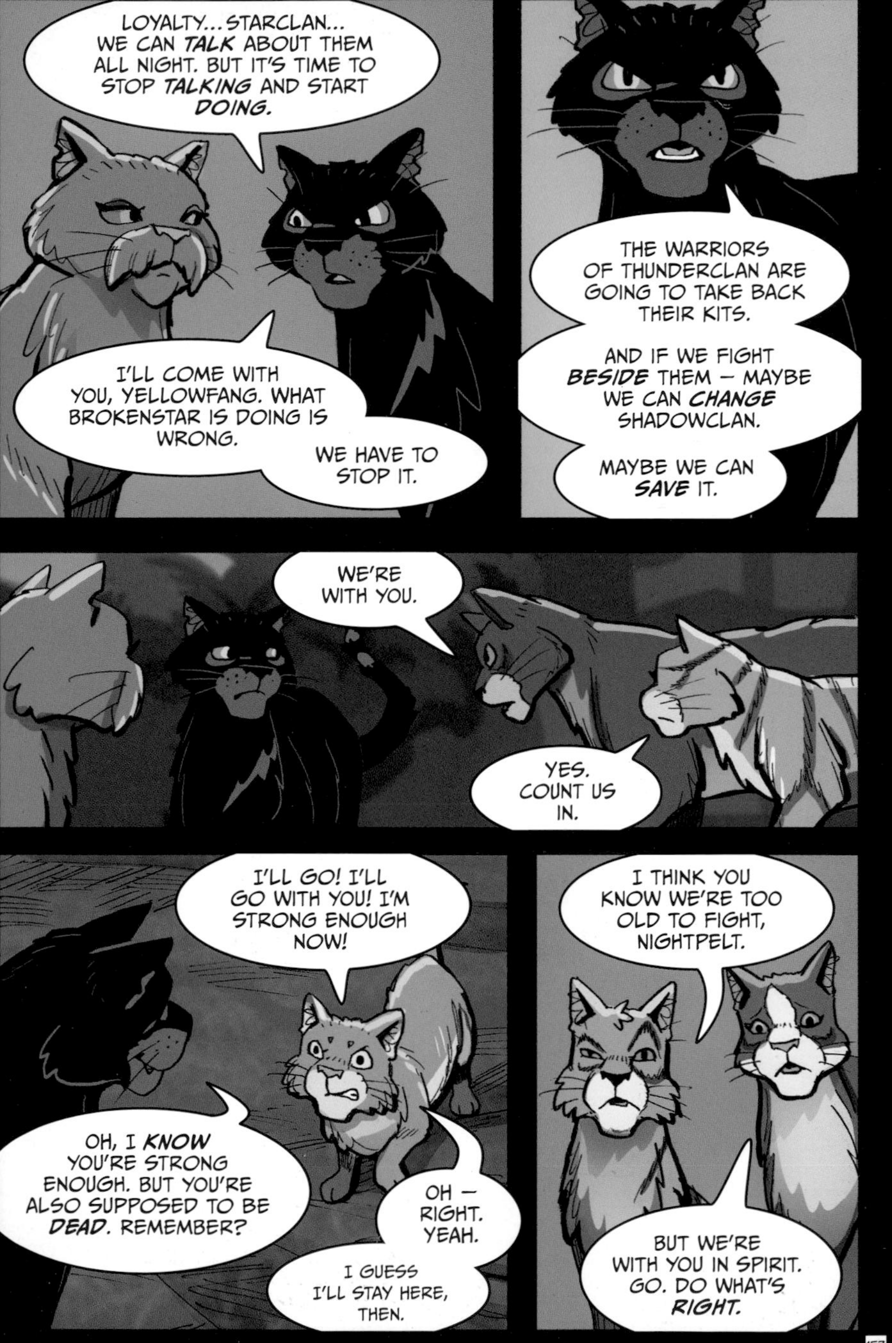
LOYALTY... STARCLAN... WE CAN TALK ABOUT THEM ALL NIGHT. BUT IT'S TIME TO STOP TALKING AND START DOING.
I'LL COME WITH YOU, YELLOWFANG. WHAT BROKENSTAR IS DOING IS WRONG.
WE HAVE TO STOP IT.
THE WARRIORS OF THUNDERCLAN ARE GOING TO TAKE BACK THEIR KITS.
AND IF WE FIGHT BESIDE THEM — MAYBE WE CAN CHANGE SHADOWCLAN.
MAYBE WE CAN SAVE IT.
WE'RE WITH YOU.
YES. COUNT US IN.
I'LL GO! I'LL GO WITH YOU! I'M STRONG ENOUGH NOW!
OH, I KNOW YOU'RE STRONG ENOUGH. BUT YOU'RE ALSO SUPPOSED TO BE DEAD. REMEMBER?
OH — RIGHT. YEAH.
I GUESS I'LL STAY HERE, THEN.
I THINK YOU KNOW WE'RE TOO OLD TO FIGHT, NIGHTPELT.
BUT WE'RE WITH YOU IN SPIRIT. GO. DO WHAT'S RIGHT.

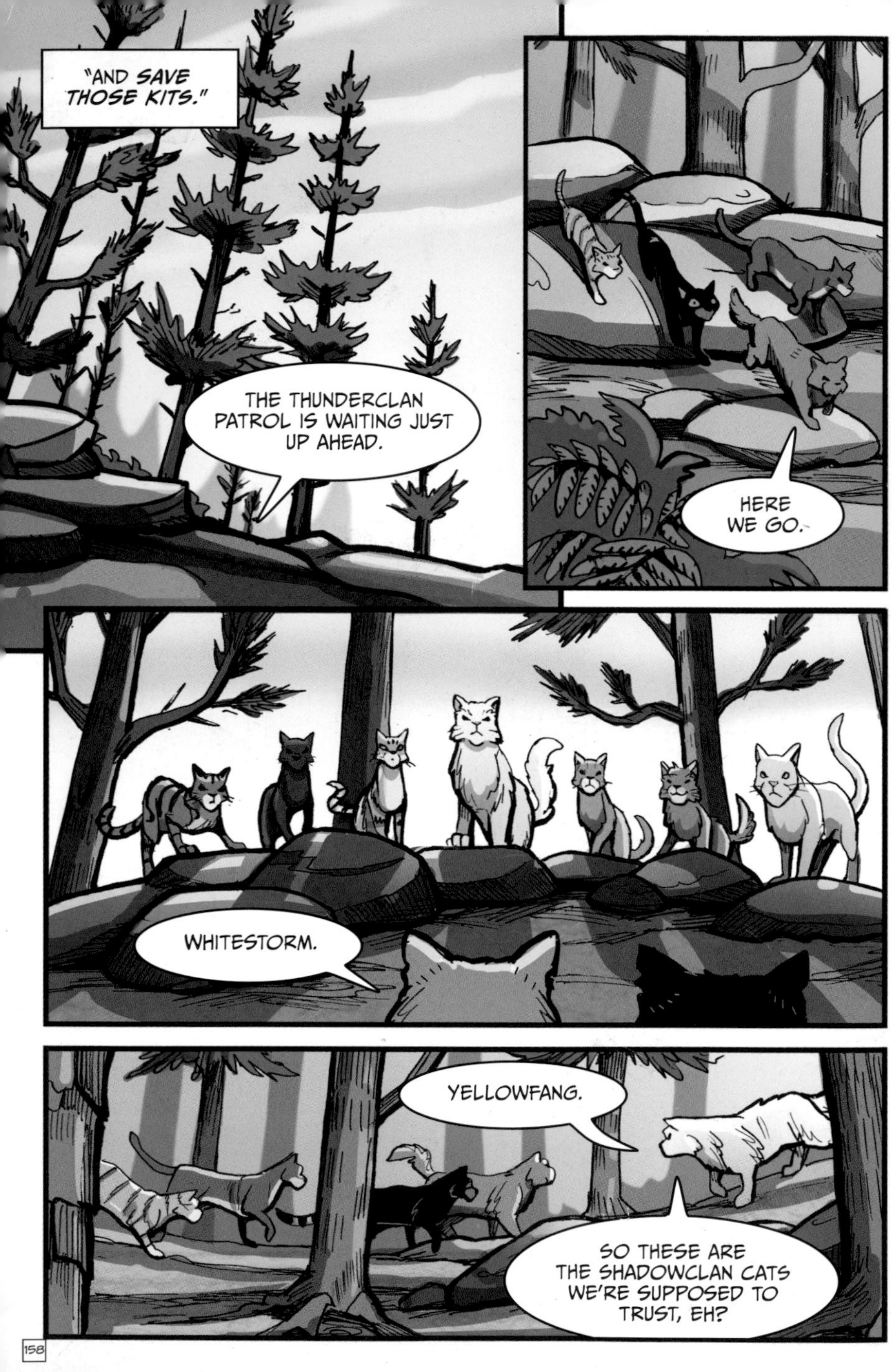
"AND SAVE THOSE KITS."
THE THUNDERCLAN PATROL IS WAITING JUST UP AHEAD.
HERE WE GO.
WHITESTORM.
YELLOWFANG.
SO THESE ARE THE SHADOWCLAN CATS WE'RE SUPPOSED TO TRUST, EH?

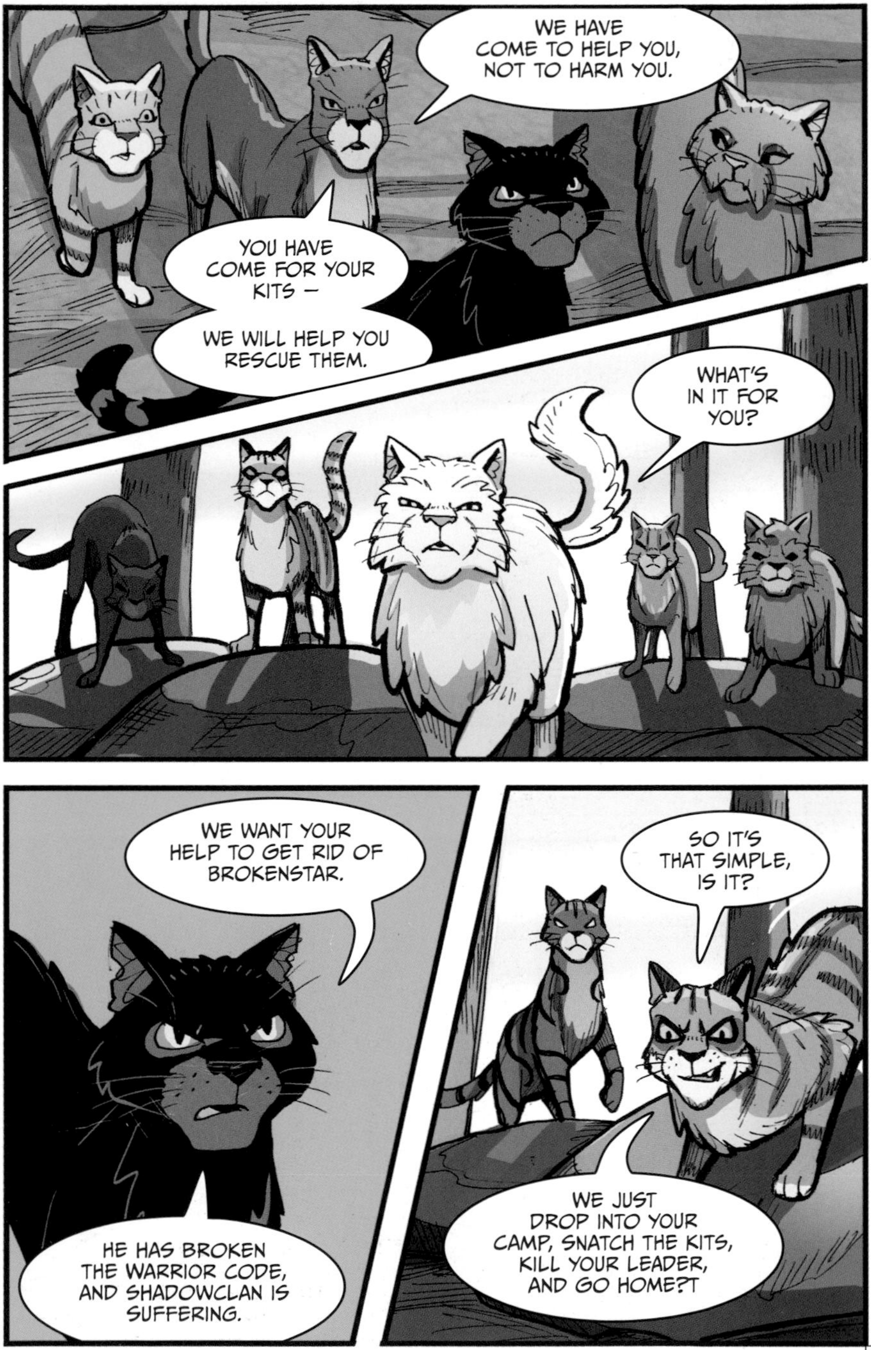
WE HAVE COME TO HELP YOU, NOT TO HARM YOU.
YOU HAVE COME FOR YOUR KITS —
WE WILL HELP YOU RESCUE THEM.
WHAT'S IN IT FOR YOU?
WE WANT YOUR HELP TO GET RID OF BROKENSTAR.
HE HAS BROKEN THE WARRIOR CODE, AND SHADOWCLAN IS SUFFERING.
SO IT'S THAT SIMPLE, IS IT?
WE JUST DROP INTO YOUR CAMP, SNATCH THE KITS, KILL YOUR LEADER, AND GO HOME?!

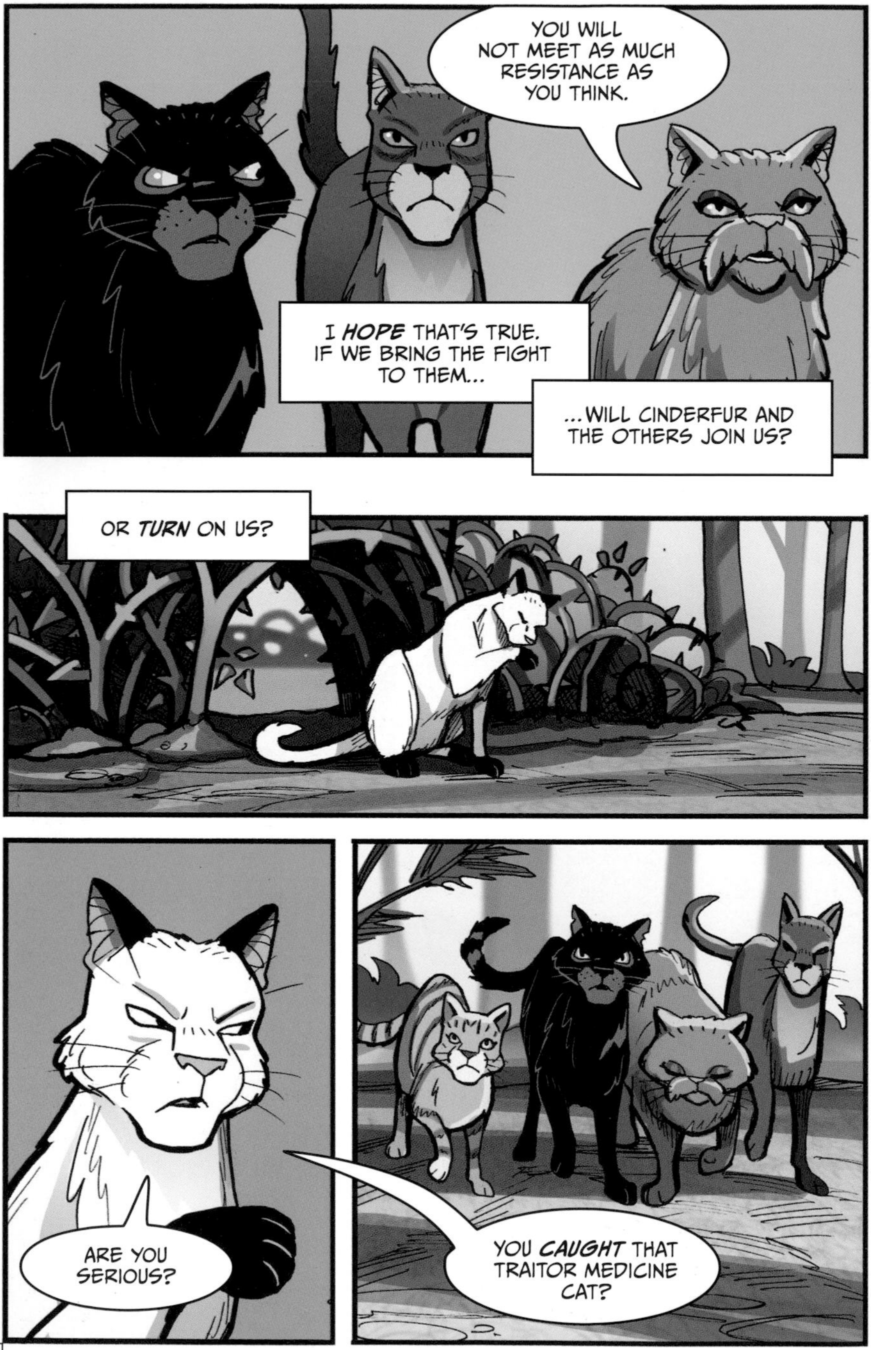
YOU WILL NOT MEET AS MUCH RESISTANCE AS YOU THINK.
I HOPE THAT'S TRUE. IF WE BRING THE FIGHT TO THEM...
...WILL CINDERFUR AND THE OTHERS JOIN US?
OR TURN ON US?
ARE YOU SERIOUS?
YOU CAUGHT THAT TRAITOR MEDICINE CAT?

DON'T LOOK SO SURPRISED, BLACKFOOT.

WE *ARE* SHADOWCLAN WARRIORS.

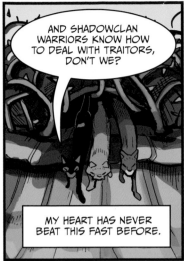

AND SHADOWCLAN WARRIORS KNOW HOW TO DEAL WITH TRAITORS, DON'T WE?

MY HEART HAS NEVER BEAT THIS FAST BEFORE.

WHAT IF BROKENSTAR AND HIS WARRIORS DON'T FALL FOR THIS? WHAT IF THE THUNDERCLAN CATS DON'T COME ON OUR SIGNAL?

WHAT IF THE SHADOWCLAN CATS WE *THINK* ARE ON OUR SIDE WON'T *HELP?*

LOOK WHO WE CAPTURED, SNEAKING BACK ONTO SHADOWCLAN TERRITORY!

WELL. THERE'S A SIGHT I WASN'T EXPECTING TO SEE TODAY.

GOOD WORK, NIGHTPELT. YOU AND YOUR LITTLE... PATROL.

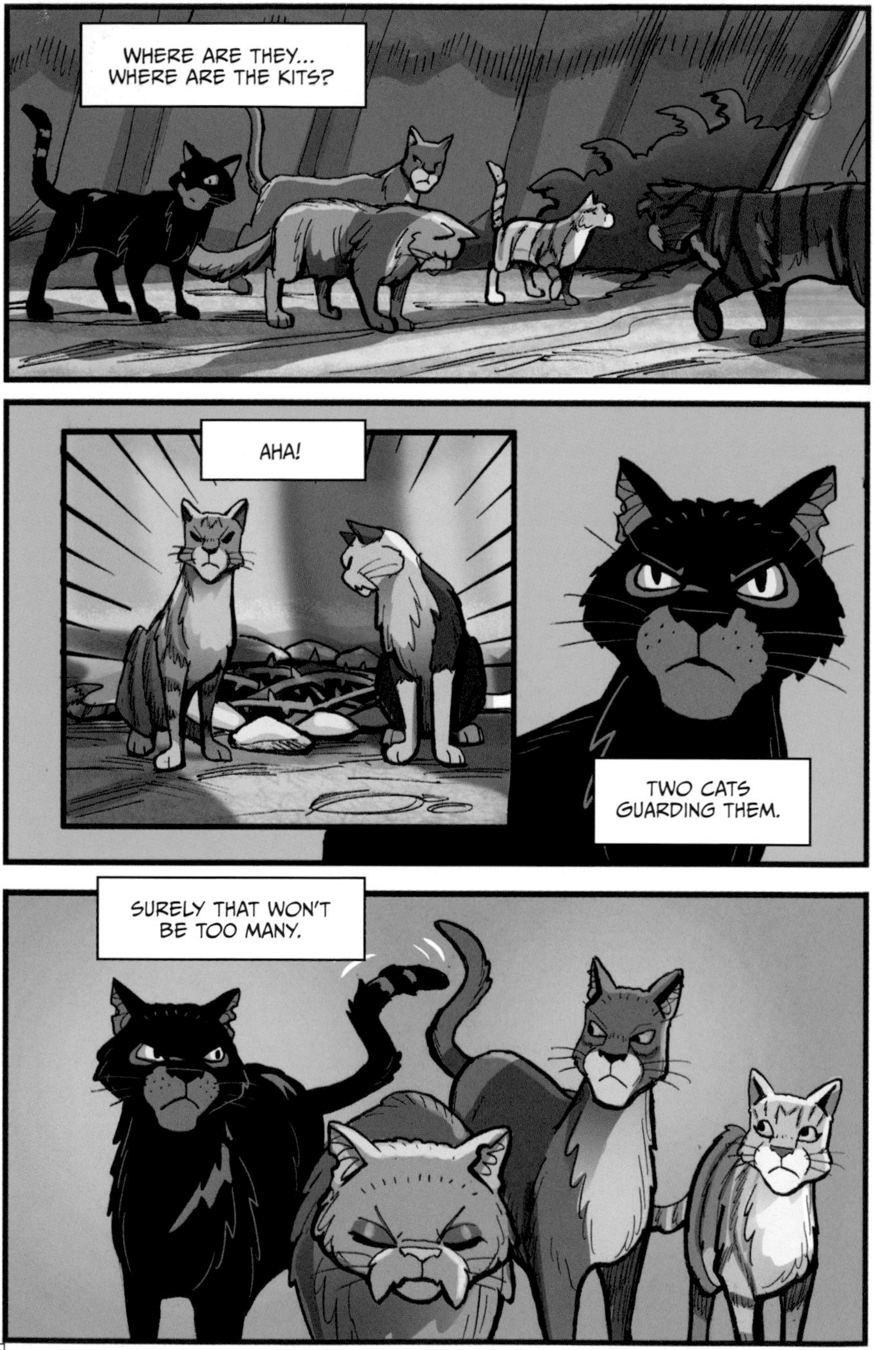
WHERE ARE THEY...
WHERE ARE THE KITS?
AHA!
TWO CATS
GUARDING THEM.
SURELY THAT WON'T
BE TOO MANY.

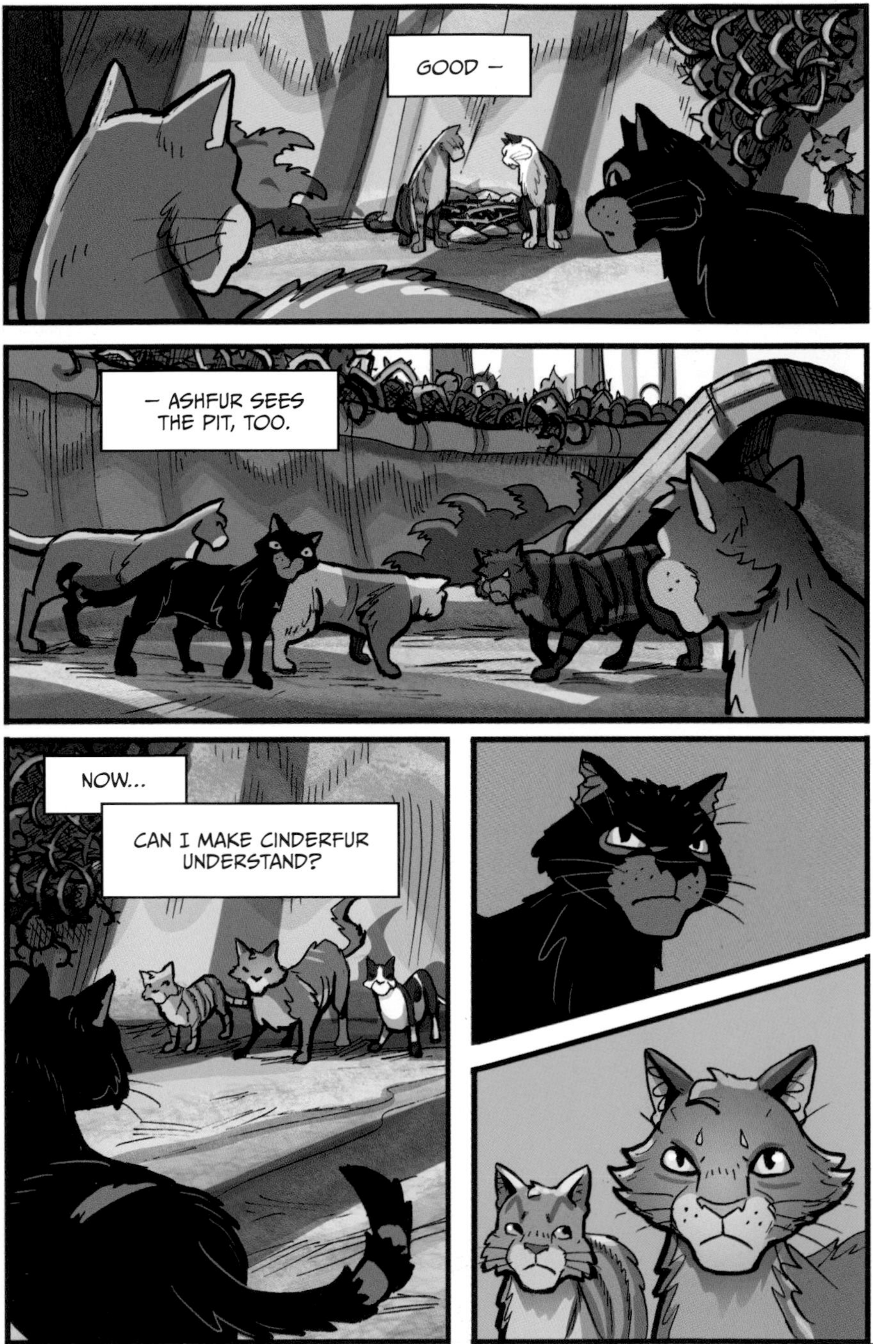
GOOD –
– ASHFUR SEES THE PIT, TOO.
NOW...
CAN I MAKE CINDERFUR UNDERSTAND?

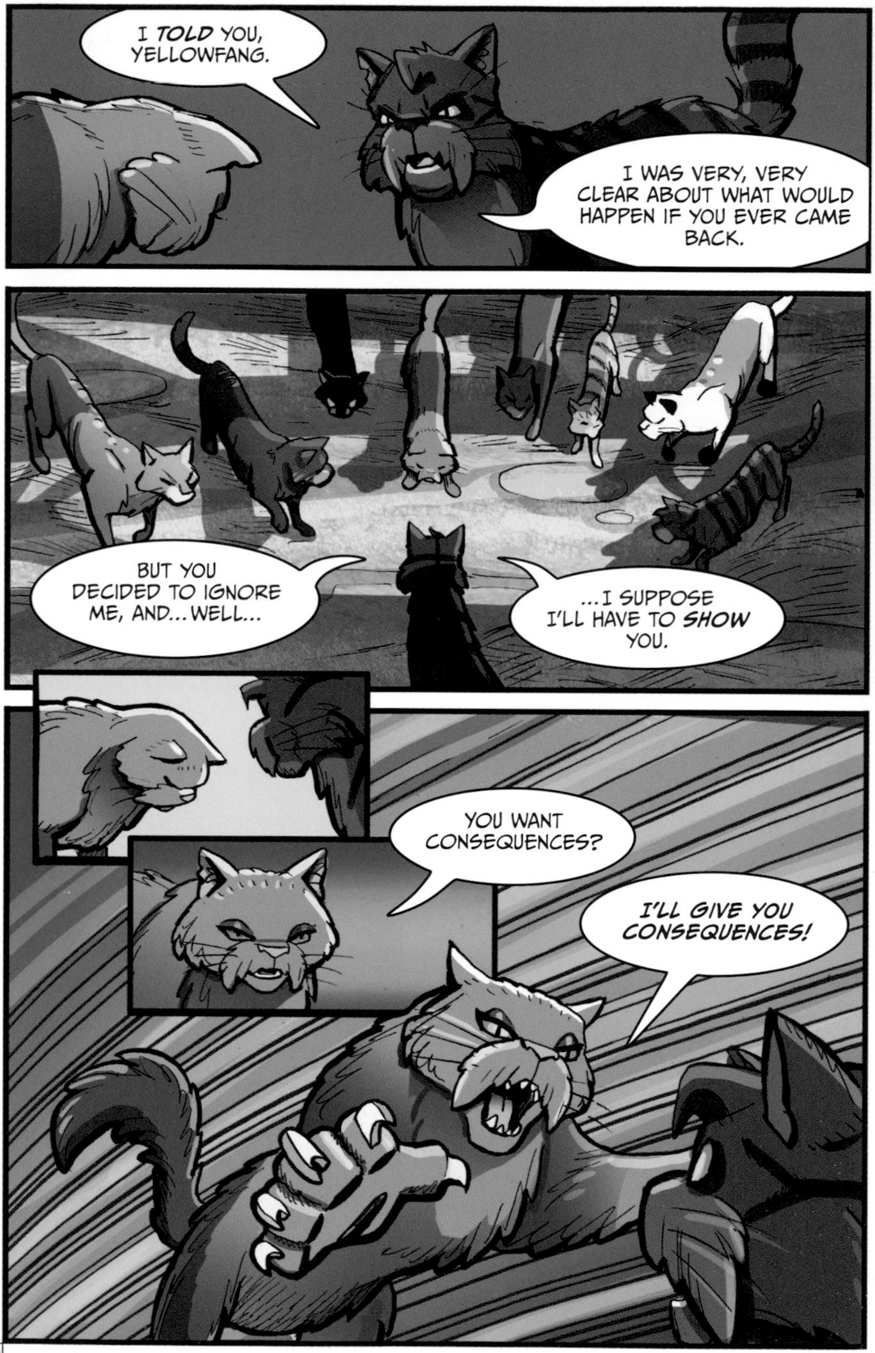

I *TOLD* YOU, YELLOWFANG.
I WAS VERY, VERY CLEAR ABOUT WHAT WOULD HAPPEN IF YOU EVER CAME BACK.
BUT YOU DECIDED TO IGNORE ME, AND...WELL...
...I SUPPOSE I'LL HAVE TO *SHOW* YOU.
YOU WANT CONSEQUENCES?
I'LL GIVE YOU CONSEQUENCES!

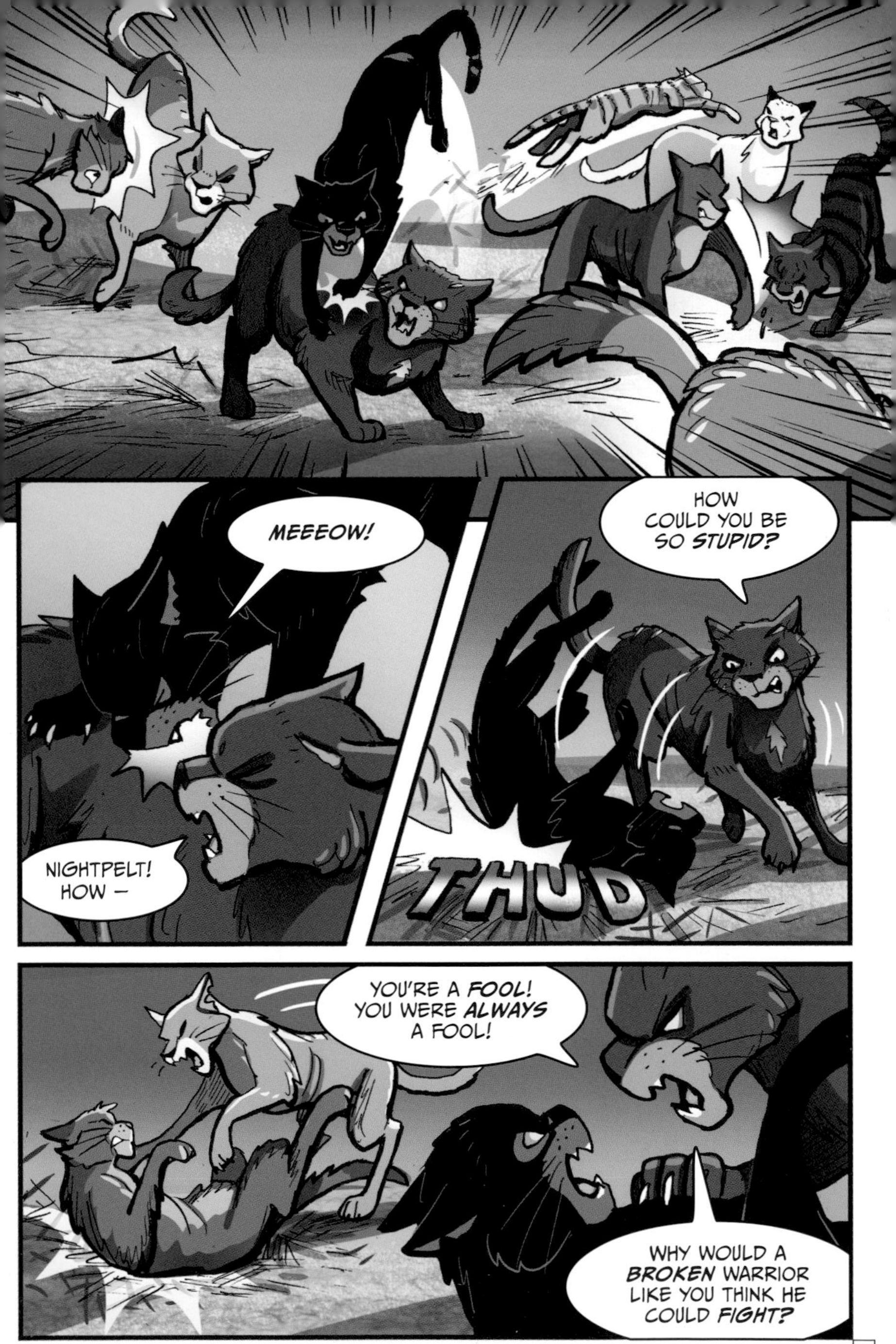
MEEEOW!
NIGHTPELT! HOW –
HOW COULD YOU BE SO STUPID?
THUD
YOU'RE A FOOL! YOU WERE ALWAYS A FOOL!
WHY WOULD A BROKEN WARRIOR LIKE YOU THINK HE COULD FIGHT?

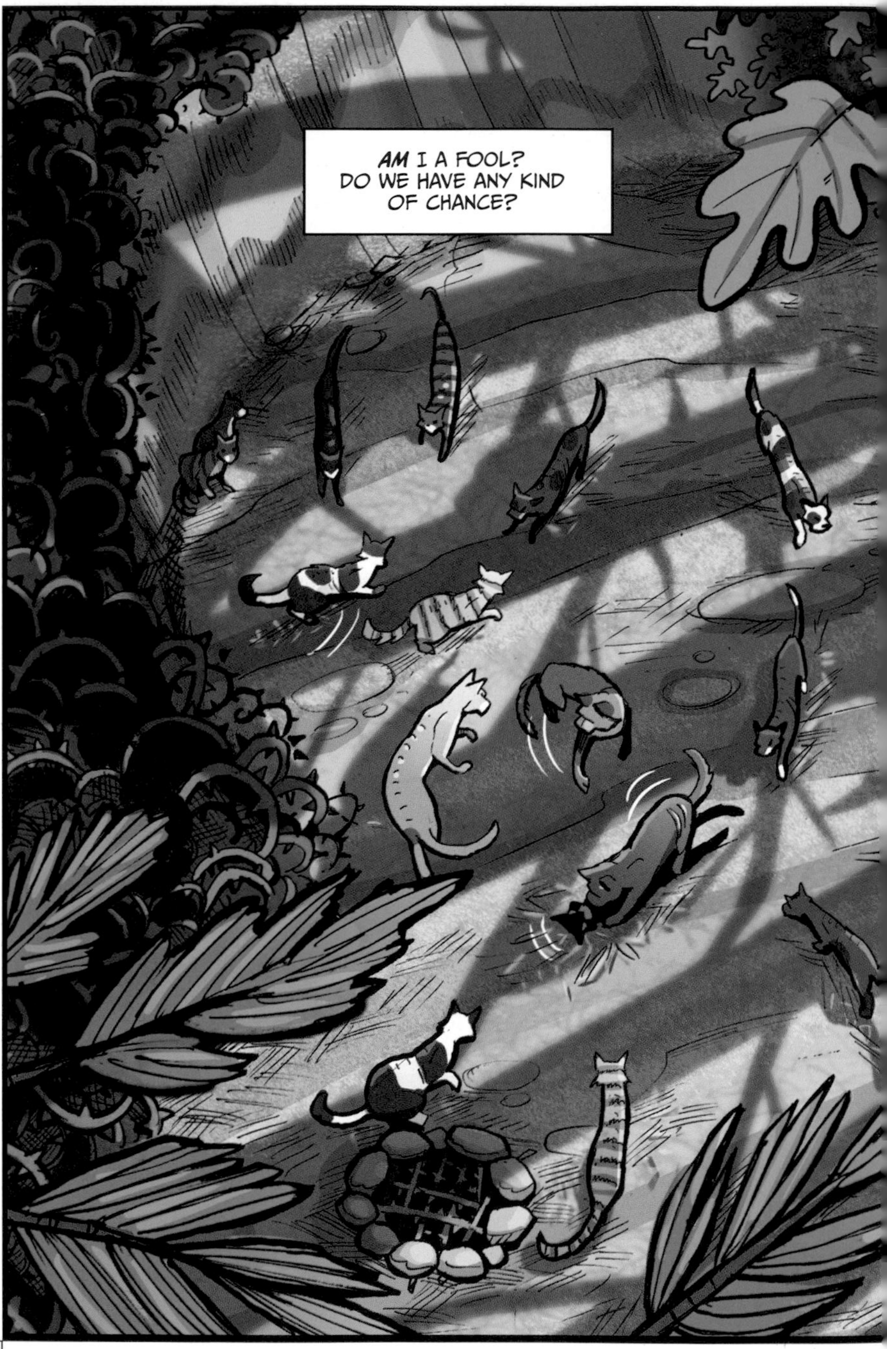
AM I A FOOL?
DO WE HAVE ANY KIND
OF CHANCE?

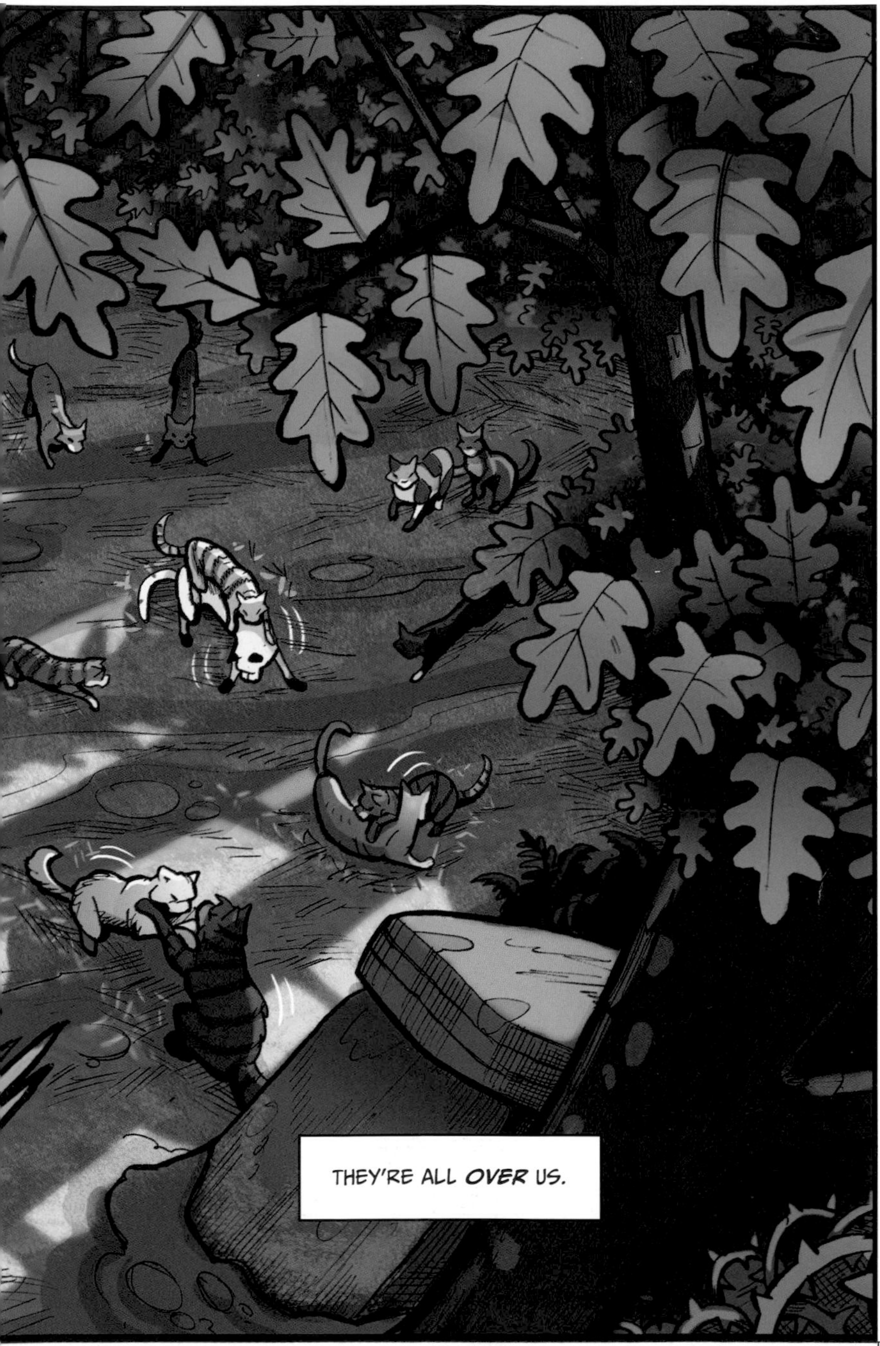
THEY'RE ALL OVER US.

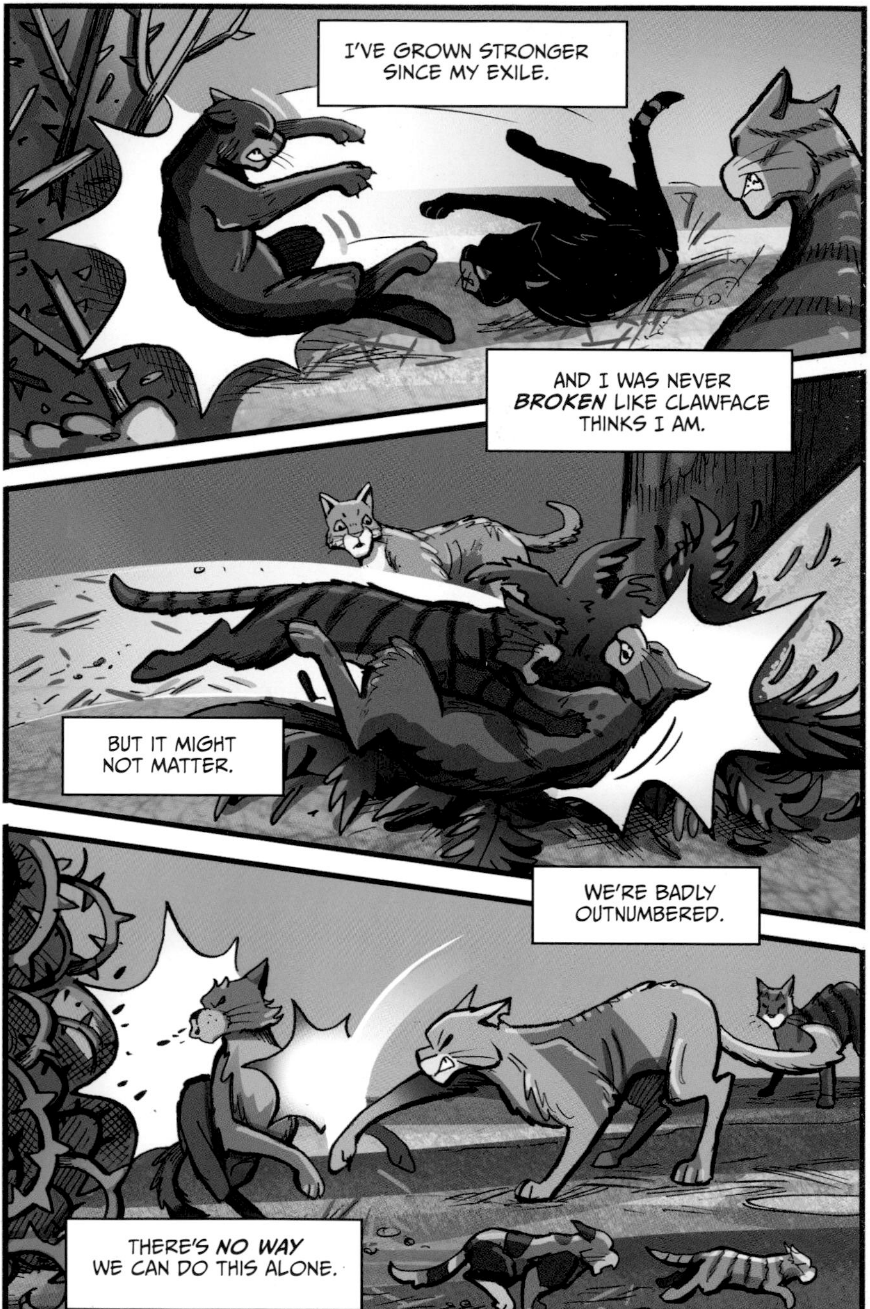
I'VE GROWN STRONGER SINCE MY EXILE.
AND I WAS NEVER *BROKEN* LIKE CLAWFACE THINKS I AM.
BUT IT MIGHT NOT MATTER.
WE'RE BADLY OUTNUMBERED.
THERE'S *NO WAY* WE CAN DO THIS ALONE.

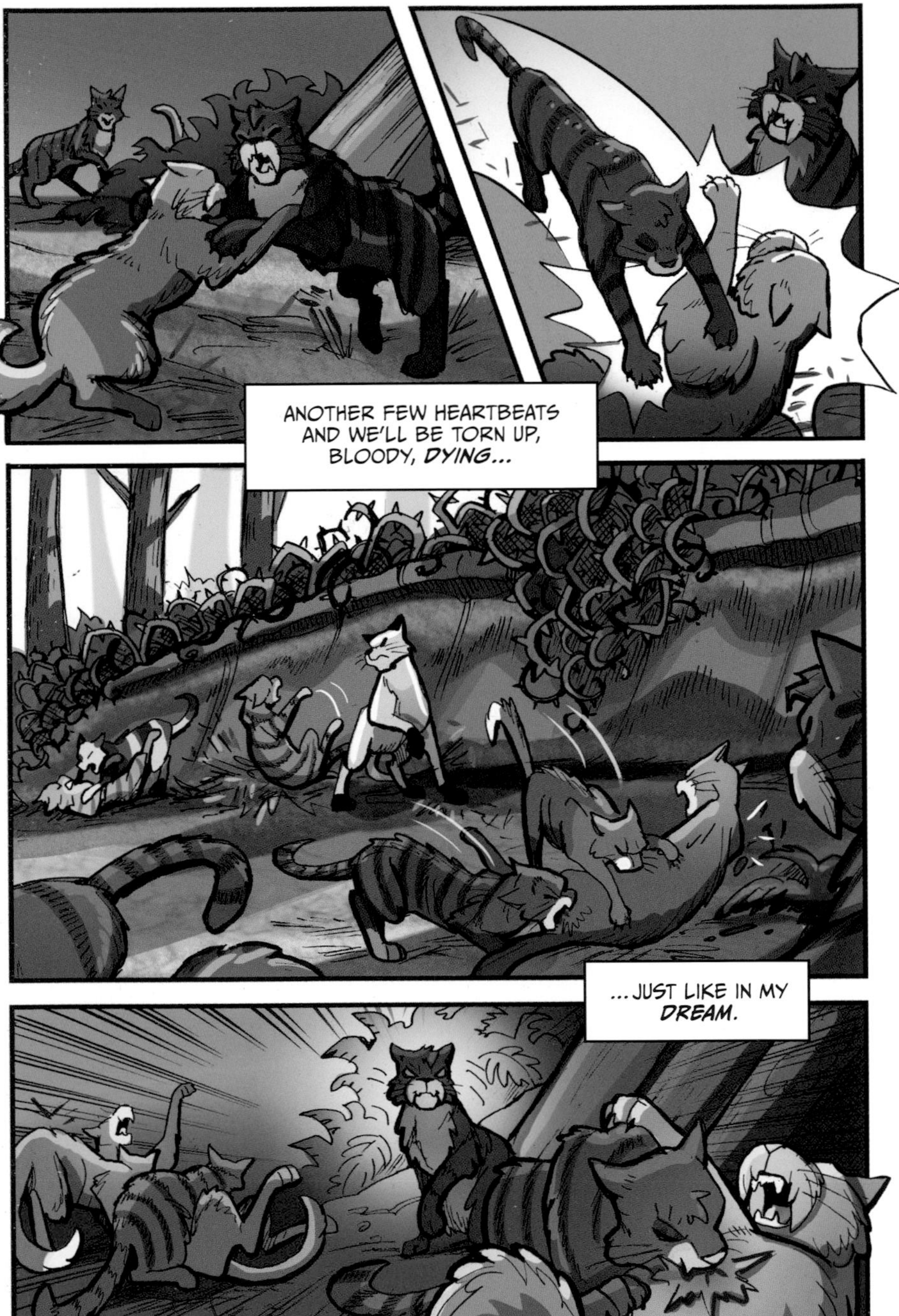
ANOTHER FEW HEARTBEATS
AND WE'LL BE TORN UP,
BLOODY, *DYING*...
...JUST LIKE IN MY
DREAM.

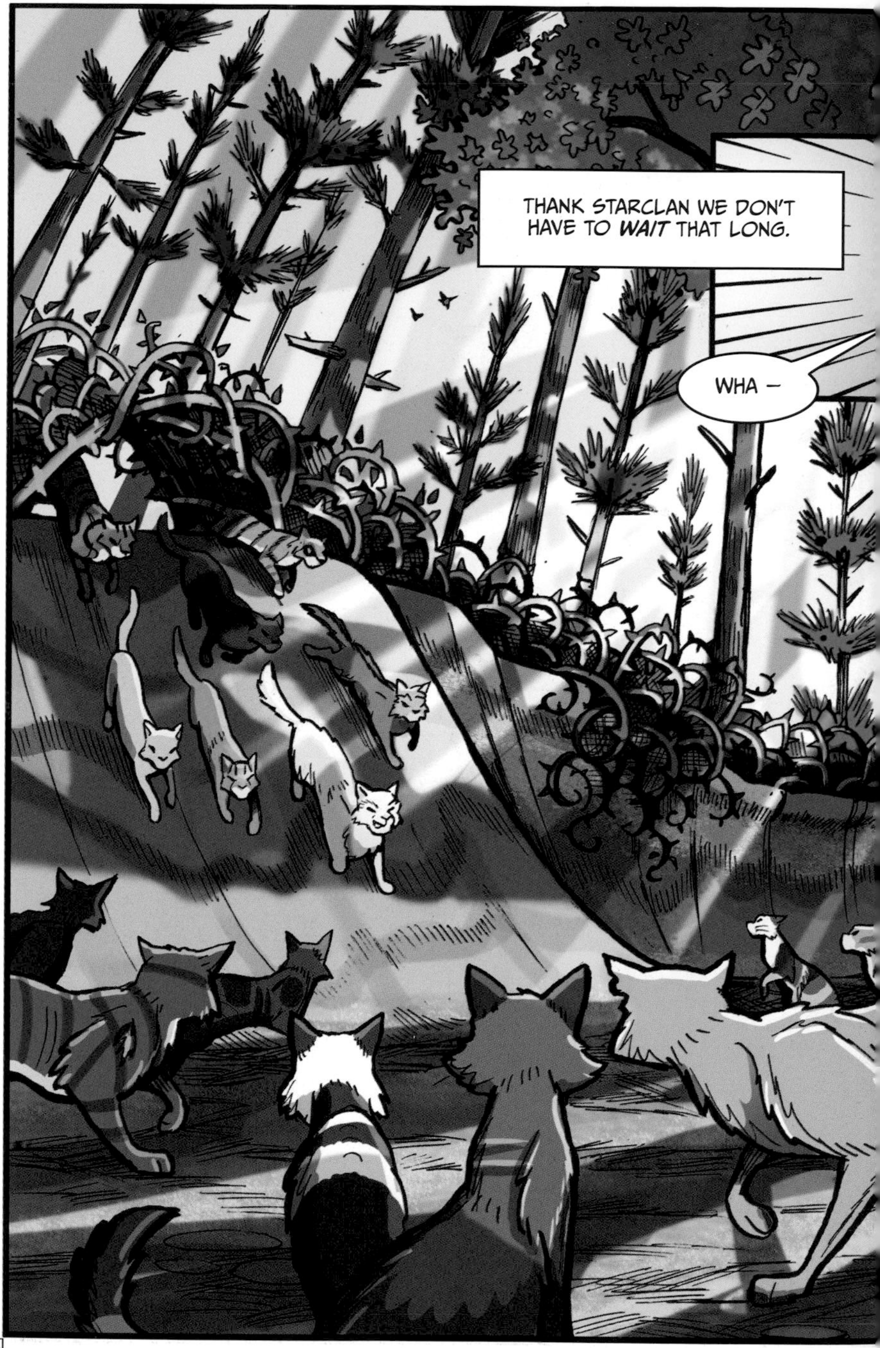
THANK STARCLAN WE DON'T HAVE TO *WAIT* THAT LONG.
WHA –

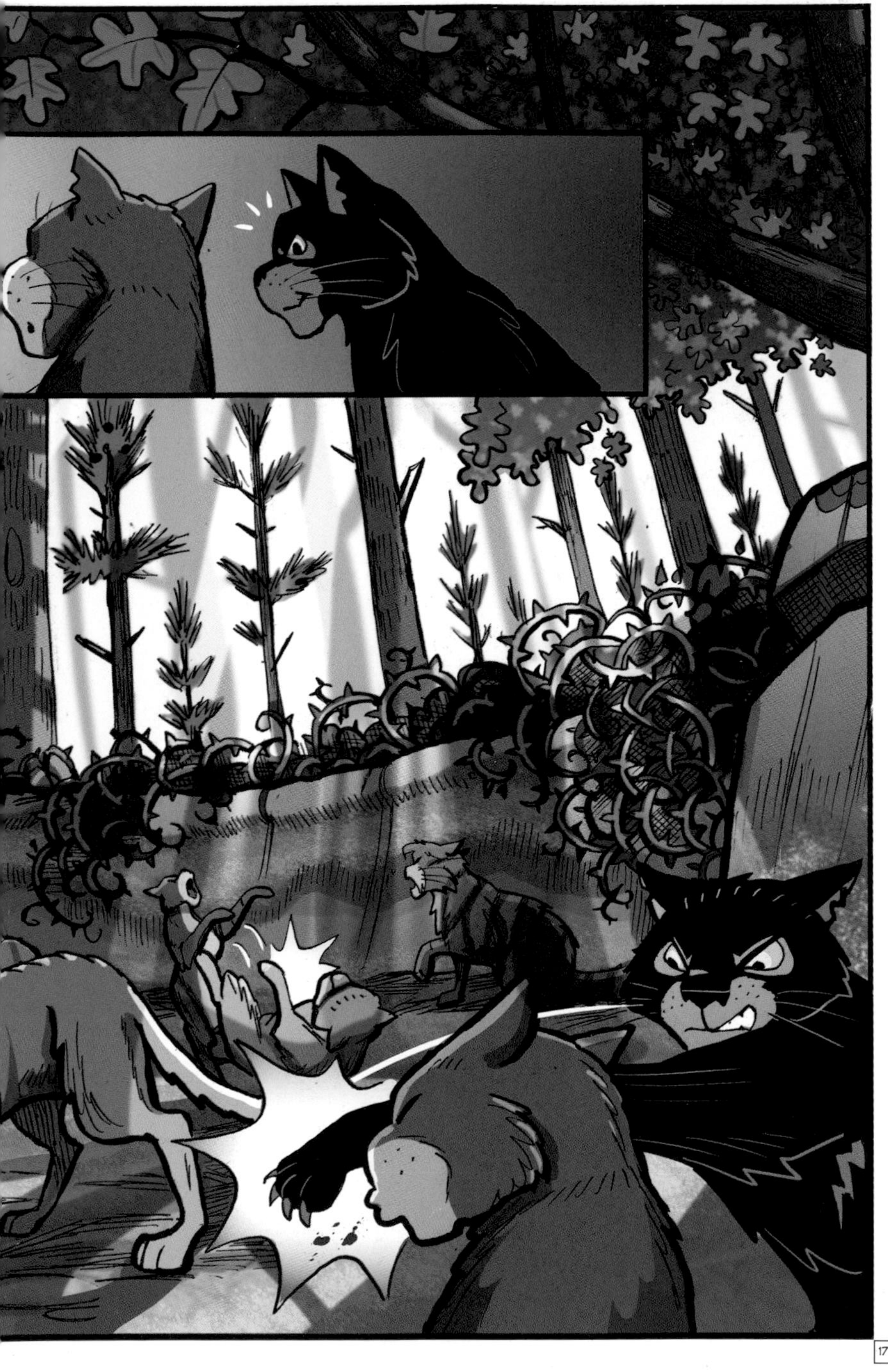

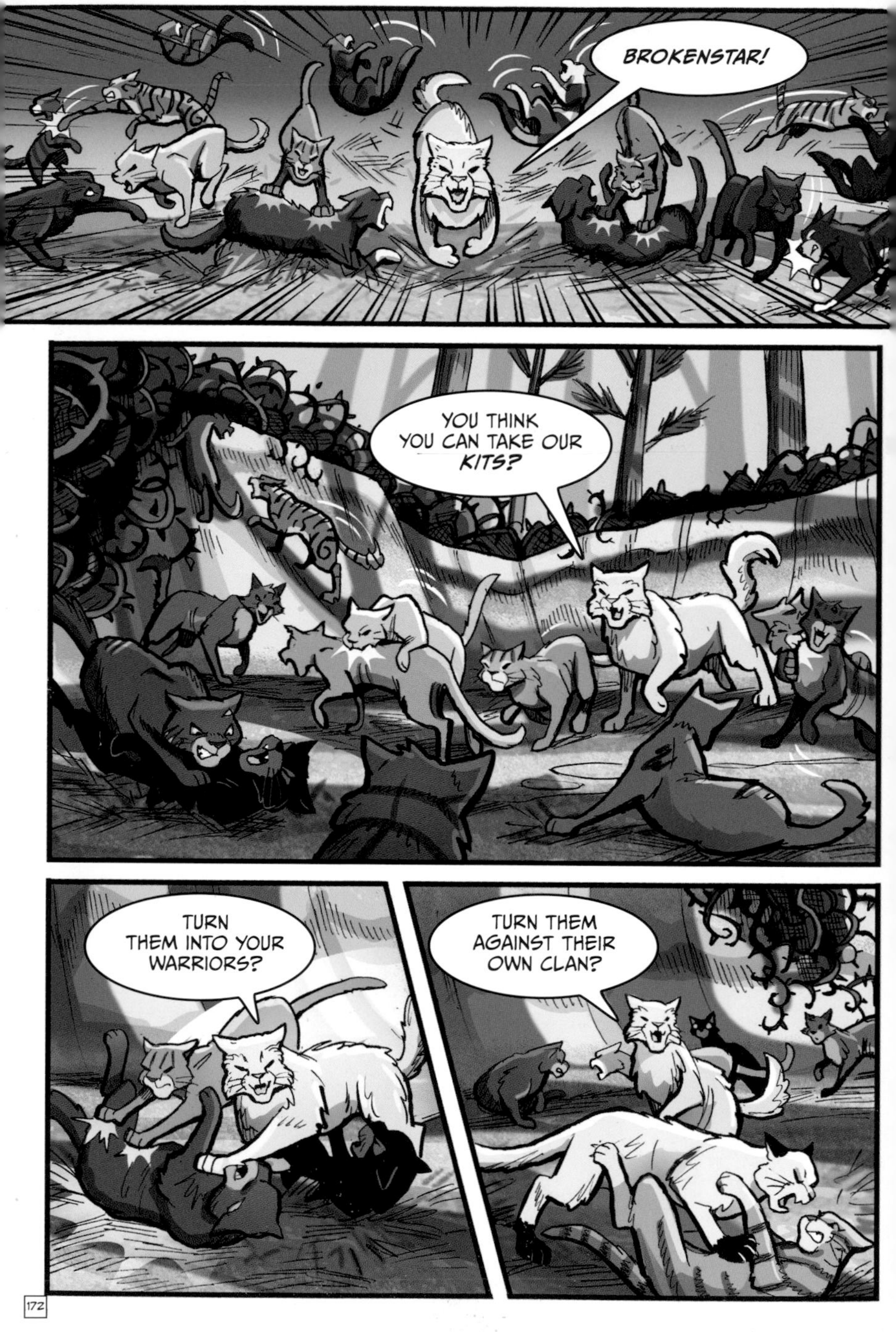
BROKENSTAR!
YOU THINK YOU CAN TAKE OUR KITS?
TURN THEM INTO YOUR WARRIORS?
TURN THEM AGAINST THEIR OWN CLAN?

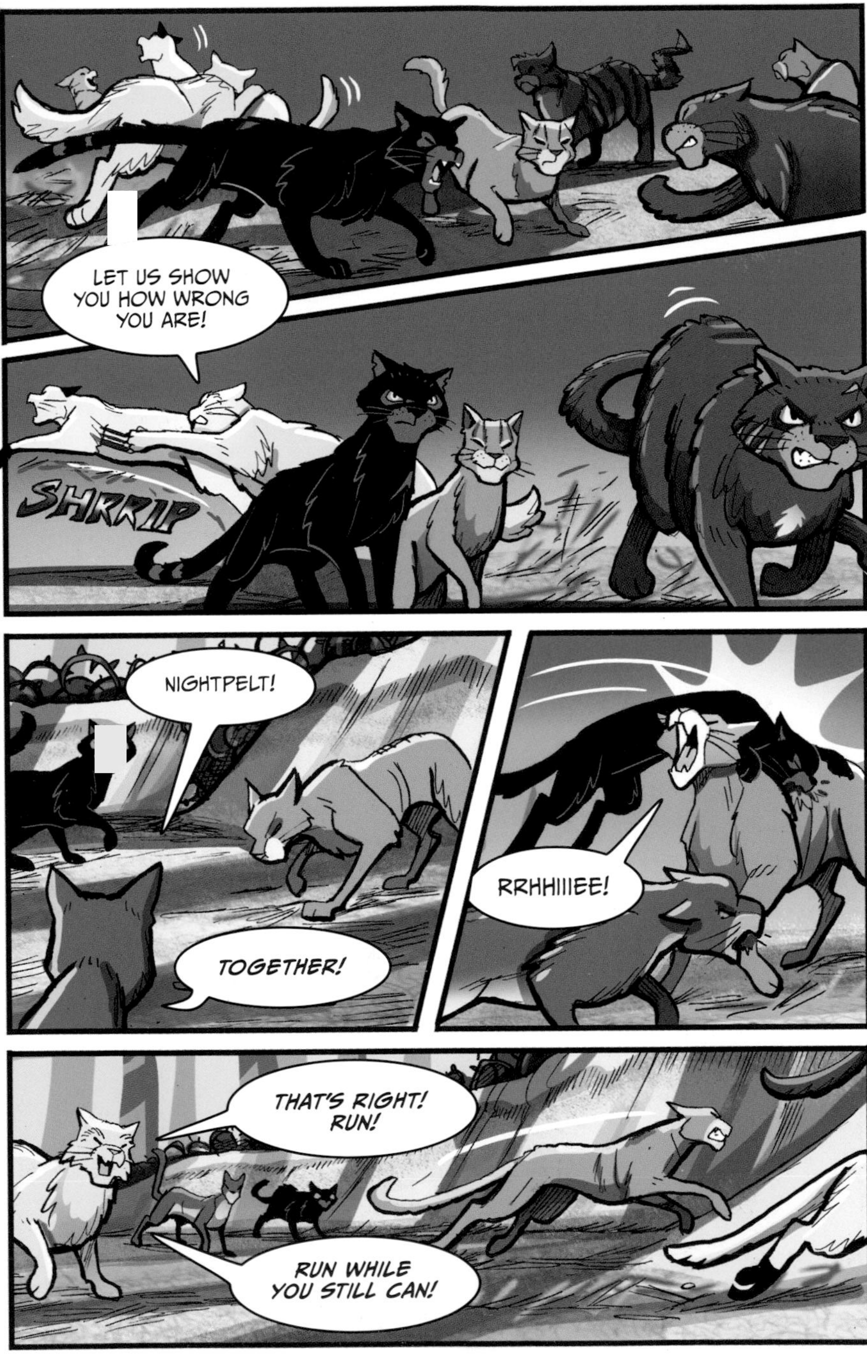
LET US SHOW YOU HOW WRONG YOU ARE!
SHRRIP
NIGHTPELT!
TOGETHER!
RRHHIIIIEE!
THAT'S RIGHT! RUN!
RUN WHILE YOU STILL CAN!

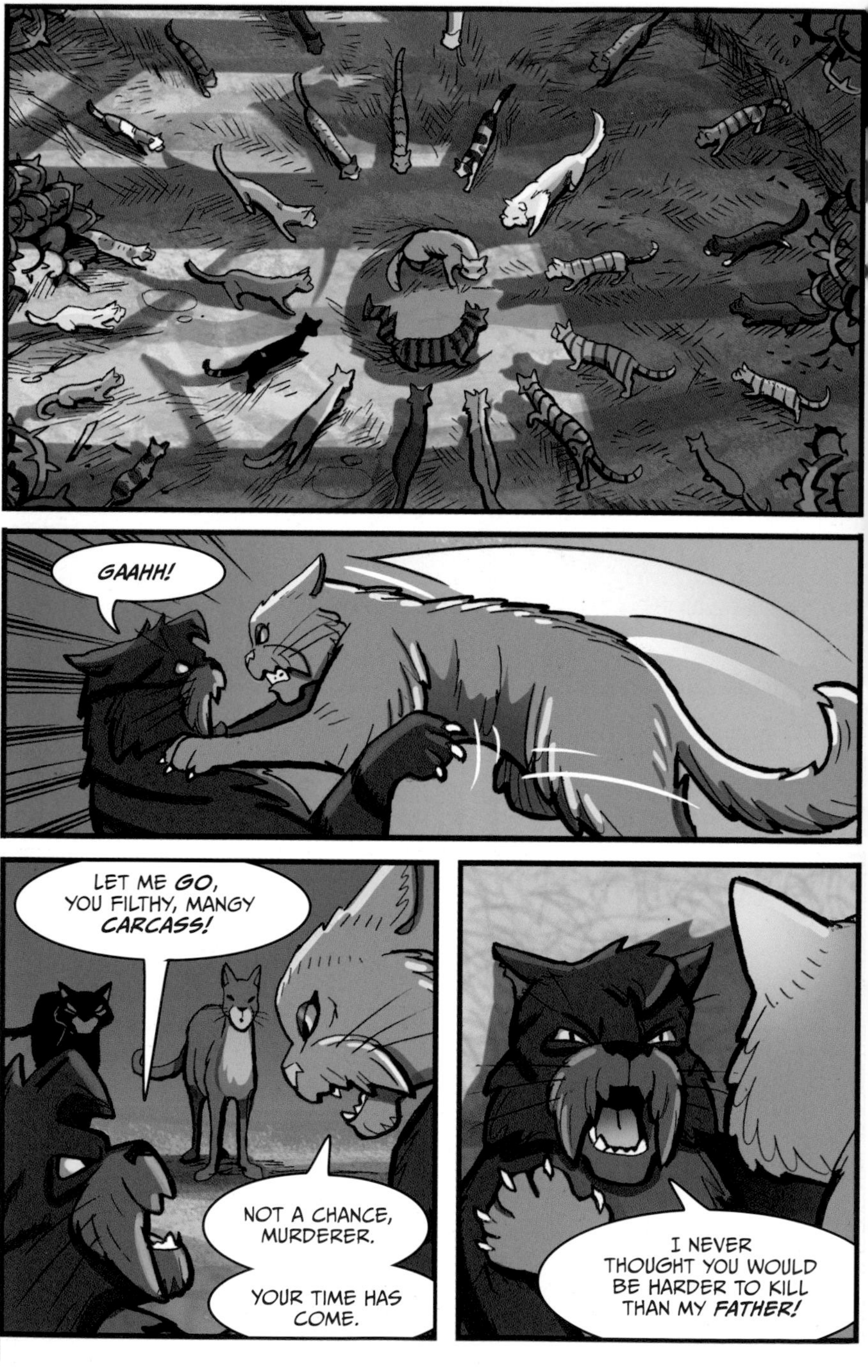
GAAHH!
LET ME GO, YOU FILTHY, MANGY CARCASS!
NOT A CHANCE, MURDERER.
YOUR TIME HAS COME.
I NEVER THOUGHT YOU WOULD BE HARDER TO KILL THAN MY FATHER!

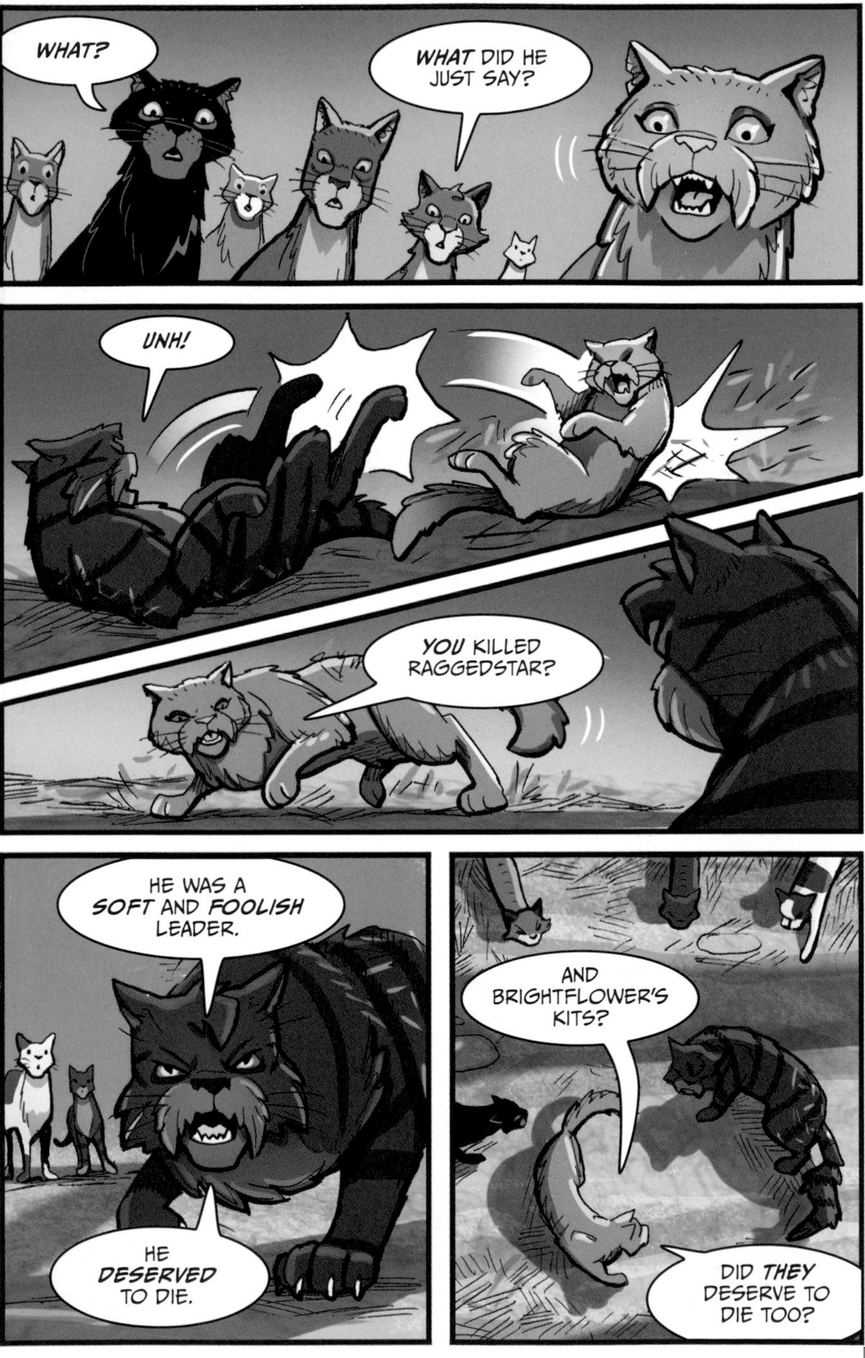
WHAT?
WHAT DID HE JUST SAY?
UNH!
YOU KILLED RAGGEDSTAR?
HE WAS A SOFT AND FOOLISH LEADER.
HE DESERVED TO DIE.
AND BRIGHTFLOWER'S KITS?
DID THEY DESERVE TO DIE TOO?

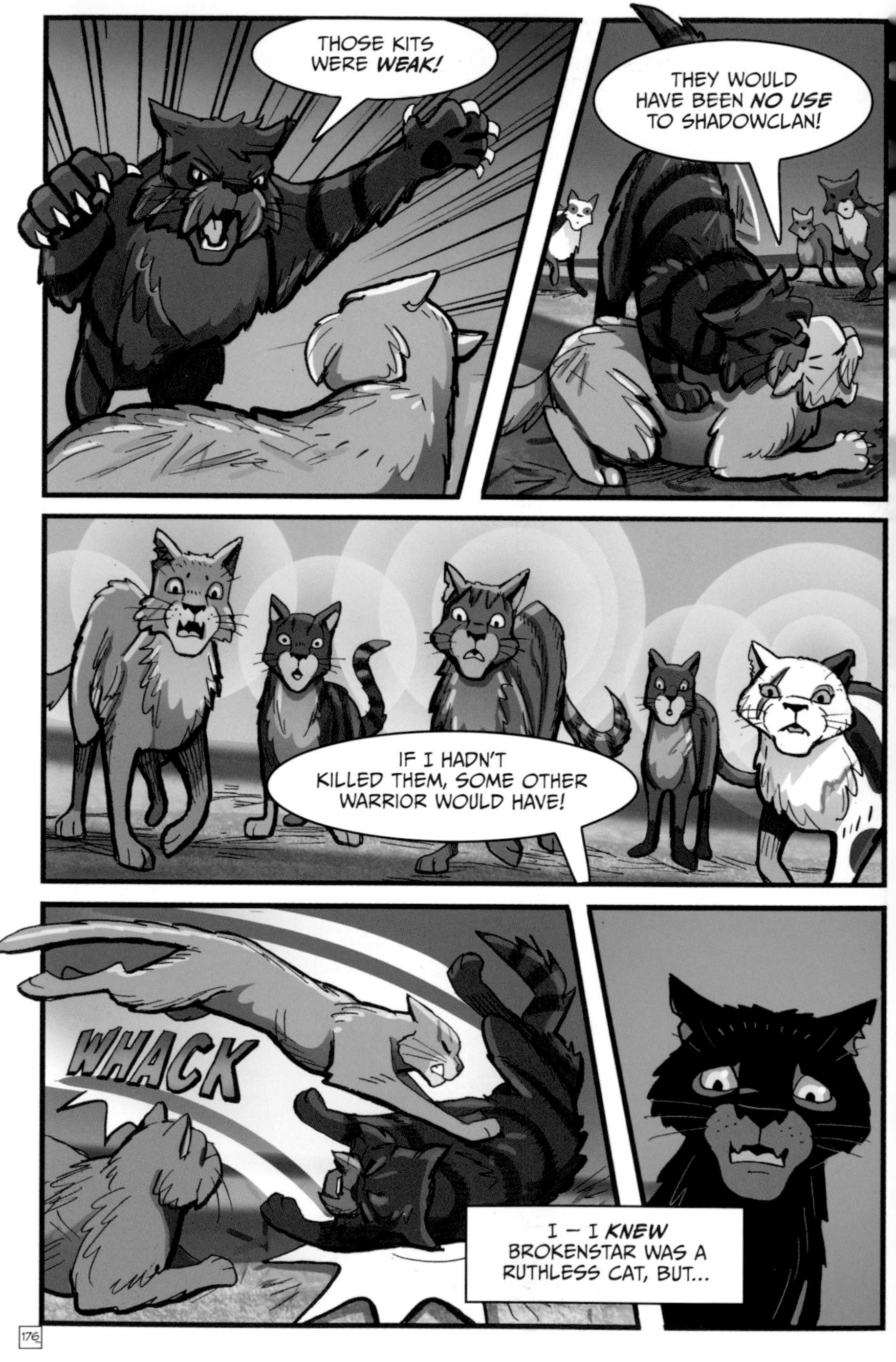
THOSE KITS WERE WEAK!
THEY WOULD HAVE BEEN NO USE TO SHADOWCLAN!
IF I HADN'T KILLED THEM, SOME OTHER WARRIOR WOULD HAVE!
WHACK
I — I KNEW BROKENSTAR WAS A RUTHLESS CAT, BUT...

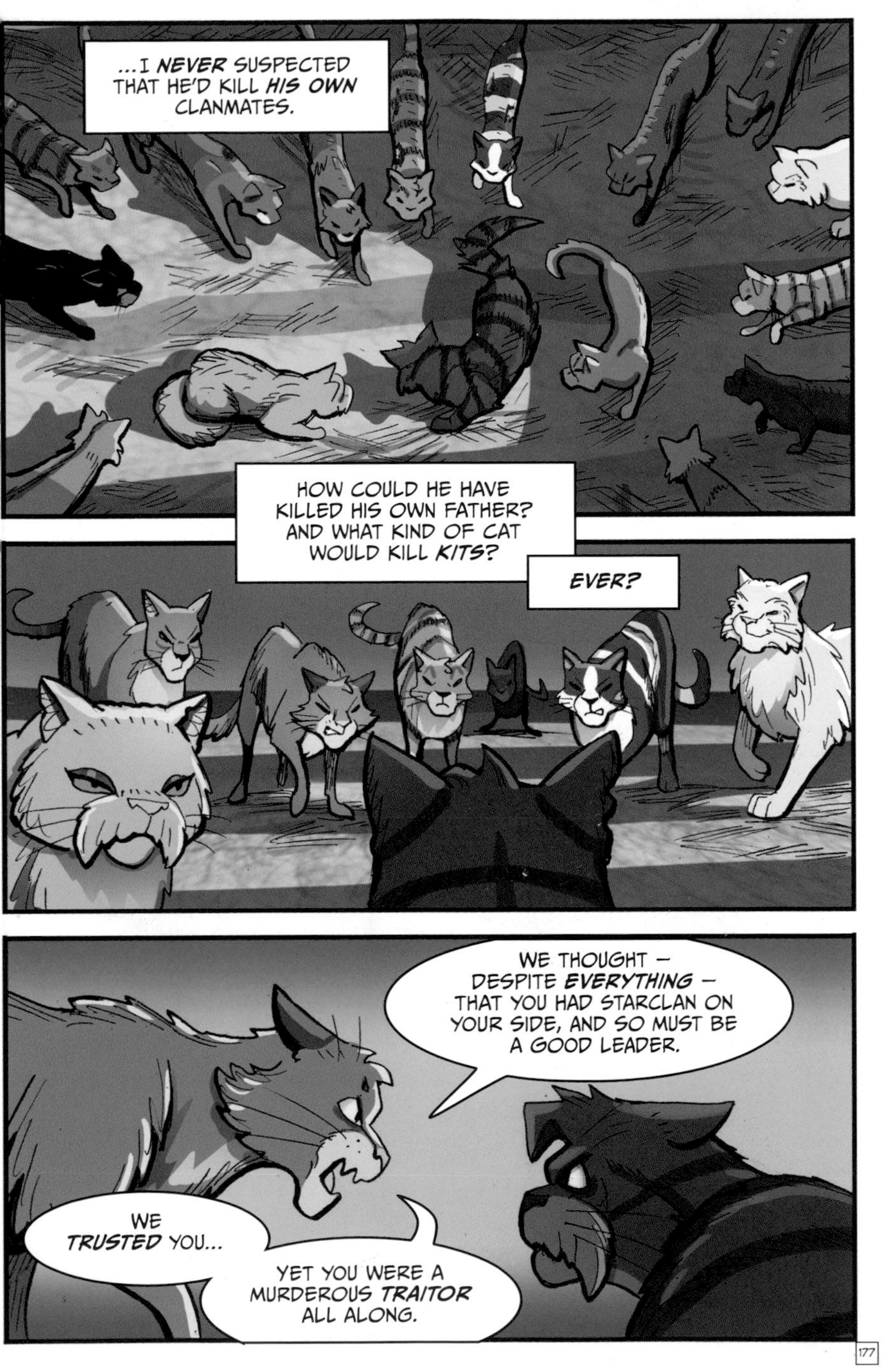
...I NEVER SUSPECTED THAT HE'D KILL HIS OWN CLANMATES.
HOW COULD HE HAVE KILLED HIS OWN FATHER? AND WHAT KIND OF CAT WOULD KILL KITS?
EVER?
WE THOUGHT – DESPITE EVERYTHING – THAT YOU HAD STARCLAN ON YOUR SIDE, AND SO MUST BE A GOOD LEADER.
WE TRUSTED YOU...
YET YOU WERE A MURDEROUS TRAITOR ALL ALONG.

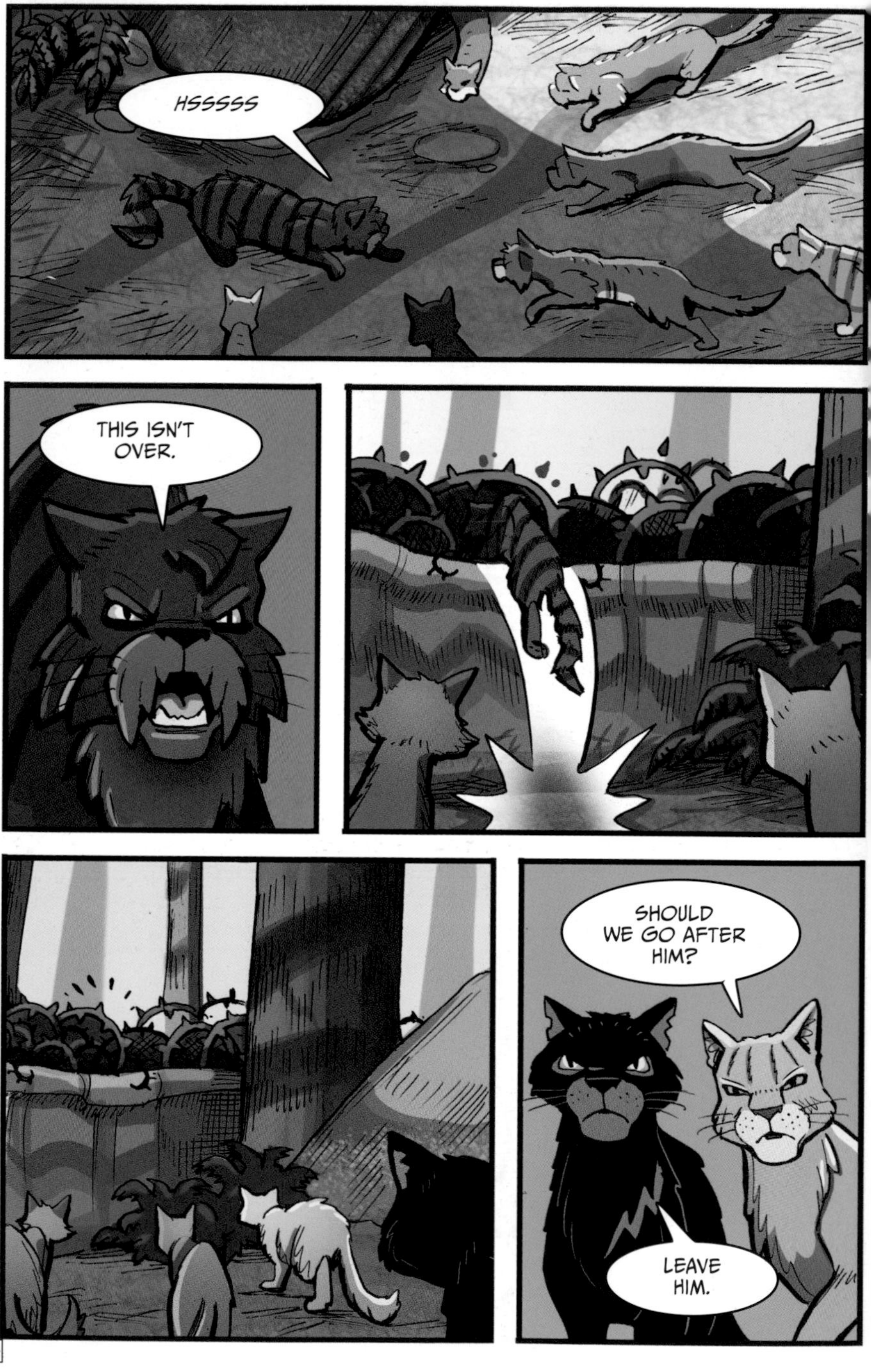
HSSSSS
THIS ISN'T OVER.
SHOULD WE GO AFTER HIM?
LEAVE HIM.

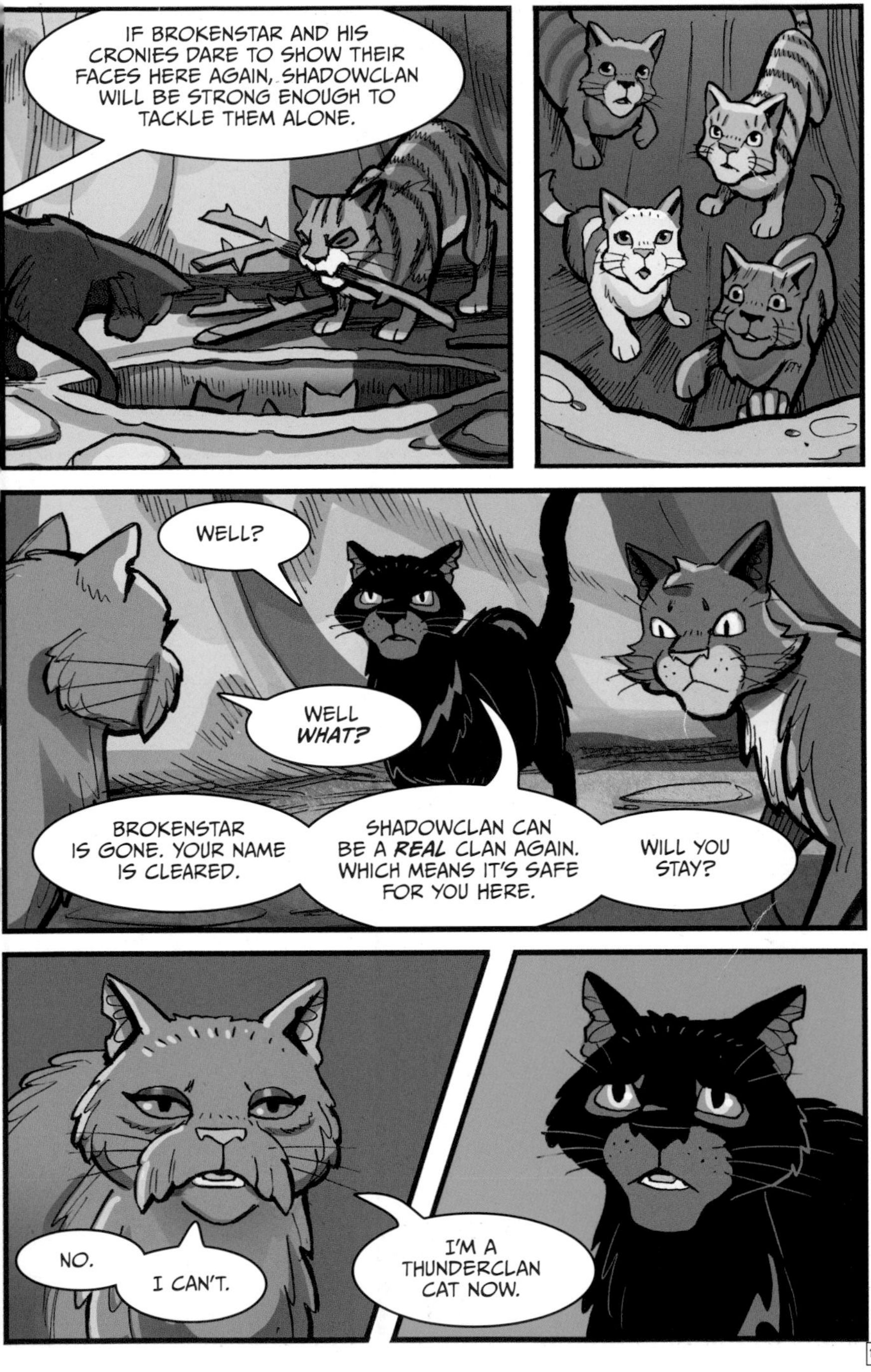
IF BROKENSTAR AND HIS CRONIES DARE TO SHOW THEIR FACES HERE AGAIN, SHADOWCLAN WILL BE STRONG ENOUGH TO TACKLE THEM ALONE.
WELL?
WELL *WHAT?*
BROKENSTAR IS GONE. YOUR NAME IS CLEARED.
SHADOWCLAN CAN BE A *REAL* CLAN AGAIN. WHICH MEANS IT'S SAFE FOR YOU HERE.
WILL YOU STAY?
NO.
I CAN'T.
I'M A THUNDERCLAN CAT NOW.

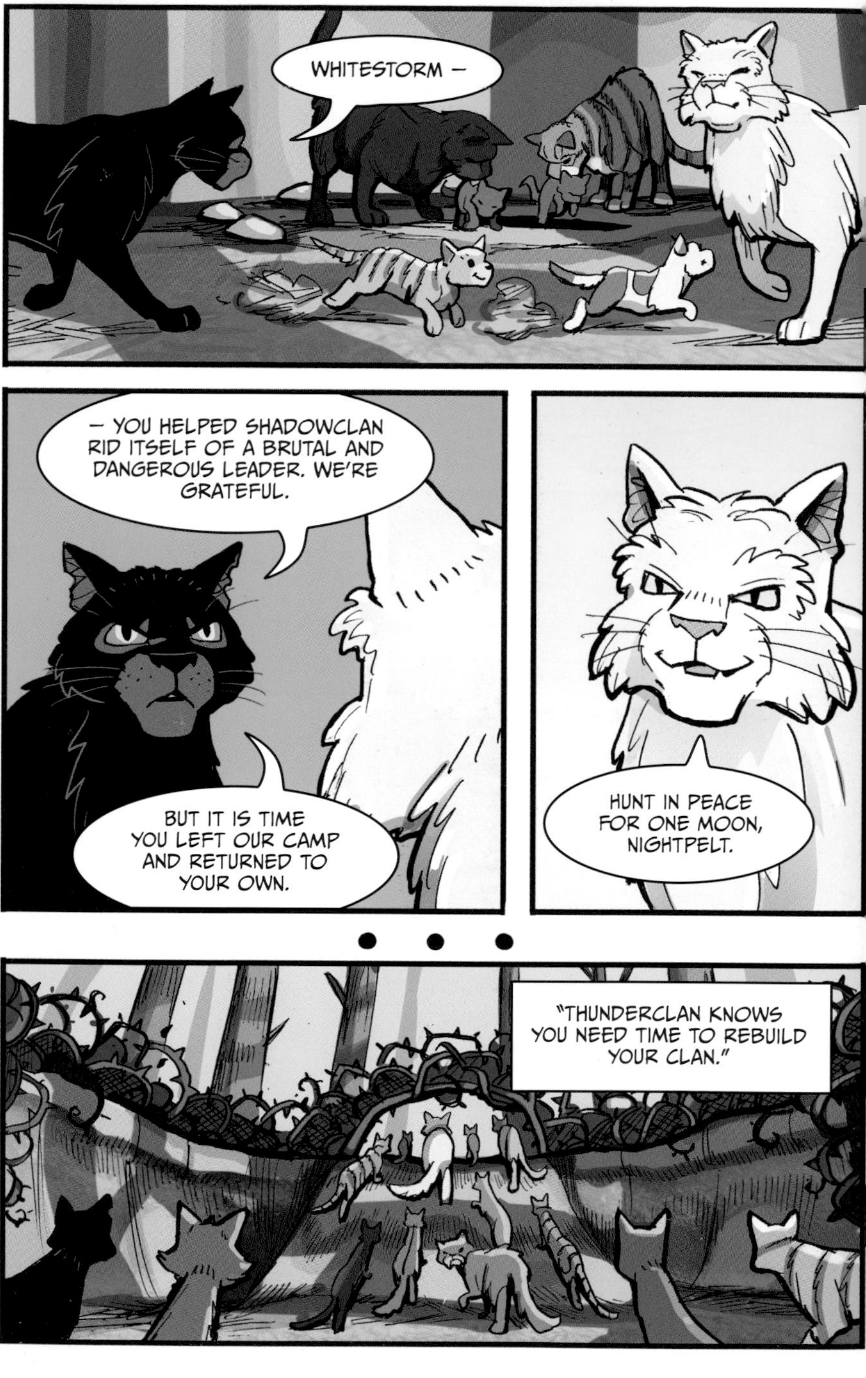
WHITESTORM –
– YOU HELPED SHADOWCLAN RID ITSELF OF A BRUTAL AND DANGEROUS LEADER. WE'RE GRATEFUL.
BUT IT IS TIME YOU LEFT OUR CAMP AND RETURNED TO YOUR OWN.
HUNT IN PEACE FOR ONE MOON, NIGHTPELT.
"THUNDERCLAN KNOWS YOU NEED TIME TO REBUILD YOUR CLAN."

WE DID IT.
WE MADE IT THROUGH.

≥ KOFF KOFF ≤
≥ WHEEEEZE ≤

≥ KOFF KOFF KOFF ≤
≥ HAKK ≤

AND I AM *EXHAUSTED.*

HERE — NIGHTPELT. CHEW THESE. THEY'LL HELP.

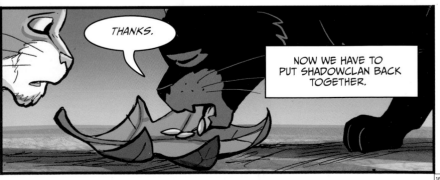

THANKS.

NOW WE HAVE TO PUT SHADOWCLAN BACK TOGETHER.

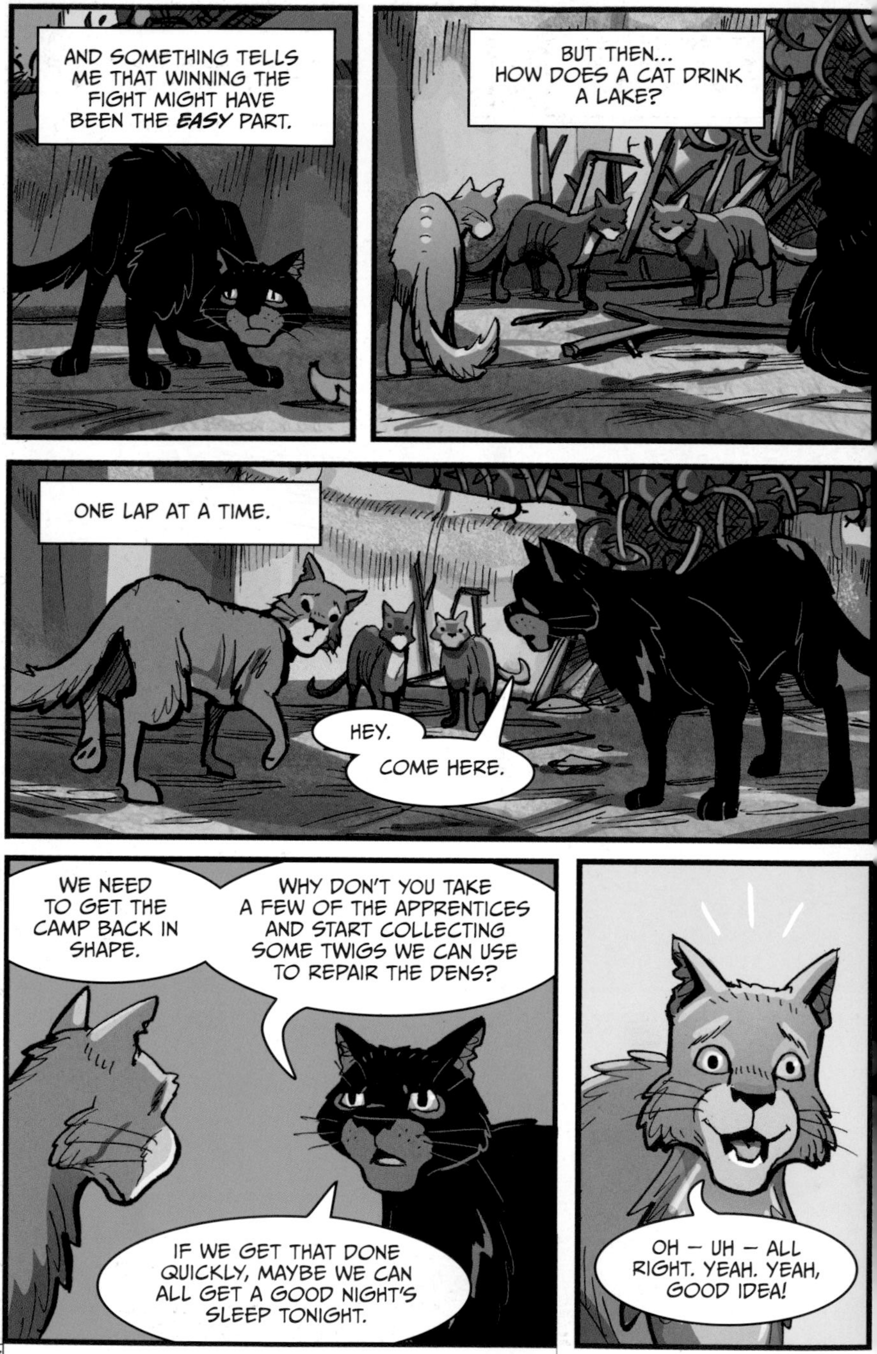
AND SOMETHING TELLS ME THAT WINNING THE FIGHT MIGHT HAVE BEEN THE *EASY* PART.
BUT THEN... HOW DOES A CAT DRINK A LAKE?
ONE LAP AT A TIME.
HEY.
COME HERE.
WE NEED TO GET THE CAMP BACK IN SHAPE.
WHY DON'T YOU TAKE A FEW OF THE APPRENTICES AND START COLLECTING SOME TWIGS WE CAN USE TO REPAIR THE DENS?
IF WE GET THAT DONE QUICKLY, MAYBE WE CAN ALL GET A GOOD NIGHT'S SLEEP TONIGHT.
OH — UH — ALL RIGHT. YEAH. YEAH, GOOD IDEA!

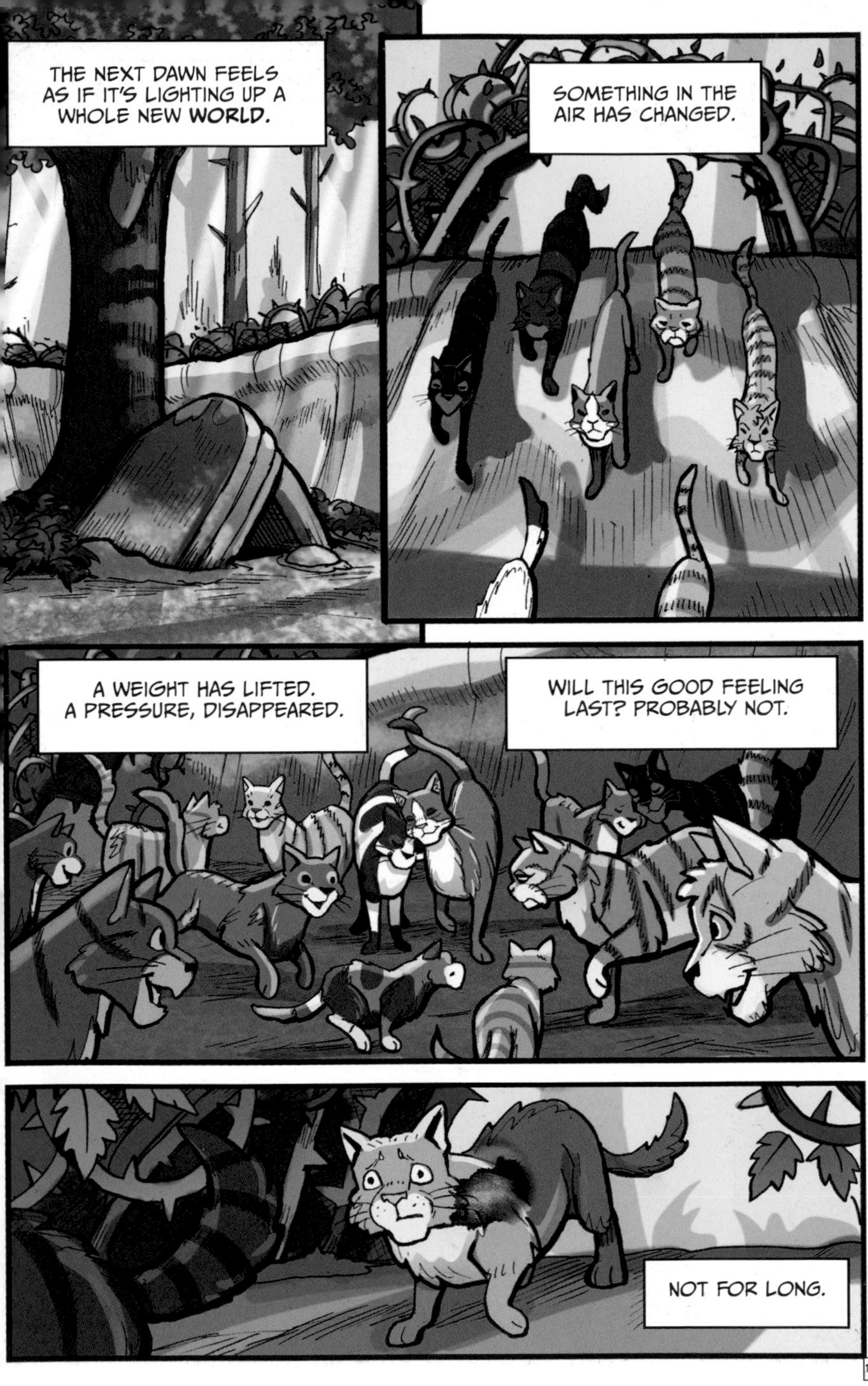
THE NEXT DAWN FEELS AS IF IT'S LIGHTING UP A WHOLE NEW **WORLD.**
SOMETHING IN THE AIR HAS CHANGED.
A WEIGHT HAS LIFTED. A PRESSURE, DISAPPEARED.
WILL THIS GOOD FEELING LAST? PROBABLY NOT.
NOT FOR LONG.

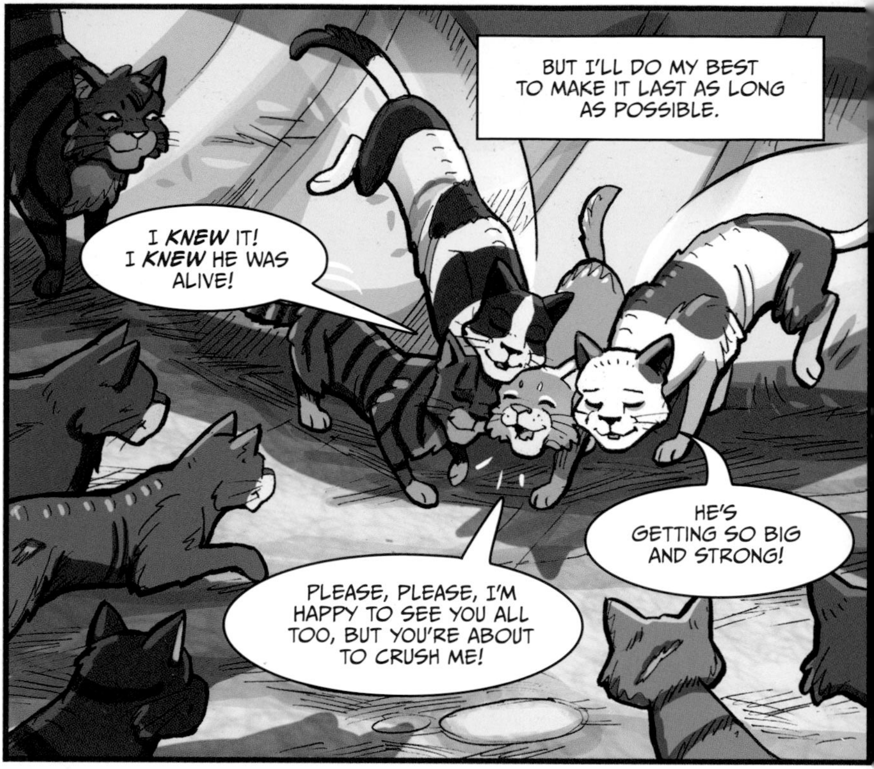
BUT I'LL DO MY BEST TO MAKE IT LAST AS LONG AS POSSIBLE.
I *KNEW* IT! I *KNEW* HE WAS ALIVE!
HE'S GETTING SO BIG AND STRONG!
PLEASE, PLEASE, I'M HAPPY TO SEE YOU ALL TOO, BUT YOU'RE ABOUT TO CRUSH ME!

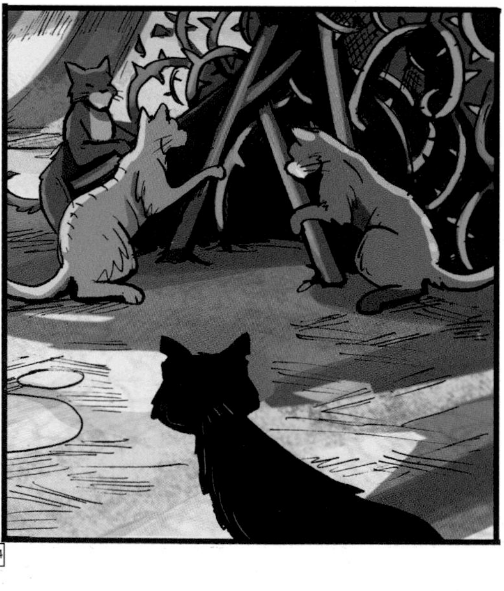

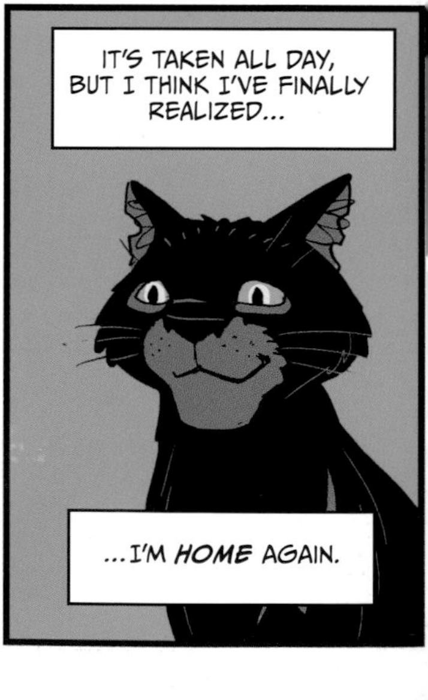
IT'S TAKEN ALL DAY, BUT I THINK I'VE FINALLY REALIZED...
...I'M *HOME* AGAIN.

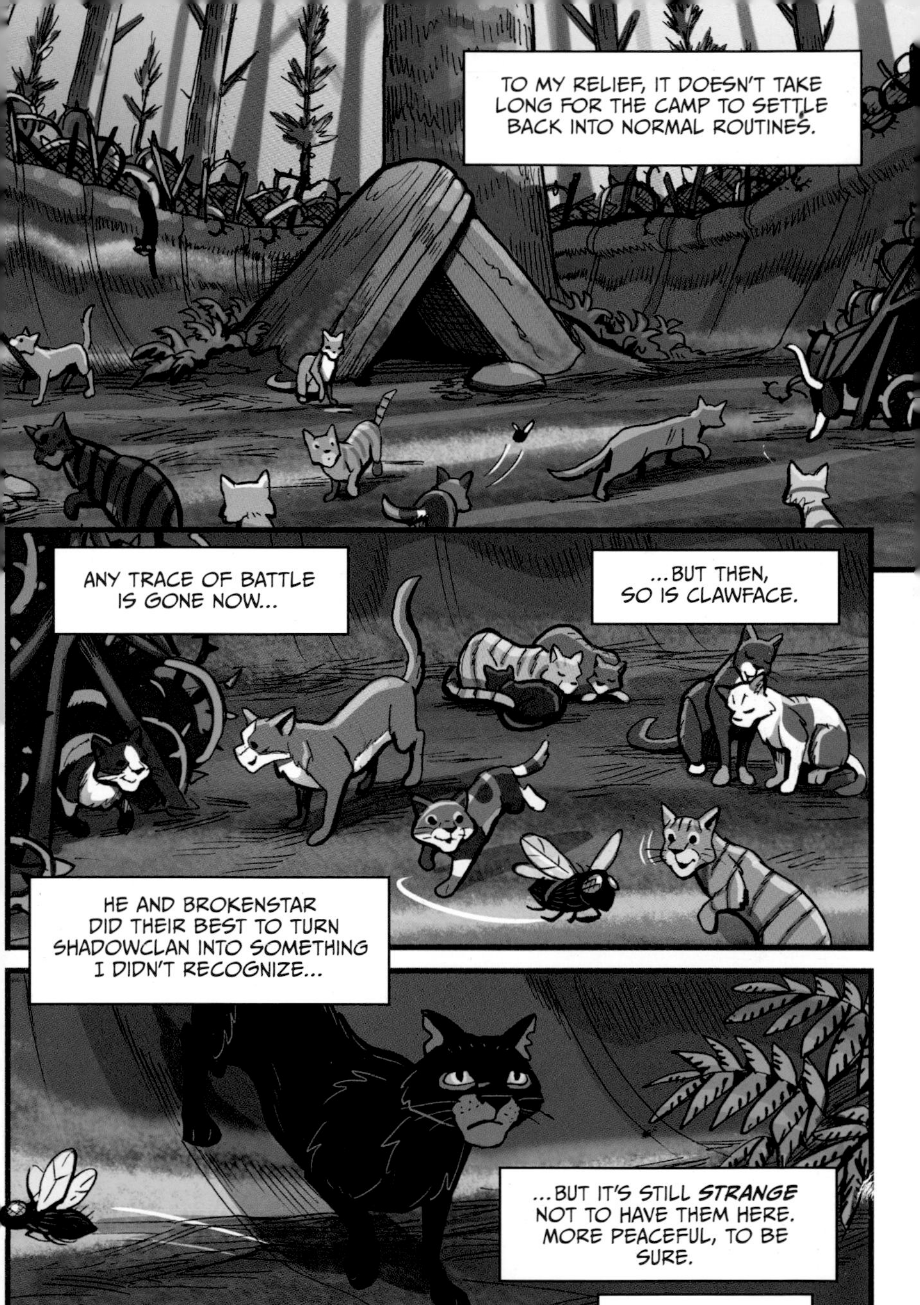
TO MY RELIEF, IT DOESN'T TAKE LONG FOR THE CAMP TO SETTLE BACK INTO NORMAL ROUTINES.
ANY TRACE OF BATTLE IS GONE NOW...
...BUT THEN, SO IS CLAWFACE.
HE AND BROKENSTAR DID THEIR BEST TO TURN SHADOWCLAN INTO SOMETHING I DIDN'T RECOGNIZE...
...BUT IT'S STILL *STRANGE* NOT TO HAVE THEM HERE. MORE PEACEFUL, TO BE SURE.
BUT *STRANGE.*

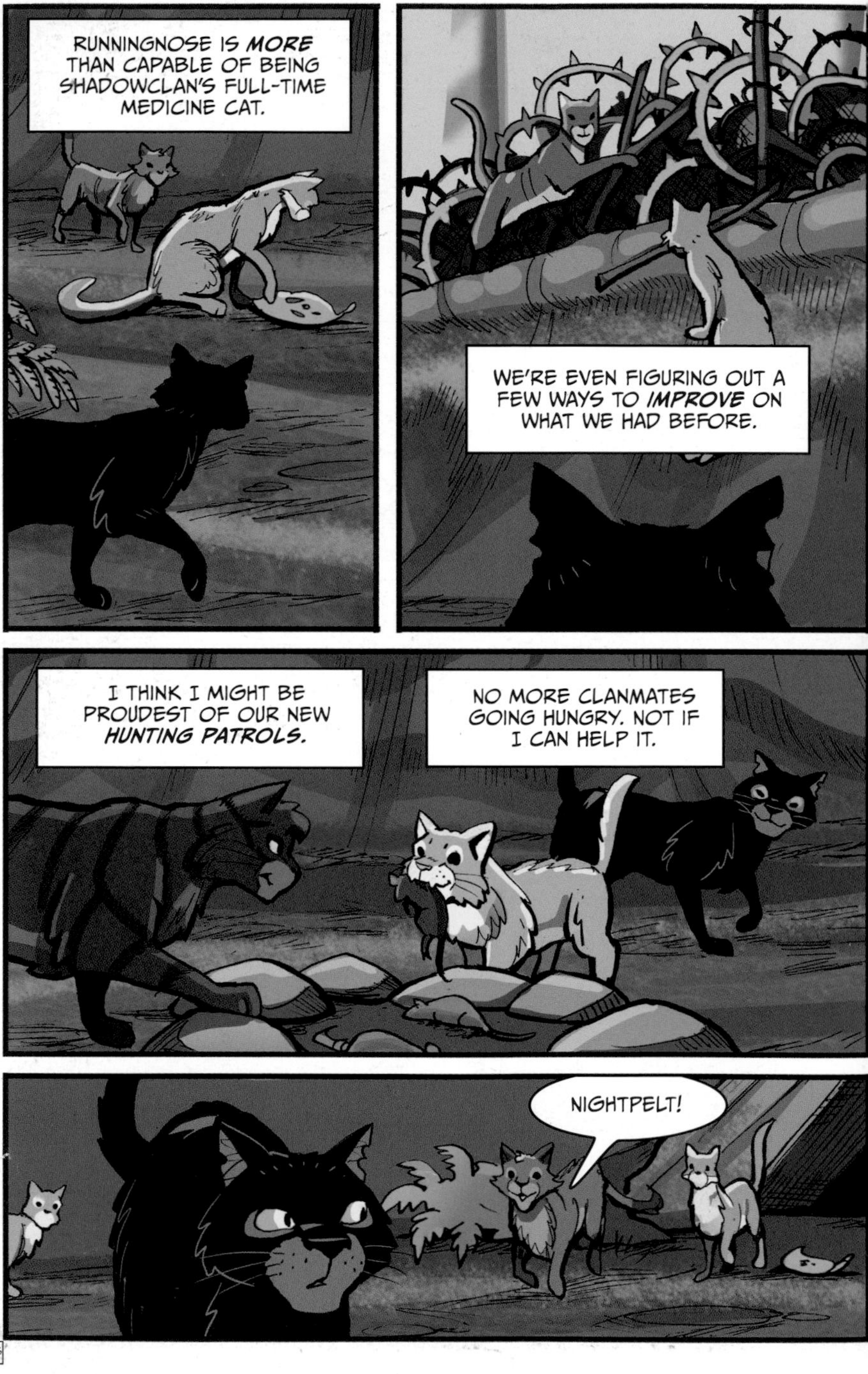
RUNNINGNOSE IS MORE THAN CAPABLE OF BEING SHADOWCLAN'S FULL-TIME MEDICINE CAT.
WE'RE EVEN FIGURING OUT A FEW WAYS TO IMPROVE ON WHAT WE HAD BEFORE.
I THINK I MIGHT BE PROUDEST OF OUR NEW HUNTING PATROLS.
NO MORE CLANMATES GOING HUNGRY. NOT IF I CAN HELP IT.
NIGHTPELT!

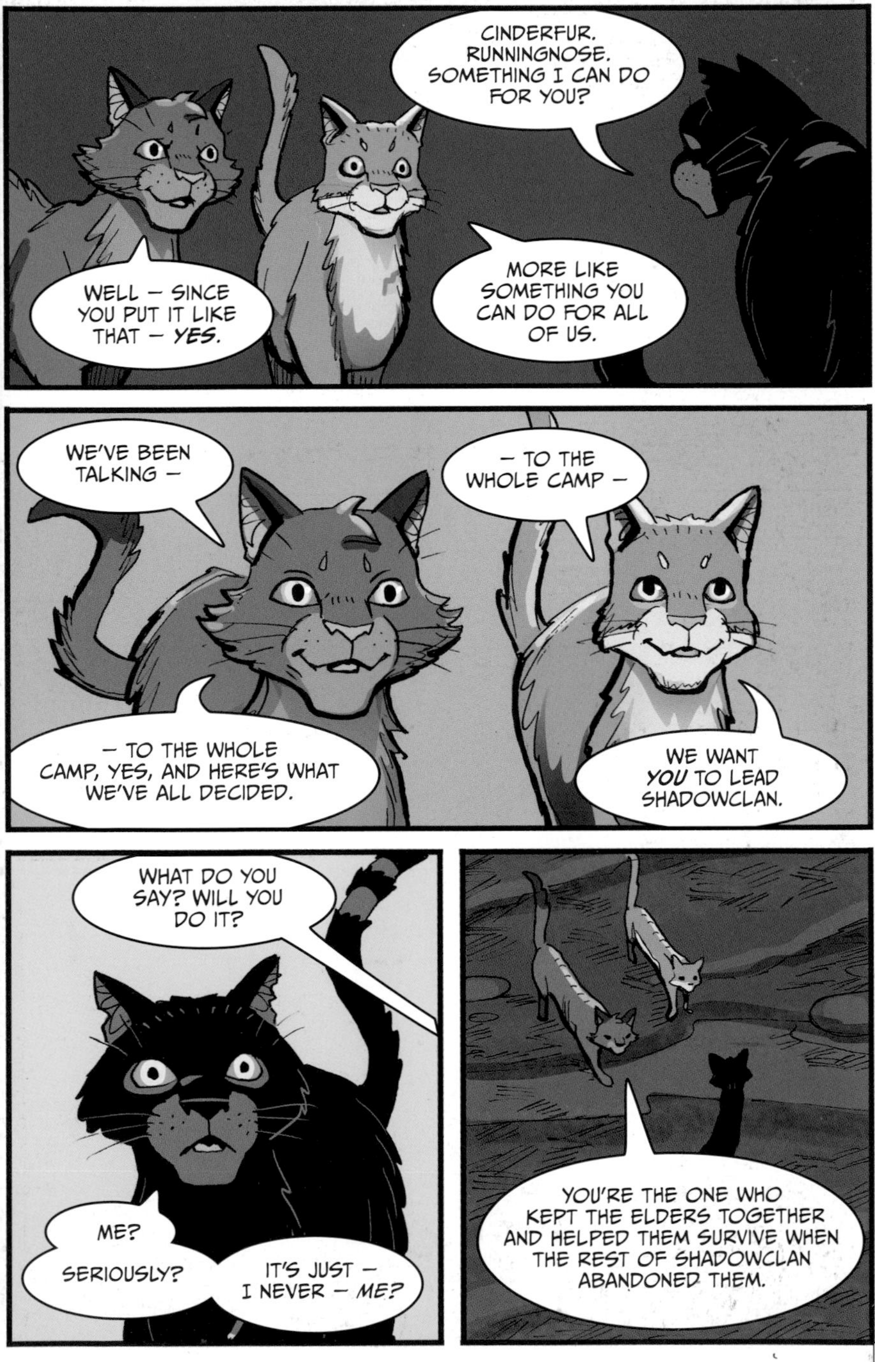
CINDERFUR. RUNNINGNOSE. SOMETHING I CAN DO FOR YOU?
WELL — SINCE YOU PUT IT LIKE THAT — *YES.*
MORE LIKE SOMETHING YOU CAN DO FOR ALL OF US.
WE'VE BEEN TALKING —
— TO THE WHOLE CAMP —
— TO THE WHOLE CAMP, YES, AND HERE'S WHAT WE'VE ALL DECIDED.
WE WANT *YOU* TO LEAD SHADOWCLAN.
WHAT DO YOU SAY? WILL YOU DO IT?
ME?
SERIOUSLY?
IT'S JUST — I NEVER — *ME?*
YOU'RE THE ONE WHO KEPT THE ELDERS TOGETHER AND HELPED THEM SURVIVE WHEN THE REST OF SHADOWCLAN ABANDONED THEM.

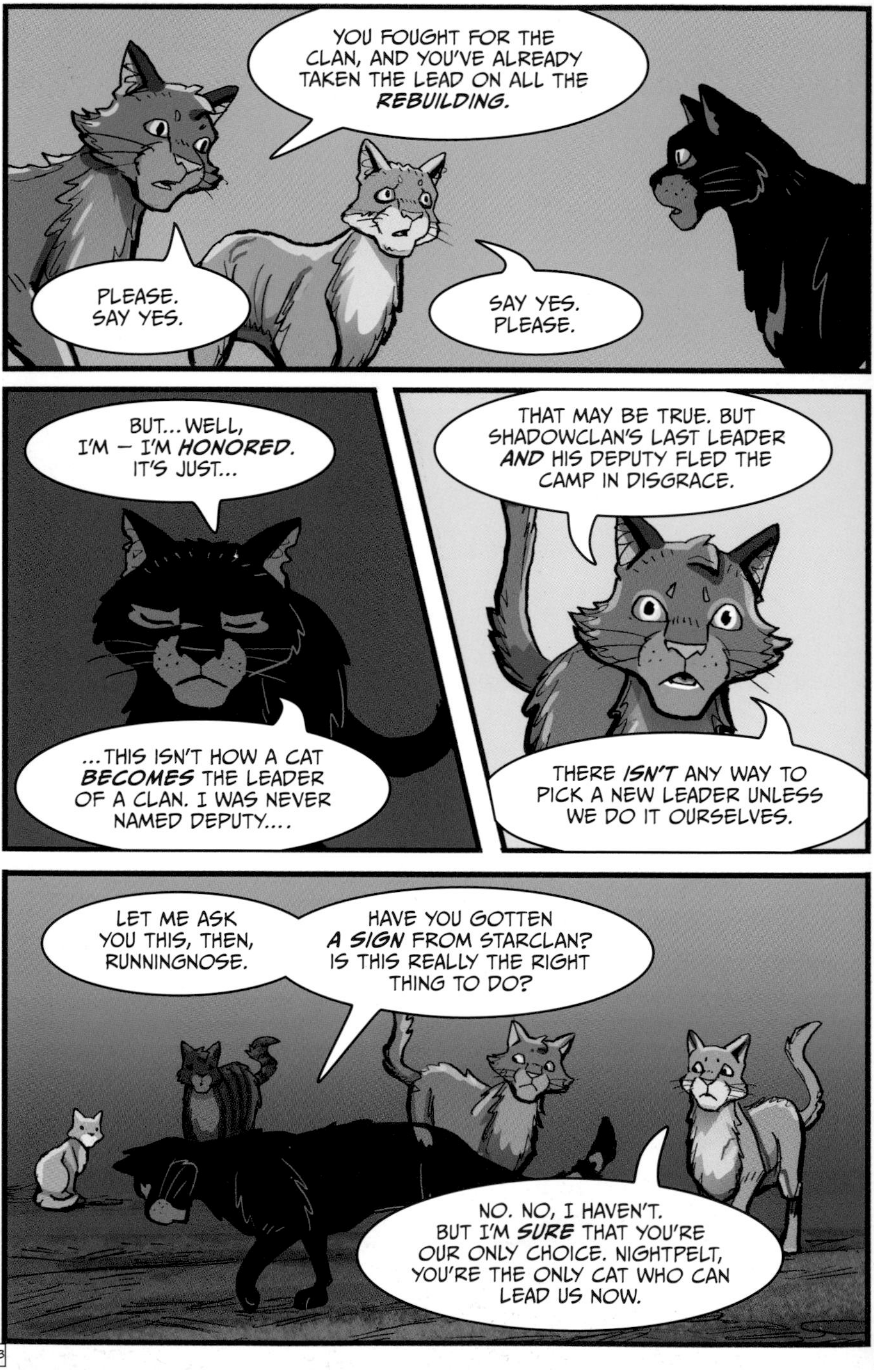
YOU FOUGHT FOR THE CLAN, AND YOU'VE ALREADY TAKEN THE LEAD ON ALL THE ***REBUILDING.***
PLEASE. SAY YES.
SAY YES. PLEASE.
BUT... WELL, I'M — I'M ***HONORED.*** IT'S JUST...
...THIS ISN'T HOW A CAT ***BECOMES*** THE LEADER OF A CLAN. I WAS NEVER NAMED DEPUTY....
THAT MAY BE TRUE. BUT SHADOWCLAN'S LAST LEADER ***AND*** HIS DEPUTY FLED THE CAMP IN DISGRACE.
THERE ***ISN'T*** ANY WAY TO PICK A NEW LEADER UNLESS WE DO IT OURSELVES.
LET ME ASK YOU THIS, THEN, RUNNINGNOSE.
HAVE YOU GOTTEN ***A SIGN*** FROM STARCLAN? IS THIS REALLY THE RIGHT THING TO DO?
NO. NO, I HAVEN'T. BUT I'M ***SURE*** THAT YOU'RE OUR ONLY CHOICE. NIGHTPELT, YOU'RE THE ONLY CAT WHO CAN LEAD US NOW.

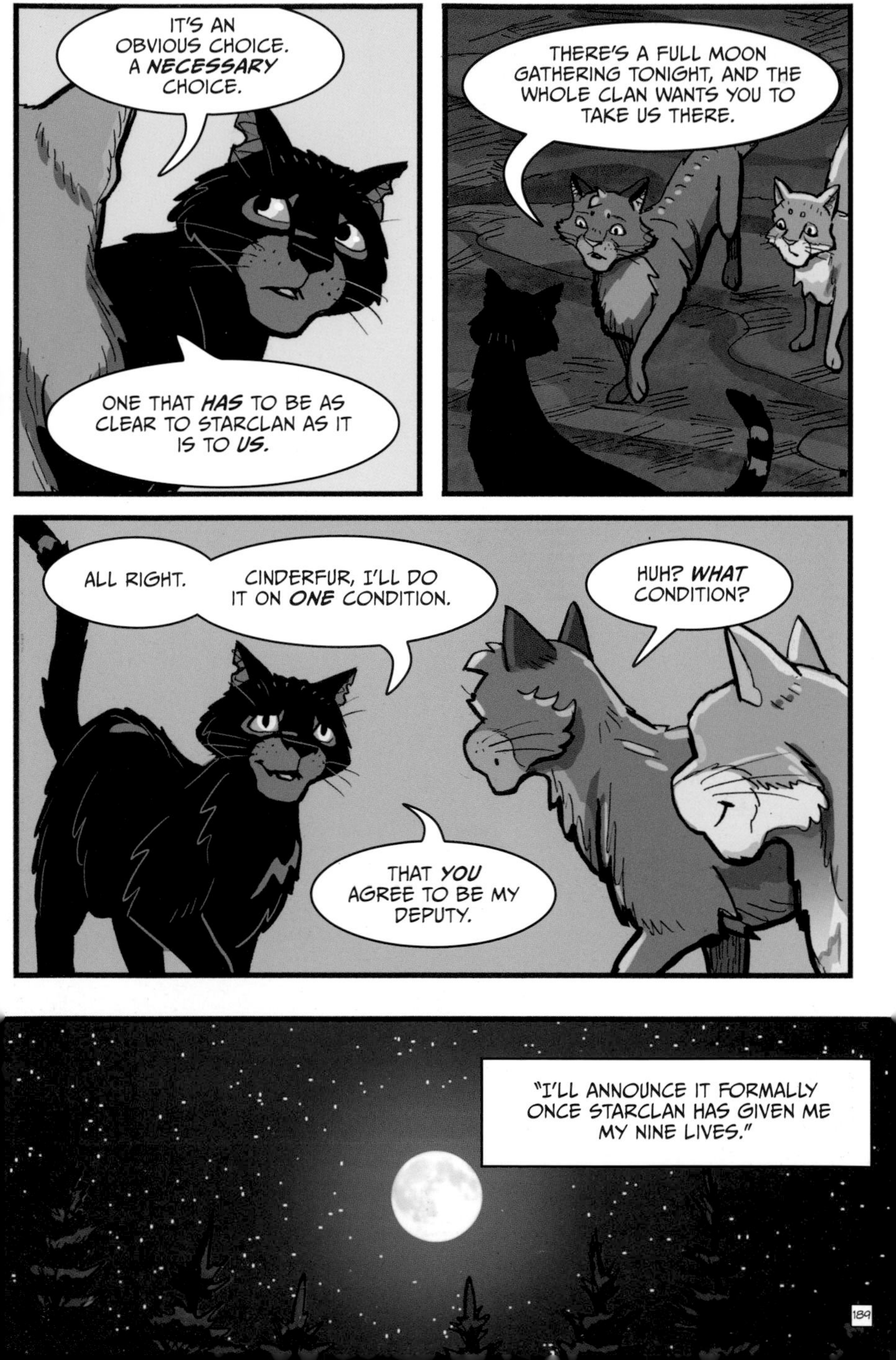
IT'S AN OBVIOUS CHOICE. A *NECESSARY* CHOICE.
ONE THAT *HAS* TO BE AS CLEAR TO STARCLAN AS IT IS TO *US.*
THERE'S A FULL MOON GATHERING TONIGHT, AND THE WHOLE CLAN WANTS YOU TO TAKE US THERE.
ALL RIGHT.
CINDERFUR, I'LL DO IT ON *ONE* CONDITION.
HUH? *WHAT* CONDITION?
THAT *YOU* AGREE TO BE MY DEPUTY.
"I'LL ANNOUNCE IT FORMALLY ONCE STARCLAN HAS GIVEN ME MY NINE LIVES."

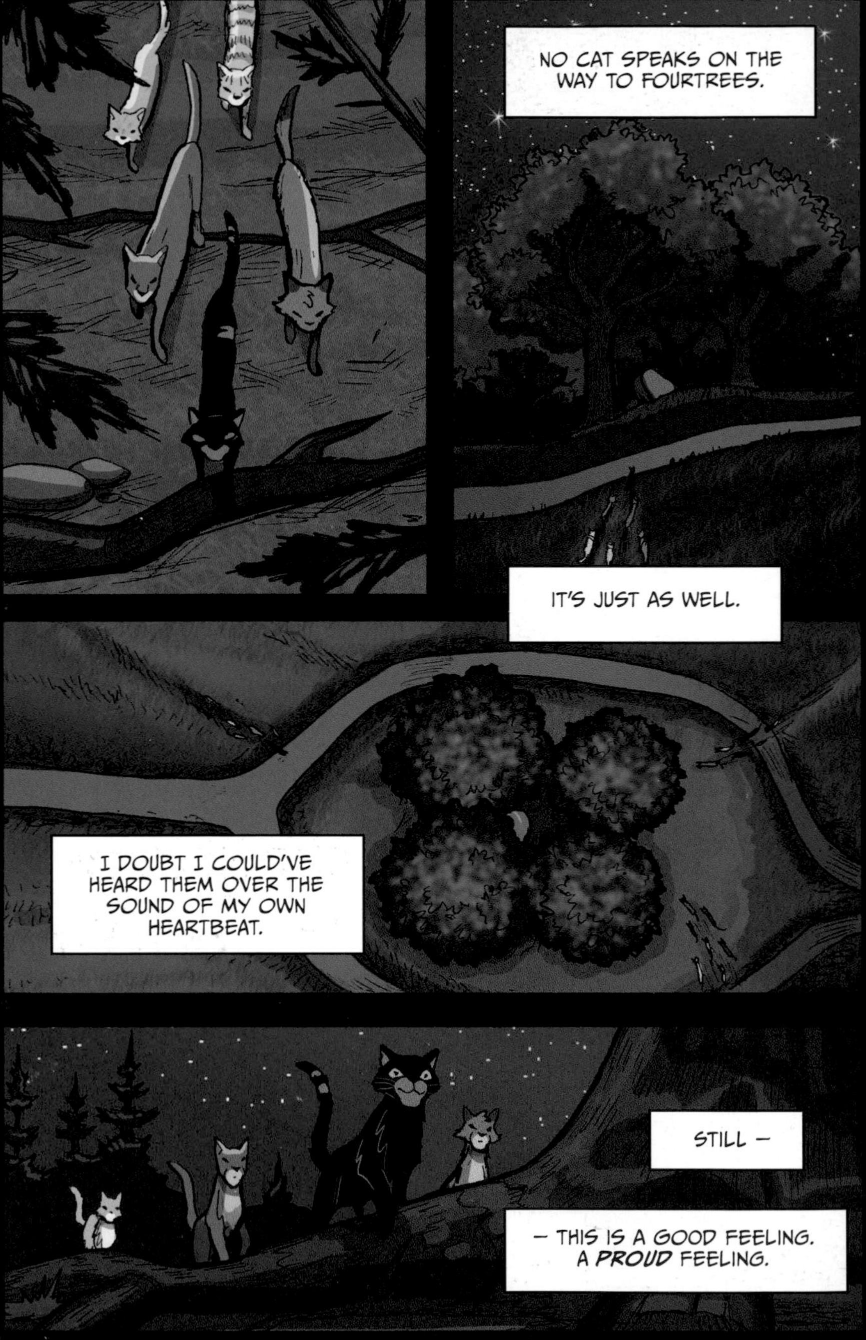

NO CAT SPEAKS ON THE WAY TO FOURTREES.
IT'S JUST AS WELL.
I DOUBT I COULD'VE HEARD THEM OVER THE SOUND OF MY OWN HEARTBEAT.
STILL –
– THIS IS A GOOD FEELING. A *PROUD* FEELING.

I DECIDE TO LET MYSELF ENJOY IT.

I, NIGHTPELT, HAVE TAKEN OVER THE LEADERSHIP OF SHADOWCLAN.

THE SPIRITS OF OUR ANCESTORS HAVE SPOKEN TO RUNNINGNOSE AND CHOSEN ME AS LEADER.

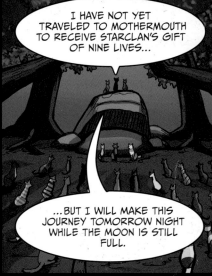

I HAVE NOT YET TRAVELED TO MOTHERMOUTH TO RECEIVE STARCLAN'S GIFT OF NINE LIVES...

...BUT I WILL MAKE THIS JOURNEY TOMORROW NIGHT WHILE THE MOON IS STILL FULL.

AFTER MY VIGIL AT THE MOONSTONE, I SHALL BE KNOWN AS *NIGHTSTAR*.

THESE CATS — THE CATS OF SHADOWCLAN — *DEPEND* ON ME NOW.

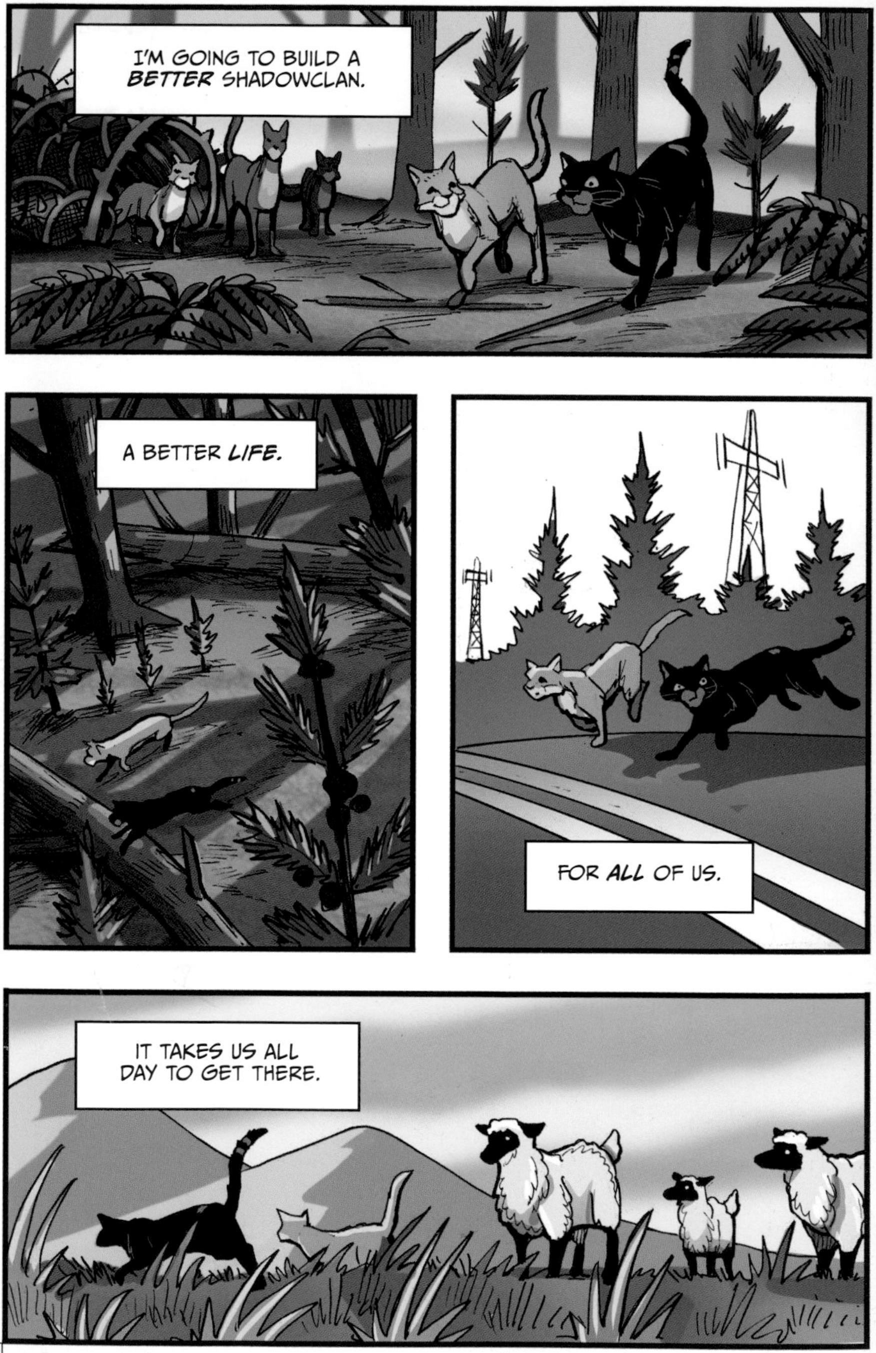
I'M GOING TO BUILD A *BETTER* SHADOWCLAN.
A BETTER *LIFE.*
FOR *ALL* OF US.
IT TAKES US ALL DAY TO GET THERE.

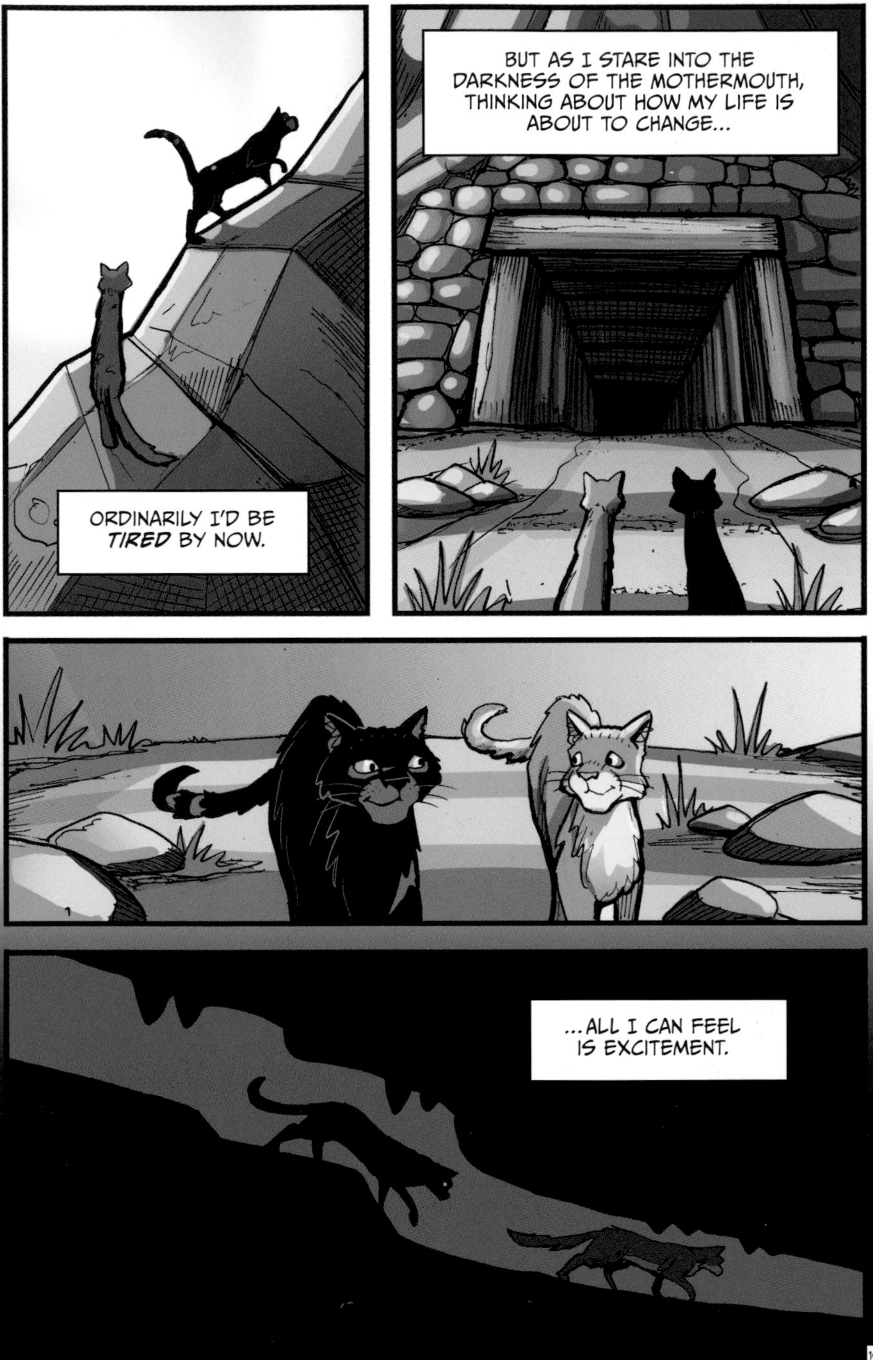
ORDINARILY I'D BE *TIRED* BY NOW.
BUT AS I STARE INTO THE DARKNESS OF THE MOTHERMOUTH, THINKING ABOUT HOW MY LIFE IS ABOUT TO CHANGE...
...ALL I CAN FEEL IS EXCITEMENT.

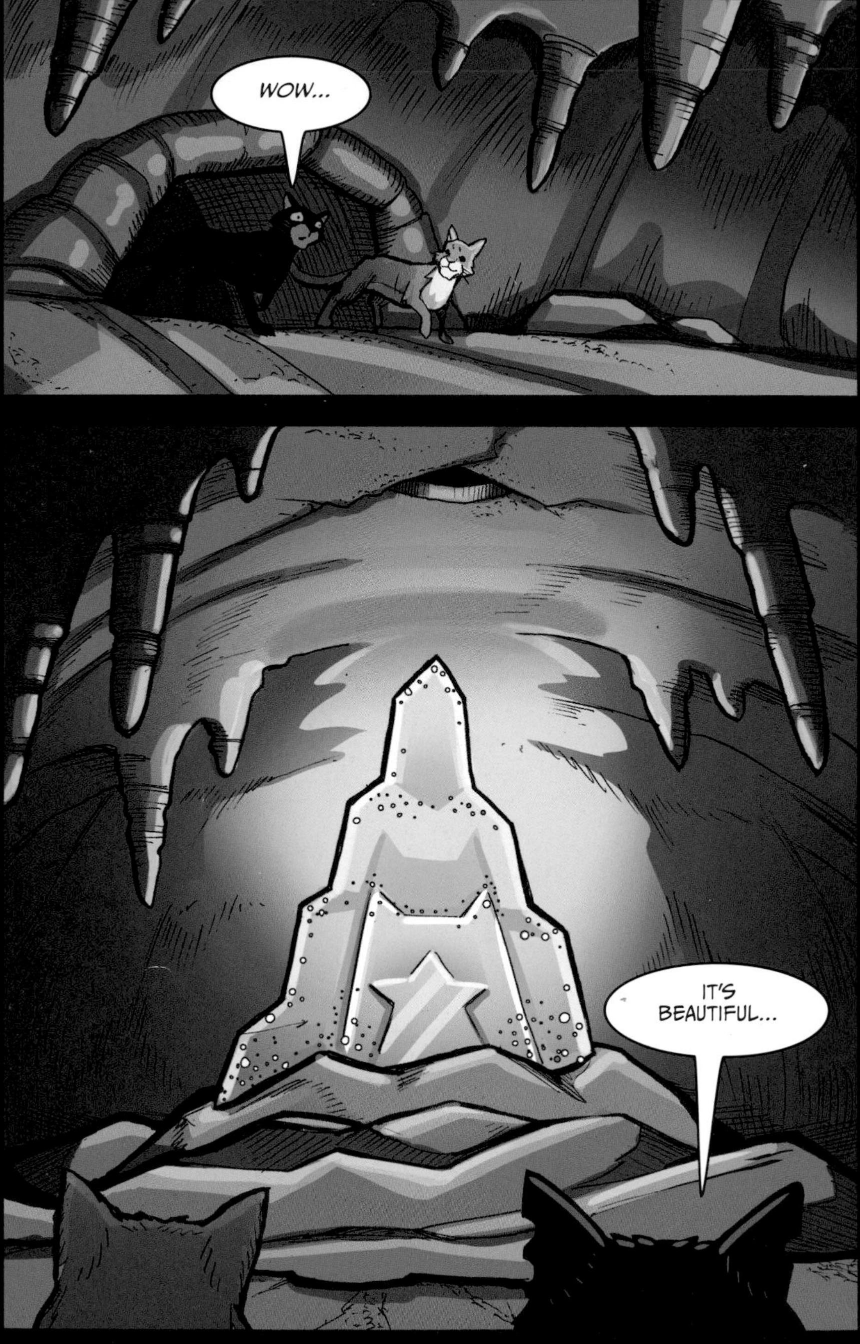
WOW...
IT'S BEAUTIFUL...

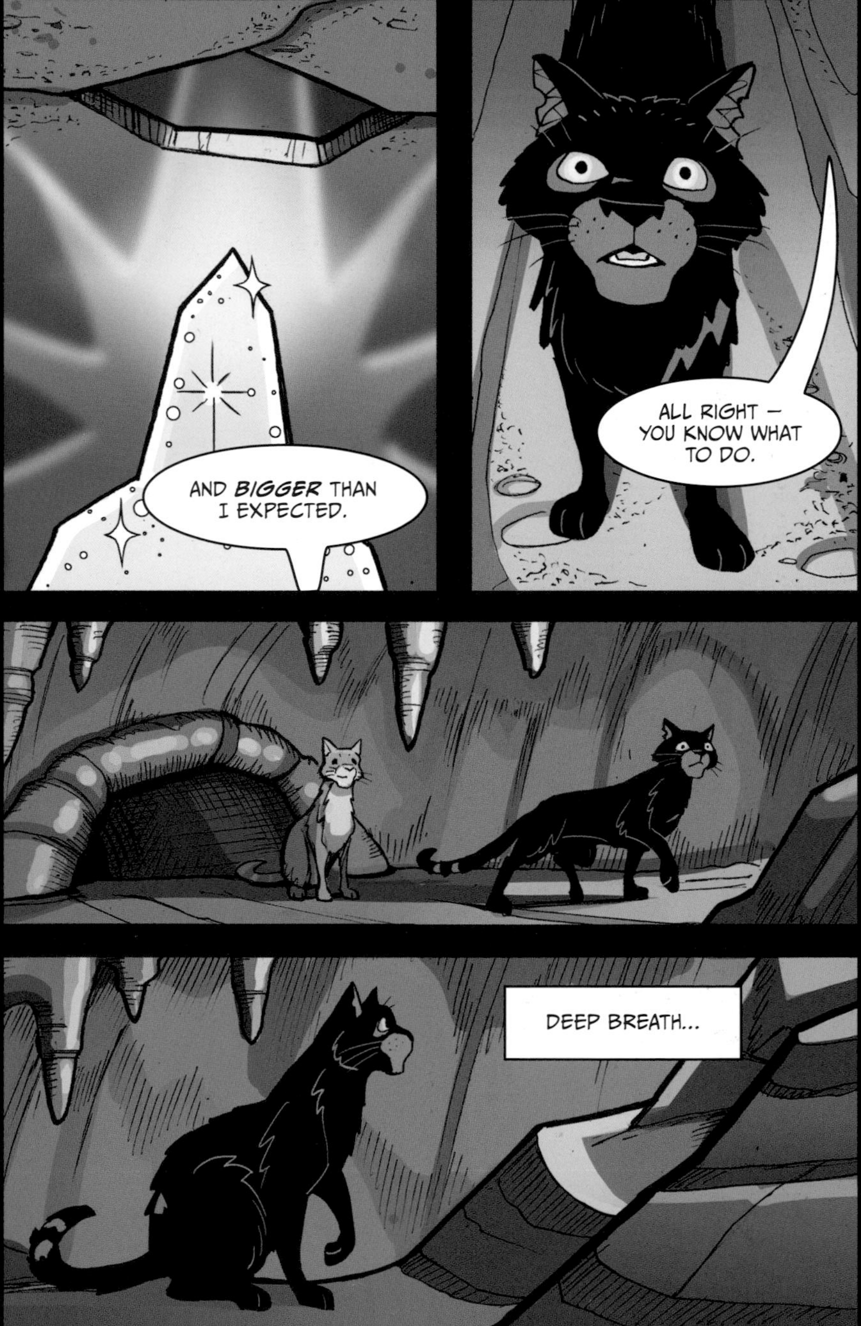
AND *BIGGER* THAN I EXPECTED.
ALL RIGHT — YOU KNOW WHAT TO DO.
DEEP BREATH...

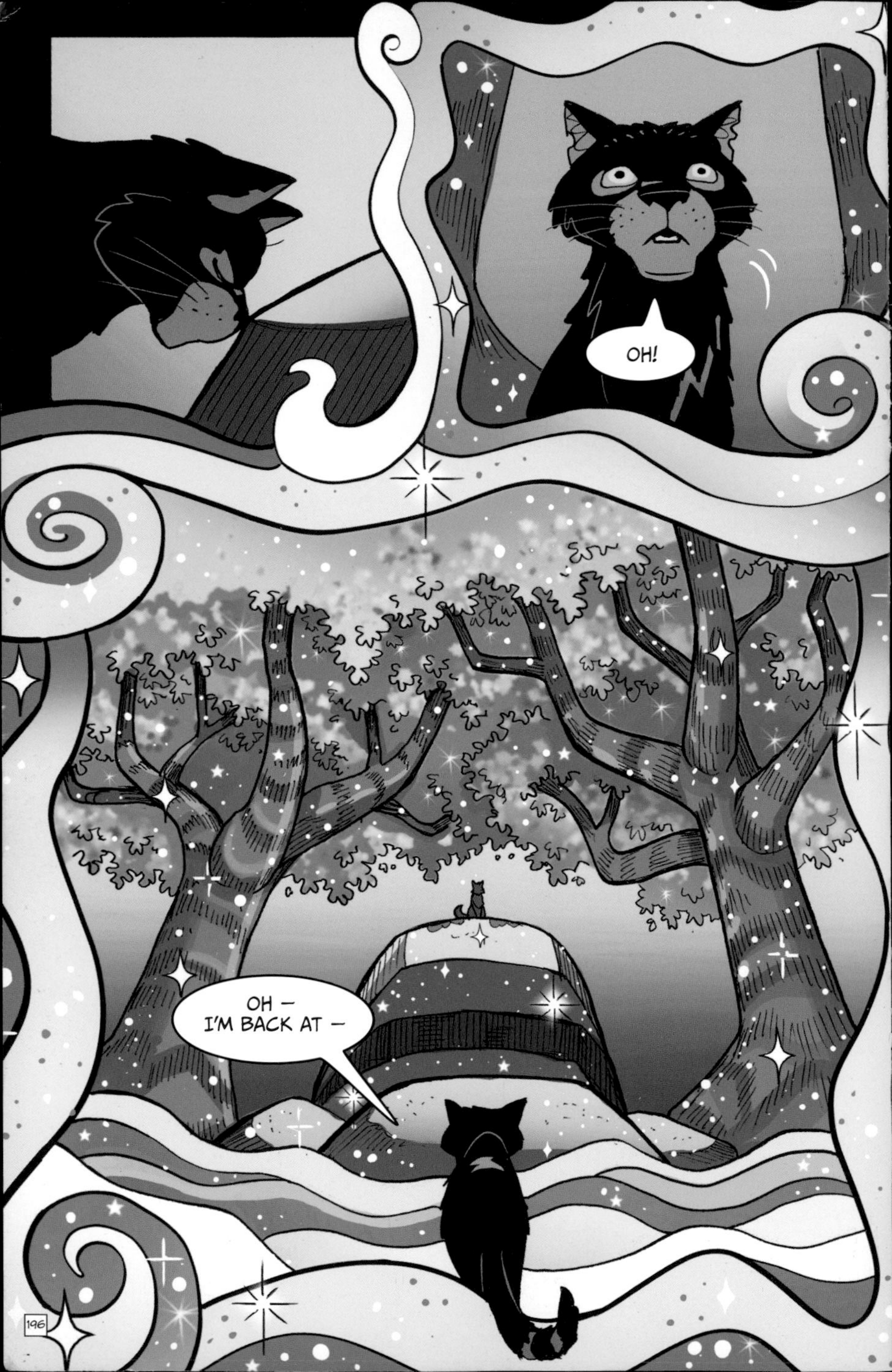
OH!
OH –
I'M BACK AT –

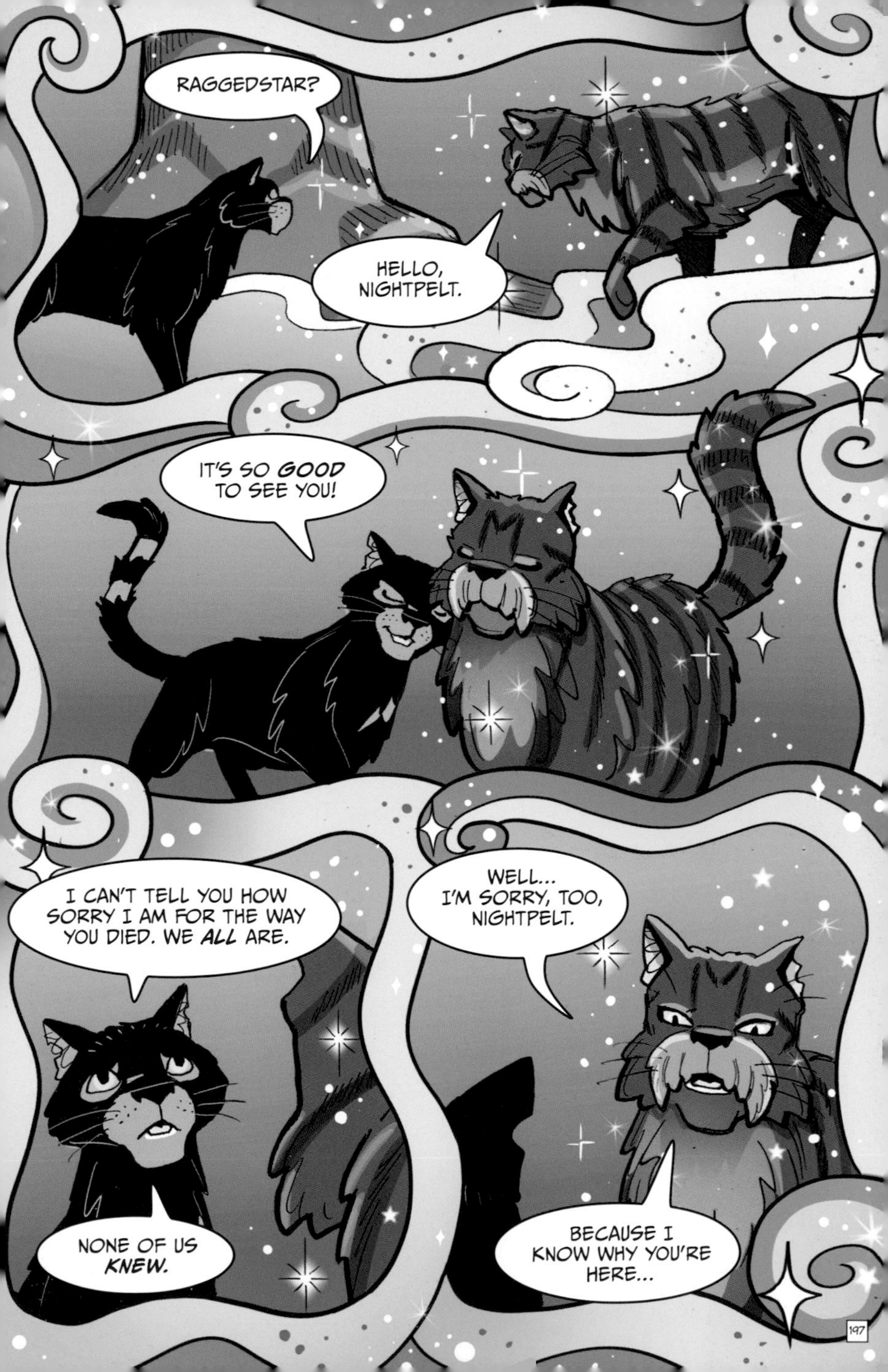
RAGGEDSTAR?
HELLO, NIGHTPELT.
IT'S SO GOOD TO SEE YOU!
I CAN'T TELL YOU HOW SORRY I AM FOR THE WAY YOU DIED. WE ALL ARE.
NONE OF US KNEW.
WELL... I'M SORRY, TOO, NIGHTPELT.
BECAUSE I KNOW WHY YOU'RE HERE...

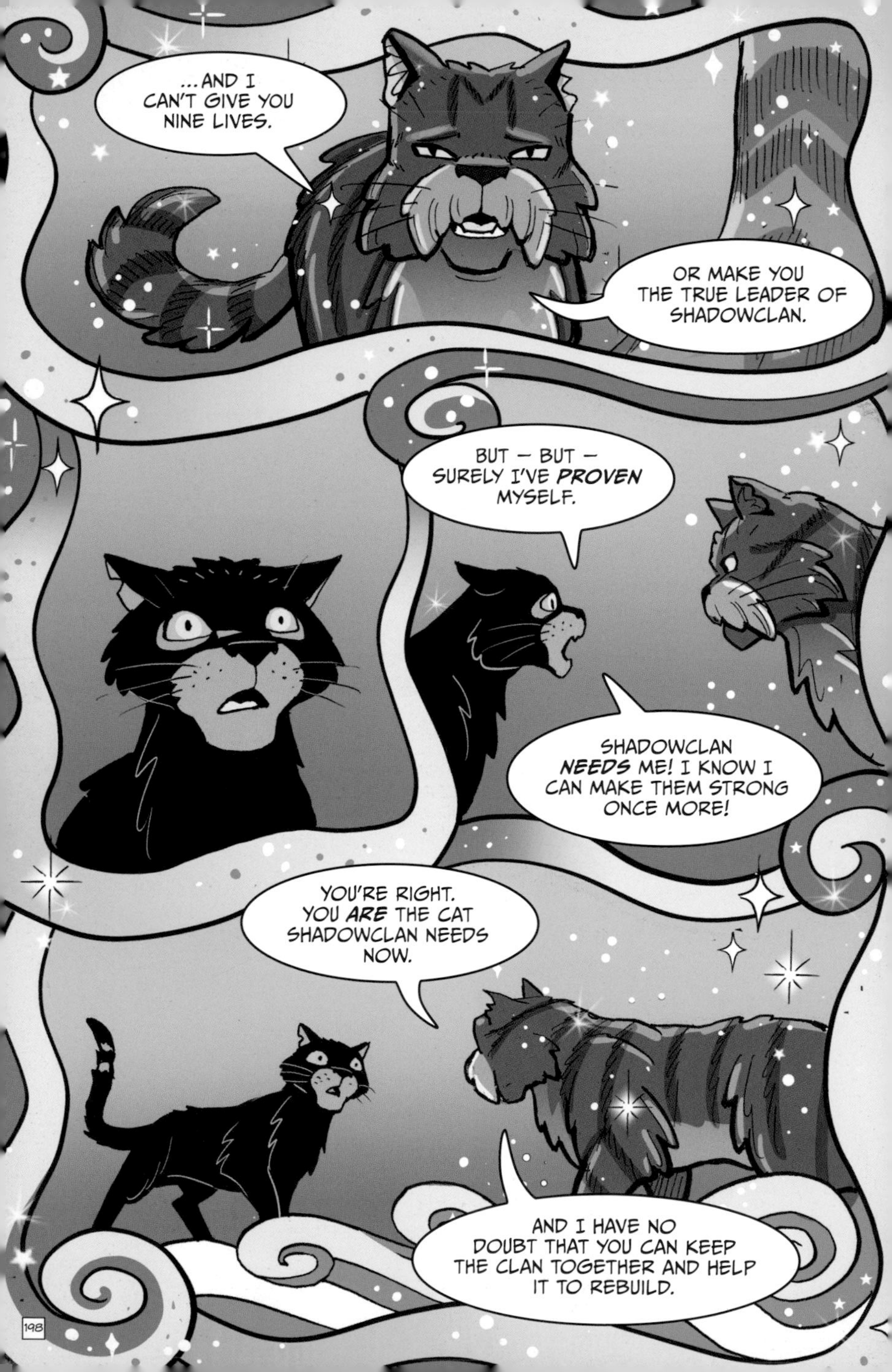
...AND I CAN'T GIVE YOU NINE LIVES.
OR MAKE YOU THE TRUE LEADER OF SHADOWCLAN.
BUT — BUT — SURELY I'VE **PROVEN** MYSELF.
SHADOWCLAN **NEEDS** ME! I KNOW I CAN MAKE THEM STRONG ONCE MORE!
YOU'RE RIGHT. YOU **ARE** THE CAT SHADOWCLAN NEEDS NOW.
AND I HAVE NO DOUBT THAT YOU CAN KEEP THE CLAN TOGETHER AND HELP IT TO REBUILD.

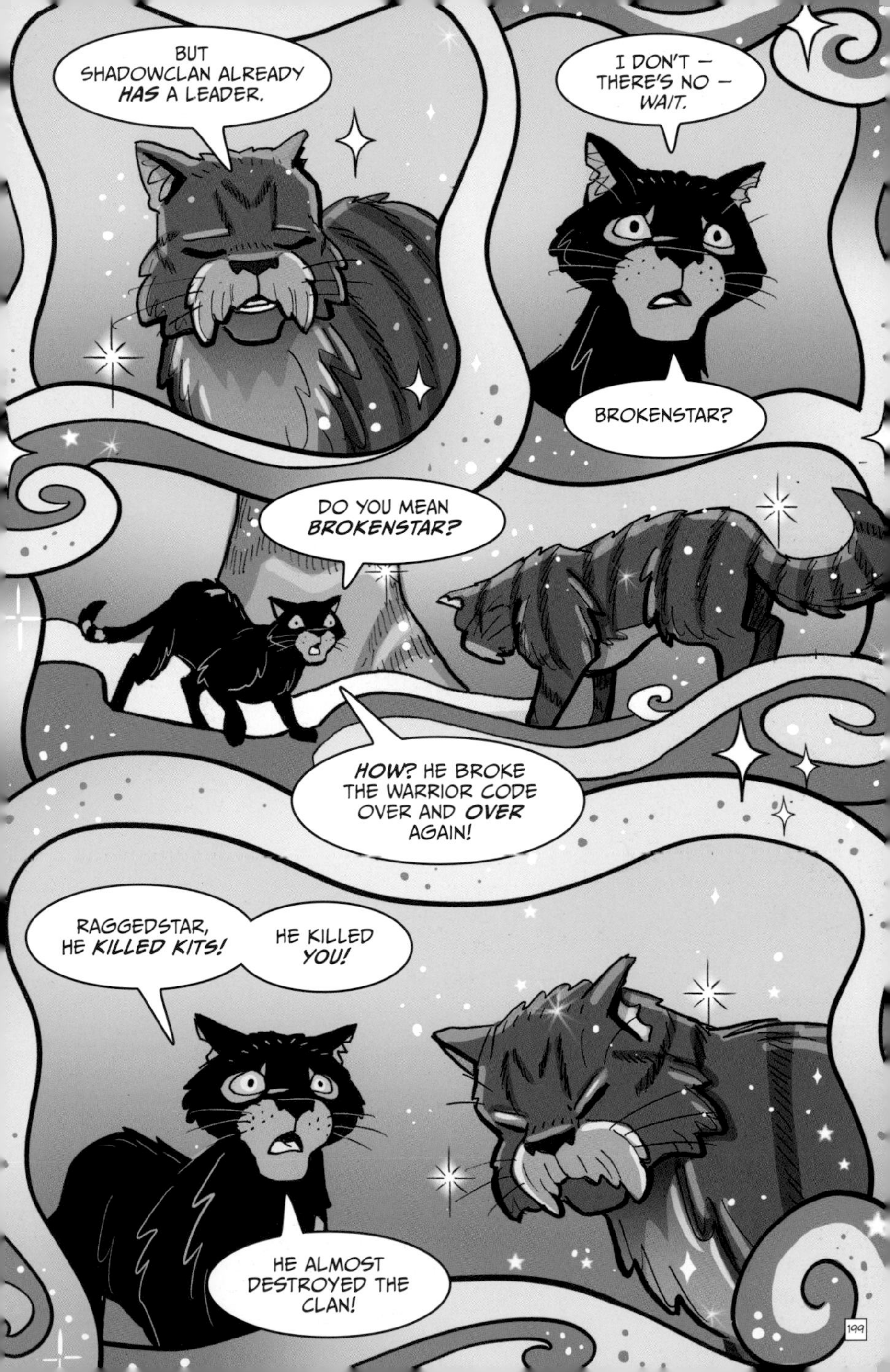
BUT SHADOWCLAN ALREADY **HAS** A LEADER.
I DON'T — THERE'S NO — *WAIT.*
BROKENSTAR?
DO YOU MEAN **BROKENSTAR?**
HOW? HE BROKE THE WARRIOR CODE OVER AND **OVER** AGAIN!
RAGGEDSTAR, HE **KILLED KITS!**
HE KILLED **YOU!**
HE ALMOST DESTROYED THE CLAN!

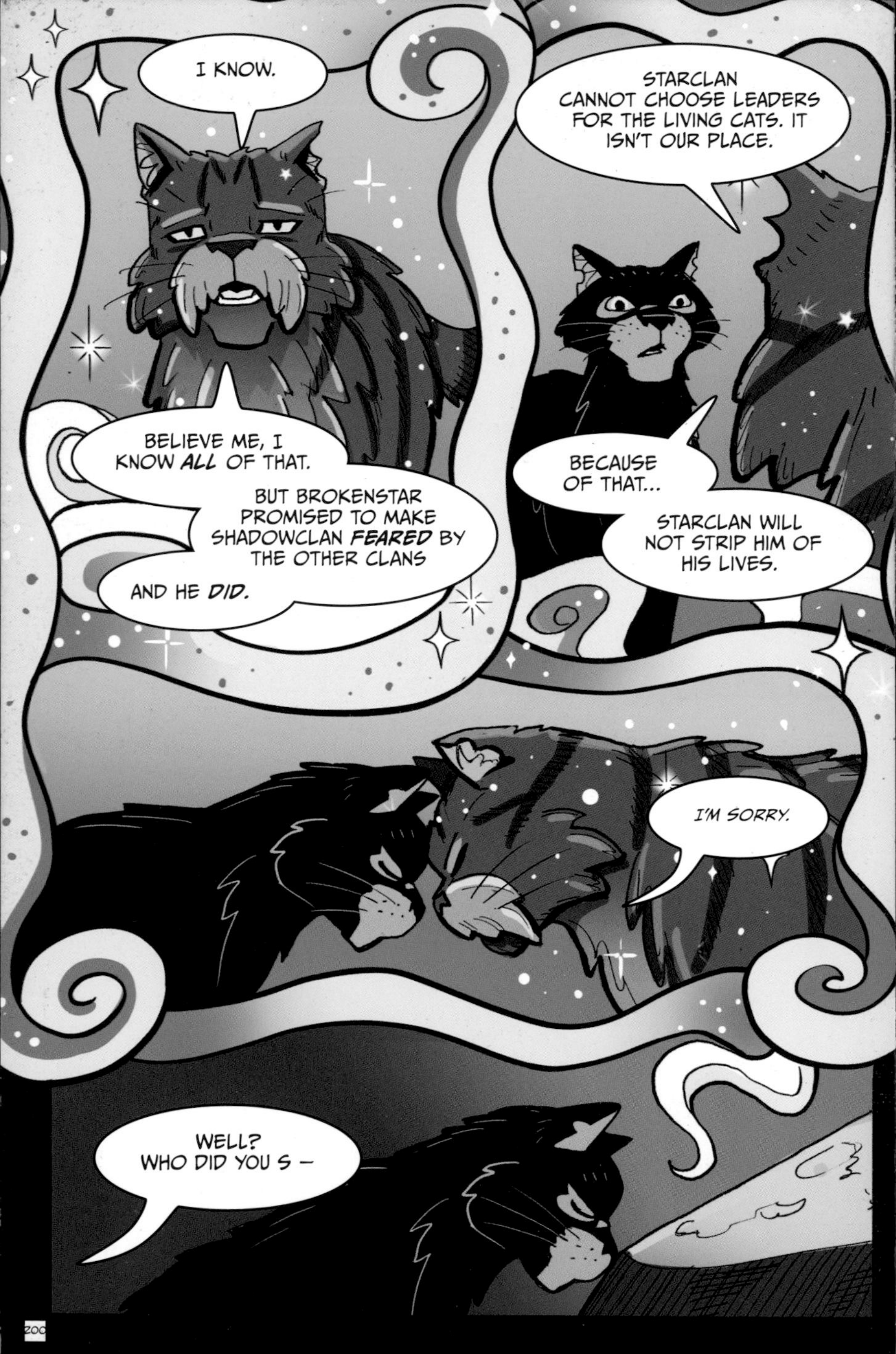
I KNOW.
STARCLAN CANNOT CHOOSE LEADERS FOR THE LIVING CATS. IT ISN'T OUR PLACE.
BELIEVE ME, I KNOW ***ALL*** OF THAT.
BUT BROKENSTAR PROMISED TO MAKE SHADOWCLAN ***FEARED*** BY THE OTHER CLANS
AND HE ***DID.***
BECAUSE OF THAT...
STARCLAN WILL NOT STRIP HIM OF HIS LIVES.
I'M SORRY.
WELL? WHO DID YOU S –

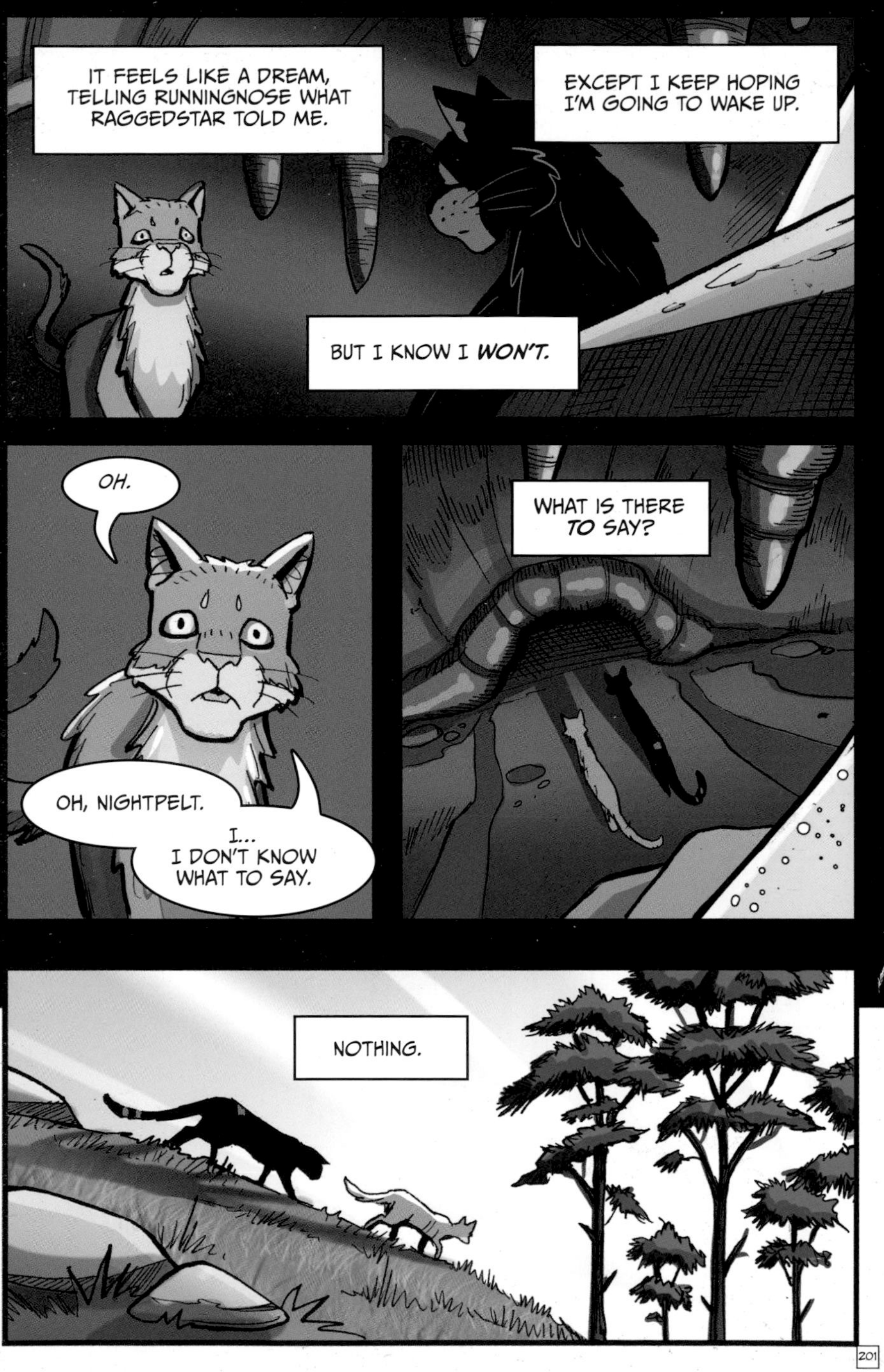
IT FEELS LIKE A DREAM, TELLING RUNNINGNOSE WHAT RAGGEDSTAR TOLD ME.
EXCEPT I KEEP HOPING I'M GOING TO WAKE UP.
BUT I KNOW I ***WON'T.***
OH.
OH, NIGHTPELT.
I... I DON'T KNOW WHAT TO SAY.
WHAT IS THERE ***TO*** SAY?
NOTHING.

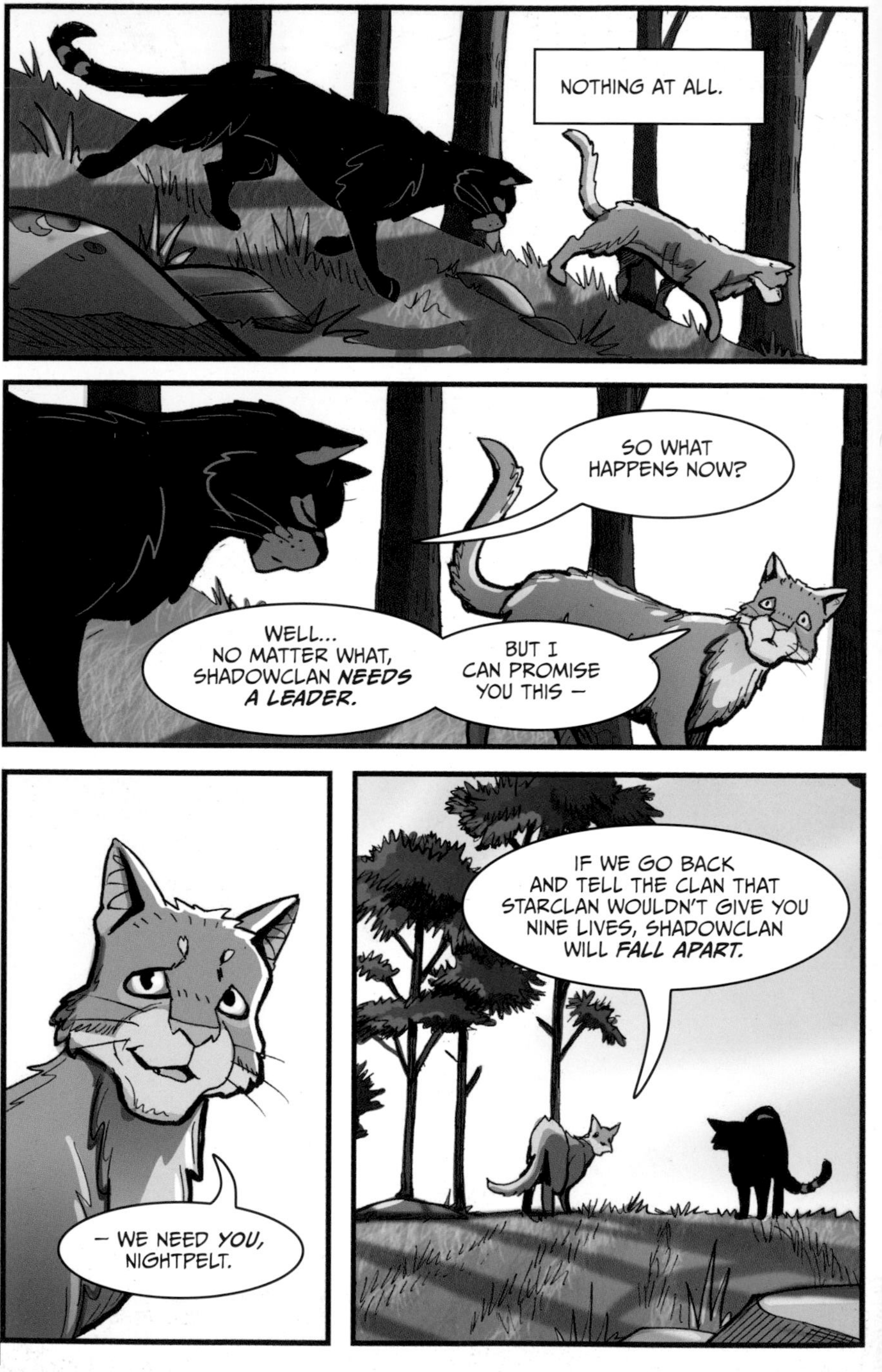
NOTHING AT ALL.
SO WHAT HAPPENS NOW?
WELL... NO MATTER WHAT, SHADOWCLAN NEEDS A LEADER.
BUT I CAN PROMISE YOU THIS –
– WE NEED YOU, NIGHTPELT.
IF WE GO BACK AND TELL THE CLAN THAT STARCLAN WOULDN'T GIVE YOU NINE LIVES, SHADOWCLAN WILL FALL APART.

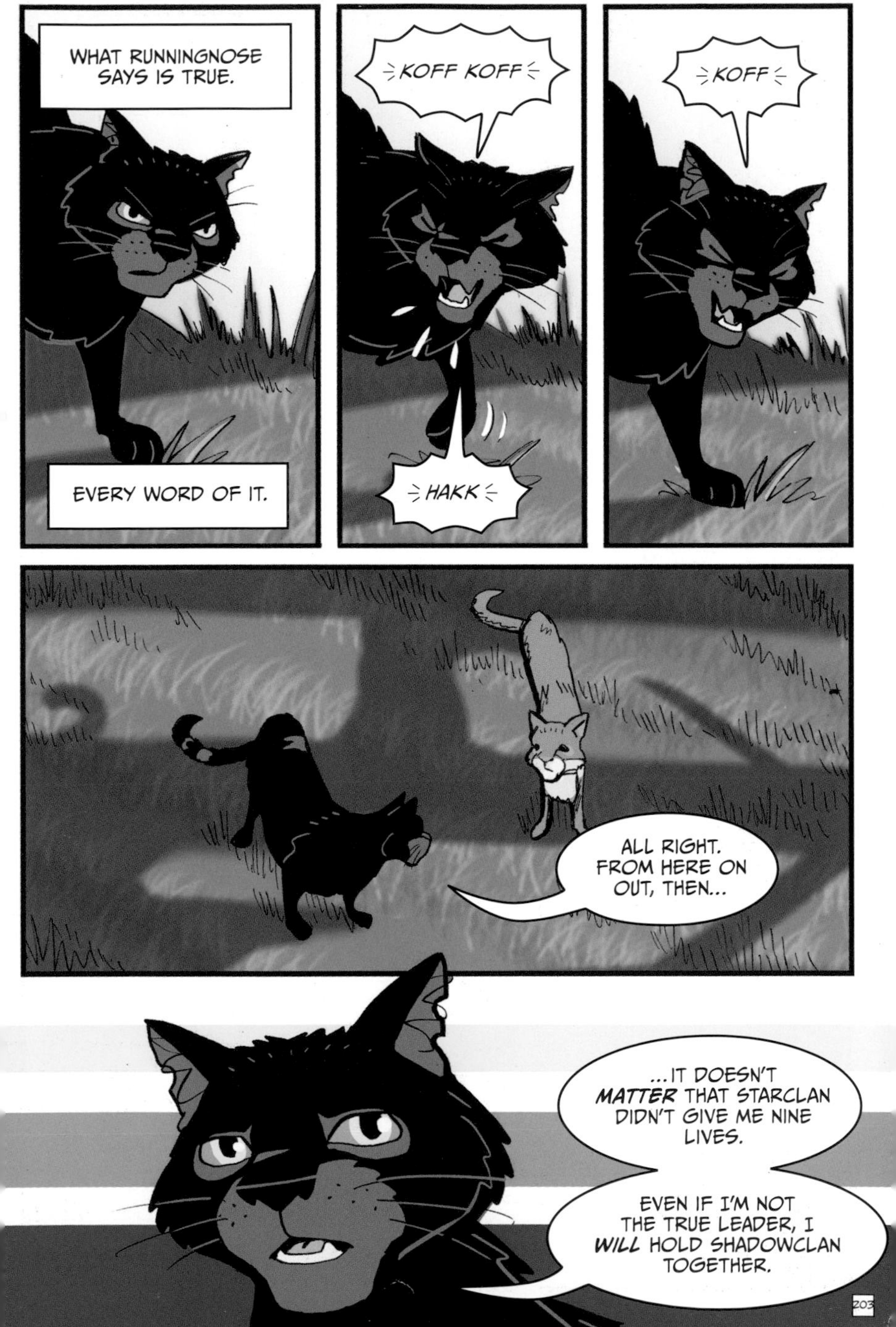
WHAT RUNNINGNOSE SAYS IS TRUE.
EVERY WORD OF IT.
KOFF KOFF
HAKK
KOFF
ALL RIGHT. FROM HERE ON OUT, THEN...
...IT DOESN'T MATTER THAT STARCLAN DIDN'T GIVE ME NINE LIVES.
EVEN IF I'M NOT THE TRUE LEADER, I WILL HOLD SHADOWCLAN TOGETHER.

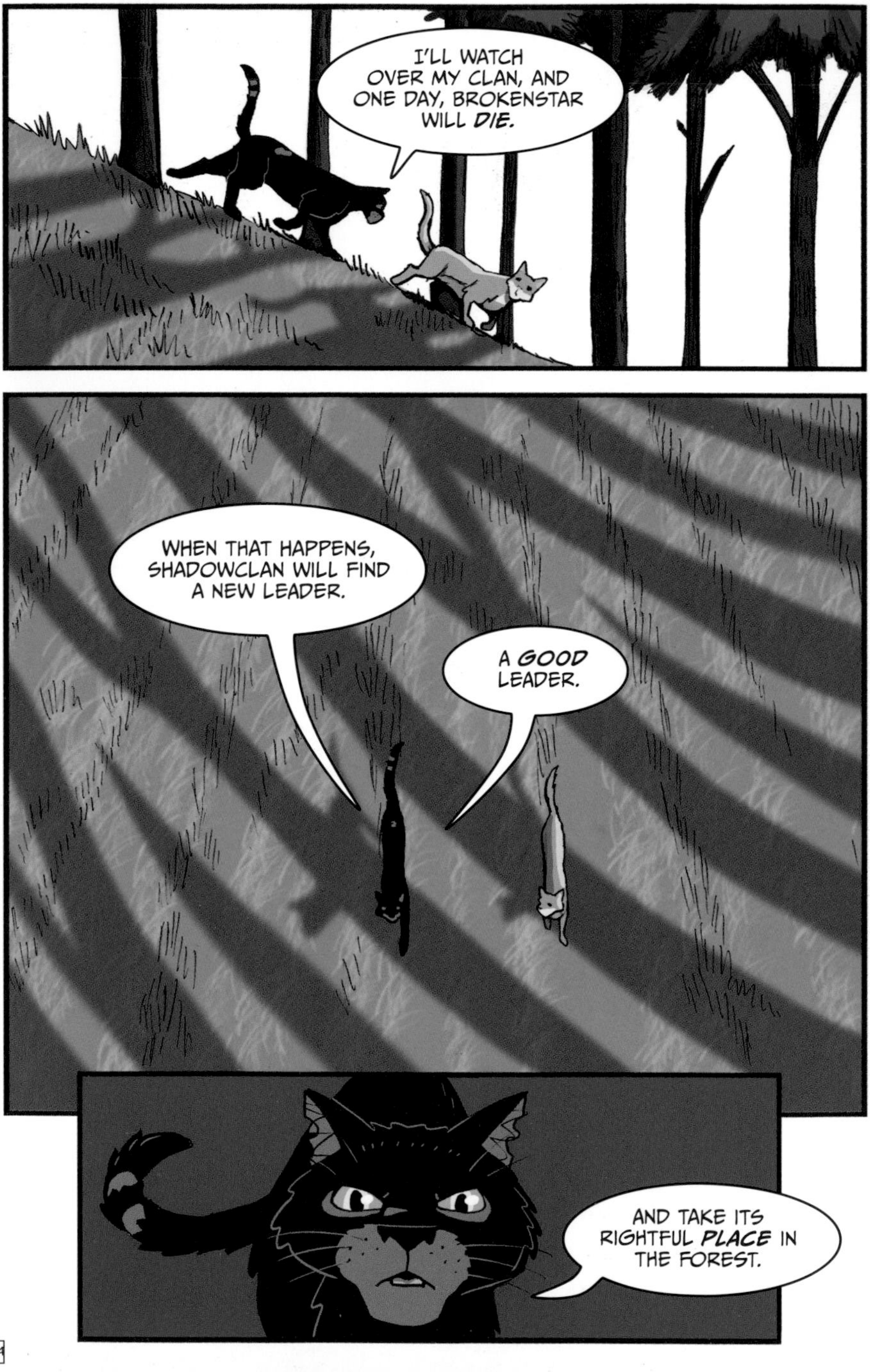
I'LL WATCH OVER MY CLAN, AND ONE DAY, BROKENSTAR WILL *DIE.*
WHEN THAT HAPPENS, SHADOWCLAN WILL FIND A NEW LEADER.
A *GOOD* LEADER.
AND TAKE ITS RIGHTFUL *PLACE* IN THE FOREST.

A NEW ADVENTURE BEGINS FOR THE WARRIORS CLANS!

A STARLESS CLAN
WARRIORS
RIVER
ERIN HUNTER
#1 NEW YORK TIMES BESTSELLING AUTHOR

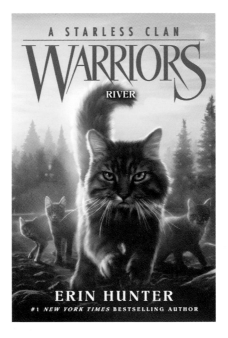

The dawn of a new age is upon the warrior Clans: one of peace, unity, and change. Now, as a new generation of warriors rises—including a young ThunderClan apprentice descended from the legendary Firestar—leaders from the five Clans agree that the warrior code must be reformed if that harmony is to be upheld. But when tragedy strikes RiverClan, old fears will give rise to new tensions—unless one young medicine cat apprentice can use her unusual connection with StarClan to calm the coming storm.

CHAPTER 1

Crouching beside the fresh-kill pile, Flamepaw tore a bite from the mouse that lay at his paws. But the succulent flesh tasted like dead leaves in his mouth, and when he gulped it down, it settled in his belly like a rock. He couldn't think of anything but his warrior assessment, which was due to start as soon as he and the other apprentices had finished eating.

Beside him, his foster littermate Baypaw, who was sharing his mouse, stopped eating to waggle his hindquarters vigorously, then took off in a massive pounce, landing with his forepaws clasped around a pebble that lay on the ground of the ThunderClan camp.

"Gotcha!" he yowled. "That was my best pounce," he declared as he bounded back to Flamepaw. His eyes sparkled with excitement. "I'm going to catch so much prey. Mice and squirrels, beware! Baypaw is coming for you!"

"Yeah, sure," Flamepaw muttered.

Baypaw crouched beside him and gave him a friendly nudge, his gaze reassuring. "Hey, don't worry," he meowed. "You'll be fine. You're a great hunter."

Flamepaw nodded and forced himself to take another bite of the mouse. Hoping to distract himself from his upcoming assessment, he angled his ears toward a group of senior warriors who were sharing prey nearby, their heads together in what looked like a serious conversation.

"I don't know what I think about making changes to the warrior code," Birchfall mewed uneasily. "Especially this idea that we could get rid of a leader. It would be like—like telling the sun not to shine!"

Ivypool let out a disapproving snort. "We would have been glad enough to get rid of Ashfur," she pointed out. "Even when we still thought he was Bramblestar. Cats died because we went on accepting him as our leader, even though he was sending cats into exile and suspecting us all of disloyalty, like he had bees in his brain."

"But how often will we have to deal with a cat like Ashfur?" Birchfall asked.

"Once was enough," Thornclaw responded with a flick of his ears. "I think Ivypool is right."

"But Ashfur wasn't a true leader," Birchfall insisted. "If he hadn't stolen Bramblestar's body, no cat would have accepted him. And StarClan never gave him his nine lives and his name. These new rules are all about deposing a leader who has been approved by StarClan. That's quite different."

"You've got a point there," Thornclaw admitted grudgingly.

"Although," Ivypool mewed, "it's not like StarClan is infallible. The first Tigerstar was given nine lives."

"That's true. Though, if a Clan deposed its leader, I don't understand what would happen to their nine lives," Cherryfall meowed. "Those lives are given by StarClan; ordinary living cats can't take them away, can they?"

"We could try, if the leader was as vile as Ashfur," Mousewhisker meowed, sliding out his claws. His eyes shone with anger, and Flamepaw remembered that the warrior had lost two of his siblings as a result of Ashfur's lies.

Shocked gasps came from two or three cats in the group, and Flamepaw exchanged a horrified glance with his foster brother.

"A leader is a leader," Bumblestripe insisted, glaring at the gray-and-white tom. "You don't disobey a leader, you don't depose a leader, and you certainly don't kill a leader. That would get you to the Dark Forest for sure."

"Keep your fur on." Thornclaw flicked his tail at the younger tom, who reared back with an offended expression. "You don't know the Dark Forest—not like

Ivypool and I do. And the code has never been that rigid. Many of you are too young to remember, but I'll never forget when ShadowClan drove out their leader Brokenstar, back in the old forest. He deserved it, if ever a cat did. But StarClan didn't take back his nine lives, and they didn't give nine lives to ShadowClan's next leader, Nightstar."

Lionblaze, who had so far listened in silence, rasped his tongue thoughtfully over his golden pelt. "That was a different time, Thornclaw." His voice was a warm rumble in his throat. "Now StarClan might agree to take the nine lives away. After all, they encouraged the Lights in the Mist to make these changes to the code."

Thornclaw flicked an ear in annoyance. "I wish Graystripe were here to explain," he muttered. "He knew how it worked, back in the day. I just don't understand what happened in the Dark Forest, and I wish I did."

"Lots of cats wish that," Lionblaze responded. "But we have to trust that our leaders understand and will do what's right."

Thornclaw's only reply was a grunt.

"What do you think, Flamepaw?" Baypaw mumbled around a mouthful of mouse. "Should we be able to get rid of our leader?"

Flamepaw dragged his attention away from the senior warriors' conversation. "Sure we should," he replied, half hoping that the senior warriors would hear him. "Except I don't think that goes far enough. Maybe the Clans would work better if we changed leaders regularly."

Baypaw's eyes stretched wide with shock, and he choked on his lump of prey, swallowing it with difficulty. "What!"

"Well, what's the alternative?" Flamepaw meowed defensively. "The way it is now, one cat chosen by the previous leader gets to boss every cat around until they've gone through nine whole lives. How is that fair?"

Recovering himself, his foster brother rolled his eyes. "You might not want to say that too loud," he pointed out, "especially considering that our leader, Bramblestar, is your kin."

Flamepaw hunched his shoulders. "It's not like any cat would listen to me, anyway," he muttered sulkily.

Forcing himself to eat more of the mouse, Flamepaw wished silently that every cat would stop judging him because of his kin. His mother was Sparkpelt, daughter of the Clan leader, Bramblestar, and his deputy, Squirrelflight—and Squirrelflight was the daughter of Firestar, the greatest leader the forest had ever known. No cat realized how hard it was, carrying the blood of cats like those in his veins.

I'm even sort of named after Firestar, Flamepaw thought. Gazing at his black paws, he added to himself, *Which is weird, because I'm not at all fire-colored. I guess Firestar was such a great cat, it was more important to Sparkpelt to remind every cat that I'm his kin, instead of looking at what I'm actually like. I wonder if my father would have gone along with it.*

Most cats never mentioned Flamepaw's father, Larksong, who had died before Flamepaw had a chance to know him. Flamepaw's mentor, Lilyheart, was Larksong's mother, and sometimes she told Flamepaw stories about him. *Maybe Larksong would have understood me,* Flamepaw thought wistfully. *Lilyheart says I look like him.*

He swallowed the last mouthful of mouse; Baypaw had already finished eating, and was sitting up, cleaning his whiskers. As Flamepaw swiped his tongue over his jaws, his mother, Sparkpelt, padded over to them.

"Good luck on your assessments," she mewed.

"Thanks, Sparkpelt!" Baypaw responded, bouncing to his paws.

Flamepaw inclined his head politely. "Thank you."

"I'm sure you'll do very well," Sparkpelt told him.

Flamepaw wished that he didn't feel so stiff and awkward around his mother. He knew that Sparkpelt loved him. *Well, she has to, seeing as she's my mother.* But he wasn't sure that she liked him very much. Sometimes he thought she didn't know him well enough to like him.

Sparkpelt hadn't raised him as a young kit; she had been too depressed by the death of his father, Larksong, and his littermate, Flickerkit. Sorrelstripe had stepped in to nurse him instead.

Later, Sparkpelt and Finchpaw—Flamepaw's surviving littermate—had grown close when they had been exiled together by the impostor, leaving Flamepaw behind in the ThunderClan camp. Maybe because he had been separated from her so young, Flamepaw still felt as if he barely knew Sparkpelt. He was not even sure he wanted to know her; he was torn between hoping for her attention because she was his mother, and resenting her for having abandoned him.

Now Sparkpelt didn't seem to know what to say to him. While Flamepaw still stood there in awkward silence, she gave a final dip of her head, then padded across the camp to where Finchpaw was sharing fresh-kill with Myrtlepaw, Baypaw's littermate. At once Flamepaw could see how much more relaxed Sparkpelt became, touching noses with Finchpaw and giving her a loving lick around her ear.

Dragging his gaze away, Flamepaw spotted Baypaw and Myrtlepaw's mother, Sorrelstripe, who had fostered him and Finchpaw. Now she gave him and Baypaw an encouraging wave of her tail. Inclining his head in reply, Flamepaw let out a long sigh. *Sometimes I wish Sorrelstripe were my mother.*

His mentor, Lilyheart, was already waiting near the entrance to the camp. As Flamepaw watched, Baypaw's mentor, Mousewhisker, and Finchpaw's mentor, Cinderheart, padded over to her. A moment later,

Eaglewing, Myrtlepaw's mentor, slipped out of the warriors' den and raced across the camp to join the others.

"Come on, Flamepaw!" Lilyheart called. "It's time!"

Flamepaw rose to his paws as the rest of the mentors summoned their apprentices, and followed the other young cats toward the camp entrance. Yowls of "Good luck!" rang in his ears from more of his Clanmates around the clearing. Flamepaw felt his sadness drain away like water into dry ground, replaced by nervous excitement thrilling from his ears to his tail-tip.

Outside the camp, the four mentors and their apprentices headed off in different directions. Before he followed Mousewhisker, Baypaw paused to give Flamepaw a reassuring nudge. "You've got this," he meowed.

"So do you," Flamepaw responded, pressing his muzzle into Baypaw's shoulder. Then he followed Lilyheart into the woods, heading toward the lake.

Once the scents of the other cats and the sound of their paw steps had faded, Lilyheart halted. "Okay, you need to go hunt," she told him. "You won't see me, but I'll be watching you. I expect you to catch loads of prey, so we'll impress all the cats in the camp with what a good hunter you are."

Lilyheart's cheerful tones, and the way she obviously expected him to do well, roused Flamepaw's ambition. *I'm going to make a really spectacular catch!*

Standing still, all his senses alert, he opened his jaws

to taste the air. Succulent prey-scents flowed in on him, telling him it would be a good day for hunting.

Almost at once he distinguished the scent of mouse and heard a scuffling. Padding forward, he located the sound among a heap of fallen leaves; he could even see the leaves twitch. *That's where the mouse is hiding—there might even be two!* Briefly he dropped into the hunter's crouch, but then he hesitated; mice weren't particularly impressive prey. *Any daft furball can catch mice!* It wasn't enough for him to pass his assessment by catching just any prey; he wanted Lilyheart to be really impressed.

Straightening up, Flamepaw padded on into the forest, passing over another mouse and a shrew that practically ran into his paws as it scuttled across his path.

Maybe a bird would be good, he thought. *They're harder to hunt.*

A few paces farther on, Flamepaw rounded the edge of a bramble thicket and came upon a squirrel nibbling at something in its forepaws a couple of tail-lengths away from the nearest tree. *It looks so fat and juicy! That would be a great piece of prey to bring back.*

Flamepaw carefully got into position and began to creep forward, checking that he was upwind of the squirrel and setting his paws down as lightly as he could. The squirrel seemed unaware of him, all its attention on what it held between its paws.

But before Flamepaw was close enough to pounce,

he remembered a move that he had practiced once or twice with Baypaw. Lilyheart had never seen it. *That would impress her, for sure!*

Flamepaw abandoned his crouch and bounded forward, launching himself into a powerful leap—not at the squirrel but at the tree behind it. He meant to whip around as soon as he hit the tree and ricochet away from it, cutting off the squirrel's escape route as it fled for safety.

But the spectacular move didn't work. Flamepaw hit the tree with one paw crushed under him; pain stabbed up his leg as far as his shoulder. Gasping, he tried to correct his position as he pushed off. But he was tangled up in his own paws and completely misjudged his leap. He thumped to the ground among the tree roots, all the breath driven out of him. The squirrel leaped over him and raced up the trunk, pausing on a low branch to chatter insults at Flamepaw before vanishing among the leaves.